The Game of the Masters

The Game of the Masters

THE MID-WORLD OF THE TRUCE
BOOK TWO

STEVE DOUGLAS

Copyright © 2022 Steve Douglas

All rights reserved. No part of this book may be reproduced in any form or by any electronic or mechanical means, including information storage and retrieval systems, without permission in writing from the publisher, except by reviewers, who may quote brief passages in a review.

ISBN: 978-1-7778868-1-3

The Game of the Masters is a work of fiction. The names, characters, businesses, places, events, locales, and incidents are either products of my imagination or used in a fictitious manner. Any resemblance to actual persons, living or dead, or actual events are coincidental.

Illustration and cover design by Thea Magerand
Typesetting by C'est Beau Designs

For my father, Don Angus Douglas.
Both my brother Dwight and I can still remember him lighting his pipe,
or sipping his beer, while he tried to extricate his characters, Julian, and
his Familiars, from the danger he left them in during previous tales.
Dad, thank you for inspiring these five books so many years ago.

Contents

Prologue:	Opening Moves	1
1.	The Wizards and Their League	3
2.	The Fight at the Ford	30
3.	The Storm	50
4.	The Broken Army	68
5.	The Tarnished Sword	97
Interlude:	The Mind of Merlin	131
6.	The Raiders	133
7.	The End of All Magic	152
8.	The Dark Emissary	177
9.	The Hall of the Dreamers	195
10.	The Many Portals	226
11.	The Siege	248
12.	The Council of the League	267
13.	The Dragon's Teeth	290
14.	The Ruined Angel	318
15.	The End-Game of the Masters	365
16.	The Aftermath	390

ONE SIDE OF
The Game of

THE MAN AT ARMS · THE MID-WORLD SPY · THE ILLUSION · THE APPRENTICE · THE CHARMED KNIGHT

THE PRINCESS · THE TALISMAN · THE WEB OF FATE · THE GREY COUNCILLOR · THE MAGI

THE ARMED HOST · THE GREAT SPELL · THE WIZARD · THE MASTER

the Masters

Prologue

Opening Moves

ON THE OTHER SIDE OF THE *oval Field, the pieces of his unseen opponent flowed forward, moving in intricate combinations of massed and focused power. A hazy glow was beginning to shift over the Field of the Masters: a symptom of his opponent's strength, a signal that powerful Sorcery was being raised against him.*

His pieces lay still, waiting for their Master's first moves. He would make those first moves, then turn from The Game of the Masters: for the Game was only a testing place, a metaphor, a mirror of what might be, where the Powers engaged in mock combat. Now for the first time, some Power was moving openly against him, seeking his destruction. The opening moves shifting over the Field of the Masters showed clearly that this contest was no longer a game, that a new and complex warfare had begun.

After so many ages of peace, which of the Powers had abandoned the pure Game of the Masters, and taken up real weapons? There were traces, obscure puzzling hints; he would locate his hidden foe and find some way to extract a great price.

He stared sadly at his pieces for a moment. It was one thing to send an object, an inanimate symbol into danger. But now, in this real, mortal contest, friends, allies, and servants would be sent into great peril, and some of them lost forever.

He signaled with his mind and turned away from The Game of the Masters. The first of his pieces shifted forward, moving toward the enchanted haze formed by his opponent. This piece was delicately carved, showing the image of a youth: The Apprentice....

Chapter One
The Wizards and Their League

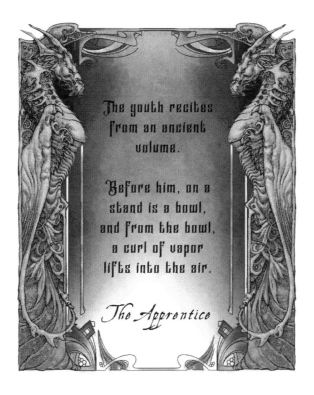

The youth recites from an ancient volume.

Before him, on a stand is a bowl, and from the bowl, a curl of vapor lifts into the air.

The Apprentice

WITH THE NOON SUN BEATING down upon him, Julian the Apprentice rode down the Greenway, passing slowly through the broad sunlit meadows that lay across the south of Alantéa the Forerunner. His pace was completely unhurried, as though his tasks were unimportant, and he had all the time in the world. Overhead, swallows darted, while insects buzzed and hummed as they busied themselves with the blossoms of the tangled clematis that lay on either side of the roadway.

An emerald jay fluttered a wingspan too close to Sebastian, and Julian's Familiar stirred from sleep, wings flaring as though to lift from Julian's shoulder and join the dance of flying creatures in the surrounding meadows. Instead of taking flight, the little Familiar stretched and yawned, staring at the cluster of houses that were slowly coming into view.

"CorumGar — is that right, Julian?" asked Sebastian.

"The name's almost forgotten," Julian replied. "But it once translated as 'Spear of the Warrior.' This village was something of a military center even before the Wild Time."

Sebastian nodded, murmuring, "CorumGar, last stop before our real destination: Gravengate, and then farther to Stone Mountain."

Julian looked about him carefully, then spoke quietly into Sebastian's mind: *We'll ride openly to Gravengate tomorrow, but for the moment we should say little of the troubles between Thorian and Balardi.*

Sebastian smiled. "They never ask about the Wizards. The little ones like stories of the Mid-World, and all its creatures. My voice will be tired tonight, but not from talking about those boring, faraway Wizards." They fell silent as they passed into CorumGar.

The Elder of the village came out to greet Julian, and, as always, the children came out to greet Sebastian. Julian watched as the younglings led the little Familiar away. Sebastian had the body of a slight monkey with brown fur, but grey wings grew from his shoulders, and they tended to droop when the little Familiar grew tired. Julian turned back to the leader and bowed.

"If I remember correctly, you are Gayal," he said, "but it's been six years. Corum-Gar looks peaceful, but sometimes looks are deceiving. How are things?"

"We've done well," Gayal replied. "In fact, it's been almost dull — the Mid-World is inclined to leave us to ourselves." He led Julian from the center of the village into a little courtyard and sat beside the Apprentice on a stone bench. In the middle of the courtyard was a low fountain that seeped water over its edge, filled from some deep underground spring. Against the courtyard's far walls, rose bushes were nestled against stone walls. The Elder looked quietly at Julian for a moment.

"Six years have passed, have they? Then you would be the lad who traveled with Orlan. I can recall your grey eyes, but the rest of you has changed."

"Six years ago, I was squire to Orlan, before my Apprenticeship to the Wizards," Julian replied, "and I remember you vividly — you were far more military in those days." Gayal laughed and showed Julian his hands, hands that were callused and worn.

"That roughness comes from farming, not from bearing arms. With the peace of the League, most of our weapons have been stored in dusty attics." Gayal looked up into the afternoon sun. "With the day wearing on, I should be letting you go about your tasks. Perhaps we'll talk more over dinner. Will you join me?"

Julian agreed, thanking the Elder, and he left Gayal alone in the courtyard, staring into his small fountain as it seeped water slowly over its polished stone edges.

As Julian walked through the village, he noticed, without surprise, that the old, lightly built wooden cottages were gradually being replaced by more substantial homes of stone and mortar. Those old cottages had been easily abandoned as violent raids and intrusions swept over them. After years of peace, more substantial homes with stone and even glass were being built. One thing did surprise Julian — he recalled that six years ago the wooden structures had seemed drab and grey, but now they had greenish hues. He peered closer so he could study the green of the old cottage siding.

"There was a long, wet season, two years back," came a voice behind Julian. "Moss and algae flourished. When the sun dried everything, it left a green stain." Julian turned and saw a man standing a few feet away, smiling down at the Apprentice. From his gloves and streaks of soot, Julian guessed that he was either a metalworker or a blacksmith.

"I like the green," said Julian. "But it seems that wood gives way to stone, and the green stain will soon be gone."

"Another change for the better," said the smith, but then his face grew more serious. "Yet not everyone agrees with me, particularly our young people. You may hear a squeak or two from them, and that's why I came looking for you. There are still many of us who came south to escape the ragged warfare in the rest of Alantéa, with its Mid-World intrusions, to enjoy the peace of the League. I came out to tell you this: don't pay too much attention to the few fools who feel otherwise." The smith smiled again and let his face relax. "Now it's back to the forge for me — it's seldom that I give such weighty advice." He gave a friendly wave to Julian and walked away.

Julian returned to his tasks, stopping by each of the houses of the village. He met with friendly interest from most, but a few of the young people seemed reserved, though none were openly hostile. Just two or three years ago, most of his time would have been spent encountering minor intrusions from the Mid-World, but now he was called on to serve as a healer rather than as a magic wielder. There was only one small sign that the Mid-World still watched, ready to interfere. At the edge of the village was a small garden, where little rows of Bindweed and Dragon's Breath were grown, together with other herbs used in simple sorcery. Here, a small creature of the Mid-World had stolen bits of this and that for its own use.

He knelt by the garden, pausing in thought: it would be best to stop this little intrusion, but it would be wise to avoid creating even a lesser enemy for the League. After a few moments, he used his staff to engrave a message on the soil at the garden's edge. First, he drew the symbol of the League, then added the name of the small thief's master, then Julian signed his own name at the base, and left a stalk of Dragon's Breath to one side. He spoke a few words over the inscription, and the lines of the symbols glowed and were frozen to the ground so that the message would remain for several months.

Now the small thief should discover the warning and depart. Hopefully, the gift of a stalk of Dragon's Breath would be understood as a gesture of goodwill.

· ⚹ ·

When nightfall came, candles and torchlights began to flicker from the windows of cottages, and the smell of stews and baked meals began lifting into the evening air. Julian returned to the courtyard of the Elder, knocked at the door, listening for a moment to the little fountain as it seeped water into the darkness. Against the far wall, rose bushes swayed gently in the evening breezes, and as he waited, the Sight within Julian brought him a sudden vision, a *flash* of insight: unseen, beneath the rose bushes, ants were guiding aphids to safety for the night.

When the Elder opened the door, he greeted Julian briefly, then led the Apprentice directly to his dining table. Julian sensed that he had been expected sooner and sat quickly down to dinner. The table was set for just two, although there was room for as many as a dozen. Large candles in vats were suspended from ceiling beams, and they lit the room without flickering or sputtering, though every now and again, shadows seemed to shift and slant over stone and mortar walls.

A young lady served dinner to Gayal and Julian, watching to see that their needs were met, then retreating quietly to a corner away from the table. They talked for a little while about the village and the League. Gayal asked about Orlan.

"In theory, he's a counselor to Merlin," said Julian, "though most of the time, he's living in the north, raising horses. Kalanin is now chief among the men at arms, and Galad too is trusted with many of the tasks dealing with raiders or intruders."

"Galad…I have an image of a tall, rangy youth, a traveler," said Gayal. "Is that the one?"

Julian nodded and smiled. "No longer rangy, but stronger and still a traveler."

Dinner was over now, and the young lady appeared again to clear the table. When she had finished, she took off her apron and came to Gayal's side. The Elder patted her gently on her back.

"I'm amazed," he said. "You didn't interrupt us, or spatter food on us. I'll ask if you may stay for a while." He turned to Julian. "This is my granddaughter, Freya, either a wise young lady, or a lazy one: she would rather talk than work and would rather discuss her chores than do them. Yet she served us well this night, without interrupting us, asking only that she might stay and talk with us. Is this acceptable?"

Julian nodded, looking into the serious face of the granddaughter. In the Elder's attitude was a mixture of affection and authority that a teacher might show to a prize pupil.

"Freya has more questions than we have answers," continued Gayal. "She asks about star movements, and crop of grain, of metalwork, and the history of the League. Lately, she asks about the Mid-World. I and the others have told her of the history of mankind in Alantéa, how the Powers of the Mid-World have claimed Godhood, forcing allegiance from mortals, but Freya is not satisfied, and asks, 'What is this Mid-World? How did it come to be?' This question I pass to you for a response if you are willing. I should add, though, that it grows late, and Freya will need her rest soon."

"I'll tell you my understanding of the Mid-World," said Julian, "though there is much that I don't know, and I doubt that even the Powers of the Mid-World completely understand exactly what they have created." He paused for a moment, searching for words that would satisfy both of his listeners. "When I was Freya's age, I asked similar questions about the boundaries of the Mid-World, and my instructor would quote — in a profound manner, 'The Mid-World lies over Alantéa as an enchanted garment,' and of the Nature of the Powers, and other beings, he would also quote, 'The Mid-World is Rich.' These explanations, or sayings, stayed with me until my Apprenticeship, and here is what I've learned from the Wizards:

"In the early ages of Earth, the Servants of the Maker warred with the Adversaries of the Maker for mastery of Alantéa, and dominion over the Far Lands. Their struggle swayed back and forth over many ages, rising, and falling, yet neither the Servants nor the Adversaries were victorious. At last, the Servants wearied, and the Adversaries lost their zeal, and so the Truce was fashioned, and their struggle ended.

"To keep the Truce, the greatest of the Servants and the greatest of the Adversaries put aside their natures and became Powers of the Mid-World. All the Seraphs and Demons, and the Spirit Lords and Dragons passed into the Truce and have not been seen since.

"Here, unlooked for, came the Mid-World, the network, the grid of the Powers. For each of the Powers feeds upon the network, and the Mid-World draws strength from each of them. Vast energies that were born in the struggle before the Truce have surged into the Mid-World, so that the Mid-World exists independently of the Powers, and it can no longer be completely controlled by them. When we say, 'The Mid-World is Rich,' we are saying that new creatures and powerful beings come to life, unplanned, into the Mid-World, so that even the Powers are surprised.... But here I'm describing my own understanding. Can you envision a network, a vast grid of energies?"

Gayal nodded; Freya said, "Those energies and Powers always seemed so immense and strong, and the League seemed such a small thing beside them. How can the Wizards possibly have held their own against the Powers of the Mid-World?" Freya's voice was clear and light, while she had the same intensity as her grandfather.

"As it's named, the Mid-World lies between good and evil," Julian answered. "The Powers are amoral, seeking their own pleasures, and they are wary, for there seem to be no lasting alliances in the Mid-World. We can't be certain, but we think that none of the Powers wishes a trial of strength, bringing that Power, alone, against all three Wizards: Merlin, Thorian, and Balardi. A time of testing came during the Wild Time and the founding of the League, yet neither the Powers nor the Wizards will speak much of that conflict." Julian paused, hesitating. "Also, there is one way that the Powers and the Wizards, and the Sorcerers test one another's strength, without open conflict, and this is called *The Game of the Masters*. But of the *Game* itself, and how it's played, I know only hearsay and rumor.

"Also, the League has set its own boundaries, keeping only a small part of Alantéa as a haven for mortal humans. As for the boundaries of the Mid-World, this is a mystery I can only dimly perceive.... But the Mid-World is not limited by the height, nor the breadth, or the width of Alantéa, or the Far Lands. By the power of the web of enchantment surrounding the Truce, many lands exist nearly in the same space, and new domains are forged each year." Julian glanced into their rapt faces, and he smiled. "Yet I am only an Apprentice, a student, and not an instructor. I hope this has helped you."

They talked for a little while about the Powers, how they had set themselves up as Gods, ruling over great masses of men. Some had trained Sorcerers to do their bidding, though these mortal wielders of magic tended to slip away from their masters, intent on creating their own domains. Freya nodded, drinking in the information.

"I can see why we both hate the Mid-World and are drawn by it at the same time," she said, "but there are so many things that aren't clear. What of the Ancient Powers before the Truce? It seems imposs—"

"Hold," interrupted Gayal. "Julian, my granddaughter would keep you in conversation all night long. I promised her only a few moments of your time, and she's had more than that. It's time for her to sleep." Freya looked for a moment as though she would dispute the matter, but she held her peace. Julian smiled at her as she rose.

"You've already learned much of what I know about the Mid-World," he said. "It's not considered wise to teach an Apprentice too much of the Mid-World: many Apprentices and Adepts have been lured away from the League by the Powers, to become Sorcerers in the Mid-World. If you wish to learn more, come to the Halls of Merlin at Sea's Edge. There you can work with the Keepers of Records, or study with the Star Charters."

Freya thanked Julian as graciously as she was able; it was clear that she would have preferred to stay. She left, and Gayal leaned across the table to pour a glass of light wine for the Apprentice, then one for himself.

"Thank you for your patience with my granddaughter," said the Elder. "She's a fine young lady but needs guidance. It would be good for her to spend some time at Sea's Edge, perhaps in a year's time when she's a bit steadier." Gayal fell silent for a few moments and Julian let silence settle over the house, tuning his mind to the village's night sounds, where a light insect chorus was interrupted now and again by the banging of a pot, or a burst of laughter.

"Really," said Gayal, "I'm not worried about Freya — she'll find something to hold her interest. But there are many, many other young people in this village and other villages who speak with longing of the old days of service and adventure in the Mid-World. Lately, a few of the boldest have drifted away, seeking adventure beyond the borders of our League. Should I forbid them? Is there guidance from the League?"

"The League feels that each village should make its own rules and that those who live within the village need to abide by those rules. Those who disagree are free to live elsewhere…and I suppose that all those who wish to leave the borders of the League are free to do so. Yet Merlin may have more to say on this matter, and when I return to Sea's Edge, I'll ask him. Have you thought of sending the adventurous to Baron Cadmon, or to Balardi? Each of them retains a large force of men in defense of the League."

Gayal gave Julian a sidelong glance, then murmured, "You didn't mention Thorian."

In Julian's mind, the Gift stirred, bringing a faint warning, as though a clash of arms echoed from a remote distance.

"Of course, send them to Thorian," he said easily, "though Stone Mountain is farther than Khiva, or Gravengate."

"Fairly answered, without hesitation," Gayal commented. "But it's not right for me to test you or take advantage of you. I knew a little of the troubles of the League, and a short time ago I sought confirmation. Though we are of the League, there are many pathways open to the Mid-World." Julian understood from his words that the Elder had a confidant in the Mid-World.

"Nothing wrong with this — if it's handled carefully. What did your advisor tell you?"

"That the League exists in name only, that Thorian has drifted away in the past year, though he has not yet openly broken with the alliance."

Julian nodded. It was becoming unraveled, as it was bound to.

"And what will this bring from the Mid-World?" he asked.

"My informant was not so mighty as to know the strategies of the Powers," said Gayal, "though he described a mixture of concern and anticipation. Nor did those of the Mid-World seem to understand the nature of our troubles."

"Merlin doesn't know either," said Julian. "The times of silence from Thorian at Stone Mountain have grown longer, and now Thorian is completely removed from us. Rumors of war have begun to echo through the League." Julian was silent for a moment, staring into the fire, wondering how much he should tell Gayal. Dark nightfall was about him, and he would need to sleep soon. This Elder was shrewd and had manipulated the conversation easily; even the Gift was no match for Gayal's perception and judgment.

"If all goes well, in four days' time I will be at Gravengate, the fortress of Balardi," Julian said, "and in ten days' time with Thorian at Stone Mountain. It's Merlin's wish that I seem a casual traveler, but in reality, I've been sent as an emissary to Balardi and Thorian, to seek the reasons for our difficulties. I was chosen because I studied with each of them. Please say nothing of this matter for a fortnight, at least, as I may be delayed."

"We are one with the League," said the Elder as he rose and led Julian to the door. "I will say nothing, not even to my granddaughter. As a child, I heard nothing but good things about the early Adepts serving the Wizards. Then, all those compliments slowly diminished as various Adepts of mixed talent and motivation came and went. As a young village leader, I had the misfortune to meet your predecessors, the Adepts Eudox and Loran, each of them higher ranked than you, Apprentice, and yet I was astonished that the Wizards tolerated them. Eudox had the bulging eyes of a fish, was wonderfully evasive, born to treachery, while Loran was completely interested in himself. The Wizards' League was better off when they slipped away into the Mid-World.

"You may be a youngling, nearing manhood, yet you seem a vastly better human than those two. So, Maker's Grace to you, lad. Keep the peace if you can. For all the grumbling, our people have flourished under the rule of the Wizards."

Gayal stood at the door, watching the Apprentice as he departed: Julian had only recently turned fifteen years old, almost fully grown, slim but wiry, pale of skin, with dark black, curling hair. Gayal shook his head, watching the Apprentice depart, thinking grim thoughts: *This lad is a considerable improvement over Eudox and Loran, but is he up to the coming challenge to the Wizard's League? I don't think so.*

· ⋊ ·

Julian readied for sleep by candlelight, in an old cottage at the edge of the village. An open window had let in several bands of moths that fluttered in excitement around his candle. Julian closed his eyes, sending the moths a vision: of bright moonlight flaring beneath clear skies. When the moths had finished racing out into the night, Julian shuttered the window.

Then a knock came low on the door, and as Julian opened it, Sebastian entered. The Familiar looked tired, his wings drooping nearly to the ground.

"How did you do?" asked Julian.

"Not too badly," said Sebastian, seating himself at the edge of a cot, "though it's good to be finished. I've been telling bedtime stories long after bedtime. I never really mind entertaining the little ones, but it leaves me tired. What of the Mid-World?"

"There's only a hint of it in the village, and that's a change. Of late the Mid-World has been leaving us to ourselves."

Julian pulled back the covers on his bed. "Did you find anyone?"

"There's a small, young girl, Mira, who has a portion of the Gift," said Sebastian, "but not nearly strong enough for Apprenticeship."

Julian settled back on his bed. "We spoke once of creating an order of Wardens for those who had only a portion of the Gift. Yet if the Mid-World has lost interest in us, Wardens may no longer be necessary. We should remember to ask Merlin." Sebastian stretched out on a smaller bed, one borrowed from a child of the village.

"There's one other matter that we should pass to Merlin," Julian continued. "The Elder of this village is far cleverer than we once thought. He and I chatted about the Mid-World, and the League, and the restlessness of his people, but he really wished for information about Thorian and our errand. I had to tell him about the real reasons for our journey." Julian blew out the candle, and complete darkness came over the cottage, with only the night sounds of the village seeping through the long dark quiet. Julian turned and slept.

· ⋊ ·

And he dreamed again the old dream that he had encountered so many times before: They were riding to a river crossing on some vital errand, their faces tense but confident as they sped along the Greenway. The faces of the riders had changed over the years, and Julian's dream was in some way different each time. Years ago, Julian had dreamt of Orlan and Kalanin, and the strong, lean faces of several Gift born wielders of magic — Magicians or Adepts, who were far along in the Study. A few years ago, Orlan had dropped away from his dream, and Galad had emerged. Then, the other Magicians had begun to slip away from his night vision, and Julian had begun to see his own image in the dream, riding beside Kalanin and Galad. Julian had never known the names of the Adepts, but he did not miss them, for now Merlin was usually close beside, or Balardi. Sometimes, a full mounted tier of five hundred men of Baron Cadmon's joined them and jostled alongside as they raced down the Greenway. Once, Thorian had arrived, just before the crossing of the ford, his silvery beard glinting in the sunlight.

Always, as they rode out on their great errand, the sun was shining on them, and they paused before the river crossing as others joined them, and then they surged forward in greater strength and confidence. Tonight, in this dream, Merlin again accompanied them, and, as always in his presence, Julian felt a powerful, calm strength flow into his night vision.

But now, so strangely, the face of Merlin shifted in the dream, turning to Julian, and the face of the Wizard was filled with a look of incredible astonishment....

· ⋈ ·

In deepest night, a distant rumble of sound drew Julian from his dreams. His eyes opened, and he saw Sebastian perched on the edge of the windowsill: the window was again open and pale lights flickered over the winged Familiar. Julian rose and stared outside. Distant pale lights rose and fell over a remote horizon, while low rumbling sounds followed each surge of light.

"Those lights have been flaring for the last few moments, but the sounds are new," said Sebastian. "I can't remember which direction we're facing. Are we looking toward Balardi and Gravengate?"

Pale lights flared green and yellow over Julian's face. "The lights are coming from Sea's Edge and the Halls of Merlin. Can you sense anything about what's going on?"

Sebastian shook his head as another roll of sound reached them. "Nothing — it's too far."

"Something terrible is happening," Julian said softly. "If I had an Adept's or a Sorcerer's strength, I could tell you more." In a few more minutes, the lights died down and the sounds subsided. Julian and Sebastian returned to their beds, and after a time of turning and thrashing, eventually, they slept.

· ❈ ·

They left the village at the first light of day, Julian seated on his Mare, Bluescent, with Sebastian riding on the shoulder of the Apprentice. Julian watched grey shadows shift over the forests and meadows of Alantéa, and his mind was troubled. *Maker's Touch, but those were strange events last night — something grim and surprising had happened at Sea's Edge. Yet what could surprise Merlin in his own place of power?*

The first rays of pure sunlight shot over the horizon, and Julian's worries eased as the incredible beauty of Alantéa rushed over him. He brought Bluescent to a halt.

"Bad moments last night," he said softly, "but sunrise is coming to Alantéa, the Forerunner. I don't think we have any choice except to press forward."

"If Merlin couldn't deal with events at Sea's Edge," Sebastian added, "what could we possibly do if we returned?" The Familiars wings sagged, and he stared blankly into the distance.

"Something like a disaster has swept over Sea's Edge," Julian murmured, "but other forces are in play all around us and we need to go forward." They rode for a while in sunlight silence, watching insects and birds swoop through the meadows and forests alongside the Greenway.

Julian's mind drifted to his time of Apprenticeship to Balardi. The Wizard was powerful and kind, but quite different from Merlin: Balardi had an incredible temper. Still, it would be good to see him again — perhaps there was still time to resolve matters with Thorian.

The Gift, waking suddenly, sent a shudder of warning through him. He halted.

"Julian," whispered Sebastian.

"Yes, I see it," the Apprentice said softly. "I must have been half asleep." To his eyes, the Greenway stretched out, long and straight, leading to the Ford of Bariloch. But the Gift and his training showed that Portal Magic had spread over the Greenway, and if they continued, they would be drawn into the domain of some Mid-World being.... He looked back. To break the spell and continue his journey, he would be forced to retrace his steps for a half of a league. But why had the spell been placed before him? Mid-World dwellers had many motives, most of them self-indulgent or malicious, and yet recently those of the League had been left to their own devices. So, who was seeking them now?

"It's my job to watch while you're asleep," Sebastian said. "I'm glad that Mer—" He broke off as his quick eyes caught a flash of color at the side of the road, and a leaping glide of his wings brought him beside the object: it was a flower of the Seferis, small, purple and red, with seven petals. In the early days of the League, the Seferis had been an emblem of those pledged to the alliance.

"So, it's an invitation, rather than a snare," said Julian. "What do you say?" The Familiar peered down the road.

"There's some humor to it," said Sebastian, "no hint of malice or treachery."

"Then we'll follow the road," said Julian. "It looks as though this spell was planned for us, alone, and not for stray travelers."

The road turned and twisted, leading over hills and down through hollows, but always deeper into the domain of the Mid-World being. Wild colors clashed in the woodlands of this portion of the Mid-World; they seemed immature compared with the lofty and somber flowering trees of Alantéa. Yet, every now and again, a gnarled, powerful looking tree would lift itself above the riot of color that ran about the forest floor — it was as though a child and an adult had collaborated in creating this portion of the Mid-World.

After many twists and turns, the road ended, halting at the door of an old cottage. Julian shook his head, smiling wryly; the old cottage was a bit of mockery — the Powers of the Mid-World were inclined to huge temples and palaces, or to impenetrable fortresses, where they lived in splendor, surrounded by thousands of worshippers and obedient servants.

Julian halted, dismounting, and he let Bluescent graze among the grasses and wildflowers. The cottage was without a garden or shrubbery, but bits of debris lay about, as though the roof's thatching had begun to shed. With Sebastian on his shoulder, Julian walked cautiously up to the front of the old cottage and knocked gently on the door.

The cottage door eased open; and at the entrance stood an old woman. She was weathered and stooped, but a sense of strength remained in her shoulders and arms. He eyes had the greyish green color of those with the Gift, but they were turning milky white, and opaque with age.

"Welcome, Julian," she said softly, voice half mocking. "Come into Granny's castle." Julian bowed, and stepped to the entrance, pausing only to leave his staff at the entrance as a courtesy.

"No!" exclaimed the old woman, laughing. "Bring it with you. Granny has no reason to fear you; you have no reason to fear Granny!" Julian entered warily, with Sebastian still on his shoulder.

"Yet I must say," the old woman continued, "you do have good manners for a youngling, and you shouldn't lose them." From within, the cottage seemed even smaller than it had from the outside. A floor of roughhewn, wooden planking was covered with straw, and scraps of hide and cloth. Sunlight poured in from dingy windows, with dust particles swirling in the sunbeams as though a tiny universe had just been born.

All this squalor has been developed in some detail, Julian thought, *but what was its purpose?*

The Sorceress shuffled about, finding a chair for Julian, then pulling one up for herself. She sat for a moment, grinning, with her opaque eyes studying Julian.

"First," she said, "the image I bear is a true one; I'm no spawn of the Mid-World, masked by illusion. Like you, I'm no more than a simple mortal."

"I sensed that, Mother," Julian said softly.

"Mother!" snorted the Sorceress, chuckling. "The lad is fair spoken — do they give you lessons in that, too?" She held up her hand to forestall a response. "Second, I'm an old friend of Merlin's. Friend now, after Merlin convinced me of my wicked ways. I won't tell you about my jaded past, lad, except to say that in the old days, the Powers of the Mid-World seemed more interesting than the Wizards." Here, the Sorceress was silent, and her opaque eyes were even more faded, as she seemed to stare into the distance.

"But that's all over now, thanks to Merlin...he even wanted me to become part of his League! To me, though, the Wizards always seemed a bit too 'nice'." Here, a look of malice and humor flashed across the face of the Sorceress and was gone. "Yes, the old Granny does ramble on! All the while, the lad sits there thinking, 'what's this to do with me? When will the senile creature get to the point?'"

Julian raised his palm in objection. The Sorceress was almost overwhelming, filled with energy, as though she were putting on a performance, and yet there was no audience in view. Julian became even more cautious.

"Those are not my words," he said gently, "and not even my thoughts."

"Fair enough, lad, but now I will come to the point: it was boredom that made me bring you here." Again, she held out her hand to forestall any objection. "No, not the boredom of some Mid-World Power, who seeks mortals as tools and toys. Granny's companion has kept her from that, but now the little trickster is bored with Granny, and he wants out. He's watched this League of yours from a distance, and now he wants to join it! Granny should have known — the little sneak always had strange tastes: doesn't like meat, eats only fruits and vegetables."

The old Sorceress shook her head ruefully and looked around the cottage for some sign.

"I believe that the little traitor is in here with us. Let's see, Julian, if you or your sniffer of magic can find him." Julian nodded and turned to glance through the cottage, letting the Gift search for him. Sebastian moved over wooden floors, peering into corners, then he flew to the highest supporting beam of the overhead roof. After a few moments, the Familiar returned to Julian, shaking his head. They and the Sorceress seemed alone in the cottage.

"There's no sign of your companion, Mother," Julian said, watching the Sorceress carefully.

"Of course, you can't find him!" said the Sorceress. "Neither can Granny! Granny has to *ask* the little sniveler to come out." She called out gently, "Rafir...."

Before them, on the floor, a few steps from the Sorceress appeared a slender, but very red fox.

"So, you really are going to leave me," the old woman said sadly.

"Just for a while," said Rafir, and the tones of the fox were surprisingly clear and pleasant. "You've given me everything, more than I could ever have hoped for, but I'm getting a little restless...you understand." The Sorceress smiled a sad, gentle smile.

"Lives change, Rafir; you probably should go out into the wide world. At the same time, you should realize that this place will not be as it was when you return. Do you understand that?"

Rafir nodded, staring up at the Sorceress. Some of the energy and posturing left the old woman. She straightened, turning to the Apprentice.

"Julian, Rafir wishes to join you. He will become one of the most secret of Mid-World Spies, for no force or power has yet proved able to detect him when he does not wish to be seen. We've tested this matter, discretely, over the years. Will you accept a new servant?" Julian said nothing for a moment, but he felt Sebastian's unease. The Sorceress peered into Julian's mind, sensing his doubt. She shook her head.

"There'll be little time for quarrels or rivalries — the three of you will be too busy. I brought you here not only for Rafir, but also to warn you: your League is entering a time of astonishing danger, and you, Julian, may well be in the thick of it. You are entering the Ragged Passages, to either gain power, or be struck from the *Game*." She watched Julian closely as she said this — and the Apprentice did not respond. "Merlin said that you might know little of the *Game*. Is this the case?"

Julian nodded. "I know little of the *Game*, except something of its history and purpose. It seems that other Apprentices learned too much of it, early, and became ensnared in Mid-World contests."

"You are already ensnared in a great contest," said the Sorceress. "The question is — can you learn quickly enough to get yourself *out* of difficulty?"

She took a key from about her neck, and with it opened what seemed to be a closet door. The cottage shuddered, and Julian felt their Portal shift, then subside.

Beyond the door was a large, chamber with a high ceiling. Sounds of an interior fountain, and light stringed instruments could be heard in the background, and there were ornaments with subtle colors hung on pillars. The far wall was covered by a huge tapestry portraying the patterns of constellations in the Southern Hemisphere, away from Alantéa. Smaller tapestries exhibited the emblems of the greatest of the benign Powers. The old Sorceress smiled at Julian.

"Did you really believe that I lived in the old cottage? Rafir, and not I, favored the dwelling of a seedy witchy creature, and so I kept it for him. Come in now, and let's have the others join us." Sebastian and Rafir said nothing but glanced at each other cautiously as they followed the Sorceress and Julian into the chamber.

In the center of the chamber on a raised table with an oval shape stood *The Game of the Masters*. Resting on many, carved wooden supports, the long oval Field of the Masters, was more than twenty paces long, like a huge banquet table. At each end of the oval were three lines of figures, each of them handcrafted and decorated in soft, deliberately understated colors. Julian walked around the oval table, noting each detail carefully. He had learned much about the *Game* and its history, but he had never himself seen a complete field.

"This is a part of my past," said the old Sorceress. "Look carefully, but do *not* touch, or you will invite one of the Powers to test your skill in the *Game*." Julian saw that the end of the Field began with eight squares, with nine for the next rank, then ten, expanding by one for each rank until the width of the Field reached twenty.

Here, the Field was at its widest, but the ranks of twenty squares continued for fifty lines until, at the other end of the Field, the number of squares again began to diminish — first to nineteen, then eighteen, until the far edge returned to the width of eight squares. Julian measured the size of the Field for a moment, counting more than a thousand squares in all; then he turned his attention to the pieces.

Each piece was intricately carved and painted with many hues. *The Sending*, on the second row, was in the image of a raven leaping fiercely from a pinnacle, and its eyes were red. Next to *The Sending* stood *The Mid-World Weapon*, shown as a stone hammer, standing upright on its wooden shaft. The stone of the hammer was plain, almost brutal, but the hammer's shaft was inlaid with tiny jewels. On the front row, *The Apprentice* was shown as an ancient scholarly book left open by a youthful student. In the last row, with the great powers, *The Ancient Secret* was depicted as an old, parchment scroll bound with stained hemp.

"In the old days," said the Sorceress, "I played with slashing movements, sweeping here and there with *The Archers* or *The Magician*, all the while testing *The Ancient Secret*, or *The Great Spell*. But now when the Board clicks, and a move is made by some distant Master, I just take my little domain a few steps further into the Mid-World, until the Board goes dead again."

Here's my piece, The Apprentice, thought Julian, looking at the open book. "What of the Masters?" he asked. "Do they have to be Mid-World Powers or Magicians?"

"Wielders of magic or perhaps one of the Power's grand counselors or generals. The Board is independent of the Powers, and of the Mid-World, so that when a *Game* begins, neither of the Masters will know the identity of the other. In the end, the Master who has lost is unmasked, or if the *Game* is hard fought until the very end, then both Masters must stand forth and declare themselves." The old Sorceress was silent for a moment as though she relived ancient contests.

"I played against Merlin more than a few times, and early on, he knew me from the way I played, so that he made little jests in his *Game,* shuffling his pieces along a little used section in mockery, and then I knew it was

Merlin. That's one of the reasons that I left the contests, as it's not wise to become so predictable."

She turned from the *Game*, back to the intent face of the Apprentice. "Do you see where you fit in, Lad? You're a piece of the front rank, useful for probing, for locating trouble, but not much use alone against a force of the second rank. Run for your life if you encounter a power of the third rank — that's what I'd do, now. Any questions?" Julian paced around the oval for a moment, taking care not to touch any part of the field. Then he stood back.

"You mentioned Passages. I've looked for trails along the Field, but there are none. Is there a pattern that I'm missing?" The Sorceress shook her head.

"The Passages change with each *Game* — those are a series of moves involving great danger to some of the lesser pieces. Should these pieces survive, their power is enhanced, but often, those sent upon the Ragged Passages are destroyed, or cast far from the center of the *Game*." Julian was silent for a moment, puzzled, frowning.

"From what you say, I've been placed on these Passages, but as yet there's been little warning of danger. Have I missed something?"

The old Sorceress regarded Julian gravely. "Did you watch the horizon last night — flickering lights, distant noises?" Julian nodded. "Then, you should know that Sea's Edge and the Halls of Merlin are cloaked in a great haze of sorcery and spell shock. I can only guess that Merlin is engaged in some terrible confrontation. Perhaps some Power of the Mid-World has arisen at last to challenge him, but I can sense neither Merlin nor God at Sea's Edge. This business makes me very anxious. You know Merlin better than I do, lad. What do you think has happened?"

Julian felt a quick flash of fear. "Who would challenge Merlin at Sea's Edge? There are problems within the League, but no one expected this...." Julian trailed off, lost in thought.

"Put Thorian out of your mind, lad. The business at Sea's Edge was not brought about by Thorian, or any other mortal wielder of magic. I'd hoped for some hint from Merlin, but we may still be able to find out a few things. I no longer play the *Game*, though you can see I haven't put aside the great Board. In *The Game of the Masters,* all the forces of Alantéa and of the Mid-World are shown." She lowered her voice. "The Field of the Masters is enchanted, an entity onto itself, aware of all the Powers while serving none. Sometimes, though, if it's asked the right questions, the Board will show what forces are on the move. Let us see."

The old Sorceress motioned Julian to a seat that was set a little distance from the center of the Board. Sebastian and Rafir followed until they faced the middle of the Board, equally distant from the two ends of the Field — the edges where the images of the powers stood unmoving. In the still air, the scent of sandalwood and mahogany rose from the Board.

At the center of the Board, the old Sorceress began to speak softly. Her eyes were closed, her voice nearly a whisper, like an old blind woman, calling up images of her lost childhood using voices remembered from her past. Gradually, her voice lowered, then stopped. Carefully, almost reverentially, the old Sorceress bowed to the Board and spread a rough powder like crystals on the center of the Field of the Masters. Then she carefully backed away and stood beside Julian.

"Let's see what the Board can tell us," she whispered.

The crystals on the Board began to glow. Slowly, at first faintly, an image began to grow from the Field... and it formed, vaguely, into the figure of *The Apprentice.*

"This, I guess, is you," the Sorceress whispered. The image blurred... and reformed into a mailed figure, who was marked by an ornament that hung over his broad chest. "Here is *The Charmed Knight,*" she whispered. "These are good tidings, as —"

Suddenly the image of *The Charmed Knight* vanished.

In its place hovered a grinning wraithlike figure. The figure was cowled and cloaked so that only a portion of its face could be seen, yet from its eye sockets came a deep glow. And its hands extended from the cloak: one hand was that of a skeleton, human, fleshless, while the other had four fingers, each covered with fur, like a beast's paw.

"This was *not* called!" hissed the Sorceress.

All the muted sounds of the chamber fell dead silent so that only the rasping breath of the Old Sorceress could be heard. The Wraith's hands held out a set of cards, and leaning forward, Julian saw that each card held the image of a piece in *The Game of the Masters*.

The Wraith turned over the first card...

The Apprentice.

The Sorceress crouched beside Julian; her body knotted with tension while she murmured in a low voice. The Wraith turned over the next card...

The Charmed Knight.

The voice of the Sorceress grew louder, murmuring the spell of *dismissal* from her choking throat.

The Wraith turned another card...

The Great Spell!

Julian was on his feet; the Sorceress was beside him, hissing like a trapped cat.

The Wraith grinned more broadly, showing...

The Archers...

The Mid-World Weapon...

The Captain.

Then, very quickly, the Wraith flashed all the other images of *The Game of the Masters,* face up. It stared at them, laughed a thin dark laugh — and vanished.

"That was not called! May the Maker save me, but the sweat's running into Granny's armpits!" The old Sorceress pushed her way out of the chamber, and through the cottage, to come out into the late morning sunlight. The others followed.

"That was *not* called!" she repeated. "That's enough to make me retire, forever!" The old woman stood outside, gathering her breath. A slight breeze lifted a grey curl from her forehead, and beneath the curl, Julian could see tiny beads of sweat. He looked away in disquiet and compassion. The old Sorceress had sought to impress each of her onlookers, but powerful forces were moving outside of her knowledge or control. He would need to reach Balardi — and quickly — the Wizard would not be turned aside by an apparition.

The Sorceress drew a deep breath and broke the silence.

"It's much worse than I thought. Rafir, do you still want to go?" The fox nodded, slowly. Julian put his arm around the shoulder of the Sorceress.

"Mother, we will start now. Thank you for your warning and your counsel." At Julian's touch, the Sorceress seemed able to see him clearly for the first time, and her greyish green eyes focused on his features.

"You *are* a good lad," she said softly. Her shoulders sagged, and she seemed to become smaller. "And you are more than an Apprentice, are you not? Yet there's a great trouble brewing that's far beyond your strength. The Wizards are wary of the Gods, and so you know little about the Powers of the Mid-World. How much was Merlin able to tell you?"

Julian laughed softly. "I've read scores of confusing texts and scrolls, but when I asked questions, I was not even allowed to whisper the Names of the Great Dark Gods."

Then Julian leaned over and touched the old Sorceress so that he could speak directly into her mind. *But I do know the names and natures of many of those Powers: Moloch the Fire God, and Dark Souled Set, and Ahriman, Master of all Lies, and Arioch, and many others.*

The Sorceress nodded, sighing. "It is good that you know of them and are wary. Some sort of truce has been maintained with those Powers, however, and clashes between those beings and the Wizards' League seemed to have lessened. Is that time of peace now ending? There's a long history concerning the Powers and their impact on the Wizards' League, but I fear there's no time for lessons. I wish that there was something else I could do to aid you." Suddenly, the face of the old Sorceress flickered with surprise.

"That's another reason I should retire — my mind is shaken, and I've forgotten something important." She turned back into the cottage and emerged a moment later, holding two carved rings of green jade. Each was about wrist size.

"These are Seeking Stones," she said. "I've dreamt many times of Rafir, lost in a far land, with no way to return. These charms will help — they are much stronger than anything I could make myself and I paid a steep price for them. Here is one for Rafir, and one for your small servant."

Julian took the Talismans from the damp hands of the old Sorceress.

"We are warned now, Mother." He embraced her gently. "I'm half tempted to return to Sea's Edge, yet I think that Merlin would want us to proceed to Gravengate. Balardi will tell us what to do after that. Farewell, for the moment." He mounted Bluescent. Sebastian bowed to the Sorceress, then joined Julian, while watching the fox warily out of the corner of his eye. They began to ride, slowly, away from the cottage.

"Goodbye, Granny," said Rafir, and the Sorceress drew the small fox into her arms, and hugged him, then set him down. She turned, suddenly an old woman alone, and went back into her cottage. Rafir watched until the door closed, then he turned and raced after Julian.

Chapter Two
The Fight at the Ford

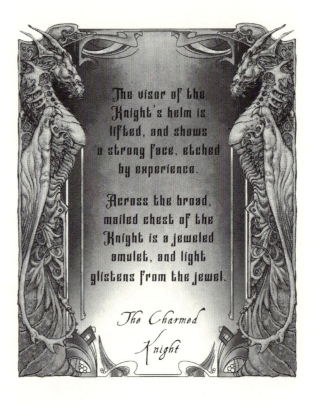

The visor of the Knight's helm is lifted, and shows a strong face, etched by experience.

Across the broad, mailed chest of the Knight is a jeweled amulet, and light glistens from the jewel.

The Charmed Knight

JULIAN LASHED HIS SADDLE POUCH higher and tightened it so that the fox could ride without swaying and flapping with every motion of Bluescent. Rafir now rode inside the pouch, fox face peering out from its leather, studying the countryside with great interest. It was only a little after noon, but the day was becoming darker as layers of clouds began to block the sunlight. Scattered trees beside the Greenway were swaying gently with gusts of wind.

Sebastian rode Julian's shoulder, and the Familiar glanced down with an unhappy expression, watching as the fox rode at Julian's side. Rafir looked too comfortable, as though he had been traveling with Julian for years, instead of less than an hour.

"What did the old woman say about getting lost?" he asked Julian. "We just found the fox, and now he's supposed to be lost soon?" From the tone of his voice, it was clear that Sebastian would be happy if the fox became lost quickly — and forever.

Julian smiled. "Nothing was said about being lost *soon*," he said quietly, "but there's always a chance of becoming separated. Rafir, what do you know about the League?"

"Granny told me about Merlin, and Balardi, and Thorian," said the fox, "and there was some warrior that began with an 'O.' Granny and I watched you and Sebastian for the last month or two, so I know about people you've met recently."

"Then you've wasted your time," said Sebastian. "We haven't seen anybody of consequence in the last while. And the name you've forgotten is Orlan."

"Well, Rafir, here is your first lesson," Julian continued. "We are on the Greenway that links the strongpoints of the League. We're traveling east toward the fortress of Balardi, called Gravengate. The Steward General of Balardi is Harmadast. Baron Cadmon is lord of the land through which we now pass, and the Baron is a key member of the League, a chief ally of Balardi's." Rafir's face was pinched in concentration, and Julian smiled. "Don't try to remember everything yet. If we become separated, follow the Greenway east to Gravengate or west to Sea's Edge, and you'll find friends. Don't go east beyond Gravengate, because Thorian's friendship is now uncertain."

"You should mention about Orlan," added Sebastian. "He's now a counselor to Merlin, and if swords or spears are needed, then Kalanin and Galad would be called."

"Good," said Julian. "Your first lesson is complete. Now let me have a few moments to think in silence."

Hoof sounds clopped on. The day grew darker, without rain yet, but mists were beginning to roll down from distant hills. In their silent, slow movement along the Greenway, Julian tried to organize his thoughts. Two events of great importance seemed to be happening simultaneously: first, the slow decay of the League, as Thorian slipped away from the alliance. Second, some great test of strength had occurred at Sea's edge. Were the two events related? It was impossible to tell. There was a third event, minor in relation to the first two: he had finally been given his first lesson in *The Game of the Masters*. No doubt, Merlin had arranged his lesson long ago, asking the Sorceress to counsel his Apprentice before he entered his first time of danger. Yet their challenge had proved greater than the Sorceress had expected, perhaps even greater than Merlin had anticipated.

The first sweeps of mist pushed by them, leaving layers of tiny droplets. Bluescent sneezed, her pace faltering then steadying.

Julian's thoughts turned back to *The Game of the Masters*. If his role was that of *The Apprentice* on the Field of the Masters, then he was moving into a greater conflict, alone and unsupported. At least he had been warned and would not be caught by surprise.

Slowly, Julian began to extend his senses into the mist, over the land that surrounded the Greenway.

His mind drifted from his body, into the bank of mists, and his hands relaxed, letting the reins go, so that Bluescent slowed, and finally stopped. Rafir was about to speak, but Sebastian hushed him to silence.

Beyond the mists and about the river before them, Julian sensed the strands of a web of enchantments, like the trap of a great spider, ready to engulf any intruders.... Great care and malice had been spent in weaving many spells together so that now the lands of Balardi and Cadmon were shielded against aid from Sea's Edge. And the ford was guarded — Julian could sense the presence of some being at the ford. He could not identify it, but the creature pulsed with power — great physical strength. Julian turned in his saddle, looking back along the Greenway, letting his Farsight drift in the other direction.

Behind them horsemen were coming, only a few, racing toward the ford, and there was something about them that turned aside his Farsight so that they were hidden from him.

· ⋈ ·

Julian drew a deep breath, clearing his mind, and then he turned, heading again toward the ford. His hand reached down and ruffled the fur of the fox beside him.

"Let's have a look at the ford," he said, quietly. "Best that you are out of sight — and silent." Rafir vanished. Bluescent pushed slowly through the mists that obscured the road before them. The river was hidden by banks of fog, but they could hear rushing water in the distance.

Julian murmured softly to Sebastian, "Watch carefully what you become, and act accordingly."

Julian took the small bells from the mare's harness, muffling them carefully in his saddle pouch. As he touched the first strands of the web of sorcery confronting them, he drew on the energies of the Mid-World, while cloaking his own power. He began to weave an illusion around them so that their appearance changed with every step that Bluescent took.

Rafir peered out and watched as Julian changed slowly, to become old and gnarled, and bent, his clothes those of a farm laborer. Bluescent became older, more like a nag, and Sebastian — here Rafir almost laughed — the little Familiar had become a snarly tomcat with one eye, riding on the shoulder of his surly peasant master.

Disguised and motley, they rode deeper into the spells' embrace, where enormous banks of low mist cloaked the road to the ford; but the rush of water grew slowly louder in their ears.

At the edge of the river, Julian bent and peered across the ford. The river flowed wide at this crossing, with much of it surging through underground caverns so that the depth of the Bariloch was less than two feet. It could be forded if travelers were careful to select the right path across it. Banks of mist thickened over the river, obscuring its opposite bank. Bluescent stepped cautiously into the flowing water. In the middle of the river, a massive figure turned toward them.

The mist cleared a little, and in the lifting gloom, a huge figure loomed, rising as tall as a troll over shallow water. A massive shield was in its left hand, and in its right hand was a heavy mace; the creature stood armed and menacing, but motionless. Bluescent raised her head and backed quickly out of the water.

Julian, an aged and confused figure, slid from his horse and his booted feet took a step into the shallows, peering up at the troll figure. Water racing over his feet was as chilled as ice. The creature's skin was a greyish-brown, and for armor, it wore a green hide over its chest and thighs; but its own skin looked to be as thick as its green hide.

The creature stared back at Julian, and perceiving no challenge, slipped the mace into a loop at its side, and slung the shield by a strap over its shoulder. Julian, showing uncertainty, stepped farther into the shallows, and called out in a loud, wavering voice, "I've got to get home...." He pointed to the opposite bank. "It's over there." The creature said nothing. Julian turned to Bluescent and began fumbling with his saddle pouch. "I can pay a toll!" Julian called out in a cracked voice. "Here, I've got coins!" But now, the creature had become bored, or annoyed, for it waded closer and pulled a large boulder from the riverbed, raising the stone above its head threateningly. "I've even got gold," Julian croaked as he edged away.

The creature hurled the boulder at them as Julian and Bluescent scurried from the river. The rock hit with a great splash of water, drenching the Apprentice as he reached the riverbank.

Julian shook the water from himself as he retreated from the ford back to the Greenway. "Not a good start — it will take more than an illusion to master this crossing," he muttered to Sebastian and Rafir. "Let's see what's coming up behind us." Rafir, too, was no longer dry, and a stray thought slipped into his mind that his first adventure was nasty, wet work, and not completely heroic.

Julian rode a few hundred paces back along the Greenway, halting beside the shoulder of the wide road. He kept the image of an old farmer for himself and that of a tomcat for Sebastian. Bluescent grazed at the roadside, as droplets of mist fell quietly around them. After a time, they heard the muffled sounds of horsemen riding in the distance. Then there came motion in the mists, with two riders approaching swiftly. Both riders and mounts were covered with ash and soot, but the insignia of the League could still be seen on their shields and armor. A team of packhorses followed them, scrambling in confusion.

Julian raised his hand in greeting, but the first horseman rode past him, swaying in his saddle, and the second rider gave only a half wave and rode on. Julian cast the illusion from himself, and called out in a loud clear voice:

"Hold, for the League! The ford is blocked!"

The riders reined in their horses and came to a confused halt. The second rider leaped from his horse to help the first, who was toppling from his saddle. Julian rode quickly to their side as the first rider was pulled from horseback. His helmet was unfastened, and Julian stared into the face of Kalanin — who was breathing heavily, while streaks of ash ran down his face.

Julian turned in astonishment to the second rider: Galad!

"What in the Maker's Name has happened to you?" he asked.

"Nothing good," said Galad, "but we should talk later. Can you help him?" Julian turned back to Kalanin who lay on his back, gasping for breath, mist droplets sliding over his face. Kneeling closer, Julian touched Kalanin, *reaching*: the Knight's lungs were choked by fumes and air filled with ashes.

Julian stared into the mists: none of the charms or potions in his pouches could deal with this kind of injury. In this case, Kalanin's body would have to cure itself, if it were able, though there were ways to aid the body in its struggle. Julian rummaged quickly through his baggage and from one pouch he drew a silver vial and a small earthenware cup. He poured a little powder from the vial into the cup, mixed it with water, and tilting Kalanin's head back, poured the mixture slowly into the knight's mouth. Galad watched on with troubled eyes.

"Will he heal, do you think?" he asked Julian.

The Apprentice stood. "I've never dealt with an injury like this before, but Heart's Ease will help, at least it will strengthen his breathing." It was raining harder now, and the droplets streaked more of the soot from Galad's face. "How in all the wide world of Alantéa the Forerunner did this happen?" asked Julian.

Galad shook his head grimly. "We'll need to let Kalanin tell you the story," he said, drawing a deep breath, "but we would not be in this sorry condition if we had obeyed our instructions." Galad waved to the pack horses. "You'll know part of the answer after you've looked at our baggage."

Kalanin's lungs seemed to be growing stronger, and he coughed every now and again as his powerful body struggled to expel the debris from his lungs. Julian walked over to the pack horses. As he touched the chest he recoiled in surprise. It had been sealed by Merlin! And sealed so that few of the League might have the power to open it. In this chest was aid for Balardi, weapons, and tools of power. So, war was upon them! How had it come to this?

Then the Gift reached out to Julian: here was the dream that had come to him so many times, of riding out on a vital errand, and meeting others before a river crossing. But where were the others? Where was the strength and confidence that had always been shown before in all his previous night visions? In all those visions there had been more than three, many more, with far greater power — and the sun had been shining. Where were the others, and where was Merlin?

In the mist and drizzle, Julian turned back to Kalanin and Galad. The older knight was sitting up, though still lying on the ground, and Galad was leaning over, talking to him in a low voice.

"So, war and disaster are upon us," said Julian, "but where's Merlin?" Kalanin put out a hand and Galad helped pull him to his feet.

"We were told that Merlin would follow, as quickly as he was able," Kalanin said, and he coughed again, bending a little with the effort, then straightening, still shaky. "We were to ride to Balardi's side or join with Baron Cadmon if we could not reach Gravengate before our foes did." Despite his injuries, Kalanin's voice struggled to seem measured and reasonable.

"That's no answer!" Julian muttered. "Something has gone horribly wrong — the Mid-World knows about our troubles, I know we are in the middle of a disaster, and even the village Elders will soon learn. Already the Bariloch is barred to us, so why don't you tell me now, without half-truths or evasions: where is Merlin?"

Kalanin and Galad exchanged looks. Rain and mist continued to sweep over their armor, with soot caking and streaking over armor that had once been polished and bright. Now, the two knights were damp, dark images of defeat and disaster.

"You're right, Apprentice," Kalanin said after a moment. "I don't understand what's happened to the League, seeming so strong one moment, then blown apart like a puff of smoke.... But I'll tell you our side of the matter with all its nasty details. Just let me sit for a moment." He sank back onto the long, wet grasses and coughed. After a moment, Galad knelt beside him on one knee. Julian stood, watching the two warriors as rain droplets pelted down upon them.

"It was yesterday morning," Kalanin said, clearing his hoarse voice, "little more than a day ago that we were instructed, by messenger, to journey to Gravengate, and to find you along the way, if we could. All their preparations were made in great haste, as though to forestall discussion; all the questions asked of the messenger were turned aside. At last, I grew angry with the man, and he retreated to the halls. Galad and I followed, pushing past sentinels, demanding to see Merlin.

"After a few moments, Merlin came down to see us. His face was grim and preoccupied. 'You must leave *now!*' he said. 'I will follow as soon as I can, but here at Sea's Edge, I am near the center of understanding: on this night, I may name the Master of our troubles.' At this point, Merlin hesitated. 'Tell Balardi what I have said. Also, Balardi will know that a dark power, a Sorcerer, aids Thorian. Tell Balardi that this Sorcerer is only a part of a greater mystery. Now, farewell! I will come when I can. Leave now!' We learned nothing more from him."

Julian stood for a moment with a misty rain seeping over him, while his thoughts raced. "So, Merlin is caught up in a great conflict with some Power of the Mid-World," he murmured. "But why should he choose this time?"

"Perhaps the conflict is not with the Mid-World," Kalanin said softly, glancing into the mists, "and perhaps the time was chosen by another Power with might greater than Merlin's."

"None of this made us happy," Galad added. "Even this solemn captain," he nodded at Kalanin, "was persuaded to disregard his instructions. Instead of leaving immediately as ordered, we waited, hidden in the hills above Sea's Edge, and we watched as the peoples of Sea's Edge fled the Halls of Merlin. About this flight from Sea's Edge, Merlin had suggested nothing."

"I think now that Merlin was sending his people to safety," said Kalanin, "and that they were probably guided by Orlan. That should have warned us away, but still, we waited, ready to go to Merlin's aid, or so we thought.

"That night, on the hillside, Galad stood the first watch, but woke me early — all around Sea's Edge a great stillness had gathered, as though the Earth was holding its breath. Then came crashing sounds, and noises of raging waters, and the ground shook, then exploded. The ash would have buried us if we hadn't fled in haste. As it was, we lost two pack horses, and we'll be searching for food in the villages if we don't reach Balardi soon."

Kalanin looked at Julian with a grim but compassionate look, then rose and placed a hand on the shoulder of the Apprentice. "I would not fault you if you wished to return to investigate the disaster at Sea's Edge — but we need your help to reach Gravengate."

Julian looked from the somber eyes of Kalanin and into the face of Galad: the Knight's usual partial smile had vanished, and his eyes watched the Apprentice uncertainly.

"That's not a choice," Julian said, "and you know it." He turned from the two men and gazed into the mists. *Merlin my Master, how did your wisdom fail so quickly, with no warning? Without your own power, all the strength has passed from the images shown so often to me in night visions is lost. Do we go forward? Is there truly another choice with Sea's Edge in ruins?* He turned back to Kalanin and Galad, drawing a deep breath.

"We'll try to reach Balardi or Baron Cadmon," he said quietly, "but you should know it won't be easy: even now the Bariloch is barred to us."

"So, you told us," said Kalanin. "How many hold the ford?"

"Only one," Julian replied, "but the river is truly 'held' by a great web of sorcery, a mass of spells woven around each another. These enchantments I see as a trap, ready to be sprung on wielders of magic who use their powers to force a river crossing. As for the being holding the ford, I know nothing of its name or origin, but it seems to be a creature of great physical power."

"But *I* know its name," came a voice from just above the ground. "It's a Gogra," and the fox flashed into view.

"Here's a new companion, named Rafir," Julian explained. "He's a most excellent Mid-World Spy — your secrets should be left unspoken unless you're certain that Rafir is elsewhere." Julian squatted down beside the fox. "So, what is a Gogra?"

"'The Gogra are large and extremely powerful, living above the foothills of Mount Evergrey, where the snow breaks and the streams flow. They do not like fire,'" the fox recited. "That's what the Sorceress taught me."

Kalanin looked up into the mist and drizzle. "Not much chance for fire," he murmured, then he turned back to the fox. "Welcome to our League, Rafir, or what's left of it. Let's have a look at this creature of yours."

· 🜛 ·

With a heavy fog gathering around them, it was difficult to know what time of day it was, but now as they rode through the mists toward the ford of Bariloch, it was growing darker, with nightfall coming in a short while. From the top of a little slope, they could see the edge of rushing water, running thin and wide, but of the Gogra, they could see nothing, nor was there even a hint of the opposite bank.

As they eased quietly down the slope, Galad whispered to Julian, "Did you try talking to it? Perhaps we can persuade it to leave."

In answer, they heard a deep bellow from the middle of the shallow river. The creature had heard or scented them.

Now, as they stood in the mist at the river's edge, they could see the outline of the creature against the gathering darkness. The creature called out again and hefted a great boulder. Galad could feel the hair on the back of his neck rise, as he saw the brutal strength of the thing. They retreated a little distance from the bank, then Kalanin left his horse, returning to the riverbank on foot, studying the ground closely. The Gogra hurled the massive stone, and Kalanin leaped away.

"It's too dark. I can't see what stones lie across the riverbed," Kalanin murmured. "More time lost." Darkness was falling over the ford, leaving them wet and tired on the wrong side of the river.

"We'll need shelter and fire tonight," said Galad, "if we intend to force a crossing tomorrow. A few hundred paces from the ford there's a shallow cave system. What do you think?" Kalanin nodded in weariness, but Julian hesitated.

"We've looked at this problem from only one side. We might also study the blockade from the inside of the fortress — in this case from the other side of the river. Sebastian, perhaps, can help us." The little Familiar's heart sank. He was cold and wet and beginning to shiver, but he stretched his wings and readied for flight. Seeing his Familiar's hesitation, Julian added, "While Sebastian investigates, we'll find shelter and begin a fire."

Galad led them to a hillside less than half a league from the ford, where one cave sheltered their horses, and a smaller, hunched one housed the rest of their party.

"With our recent bad fortune, we'll probably find a bear — or an ogre," Galad muttered, but the caves were empty. A fire was built near the entrance, and they sat back, beginning to dry. After a few moments, Sebastian fluttered into the cave, shivering as he edged closer to the fire.

"I can't pass," the little Familiar said, teeth chattering. "Both above, and on either side of the ford, the way is barred, to me, at least."

"I'm not surprised," Julian said, "but we needed to test the passage."

They ate in silence. When they finished, Kalanin and Galad spoke quietly together about methods of countering the size and strength of the creature at the ford. Julian sat, warming himself, a little apart from the two men, watching them from beneath half closed eyes.

Kalanin and Galad were two of Merlin's most trusted servants — emissaries, messengers, warriors as required. Galad had brown hair, and was broad, powerful, and quick. In his youth his mood was light, bantering, humorous, but the disaster at Sea's Edge seemed to have sobered him for the moment. Kalanin was older by seven or eight years, a little taller, a little less broad; his dark, close cropped beard showed flecks of grey, but he was dangerous, extremely dangerous, and there was a powerful, measured intellect hidden behind his somber, unruffled exterior.

Yet neither of them was whole; beyond the dust and ash wounds, the fall of Sea's Edge had stunned and blunted them — the Gift showed them healing, but would they be a match for the Gogra, a creature that looked larger than a troll? As for the "Gogra," he turned to Rafir and touched his soft fox fur.

"How were you certain that it was a Gogra? There must be many tribes of troll creatures."

"By its smell," Rafir murmured, half asleep. "The Sorceress had me memorize their smells as well as their shapes." Julian nodded thoughtfully, staring into the flames.

· X ·

By daybreak, the rain had stopped, but the forests and meadows of the land were wet, and Alantéa was bathed in fragrances as many trees and shrubs were blossoming so that the air was rich. Julian watched as Kalanin and Galad armed themselves in their linked mail, checking each other's armor. In addition to their spears, each bore a shield and sword for close fighting. With their great chargers and heavy armor, they hoped to ride down the creature in the shallow waters of the ford.

They rode slowly down to the river, horses snorting and blowing winter breaths from their nostrils. At the ford, they came to a halt; before them, in the middle of the driver, the Gogra rose as before, armed with a shield in one hand and a great mace in the other. Now they could see that beneath its bulky hide, a sheet of metal was banded about its waist. Kalanin measured the creature with his eyes — it was far taller than Galad, even with the knight on horseback, and it was more than twice the thickness of a man.

"Very lovely," Galad muttered under his breath. "I'm glad I took only a bit of food this morning. But should we not speak to it? Convince it to leave?" Kalanin edged his way to the river and called out in a loud voice,

"By the League of Three Wizards, I call upon you to return to the Mid-World! Leave now, or be—" Here, the Gogra again swooped into the waters, raising, and hurling another great boulder onto the riverbank. They scrambled quickly out of range.

"It's charming, too," said Galad in a quiet voice. "Does it speak or just grunt?" He shook his head at Kalanin. "And by reputation, you were such a skilled diplomat." Kalanin did not respond, turning instead to Julian.

"Note that it does not seem inclined to leave the river and pursue us. What's next?"

"I might try to move it," said Julian, "but I think that we are faced by a trap for wielders of magic. We should try to force our way forward but by spear and sword."

"Has it a weak point, do you think?" asked Kalanin. Julian shook his head as Kalanin turned back to Galad. "We should be able to get one spear point into it. I'll take the shield side if you look to the club hand."

The two warriors drew their horses back to gather speed before reaching the running water. Their chargers began moving slowly down the slope, gathering speed as they entered the ford. Kalanin was a few feet forward. Both spears were aimed at the great head of the creature. Water foamed about the legs of their chargers as they plunged through the shallow river. The Gogra tensed, snarling. Kalanin's spear was met by the Gogra's shield and glanced off, while Galad's spear struck the Gogra in the shoulder of its club hand and shattered. Galad was hurled into the rushing waters.

The creature let out a great piercing cry of pain and rage, so loud that Sebastian, on the riverbank, covered his ears.

Galad struggled out of the rushing shallows, drawing his sword. The Gogra moved to destroy him, but Kalanin slashed at the shield arm of the creature, diverting it. The Gogra took the stroke on its shoulder armor and glanced a wild blow off the shield side of Kalanin, numbing him, nearly felling him from his charger. Galad leaped through the shallows and took a sweeping cut at the exposed leg of the Gogra. His blade bit and he could see green skin under the opened wound. The Gogra wheeled, swinging its mace, and shattered Galad's blade. Galad stumbled back and catching the bridle of his charger was dragged to the shore. Kalanin followed, reeling in his saddle.

The Gogra was stronger than two powerfully armed and dangerous Charmed Knights.

Julian watched the creature as it stood triumphant in midriver, powerful and menacing. He went to Kalanin's side, examining the warrior's arm and shoulder: nothing seemed broken, but his ribs and shoulder were badly bruised. Julian passed Kalanin a mixture of Serpine and Bindweed for his wound, then turned his attention again to the ford of Bariloch.

"So, it's my turn to force a crossing," Julian said, drawing a deep breath. "Perhaps if sorcery is not used openly...." He watched the Gogra for a moment, then turned to Kalanin and Galad. "As a healer, I've been called to the Mid-World at times, and a few have promised me aid in payment. There's one I may be able to bring through a small, enchanted passageway, perhaps small enough so that it would not be observed." He looked down at Sebastian and Rafir. "Sebastian knows Kath, but you do not, Rafir. Best you were not shown to distract him." The fox vanished but watched on with large, curious eyes.

Out in the water, the Gogra pulled the spear point from its shoulder and was washing its wounds in flowing river waters.

Julian sat quietly on his cloak for a moment, letting his concentration strengthen. He sought the great serpent, Kath, who had pledged service to Julian a few years ago. He whispered spell words, and within those words, he wove the serpent's secret name, one that pledged him to Julian. The Apprentice was silent again for a moment, then whispered, "Kath," first in the lightest of tones, then gently, and finally aloud, as Julian felt the being move closer to him.

Sebastian felt a surge of fear, as the head of the serpent appeared in Julian's lap. Kath's head was more than a foot in width, with a darting red tongue that flicked in and out of enormous jaws. Only its head had appeared, but Rafir could sense the power of the creature. Galad let his hand drift to the hilt of his broken sword.

Julian sat, stroking the great serpent's head. "Kath, I am barred from my river passage, and I sought you to clear it for me." Julian nodded toward the Gogra. "Let us see if that creature is stronger than mighty Kath." The serpent stared at the Gogra, then began to spill out from the portal, fully forty feet of its thick body racing toward the shallow river.

The Gogra leaped up, grabbing both club and shield as Kath surged into the water. Only flashing coils could be seen as the serpent raced through the shallows of the ford.

Suddenly, the head of Kath shot up and sank its fangs into the wrist of the Gogra's club hand. With a bellow of surprise, the Gogra dropped its club and smashed the serpent's upper body with its shield. Kath recoiled but now caught his lower body about the huge leg of the Gogra, struggling to pull the creature down into the waters. As the coils wrapped about its body, the Gogra dropped its shield and seized the neck of the serpent with both hands.

Now a trial of strength began between two powerful beings of the Mid-World. The Gogra's huge arms knotted as it applied all its massive power to squeeze the life from the serpent, but its breath came in great gasps as coils tightened about its body.

The two strove in midriver as the waters of distant mountains flowed about them — to Rafir, they seemed like giant statues, frozen in the middle of surging waters. Then, first a flicker, then a blink, and then the eyes of the great serpent began to close; its body shuddered as its hold on the Gogra began to lessen. The Gogra, gathering itself, hurled the serpent into the water and against the stones on the riverbed, then reached for its club, moving to break the serpent's spine.

Julian sent Sebastian hurtling through the air, soaring and waving, then shrieking at the Gogra. The creature was distracted for a moment, and when it turned back to its foe, Julian had opened a passageway and sent Kath back into the Mid-World. On the riverbank, Kalanin and Galad stood silent, awed by the power of the battle and its finality.

"Well done, and timely," Julian said to Sebastian, then he shook his head. "Kath nearly mastered him."

"Is there anything else we might call upon?" asked Sebastian.

"Only my wits," Julian said grimly, and he walked forward, wading into the shallow river. The Gogra, exhausted, was seated in the water and made no move to stand when Julian approached midriver.

The Apprentice halted a little beyond the Gogra's reach.

"We seem unable to move you by force," Julian said quietly. "I thought perhaps that our reasoning might sway you." The Gogra said nothing, but kept its head downcast, face toward the water. Julian looked closely at the creature: sheets of sweat rippled down the Gogra's head and chest, although the water was as chilled as ice and the day was overcast. The Gogra's wounds were seeping blood that was brown and touched by red, but even now flesh seemed to be closing over both spear and sword wounds, and the gash in the Gogra's wrist made by Kath had almost vanished.

"Your task is great, being of the Mid-World. Even if you succeed in barring us, others will come who have the power to move you — we are servants and allies of the Wizards. Keep your victories intact and return to the Mid-World in peace."

The Gogra looked up, and its eyes were like those of a pig, squinty, and bloodshot, filled with malice. It spoke at last in a voice like grating stone: "None will come — ever again, for the day of the Wizards is done," and it lunged toward the Apprentice. Julian dove away, sweeping his staff at the Gogra, lashing its outstretched hand with bolts of force, so that it drew back. Wet and shaken, Julian reached the riverbank, then turned and faced the creature.

"*You* cannot judge the Wizards and their time," he cried. "But by the Maker, your time in Alantéa is at an end!"

He took a deep breath and turned to Kalanin and Galad. "So, at the last, I must turn to magic. We need to fight our way forward, no matter what weight of power is raised against us."

Julian stood by the riverbank, staff in hand, with Sebastian, his Familiar at his side. And he caused a *whisper* to sweep up and down the river, a hint to the fishes of better feeding, warning frogs and serpents of coming frosts, rumors to the otters and beavers of roaming wolf packs so that all living things cleared this section of the Bariloch. Julian then went upstream, intoning quietly all the while, drawing on the lessons of his Wizard masters, and he cast a potion on the waters, a substance that was carried swiftly down the river. Then he returned to stand beside Kalanin and Galad on the western bank of the Bariloch.

"Now comes our third attempt to clear the ford," Julian murmured. "If it fails, we may have to make our crossing much farther to the north." Kalanin and Galad watched the Gogra and the riverbed closely: nothing seemed changed.

Galad opened his mouth to question Julian, but then he saw that the Gogra was standing again in the river, showing signs of uncertainty and discomfort. Sheets of sweat were pouring from the Gogra's body, and it was swaying back and forth on its feet, low moaning sounds slipping from its gaping mouth as the river began to heat.

As steam began to curl from the swirling waters, the Gogra gave a great bellow of alarm and raced with huge splashing feet to the opposite side of the river.

Julian raised his staff as high as his chest, holding it with his right hand, and cried out in a loud voice:

"Halt! By the emblem of the Wizards' League in Merlin's land; by your broken oath; and by our pact with Taurog, the Father of Trolls, I command you to remain here — until Merlin or your Master shall come to free you!" The Gogra twitched and shook, as its body locked to the ground, then, as frozen as a statue it did not move again.

When the heat died down, they crossed with ease.

"That surprised me," Galad said, watching Julian closely. "Just a year ago, the outcome would have been different, I think."

Weariness tugged at Julian and a grim foreboding weighed him down. "Don't celebrate this as a victory," the Apprentice murmured. "We are like rabbits who have escaped a weasel, but now a fearsome tiger is awake, stalking us on the forest floor: the Gogra was no more than a tripwire, and now the trap is sprung. Be very, very careful."

Chapter Three
The Storm

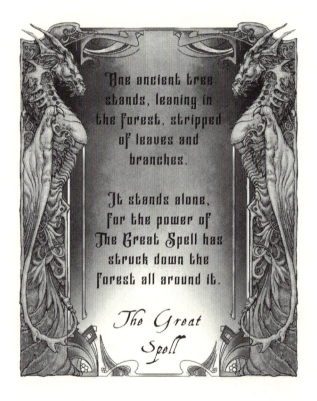

One ancient tree stands, leaning in the forest, stripped of leaves and branches.

It stands alone, for the power of The Great Spell has struck down the forest all around it.

The Great Spell

A**S THEY RODE DOWN THE** Greenway through the overcast afternoon, Galad imagined their passage as though seeing themselves from a distance: they were grey figures, clad in drab cloaks, hunched in their saddles, armor tarnished, skin still streaked with ash; and those grey men were leading tired packhorses into an even greyer afternoon. Galad drew his shattered, partial sword and laughed ruefully.

"We're a sad, dingy lot to be riding off hoping to save our great Wizard's League. Grimy, and not too well prepared." He held up his shattered sword. "Here's one warrior that's nearly weaponless, another struggling with injuries, a shivering Familiar, and a Mid-World Spy who may or may not still be with us." Rafir could not be seen, except for the bulge he left in Julian's saddle pouch. "Our one hope is that Julian will conjure his way through to Gravengate and deliver us with the baggage." Galad smiled cheerfully at Julian, but his smile passed quickly when he saw that the face of the Apprentice was drawn, pale, and his body was slumped in his saddle. "So, not all's well with you either," Galad added softly. "What's happening?"

"The spell's shock, a backlash." Julian drew a deep breath. "It's not something I've felt before, but I think it's a measure of the strength of our foes. I should be better in a while." He managed a strained smile. "It's only fatigue, a weariness, no damage to the Gift within me. It will pass."

Another promising sign, Galad thought grimly as he sheathed his shattered sword.

Julian rode in silence for a while, studying the road before them. The great Greenway that linked the fortresses of the League ran west from Sea's Edge to the east, ending at Stone Mountain. The Greenway ran wide and mainly straight, and it was kept clear partly by the enchantments of the Wizards. Other roads crossed Alantéa, through all its towns, fields and forests, villages, and meadows, and were maintained by the peoples of Alantéa. Both the Greenway and the other roads of the League had been built originally as highways for the petty kings of Alantéa, who looked to their fortresses, and their raids, and the swift movements of their small armies, only dimly understanding how the Powers of the Mid-World — the Gods — played them as minor pieces in their far larger contests.

Now, as he stared east down the Greenway, Julian saw that a storm was gathering over the eastern horizon, with a slow pressure of wind building all around them. And he could feel the unwavering Farsight of their enemies as it followed their progress with the sharp eyes of raptors seeking prey.

"I was afraid of this," Julian murmured, watching the storm as it gathered over the Greenway. "They know we are coming."

"But who are 'they'?" asked Sebastian. "Is Thorian blocking us, or is it that Sorcerer that's helping Thorian?" Julian looked to Kalanin for confirmation; the Knight only shook his head, as though to answer in the negative, or to say that he didn't know.

"It seems more likely that Thorian and his Sorcerer ally would deal first with Balardi and Baron Cadmon," said Julian, "but powerful forces have been summoned to prevent aid from reaching Balardi. Did Merlin say anything of this to you, Kalanin?" The Knight shook his head and did not speak. Ash and fumes were clearing slowly from his lungs, but his ribs throbbed with pain as the charms of Julian struggled to heal his battered side.

"Here's what troubles me," Julian continued. "I'm afraid that they have enlisted one of the Powers of the Mid-World to check Merlin, and without Merlin, using some Power of the Mid-World against us is like using a mace to crush a fruit fly."

"Let's hope that the wings of that fruit fly are swift then," Galad said, staring into the oncoming storm.

Rafir sat in the saddle pouch carried by Bluescent, trying to sort all the new pieces of knowledge into neat piles of wisdom. He flickered back into view.

"But what are these things in the chest, that we're taking to the Wizard?" he asked. "Can't these help us? Why can't we use them against whoever's opposing us?"

"It might be better not to think too long about our baggage," Julian said quietly. "Their contents are hidden from the Farsight of our enemies, but they might learn about them from your stray thoughts. I will tell you this much: in my hands these gifts are nothing, but in the hands of Balardi, they might well be extremely powerful tools. It's more important for the luggage to arrive than the baggage carriers."

Galad stared into the darkening eastern skies that were spreading rain and gloom and wild winds across their path. "One thing is certain," he said, "if we thought that this task involved only a pleasant ride down the Greenway, we were badly mistaken." Just then a flurry of raindrops swept over Rafir's face and all the neat piles of knowledge he had constructed spilled away from him, and he felt that true wisdom lay in staying dry, so he burrowed deeper into the shelter of his saddle pouch.

And now each of them began to feel the dampness and cold of the coming storm. Kalanin and Galad drew cloaks over their chainmail, while Sebastian hunched his wings closer to his body and wrapped himself in folds of Julian's cloak. Ragged winds began blowing chilled mountain air through their bodies, like winter ripping through summer wildflowers.

Julian stared up into the darkening sky. Far above him, the afternoon sun was blocked by distant sheets of dark clouds that covered the upper reaches of the sky from horizon to horizon. Beneath those higher clouds, low and fat grey ones lumbered toward them, full of thunder and lightning and dark rain. Rafir peered out again: the oncoming storm was like smoke from a great burning; and now heavy winds were beginning to whistle through the woodlands. Leaves were being torn from the forest, swirling westward toward Sea's Edge. When broken branches began toppling to the ground, the fox pushed his small body deeper into the saddle pouch.

The three riders were forced to dismount from their horses, leading them by the reins, as the winds beat against them with increasing ferocity.

"Is there nothing you can do to stop this?" asked Kalanin, coughing, his voice raised to counter the noise of the wind.

"I might," Julian called back, "if, like our enemies, I had time. If I were dry." Kalanin shook his head and pressed forward. Rafir's thoughts turned to the comfort and warmth of the cabin's hearth where the old Sorceress told her stories, but then with a determined effort, he pushed those images from his mind.

For now the storm had moved beyond speech or stray thought. Frigid winds blew through their clothing as they led their horses, faces bent to the ground. Water was streaming over the Greenway, first clear, then muddy, as hooves and boots broke its soft, grassy surface. In nearby fields and forests, dead trunks of ancient trees began toppling to the ground. Lightning flickered briefly over the countryside, with low rumbles of thunder rolling toward them. Galad brought himself closer to Julian, struggling to make himself heard over the noise of the storm.

"With the metal we carry, we are magnets for lightning," Galad shouted. "We'll need to find shelter and wait this storm out!"

Julian nodded, looking up at the darkened sky. "But what shelter, where?" On either side of the Greenway, the land was heavily wooded, dark, and uninviting. "We can't go back to the ford."

Galad shook his head, pointing to the north. "I know this part of the League. There's shelter — I can get us there before nightfall if we start now." Julian nodded and pulled his hood back over his face. Again, bent to the ground, he plodded onwards with sheets of rain washing over a muddy

Greenway. Galad pushed forward to convince Kalanin, and after a brief argument, Kalanin also nodded in agreement.

Galad led them along the Greenway for a few hundred feet, then turned left off the great road, taking them north over an overgrown trail. They passed deeper into the forest, picking their way past the trunks of gnarled trees and through tangles of brush. Winds were checked by thick woodlands, but rain poured through the canopy of leaves overhead, and every few moments a thrashing tree limb came hurtling to the forest floor. Julian could see now that their trail was lined with boulders and stones on either side and so it had been made by men, long ago and overgrown decades ago.

The sky darkened and nightfall was coming. Lightning still flashed, but the sound of thunder drifted farther away, heading west along the Greenway. Soon, thought Julian, the lightning would provide their only illumination as they stumbled, lost, through a tangled dark forest. But then he caught the first glimpse of a rock face that stood in a little clearing in the distance.

As they drew closer, they found that the rock face was part of the ruins of an old fortress. Just one wall and part of the tower were left standing, while other walls had been reduced to mounds of stone and rubble, grey and wet with rain, some layered with green mosses. The old tower had just one door and one window at its base; these had faced to the outside of the fortress so that guards could watch for movement along the forest pathways.

Galad pushed the ancient door open, and creaking sounds echoed through the tower's interior. It was dry inside but pitch black. Light flashed from Julian's staff, and they stared up at the walls and high roof of the tower. It looked as though the ancient stone roof had collapsed many years ago, but another made of planks and mortar had replaced it, and now kept the tower mostly dry. An upper part of the tower wall had collapsed more recently, and beyond the shattered wall they could see wet branches still waving in the storm.

They led their horses in through the tower door, out from the storm's rain and wind. Once inside, they found that a ruined staircase curled about the tower's interior — at one time it had led to the top of the tower.

"At least there's firewood," said Galad, and he began to pull apart a few of the tower stairs to build a fire. Kalanin gathered several other boards, breaking them and wedging them in the space where the window had once looked to the interior of the fortress. Outside, the storm battered away at the rock of the tower, though they could hear from the distant rumble of thunder that the eye of the storm was rolling farther from them, drifting toward Sea's Edge.

Dry boards caught fire after a few sputtering moments, blazing into high flames in the center of the tower. Sebastian crept closer to dry his small body in the warmth. Clothes were put out to dry, and their rainsoaked provisions provided them with a small supper. Rafir declined an offer of cured meat but munched unhappily on a portion of soggy bread until his hunger left him.

As they ate, Galad led their horses to the far side of the chamber, fed them from saddle pouches, and then tethered them so that they could still see their masters and the tower's lone fire.

When Galad returned, Kalanin lit his pipe and began to draw slowly on it, turning his side and shoulder to the flames, hoping for a healing warmth.

"So, we've lost another day," he said quietly, watching Julian, "and perhaps Balardi's struggle is already over. Is this possible?"

The weakness had left Julian, and as he began to dry some of his grim mood lifted. "I have to believe that they still hold. Balardi is among the most powerful of mortal wielders of magic, and Baron Cadmon is a formidable leader of men. Yet news would be useful, whether good or bad."

He turned to Sebastian. "What do you say to a chat with Pervish?" Despite his chill, Sebastian smiled at the thought. "Pervish is my Mid-World gossip," Julian explained. "In his own eyes, Pervish is a wise counselor, filled with deep meanings and hidden understandings. In truth, he is mostly a source of rumor, but he's often useful." Julian stood, smiling. "Let's ask Pervish how matters stand with Balardi and with Gravengate."

Sebastian began to clear an area on the floor of the tower. In its original form, the floor of the tower had been built with mortar and paving stones, but over the years so many layers of dust had collected that the stonework was buried. In the dust, Julian inscribed a simple pentagram with five sides, a frequently used gateway to the Mid-World. Within the figure, he traced several runes with his staff.

"If you have questions, ask them through me," Julian told Kalanin and Galad. "Pervish will respond only to myself or Sebastian."

Julian stood outside of the pentagram and began to retrace the lines of the runes within, all the while whispering the binding name of his small counselor. The fire on the floor of the tower grew less bright, but the lines of the rune within the pentagram began to flicker with light. After a few moments, the shape of a small, squat being formed inside of the pentagram. Galad peered closely at the creature: it was colored bronze, with soft eyes, a slight nose, drooping ears, and a wide mouth that seemed made for the laughter of a villager who was filled with gossip.

But now, the creature was stonefaced and filled with panic.

"Pervish! What's happening?" Julian's voice was filled with alarm. The imp looked wildly around the tower — then vanished.

"No outside force has ever done this before!" Julian said. "Some being dares greatly to interfere with the Wizards' League!" He placed his staff on the runes once more and called out a command: "Return!" and his staff crackled with a charge of energy. The small creature again appeared, looking terrified.

"Pervish!" cried Julian. "Who interferes? Who treats the League so lightly?" Pervish was shaking with fear. His small mouth opened, and he tried to speak, but no sounds came. Looking frantically about him, Pervish knelt on his stubby hands and knees — and began to scratch something on the dust of the old tower floor.

Suddenly, the pentagram exploded. Julian was blown back from the imp. Bits of their watchfire were scattered around the base of the tower; Kalanin and Galad hurried to stamp them out, then they returned and pulled Julian to his feet.

"Why would they do this?" Julian cried. "There was no need to kill!" Where the pentagram had been carved lay the body of Pervish, dead in the floor's dust, with a gaping wound in his small chest. "I never expected this. If danger threatened, Pervish would have sent word not to contact him." Julian seemed half frozen in shock. Kalanin studied the Apprentice in silence, listening to the sounds of rain on stone, and wind on branches. Galad peered closer at the wound of Pervish: no spear or sword or dagger of Alantéa had caused it; some clawed creature had casually ripped the heart of the imp from its body.

Julian knelt beside the small figure for a moment, thinking about their many conversations, and the way in which each of them had taken so much pleasure from their talks. Then he carried the body of the little Mid-World creature to the far side of the tower and built a small tomb over Pervish with fallen rocks from the ancient fortress. When he was finished, Julian stood and spoke a short prayer over the imp's body: "Maker, God of Gods, at the Awakening, may you draw Pervish to you, and may he delight you with his gossip." He then returned to the other side of the tower, filled with sorrow and weariness.

"Let me rest for a while," he said quietly. "If Galad will take the first watch, and Rafir the second, I will take the third and Sebastian and Kalanin the fourth and fifth. But wake me if there's the least disturbance: now we know that our enemies are grim and merciless." Julian lay with his face turned from the fire, and in his sorrow and deep fatigue, he was asleep in moments.

Galad began tending the fire, feeding it with bits of wood from the ruined staircase, listening to the sounds of wild wind and rain on the outside of the tower. The storm seemed to be dying down, as though it had done its greatest damage to them and could now move on to trouble others. Galad moved to the far side of the tower where the horses were tethered, making certain that their needs had been met. He fed them more grain, then cleared some of the rubble away so that they could sleep as best they could on the floor of the old tower.

As he cleared the area, a flicker of light briefly illuminated the wall, and Galad could see that there was an inscription in the mortar at the base of the tower wall. He peered closer, reading the vague writing:

Orantes: Flee this place and find Sentauris — Wylar.

Nothing but scratches from the staff of some unknown Adept or Apprentice, Galad decided. None of the three names were familiar, so it was impossible to tell whether these people were ancient allies or adversaries of the League.

Galad stared up into the broken wall above, where rain blew leaves through the night skies, and so he never saw see how the letters inscribed in the mortar glowed bright green, as though calling to him across a distance of many years. As he turned back to the fire, the fox joined him, and they watched the flames together for a time. After a little more than an hour, Rafir broke the long silence.

"I can watch now if you like. I'm awake, and it's fox time, in the darkness." Galad hesitated for a moment, thinking that the fox might simply vanish should trouble arise, but then he considered that the fox could have slipped away several times during their journey, stealing away from discomfort and danger, so Rafir could be trusted.

"Good," Galad murmured in hushed tones, "but wake me first if there's even a hint of trouble. Kalanin is twice wounded, first from the ashes, then from the Gogra, and Julian is weary."

So Rafir, at midnight, watched the flames of the fire slowly die down. As the light and smoke diminished, the night vision and senses of the fox grew stronger in the gloom. The tower was silent, except for the sounds of sleeping horses and men. Rafir padded about, investigating each corner with his nose.

The door had a great bolt across it, and seemed firm, though weathered. The window that Kalanin had barricaded would hold the wind — at least if the wind didn't get any stronger. The storm outside was subsiding, with the sound of thunder becoming faint and distant. Now as smoke from the dying fire grew thicker, it began to dull his senses. Rafir padded back to stare at the embers. He didn't sleep, but he let his mind drift to the thoughts of a fox, of slinking through warm summer nights under clear skies, and the sounds of breezes blowing over dry meadows.

Suddenly he became alert. Snuffling noises were coming from the door, noises that a large dog might make. Carefully, so as not to move even a particle of dust, the fox crept toward the door...the smell was made stronger by the rain...he tried to recall the lessons of the old Sorceress. No, it wasn't the smell of a Mid-World creature, it was the smell of a common predator of Alantéa — a wolf! A second snuffling sound came from the door: at least one wolf was at the door!

Rafir turned quickly from the entrance and raced across the tower floor to wake Galad — the Knight was up instantly at Rafir's touch. The fox made no sound but pointed with his paw at the doorway. At the top of the entrance, the door was bending a little as weight from the outside mounted against it. But the door held. Galad broke the silence with a cry: "Intruders! Kalanin, Julian, up now!" He kicked more wood on the flames, lifting a smoldering branch for his own use. Kalanin rose and drew his sword. Julian staggered to his feet, staff in hand.

Pressure on the door ceased, but suddenly a great grey shape burst through the shuttered window, quickly followed by two smaller wolves. With a snarl, the great wolf leaped at Galad but was smashed back with Galad's smoldering branch. Kalanin hewed another, severing its neck. Julian's staff sent a jagged bolt of force through the third wolf, and it fell dead on the floor of the tower. The great grey wolf stood at bay, facing his enemies, fire gleaming in his eyes, snarling through his singed muzzle.

Without warning, a fourth wolf leaped from the top of the ruined stairway. To Sebastian, helpless, paralyzed, it seemed to float down like a grey ghost. Julian was struck in the back and smashed to the ground. The wolf scrambled to close its jaws on the neck of the Apprentice, but a sharp pain struck the wolf as Rafir's teeth sank into his hind leg.

As the wolf turned to destroy his small, invisible adversary, the sword of Kalanin bit into its skull, leaving the intruder twitching in death on the fortress floor. The great wolf faced Galad and the flames behind the Knight, tensed to spring, then darted to the side past the fire. Leaping back through the window, he was off into the night, howling with menace.

On the other side of the tower, the horses bucked and neighed, rising on their hind legs to trample the grey intruders. Galad and Kalanin stepped quickly over to control them while Julian picked himself off the floor.

"That was a near thing," he told Rafir. "Thanks for your quick thinking." Julian walked over to the ruined stairway: a frame of wood, just above his reach, led along the side of the tower, close to that part of the tower wall that was broken and open to the night.

"It must have come over the rubble, along the wall of the fortress, and through that opening." Kalanin said, "But that's more than the simple plan of a wolfpack, is it not, Apprentice?"

Julian stared at the intruders: they lay still, though small streams of blood were still seeping onto the tower floor. "An attack by our enemies at least. It may even have been another test to see if Merlin was present."

Galad began to pull sections of the ruined stairway down from the walls so that the stairway could no longer make a pathway for their foes. Kalanin again blocked the window but reinforced the planks with beams wedged with one end against the boarded window, and the other ends planted firmly into the ground. More debris fed the flames so that their fortress grew brighter. Strangely, Julian felt his mood lift somewhat.

"One problem has been solved at least," he said. "My serpent ally Kath hungers and he's too wounded to hunt for a time." He pointed to the wolf carcasses. "Our intruders will make an interesting meal for Kath." Rafir recalled the bitter, hairy taste of the wolf's leg, and he gagged.

So as their fortress was strengthened, Julian dragged dead wolf carcasses together, then sent them through a small portal into the Mid-World, as a gift to his serpent ally, Kath. Kalanin watched the carcasses vanish, and lay back again for a few moments, nursing his bruises. Then he rolled to one side, propping himself up, looking at Julian.

"We've lost three days now," he said softly. "With every league, our foes have raised a new and different force against us. At this pace, many more days will be lost — if it's not too late already."

Julian nodded his head. "You're right, and there must be a way to speed our journey. Let me think about it. I'll take the next watch, and perhaps some device will come to me."

Julian stood, watching the fire seep and pulse and again begin to diminish. The Gift was calling to him, suddenly filled with a confusion of images and messages. The tower itself was haunted by some old adventure, with ghostly figures struggling to take shape and tell their tales of triumph and woe. What would they have to say to him?

Julian stood and paced. What was happening? Magic stirred and his eyes were caught by a distant flash of green. Moving slowly, filled with tension, he was drawn by the same inscription that Galad had seen earlier:

Orantes: Flee this place and find Sentauris — *Wylar*.

Who were those people? But now the green glow had leaped from the carved words onto his own form, and from there the cold green gleaming color sprang toward Kalanin and Galad. Lying asleep on the tower floor, Galad's hand still clenched the hilt of his shattered sword. But now bathed by a green glow, the blade was renewed, gleaming with new power. And around Kalanin's bare head a diadem seemed to glow, and his beard was greyer in the darkness as though he had become a warlord and leader of men.

Then suddenly, the green was gone, and only the fire remained to light their night refuge in the broken tower.

Julian stood blinking for a moment, then he turned back to the fire, and sat. What had just happened? Some signal had been sent — but was it from the past or from the future? And that strange signal that gleamed so brightly with rays of green, was not the only mystery. Absentmindedly, he traced forms in the dust with his staff, while his mind considered the events of the past few days and the journey before them. Now, the Gift was focusing on the image of the great grey wolf: there was something strange about the creature, an intelligence and a lack of true fear. His staff drew more diagrams in the dust.

A soft coughing sound broke Julian's concentration, and from the shadows, Sebastian moved slowly over to the fire, touching Julian's arm with his own small hand.

"I'm sorry that I couldn't do what the fox did," Sebastian said sadly. "I watched that wolf, and it seemed to float toward you, slowly, forever, and yet I couldn't move." Julian smiled, covering the small hand with his own.

"We each do what we can. You were fierce at the ford. In this encounter, a wounded Kalanin was by far the most effective — it was sharp metal that did the real damage." His staff shaped another diagram on the floor, then Julian stood and began to clear his tracings from the dust. "Help me now, Sebastian. Maybe we can learn more about this wolfpack."

With Sebastian's help, the dust was smoothed, and a square ten paces wide was traced in the tower floor, and within the square, divination symbols were inscribed. Julian then stepped outside of the form; holding his staff to the border, he sent a surge of power through the lines so that lights flickered around its edges, and over the symbols within the square.

Sebastian looked for images to form, but the pattern offered nothing. Julian sighed. "So, it was more than a simple wolf," he murmured. "We'll need some remnant of the creature to capture its image." They hunted about the tower floor, searching for traces of the intruder. Finally, Sebastian found a few tiny, singed strands of hair closer to the window, where the wolf had been struck by Galad. Julian took these and carefully placed one upon each of the symbols within the square.

The Apprentice again stood back as light from the fire flickered and dimmed. Sebastian peered closely into the square: within the diagram, the image of a wolf formed, tiny in the dust, as it raced through the stormy night, stopping now and again to howl at some cave or outcrop of rock.

"He is gathering his brethren," whispered Julian. In a moment, the image showed a pack of wolves racing through the night, the largest leading them toward the ruined fortress. In the dust, the image of the tower was less than three feet high, and Sebastian watched as the great wolf nosed about the outside of the fortress, then led another wolf to one edge of the ruined wall that was heaped with fallen rock more than halfway up the tower's side.

"Here, then, is the planner," Julian again whispered.

Then the image showed the fight in the tower, with the great wolf leaping back out of the window. The mouth of the wolf was opened in its howling defiance, but no sound came to the watchers except for the muffled crackling of their fire.

"Now, this is what I most wished to see," whispered Julian, and the image of the wolf in retreat flickered in the dust. The wolflike figure sped quickly through the rain soaked forest, its face darting from side to side, as though checking for pursuers. Then its pace slowed, and it reached the edge of the Greenway and stopped. The figure of the wolf shook and seemed to straighten...to stand on its two hind feet...then it formed into the image of a man.

The creature now shaped as a man turned around, as he stood on the Greenway, and stared directly into the eyes of Julian, and he perceived the spell of the Apprentice: with a wave of his hand, he broke Julian's divination search, and the image on the tower floor vanished.

Julian recoiled as though struck by a blow in the face. "Not good," he murmured, steadying himself. "It's not a wolf, nor truly a man; and it has the Gift."

"Greater strength than you?" asked Sebastian.

"It's more than an Apprentice," Julian said slowly. "I think that they were probing, perhaps wondering if Merlin was hidden among us." He was silent for a moment, lost in thought. "With any luck, they'll have decided that we're unimportant, and we'll be left alone for a time." Julian turned to his small companion. "But now you should sleep for a while. You have the last watch, before dawn, and that's sometimes the hardest." He covered

Sebastian with his cloak, watching the little Familiar until Sebastian drifted back to sleep.

Silence slipped once again over the old fortress. Julian sat in front of the fire, staring up at the tower's roof: the upper part of the tower was laced with spider webs, tangled nets that were turning black from the fire soot, as they flapped in the updrafts.

What should we do next, and how can I force a passage to Gravengate? It's truly only three days journey, but with opposition from beings like the Wolflike Adept and the Gogra, it might easily be three weeks.

He peered closer into the flames, the Gift within him sifting, reaching to bring forth the vaguest of images — of minor pieces in *The Game of the Masters*, *The Apprentice*, *Charmed Knights*, and *Mid-World Spies*, a small cluster moving down a narrow lefthand passage, while the great powers of the *Game* warred at center rank.

Maker's Touch! Now I feel fear too, I remember how the old Sorceress stood, sweat beading on her forehead. How to speed a passage to Balardi? The Wizard remained fearless, a power in his own domain.

As he sat, considering ways to speed their journey, the first tentacles of *The Great Spell* reached out to him through the darkness.

A *Great Spell*! A force of the Third Rank in *The Game of the Masters*!

He leaped to his feet, both hands on his staff, his mouth open in shock. They had only toyed with them before! Now they had grown tired of the *Game* and were going to end it! As in a dream of horror, Julian looked about the old fortress where all seemed peaceful, but terror surged through him as the Gift cried out, calling on him to flee.

Julian steadied himself. There were still a few things he could do. He raced to the sleeping Kalanin and Galad. Each was under the protection of the League, charmed against sorcery. They might survive...but one should be doubly shielded, maybe even to fight through. It would have to be Kalanin, more experienced, more resourceful than Galad. And Kalanin had been Merlin's emissary to Baron Cadmon who served Balardi, and to Harmadast, who led Thorian's fighting men.

His staff sped as it traced a great diagram around the sleeping form of Kalanin. The chest of Merlin he could protect; it was already charmed... for their horses, only sleep...his staff wove a healer's sleep over them. Panic again lapped at Julian, but it ebbed and sank farther back.

He looked at his small companions in fear and horror: nothing could be done, and no time remained. But there were the gifts given by the Sorceress! He raced to his saddle pouch, taking, and placing one of the Seeking Stones on Sebastian and the other on Rafir. For himself, there was nothing. Nothing but the Gift — and his own bitter determination. He turned to face the spell, in mounting anger, his staff clenched in both hands.

Then unexpectedly, from the chest sent by Merlin, powerful counter spells surged skyward. The Wizard had prepared for this moment and so they were not left undefended!

From the tower itself, gleaming strands of blue and gold reached skyward. Where had that force come from? And was it sent by foe or friend?

But then *The Great Spell* was upon them.

A dreadful cold surged through the chamber. The tower walls began to shake — and the roof of the tower burst in a flash of light, as though the hand of a giant had swept it away.

The storm of magic that raged overhead through the night skies, hurtled downward.

And when it burst over them their lives were changed forever.

Chapter Four
The Broken Army

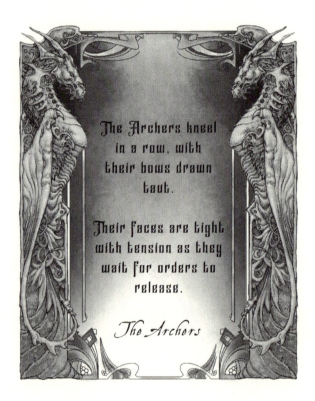

The Archers kneel in a row, with their bows drawn taut.

Their faces are tight with tension as they wait for orders to release.

The Archers

DAYLIGHT WOKE HIM — NOT the pale light of daybreak, but a bright noon sun beating down hard upon him. Kalanin peered out from blurry eyes. Most of the tower was gone, shattered, joining the ruined walls of the ancient fortress. His body warned him against moving too abruptly, but he shifted a hand, gingerly, over his face.

Blood had flowed freely from his nostrils, spreading, and caking as it dried over his beard.

Fresh blood pulsed out as he pushed himself over on to his side and finally struggled to his feet. The tower was gone, along with his companions. For some reason, their horses seemed alive — he could see their chests rise and fall, free from the wreckage of the tower. Though as he drew closer, he saw that one of their pack horses had been crushed by a block of stone, and it no longer breathed.

His eyes cleared and he walked through the tower, searching carefully for any signs of his companions. Nothing remained — no damaged weapons had been left, no blood, no scraps of clothing, and if there had been a struggle, the wreckage of the tower covered any signs. He returned to the diagram that had been drawn for his own protection. The lines of the diagram were engraved in the ground and were still clear, even after the destruction of the fortress. At the edge of the diagram, the letter *"J"* was engraved as the signature of the Apprentice. Kalanin knelt beside the engraving, shaking his head to clear it.

So, he alone had been spared, while his companions were destroyed or captured. Over with the horses, the chest sent by Merlin remained to be taken to Balardi by the lone survivor: a fool's errand, always more difficult, less realistic.

He felt a great temptation to drag more of the rubble over the chest, to free himself from a doomed undertaking. With a discipline of long practice, he cleared the bitterness from his mind and returned to their horses. Four still breathed, but deeply, as though drugged. Bluescent lived, and his own steed, Great Hoof, with Molise of Galad, and one pack horse. These were dragged awake, still groggy and swaying. To his everlasting sorrow, Kalanin found that the front legs of Great Hoof collapsed, and the Charger sank back to the rubble neighing in pain. Grimly, he drew the other three horses a distance from the ruin, then returned to cut the Charger's throat.

As Kalanin walked with a grim face from the ruin, he turned once to look back at the fallen tower: a tomb for Pervish, an open grave for Great Hoof, and the end, perhaps, of the League.

· ⋈ ·

He rode on into midafternoon. Their horses stumbled and straggled as Kalanin led them, then rode each in turn as they slowly woke from their enchanted sleeps. A stream ran close by the Greenway and there Kalanin let his horses drink deeply, then he knelt and washed the blood from his matted beard, watching as the waters slowly ran clear again.

As they continued, he took inventory of his resources: one chest filled with sorcerous devices, useful only to a skilled Wizard or Adept, three steeds, one swordsman armored with light chain mail. A little food was left, but no spear, no dry clothes, and worst of all, no one to guard his back. His ringed mail and helmet would turn back the darts and arrows of an opponent, but a small party of lightly armed men might easily drag him down, or one little thief could end his life with a dagger in the night. After all his service to the League, to be struck like a pig in a slaughterhouse! He growled deep in his throat then cleared the thought from his mind.

The Greenway took them through many wooded areas, and they were forced to pick their way over fallen branches and shattered trunks that had been felled by the previous night's storm. If the Wizards' League were ending, the Greenway might never be cleared again; then the great forests of Alantéa would surge over the great east to west passage. In the midst of these gloomy thoughts, he was pleasantly surprised to see that his troupe of horses followed him without hesitation as he led them over and around the fallen branches. Perhaps they recalled yesterday's storm and were glad for sunlight.

By early evening, his mind had thought out a device that might protect him with a measure of safety at night. Among the rolling hills were rock faces and cliffs, though no caves. Kalanin sought out a steep cliff, with rubble strewn over its face. No one would be able to approach silently from the cliff side, so he made his camp at the cliff's base. In front of the cliff face, the horses were bedded in a semicircle, and where there were gaps in the arc, he heaped dry branches. Now, an assassin might stumble over a horse, or make enough noise to wake him. Against an intruder from the Mid-World, the charms of the League should afford some protection. He slept with his sword close to his hand.

In the morning, the sounds, and smells of Alantéa rose from its great sunlit forests, and he felt his spirits rise. He was alive, and he was healing. Perhaps Julian and Galad lived and would win through to him; or Balardi, of his own Wizard's power, would cast down his enemies. And Merlin might emerge from his great confrontation, surging with power over the Greenway to renew the Wizards' League.

As he rode through the forest paths, Kalanin wondered again if any of the Great Dark Gods were involved in their battles. A time of peace was said to have settled over the League after its early struggles. Refugees coming from other parts of Alantéa still told stories of the Vengeance of the Gods: if Moloch's name or Set's or Ahriman's were spoken without proper reverence, then assassins were sent to deal with the offender. Was it any wonder that the Wizards has trained their peoples not to speak those Names?

The next section of the Greenway led them beyond the wooded areas, and up into a hilly section, with brush on either side of the road, and only a few parched trees overhanging the roadway. As they traveled over the hills and down into the little valleys, Kalanin hummed a little as he rode, and made small pieces of conversation with Molise and Bluescent, who could not reply. If he were fortunate, and if their foes would let him be, he would reach folk who were loyal to Baron Cadmon, maybe even before nightfall and with those allies, he might find shelter and news of Gravengate.

They passed down through another hollow and up the slope to the crest of another hill. Looking back, he saw that they were higher now, and they could view the roll of the surrounding countryside. Here the Greenway was dry and dusty: even the long grasses were dead for lack of water. One of the limbs overhanging the road seemed to droop heavily, and as Kalanin approached, he saw that an eagle perched there, his weight causing the tree limb to sag. The wingspan of the eagle seemed unusually large, and it made no move to fly away as the horses approached; instead, the eagle perched on the limb grimly and stared at them with fierce eyes. The image was strange to Kalanin's eyes, and he laughed, for the first time in days.

"Here's an overfed eagle," he murmured to Molise, "who is studying to become a buzzard. Maybe he thinks that his dinner approaches, and so we should look lively."

To his enormous surprise, the eagle spoke: "Where is Julian?" the eagle croaked at him.

"What!" Kalanin said, halting. "Whom do you seek?"

"I asked," croaked the eagle, "where is Julian, and where is Galad, and where is the small servant of the Apprentice?"

Kalanin slipped from Molise, as though to speak more easily with the eagle, but his eyes darted over the ground, seeking a stone to hurl at the huge bird.

"What do you know of my friends?" he asked, "and what is your interest in them?" Now, he was under the eagle's perch, but still weaponless. The eagle looked far over the hills before speaking again.

"The voices of humans betray them — yours is full of fear and the desire for revenge, for your foes have struck at you many times. Behold! Your Master is my Master!" The eagle dropped to a lower branch so that its talons were at a level with Kalanin's eyes. "Come forward, but slowly, and without weapons." Kalanin walked forward warily, watching for signs of treachery. The eagle flared its wings as though its wildness called upon it to flee.

"Although I serve, no man has tamed me. I am the Eye of Merlin. Behold!" And the eagle lifted its talon to show a tiny band of gold upon which was imprinted the emblem of the League. "I see for great distances in the darkness and the light. I perceive matters of sorcery that are far distant from us. But my sight is now blocked. I ask again: Where is Julian? And where is Galad?"

Kalanin stepped back for a moment beneath the fierce gaze of the eagle, still uncertain about the creature — and yet an adversary would know of the Great Spell, and the fate of his companions, while an ally might not.

"They are dead or taken. I am alone." In a halting voice, Kalanin told the eagle about waking, under Julian's protective spell, in the ruined fortress.

The eagle gazed over the rolling countryside. "So, defeat before us and defeat behind us. Merlin is beyond my sight. Julian is gone, and Galad has vanished, to what places we may never know. Before us, a broken army flees in our direction. Baron Cadmon is dead, and his tier groups are no more. Merlin is gone; who will now bring aid to Balardi? He stands besieged, confronted by two great masters of magic and hosts of armed men. Where do we now turn?"

Kalanin sat down and pulled off his helmet. Baron Cadmon was a mainstay of the League, no magician, but a noted captain, a battle hardened and tenacious leader of men.

"How can all these things have happened in such a brief time?" he asked softly, shaking his head. "Just a few days ago, the League seemed so powerful, even without Thorian. Are you certain that Cadmon is dead?"

"I am the Eye of Merlin," said the eagle. "Many things I see from afar, while others I can sense. I know of death. Cadmon is dead, and his tier groups have been defeated. Julian and Galad are alive — perhaps — but they are so far from the League, that they may as well belong to another universe. Balardi holds but cannot last forever." The eagle stared, fierce and unblinking, into Kalanin's face. "Yet I do not see everything. Soon you will be able to speak to those who fled this morning's battle, though you may wish to save yourself and turn back."

"I refused my instructions once, waiting for Merlin at Sea's Edge; the results were a disaster. Now I will do as originally told — and more if necessary." Kalanin remounted Molise. "But what will you do, Eye of Merlin? Will you aid me? Will you be my eyes and my advisor?" The wings of the eagle flared as though bristling at the thought.

"I have been subject only to Merlin...yet our cause has gone so evilly that I must help you, Giftless mortal. I will be the eyes of those serving the League if you wish. First, you will know of the broken army that flees toward you." The eagle cast himself from the branch and rose with a heavy flapping of wings to a great height.

Kalanin continued along the Greenway at a slow pace, but his mind was racing. Before him was the remnant of a single broken tier, normally five hundred men. How badly broken? He would learn in a while. For the moment, it was only important to be traveling in the right direction. He rode, slowly, along the Greenway towards Gravengate.

In a while, they were out of the dry hills, and the Greenway led through a stretch of level meadows and ranges where farmers of the League let their grazing animals roam. In the distance, Kalanin could now see the first riders of the broken army, streaming down the road. The first group pushed past Kalanin, without speaking a word. Both men and horses were exhausted and filled with fear; they would have ridden Kalanin down had the Greenway not been wide enough for them to push by. A second cluster was also weary and beaten, but a few called out to him:

"Flee, the Baron's dead."

"They're coming behind us — go far from here!"

One said simply, "Wrong way!"

A grim, white faced soldier caught the reins of Molise, crying to Kalanin, "Don't you understand? The Maker has turned against us! One of his ancient First Servants rose up to strike down the Baron!" Kalanin pulled the reins from the man's hands and continued, saying nothing.

The eagle descended to the Greenway, lighting on a branch in front of Kalanin.

"Why did you not stop them?" the eagle asked. "You wished news of the battle, did you not?"

"Not from them. Those who have gone by us were the first to flee and likely the last to be believed." He hesitated. "I will try to find one to speak with, and when I do, I would like you to descend, come to rest on my shoulder, and tell me the size of the force that pursues the Baron's broken tier groups. Will you do this?" The eagle looked at Kalanin with his huge, unwavering pupils, as though trying to read the Knight's mind. Finally, the eagle nodded.

Now, the men that streamed by Kalanin were grimmer looking and less fearful. Some of their shields were marked, others bore light wounds, and still, others had not been wounded, but stained with the blood of their foes. One of the older bloodstained men rode a little apart from the others and seemed to be leading a small band of men. Kalanin guessed that he had been the leader of a sub tier, maybe a sergeant. Kalanin picked his way through the stream of men, and halted just before the band, holding his hand up in a gesture of peace.

"Hold, for a moment only," he said in a soft voice. The Sergeant halted, reaching for his sword, but stopped when he saw the emblem of the League on Kalanin's shield.

"Matters are bad enough without cutting an ally," the man muttered, "but you're going in the wrong direction. The Baron is dead. An ancient Power struck him down. Balardi is doomed. Go back to Merlin and tell him his League is finished."

The Sergeant motioned his men to continue. Kalanin again stopped them, saying "Wait, just a moment more," and he signaled to the eagle, who hovered then dropped to Kalanin's shoulder. Men about them halted in surprise. The eagle spoke in a clear voice:

"They are pursued by a few hundred, perhaps no more than six hundred."

"That number should not present too great a problem," Kalanin murmured; then to those around him, "this is the Eye of Merlin. We are the forerunners, bringing aid from Merlin. Others will follow." More men began to halt around them, and a few that had ridden past turned and came back. "What of those who pursue the Baron's men?" Kalanin asked of the Eye. "Are they fresh or weary? How quickly do they come?" The eagle raised his voice so that those around him might hear.

"They wear the badge of the vanguard of Thorian, and seem well trained, but weary, and move slowly. Neither the Wizard nor the Sorcerer accompanies them."

Kalanin lifted his voice so that those along the Greenway could hear clearly: "Aid from Merlin is coming, but we should turn and check the vanguard of the foes of our League!" In a lower voice, he murmured to the Sergeant, "Will you aid me? There are places where we might be concealed and surprise them." The Sergeant looked at Kalanin with grim understanding, then spoke in the same hushed tones:

"Aid from Merlin, is it? You look in worse shape than some of my lads did after we lost the Baron." Kalanin had washed, but his armor and cloak were still stained with blood and ashes. The old soldier then raised his voice, "But I'm tired of running! Let's stop and fight! No more of this Maker-cursed retreat!" He signaled to the three soldiers who had followed the Sergeant, and these three began to check others who were fleeing in their direction: those who had retreated last from the battle seemed more willing to halt their flight than those who had broken first.

The Sergeant turned back to Kalanin. "Are you thinking of using the Badlands?" He pointed back along the Greenway to the place where Kalanin had met the Eye of Merlin.

Kalanin nodded. "Unless there's a better place."

The Sergeant shook his head. "Only place good for an ambush in this part of the Baron's lands." He called over the three men who had been following him. "I'm Dargas, once a Sergeant in the Baron's forces, and here's Harlond, and Envar, and the one with the nick in him is Rurak." These three seemed between twenty and thirty, strong, cool professional soldiers. "They're good lads — they'll take orders, lead men for you. Likely they'll never be Generals." Dargas looked at Kalanin coolly, without a trace of affection, as his own horse shifted a few paces, seeking fresh grass. "We'll let you be the General, for the moment, but let's get on with it."

Kalanin rode at the head of the group of men, with the eagle still perched on his shoulder, while Dargas and the others passed news and instructions up and down the Greenway. More men began to join the column.

"Do humans always tell such falsehoods?" asked the eagle.

Kalanin shook his head. "Others lie each day; for me, I lie only in great need, and yet everything that I've said may come to pass. What these broken tier groups needed was some purpose, a chance of success. They'll fight again if they are organized, and if they meet a foe on even terms. What's your judgment?" The eagle was silent for a moment.

"In *The Game of the Masters*, you are like a piece of the first rank that has emerged from the Ragged Passages: you are free to do some damage before the greater powers take note of you."

"I know something of the *Game* — though I was never happy thinking of myself as the pawn of some distant Master. Specifically, what of Adepts and Sorcerers? If powerful magic is again hurled at us, all of our little plots will come to nothing."

"You may be free for a while," croaked the eagle. "Your enemies have launched a great torrent of power against Merlin, and against Balardi, and against your errand. This power is not without limit, and there may well be a lull before they are able to strike again. As for the humans that pursue you, I can say only that you are traveling in the wrong direction if you wish to contest their passage."

Kalanin laughed. "We're going in the right direction. Many of those who were fleeing will now discover that they were not truly running — they have merely joined a raiding party that happens, for the moment, to be heading away from their foes.

"One thing is clear to me though — we must win the first skirmish. To do that, we must know everything about our enemies." He turned to the eagle; the Eye of Merlin looked back at Kalanin evenly.

"You will know everything, down to the color of their buckles." The eagle sprang with a jolt from Kalanin's shoulder and surged into the afternoon sky.

Now, more than ninety followed, but many others, worn from their flight, sat by the side of the road, and looked on with dazed expressions. After some hurried discussions between Dargas and Kalanin, Dargas was made Tier Leader, and the three men most trusted by him, Harlond, Envar, and Rurak, were given Sergeant's badges. As the afternoon waned, more gathered to their group, until by evening, there were more than one hundred and fifty men from the broken tier groups. At sunset, the eagle returned, advising that their pursuers had camped less than two leagues away, on a field near the road. The men of Thorian kept a heavy guard but did not seem greatly concerned about those they pursued.

With this news, Kalanin called a halt to their journey. They were now well into the dry hills, where the Greenway rose and fell; curling around hillsides, it blocked the sight of their pursuers. During the day, Kalanin had quietly marked a few more than twenty five who were still harried, or worn, or hampered by wounds. These he took aside for a separate task.

"More help is coming from Sea's Edge," he told them, "and we have begun to reform the Baron's tier groups. Yet more still will be needed. We must raise the countryside and rid ourselves of the invaders. For a while, you will be our messengers. Every village must know of this struggle and send men to our aid. Most specifically, we need those who are skilled in metalwork. Tell them to gather at Amalric, and we will meet them there, or have instructions for them in twelve days' time. Tell all that the League will rise in their defense. For now, you should sleep and be ready for the morning."

He was left with roughly one hundred and twenty men. These he divided into three groups: those on foot who were armed with a bow or javelin; those who were on horse and armored; and a third group that was lightly armed, but quick and stealthy. Kalanin, having noted the substantial girth of his Tier Leader, decided that Dargas would lead the heavy armor. To lead the archers, he would need someone who would obey instructions… after some thought, he chose Harlond, who seemed perhaps the steadiest of the three originally attached to Dargas.

The rest periods of his three groups were rotated so that he would be able to work with each, while the other two groups slept. A little after midnight, he decided that they might succeed, if they were fortunate, and if the night vision of the eagle proved accurate. Three hours before dawn, Kalanin raised each of the three groups and went over their instructions briefly. Then he led his group of twenty five into the night, moving quickly at first along the Greenway. Later, they would be forced to move more slowly as they passed through wooded areas.

The night was clear and mild. They walked quickly, speaking only in hushed tones, though there was excitement in the air, and exhilaration as they passed under starry skies. Kalanin guessed that a few had come resigned to dying, but even those were becoming infected with hope, a feeling that it might all come together. The eagle had told them that a heavy guard was at the roadside, that the camp lay by a field just to the north of the Greenway, and that the vanguards' horses were penned in a wooded area, beyond the field, and that the horses were only lightly guarded. If they could free the mounts of their enemies, great confusion would follow — then the second party, the archers, would strike.

They came to the bend in the Greenway that the eagle had marked earlier. Half a league further was the camp of the vanguard of the men of Stone Mountain. Kalanin held his group up. A predawn breeze was rustling through the trees, and with good fortune, it would help to mask their movements.

They began, slowly, to feel their way through the forest, testing each step. Through breaks in the leafy canopy, they looked to the starry skies of Alantéa for direction. By now, the night travel had sharpened their hearing and vision, so that they were able to pass through the forest floor with care and quiet. After a while, an uneasy, lost feeling began to slip over him, but the feeling eased as the night air began to carry the smells of watch fires and horse droppings. A little farther on, they were able to hear the sneezing and snorting of many horses. The Eye of Merlin had told him that much of the tier was mounted, perhaps as many as two of the five hundred. They were at the edge of the clearing now, just north of the camp. Each of them was clad only in light leather, but each wielded a heavy weapon, a sword, or an ax. Kalanin peered forward: a little light was beginning to seep over the horizon.

· ※ ·

He knelt at the forest's edge, hesitating. As the eagle had said, there were four sentries. Their features were masked by shadows, but they were men he might have ridden with years ago when he traveled with the men of Stone Mountain before the League began to fail. Even now, his instinct was to step forward from the forest, saying, *put down your weapons, there's been a great misunderstanding.* But Cadmon was dead, Merlin was gone, Julian and Galad had been swept away — so this conflict was beyond confusion. He had no choice now but to act, swiftly and decisively to preserve the League.

At a signal, Kalanin and three others drew weapons and crept out of the forest toward the sentries. Two guards were killed instantly, slumping in silence. A third sentry cried out in pain as he was struck, and the fourth parried the cut of his attacker, felled him with a counterstroke, and raced away to the camp, calling out the alarm.

With the sounds, others of the raiding party leaped from the forest, pulling down the horse pen, shrieking and yelling, lashing at the ties of the mounts. Neighing and rearing, the horses broke free, fleeing in great panic as they stumbled through the camp, knocking down men and tent riggings, racing wild into a creeping red sunrise.

Kalanin shouted over the noise of the camp, and men gathered back to the shelter of the forest. He held one of the chargers, though it backed away from the raiding party. Men were breathing hard, standing with drawn weapons.

"Let us go back!" one said, and another added, "We can strike them from this side!" Grim eagerness showed on their faces as they pressed closer to him.

"Not this time." Kalanin leaped up on the horse. "There will be other times, many other times. You must go back now, as planned. If we are pursued, you must be in place to check them. Quickly!"

Then Kalanin was away, speeding over the field past the camp of their opponents. In the new light of day, he could see the second part of the raiding party move to attack from the hills that faced the south side of the Greenway. Archers and stone casters advanced to the road and fired volley after volley of arrows and stones into the confusion of their enemies' camp.

He sped around the seething campsite, racing toward the Greenway and red daybreak. Exhilaration surged through him as he saw the confusion of their enemies: some dodged arrows, some tried to control the great chargers that still reared in panic. Others remained trapped in trampled tents. Several tents had been dragged into the watch fires and now burned, flashing red against the crimson sky of morning. As he sped past them, he called out in defiance, "One stroke for the League!" But in the noise and confusion, none heard.

Now, in the camp, a knot of mailed men opposed the archers, while others gathered to them. These began to advance on the archers, shields, and mail protecting them. The archers left the Greenway, moving south toward the low hills before firing another volley. More of the men of Thorian emerged from the confusion of the camp and moved toward the Greenway, but as they reached the great road, Dargas led the third party of more than fifty mounted spear. A tide of horse and man and metal surged over the surprised vanguard, leaving many men trampled and lifeless. Others from the vanguard returned to their camp where commands of captains and tier leaders could be heard above the confusion. The armored horses halted on the Greenway, readying for a charge in the other direction, returning west. Kalanin reached the side of his tier leader. Dargas, breathing heavily, lifted his visor.

"One charge might yet break them," he panted, watching the tangled camp sight. Kalanin shook his head.

"We're too few for a pitched battle — and at the moment we need them alive and in pursuit." A look of astonishment passed over Dargas' face. "Wait and see," Kalanin continued. "For the moment, we need to follow our plan, and return to the others." He turned to go, but Dargas caught at the reins of his horse.

"It's a rough and dirty little war you're going to fight if I understand you right," Dargas said grimly, "but for now we'll do it your way."

They rode back along the Greenway for a while, then halted, waiting for the other raiding parties to join them. The eagle could be seen circling high above them in the early morning light. As they paused the eagle descended, coming to rest on Kalanin's shoulder.

"Your enemies tend their wounded and seek their horses," croaked the eagle, "but a half score of men ride swiftly east to Gravengate."

"They will seek more men," Kalanin said, "perhaps another tier. But what of our archers, and those who passed through the forest?"

"Look..." said the eagle, as he nodded to the hills, where Kalanin could see in the distance that the archers were pushing their way through the brush on the hillside, "and listen." On the other side of the Greenway, the voices of the raiding party could be heard, some laughing as they made their way back through the forest.

"Do all humans have such weak senses?"

"You will be our eyes and ears," Kalanin murmured, and some of the tension left him, as the various parts of their small group gathered. Men laughed and exchanged stories in the sunlight. Others who had been held aside for their weariness or wounds joined the main body, and hope seemed to return to many.

In all, they had lost only five, and such was the surprise and confusion of their enemies, that none were severely wounded, only a few with light cuts and bruises. These men, Kalanin tended as best he could: Bindweed to heal the cuts, Dragon's Breath to seal away infection.

As Kalanin looked to the wounded, Dargas sought him, and there was a concerned look on the Tier Leader's face.

"Word's come that men of Thorian have returned toward Gravengate for aid. If they send another tier, then we'll face a full thousand, less those they lost this day. What of this aid from Merlin that you spoke of before?" Kalanin drew Dargas aside so that they were apart from the others.

"You and I must be as brothers, with no secrets between us. I will tell you our true state of affairs: there is only myself and the eagle, and a few trinkets that are useless unless they reach Balardi."

"What of Merlin?" asked Dargas. "By reputation, he was the most powerful of the Wizards."

"Gone," said Kalanin. "Destroyed or captured, we know not. We must do what we can with what we have here."

Dargas laughed, a short, bitter laugh. "We have less than two hundred, and about Gravengate there are more than twenty five thousands of our foes, and Balardi perhaps with five thousand, and these locked away from us by the siege. These are poor odds!"

"Would you prefer that we were back on the Greenway, fleeing once again from our enemies?" Kalanin asked, and Dargas shook his head. "As for the odds, we will raise the countryside; we will form a new force in the name of the dead Baron, and of the League. Soon, we'll turn from the Greenway and travel north. How far is it to Amalric?"

"Less than twenty leagues, to the north, but over bad roads," Dargas said, "though it's a fair town and sad to see war come to it."

"They will never reach Amalric," Kalanin said quietly.

· ⚔ ·

They turned north, off from the Greenway, and began to journey toward Amalric. It was a journey over side roads and paths, through Alantéa's forests and meadows, with only a few farms scattered about this part of the League. As they traveled, Kalanin called the Heralds to his side.

"Dargas will give each of you a group of villages, or towns, and you will pass these messages to each: We have struck back at the enemies of the Baron; the League is coming to our aid; the tier groups commanded by Baron Cadmon are reforming at Amalric. Those who wish to join may earn a place by harassing the vanguard of those attacking our League that follows behind us. Those attacking the vanguard should seek the counsel of the eagle, the Eye of Merlin."

He made each of the Heralds repeat his words several times. To the Eye of Merlin, Kalanin added, "We want live fighters and not dead heroes. A night skirmish, a trap, a small ambush, even some distraction at nightfall is sufficient. But every day that passes must leave them weaker, and fewer, while we gain strength. Can this be done?"

The eagle looked at Kalanin as though studying the motions of some small creature from a thousand feet in the sky. "It might be possible — if the people of the countryside support you. If your enemies are preoccupied with the siege. If the Mid-World does not intrude...."

Dargas was left with the task of assigning areas to the Heralds; he stood with men all around him, puzzling over a stained, rumpled map. The rest of their force moved on, with Kalanin conferring with his three Sergeants as they rode.

"We'll be moving quickly, with few supplies. Wild game is best, but where you must draw from the villages and farms, you must sign for goods in the name of the League. Look for the Elders — they may recall that the Wizards have always paid for provisions, and the script of the League has always been redeemed." Rurak looked a little uncomfortable with this, and Kalanin, guessing, added, "If your writing is not altogether impressive, we'll find a scribe for you." Rurak seemed to relax. "Also, we'll be moving quickly and growing larger all the time. Watch for men who can assist you. Pass their names to Dargas."

Dargas caught up with them, having dispatched the Heralds.

"I've sent them off," he said. "They're eager; perhaps people will listen." Kalanin nodded. They were little more than a hundred now, moving north toward Amalric. Some of the time, they found themselves breaking into smaller groups to pass in single file over narrow paths. As they journeyed into the afternoon, they found that bit by bit, in twos and threes, more men of the broken army were riding to join them. Some were heartened by news of a victory, however small. Others had simply fled into the wild and were glad to have a new purpose. The tale of their morning's work grew in the telling so that it became an effort to recall that they were still fleeing from a much larger force.

Throughout the afternoon, Kalanin scanned the sky above, watching for the Eye of Merlin. At last, at the edge of the afternoon sun, he saw the great eagle, soaring effortlessly. Though now a flock of crows rose to harass the eagle. Kalanin expected to see the eagle forced higher, but in its ponderous midair passage, the eagle seemed to *spurt*, and two crows tumbled with broken wings down to the earth, with clusters of feathers floating in their wakes. Other crows fled, calling out in fear.

Not your average overly heavy predator, thought Kalanin.

Suddenly, the eagle dove; Kalanin halted. Had something gone wrong? Then he saw the eagle strike a ground creature, a hare, or some other small, forest creature. He had not thought of the eagle as a predator, but the eagle must eat, as did the humans. In a few moments, the eagle was again perched on Kalanin's shoulder, but now its beak and claws were touched with the blood of its victim.

"So, Eye of Merlin, was that noon or evening meal?"

"Food for dealing with humans, who chatter like songbirds in the morning dew."

Kalanin laughed.

"I'm sure you know more about songbirds than I do. But how does it go with our enemies?"

"They follow, but warily," said the eagle. "They remain about half a day behind you but are losing more distance each hour. Already, they seek safe havens for the night. A second tier has left the siege of Gravengate and is moving toward you — far more swiftly than the first tier."

"We cannot let them reach Amalric," murmured Kalanin.

It was late afternoon, but the day's heat was broken by winds from the west. The eagle dozed after its meal, and it must have dreamed of hunting, for every now and again its talons would dig into Kalanin as though clutching prey. Just before evening the eagle woke and lifted into the sunset.

When they halted at nightfall, Kalanin went carefully to each group, seemingly to see that all was well, but in reality, to count their numbers. In all, there were one hundred and eighty four, but he reduced this count in his mind by two — these last two seemed uneasy, restless, and likely to depart before morning. Much of the area through which they had traveled had been wooded, with few farms and villages, so the only food at evening came from provisions that men had brought with them. Dargas sent his Sergeants to ensure that all food was shared. Perhaps, thought Kalanin, the Eye of Merlin would help them to hunt on the next day.

Sentries for the night were chosen from those who had not taken part in the morning skirmish. Others were encouraged to an early rest so that they could forage in the morning. Most rested beside campfires, talking among themselves. Kalanin found a stream and bathed, in spite of the evening chill; the light was dim, but he could still see the water darken with the last of the ash from the ruin of Sea's Edge.

Later, he found Dargas, alone, by a watchfire. Kalanin joined his Tier Leader, sitting in silence for a while, watching the flames. Kalanin lit his pipe with a coal from the fire, and puffed away, letting his mind relax while his body dried. There were matters he wished to discuss, though he needed to be cautious. After a few more moments of hesitation, he broke the long silence.

"What I said before, I should repeat: you and I must be as brothers; we cannot hold information from one another. I held nothing back concerning aid from Merlin. I hope that you, also, will hold nothing back...I need to know what befell the men of Baron Cadmon of the Plain of Gravengate. Tell me now, as though you were the Eye of Merlin, seeing all." There came a pause as Dargas eyed Kalanin narrowly, pursing his lips.

"All right. There's no shame in it for me or for the Baron. I'll tell you, but I'll start at the beginning. I don't know much about the Wizards' League, only what the Baron shared with a few of us...but I could see that trouble was brewing. How long has it been since Thorian withdrew from the councils of the League?"

"More than a year, now," said Kalanin, "and before that, there was uncertainty and hesitation for again another half a year. No one seemed to know much about the cause."

Dargas pulled himself up and threw another log on the fire. "It was more than just silence because there was trouble along the border, forays, raids, and such, with more men always being drawn into the service of Thorian. At first, the Baron tried to pass matters off as rumor and misunderstanding, but after a time, he added a few more tiers of his own…the Baron! Now, there was a man and a man with a temper. We watched, waiting for the explosion. But you know that Balardi's a fierce one too, and somehow the two of them tiptoed about, each afraid to set the other off, and they let things go by that neither would have accepted from the Mid-World. War would have come early if the Mid-World had been pushing at our borders." Dargas shook his head, looking into the darkness. "What of you at Sea's Edge? You must have given some thought to a stray Wizard — and your League."

"Merlin did, I'm sure," said Kalanin. "As for me, I thought it might be the attraction of the Mid-World, perhaps that Thorian wished to be chief among the many Sorcerers, rather than second to Merlin. Over the years, the League has lost many an Apprentice and Adept to the Mid-World — it's easier for many to satisfy themselves than to serve the Wizards. Julian, I think, was different, but he's gone."

"I don't know about this lure of power," Dargas muttered. "There's an ugly smell to this thing — Thorian turned on us, as though *he* had been betrayed, and he had this Sorcerer, this Nergal at his side."

"Merlin told us of a Sorcerer, but he wasn't named. How did you learn of him?"

"There was some great sorcery worked," said Dargas. "The Baron's councilors told him of a divination — but it was such that it troubled our sleep, and all of us dreamed similar dreams, very strange night visions. After, we were told that a powerful Sorcerer called Nergal had come from the Mid-World to aid Thorian. We had not much time to think about it, as war swept over us only a few weeks later." Dargas paused once more, as though organizing his mind.

"Thanks for letting an old soldier ramble on. Here's the meat of this sorry tale: it was but eleven days ago that men of Thorian and Nergal swept past us before we could warn Balardi, or ride to his aid. They were said to number more than thirty thousand, as counted by our frontier posts, and Balardi with maybe five thousand, now trapped in his fortress. The Baron had only twenty tiers, but a few were under strength, so you can count his force as less than ten thousand...yet we marched to the Plain of Gravengate, some of the Baron's councilors telling him this, others that." Dargas sighed.

"I led the scouts to the edge of the Plain that morning and watched the first assault against Gravengate. There was war on the ground that day as thousands surged over the Plain, but there was war in the air, too, as Elementals and servants of the Wizards fought in the sky, and great blasts of power from the Wizards shook the earth. I don't know how Gravengate stood.

"Now the councilors of the Baron — a prissy lot, I don't know where he got them from — but some said, 'Wait for Merlin,' and others, 'Draw them away with the pretense of an attack.' But the Baron would have none of it, and he called upon the tiers to form at the edge of the Plain, vowing to fulfill his oath." Kalanin sensed something unsaid.

"And this, the oath, was the only reason?"

"Not all," Dargas continued. "The Baron was hot, really hot. These men of Nergal are a filthy lot, burning villages, attacking farmers. But don't misunderstand: the Baron may have been angry, but he was a good soldier, and he would have bashed them good if it hadn't been for that Maker cursed Angel."

"What, a Seraph!" cried Kalanin, stumbling to his feet. "So that's what they were talking about! But how could it be, a First Servant of the Maker on a battlefield against us? Surely, they were watching an illusion!"

"Sit down," said Dargas in surprisingly mild tones. "No need to stir the men while they're resting...I said that there was no shame in it. Did you think that we fled some mongrel creature of the Mid-World? Or an illusion? There were those with the Sight among us and they were the first to flee. It was an Angel, or as you call it, a Seraph.

"Before the thing appeared, the battle didn't go badly. The Baron surprised them and smashed their right tier group. We could hear the men of Gravengate cry out in encouragement as Balardi struck at our foes, and for a moment, they seemed to waver.

"But then the Angel appeared on the Plain. It stood taller than you by about two heads, strong and noble looking so that it made even the fairest human seem like some poorly made beastlike creature. In its left hand, it held a light shield, made of wicker and in its right, a long cane, a wand maybe. When his cane touched our men, they fell senseless or dead — we couldn't tell which. Men began to pull back from it in fear, for those who had fallen were hacked to pieces by the men of Nergal. Archers fired volley after volley at it, but every shaft veered skyward. It seemed that the Maker had turned against us.

"But the Baron didn't fall back; he was mad as a Pit Fiend. He called on his bodyguard to hold his flanks, and he forced his way toward the great Seraph. I took some of my lads and broke off to protect the Baron's right flank, so I was there as the Baron slashed at the Angel. I could see the Angel's face, filled with sorrow, as it brushed aside the Baron's sword, and reaching over the Baron's head, touched him lightly with his cane. The Baron fell like a stone, but it was Nergal's men who hacked at him with broadswords and axes, laughing as they chopped the Baron into chunks of dead meat.

"And I saw, with a few others, that the Baron's first cut had been a good one, that he had struck the Angel, yet left no mark. After that, we couldn't keep our strength together. Within a brief time, even our rear guard was broken. I fled with the rest." Dargas fell silent, but Kalanin was on his feet, pacing by the watch fire.

"A Seraph!" he muttered. "It wouldn't shock me to learn that some Mid-World Power had aided Thorian, but a Seraph, a First Servant! All the Seraphs and Demons, Spirit Lords and Dragons — all these were said to have passed into the Truce and vanished with the birth of the Mid-World. And that a Seraph, a First Servant, should come against us rather than aiding the League is astonishing! We have always counted ourselves as Third Servants, after Seraphs and Spirit Lords.

"Thorian turns, Merlin is truck down, a Seraph comes against us: an amazing series of events. More than the future of the League may be at stake — Merlin should be here!" Kalanin calmed himself and sat again beside Dargas. "Yet now I see how a great force might be brought down and broken. On the other hand, I should tell you that the Eye of Merlin advises that there is often a calm after these many Sendings, a time when we might build our strength to strike back."

"I don't think much of our chances in dealing either with the humans or the Powers," Dargas said softly, "though it's better to be here than being chased down the Greenway."

· ⋇ ·

The next morning, they began the second day of their journey to Amalric. Kalanin and Dargas rode a little to the rear, watching for the Eye of Merlin. It was still early morning when the great eagle reached Kalanin's shoulder.

"So?" asked Kalanin.

"You expect great tidings this quickly?" croaked the eagle. "Here they are: a few farm hands crept to the edge of the camp guarded by your foes, casting javelins and stones at the camp. There was some loss of sleep, but that is all. This morning, a second tier of five hundred reached the first so that nearly nine hundred now pursue you, and they move swiftly with greater purpose than before." Dargas shook his head in dismay.

"Yet I still think we will prevail," Kalanin said. "Let them pursue us as the land grows hostile. Also, we have here in the Eye of Merlin, the greatest of the Mid-World Spies — worth perhaps half of a tier in himself." The eagle hesitated for a moment, then continued grudgingly.

"I have found a few who will listen. We may yet do some damage."

Again, the next morning, the eagle brought tidings: "The first part of the night was still, but beyond midnight, a group of perhaps twenty stumbled to the edge of your enemies' camp. How they escaped notice with all their noise and rumblings I do not understand."

"Few have the senses of the Eye of Merlin," Kalanin said with a trace of a smile.

"Once in place," continued the eagle, "some drew arrows against the sentries, doing some slight damage, but others kindled flame arrows and shot them into the camp, setting fire to many tents. Several of our foes were wounded in the confusion. The archers escaped and are traveling to Amalric." Kalanin straightened and let out a sigh of relief.

"Perhaps we have now begun," he muttered, almost to himself.

"Wait, there is more," said the eagle. "Before daybreak, a separate group of fourteen attacked and killed two sentries before being driven off. Several were wounded, one gravely, but the others journey now to Amalric."

During the next few days, Kalanin led the remnants of Baron Cadmon's force to the south of Amalric, staying always a day's march from their enemies. With stragglers returning each day, and with new forces joining as they marched, Kalanin now counted nearly four hundred. And under the direction of the Eye of Merlin, bands of men hung night and day at the edges of Thorian's vanguard, so that they had no peace, and more of their foes were lost each day. Word also came from the eagle of a young man of considerable cunning, who had tampered with the axles of their enemies' provision wagons, so that they shattered over uneven ground, and the provisions were abandoned.

The Eye of Merlin sent this young man to Kalanin, and when he arrived, Kalanin looked him over carefully, meeting a young man with a wispy beard named Rostov: the youth looked to be more at home at an inn — as a musician perhaps — rather than on a battlefield. Yet there were flickers of intelligence and humor in the eyes of the young man, and he was sent to serve under Dargas.

· ⋊ ·

On the sixth night after their first skirmish, Kalanin readied for sleep, turning events over in his mind, feeling a certain grim satisfaction: more men joined them each day; his body was slowly healing; and their pursuers faltered. If each part of the League held up its end as well, then the League might still survive.

He drifted into a peaceful sleep — but woke in the darkness, covered with sweat, groping for his sword. His friends were in trouble! They needed him! He stumbled up, and walked out into the starry night, trying to calm himself, to pass off his fears as a nightmare left over from childhood.

Kalanin was still out under the stars when the Eye of Merlin returned, sweeping through the darkness, seeking Kalanin as he stood beside a watch fire.

"So, the message has reached you as well," said the eagle, watching Kalanin's grim face. "What were you shown?"

"No message for me...I had a dream, of Galad, and Julian, and the small ones. They were in great peril so that I felt their fear. It was only a simple dream; it will pass, and in a few moments, I will be asleep again."

"It was more than a dream," said the eagle. "It was information, grim tidings perhaps, but news of your friends. I was awake when it came, and my Sight is greater than yours, so the images were clear as life to me:

"I saw Galad turn and flee from a powerful being of the Mid-World;

"I saw the small servant of Julian, and another small one, pursued by an evil Sending through an enormous, dark city, and they were not aware that they were being hunted;

"I saw Julian, racing in great fear from a holy place."

"But what are we supposed to make of these night visions?" asked Kalanin. "Are they not simple illusions, disturbances sent by enemies who are trying to confuse us?"

The eagle was silent for a while. "I must guess that one of the Powers of the Mid-World has given us a little aid, with small risk to itself so that in the unlikely event that we survive, it can claim our goodwill — though no Power has ever before attempted such a thing." The eagle trailed off.

"Wait, now wait!" the eagle croaked, voice straining in the darkness. "At the edge of each vision, a figure lurked — cowled, cloaked, with glowing eyes — showing the innermost force of *The Game of the Masters*! So, *The Game of the Masters* has itself stepped forward, something that has never happened in the long history of the *Game*! Merlin my master, aid us now, for we are trapped in a very great *Web of Fate*.... But be comforted, Giftless warrior — your friends are alive, though in great peril."

X

As the days passed, it seemed to their foes that all of Alantéa had burst into violence against them, with the raids and harassments becoming pitched battles, fought every step of the way against men who struck then melted into the countryside.

At the beginning of the tenth day of their pursuit, the vanguard of Thorian's tier force — fewer than seven hundred, the remnant of two tiers — turned, marching southeast, away from Amalric, and back to the siege of Gravengate. That night, Kalanin and Dargas rode at the head of many men into Amalric, where there were thousands gathered of all ages, cheering, and calling out for the League; and bonfires in the broad city streets flamed red into the night.

Later, Kalanin stood with the Eye of Merlin, staring into the embers of one of the great fires.

"So, we have begun," murmured Kalanin. "The League will not be put down so easily."

"There has only been a lull. They will again send great powers of sorcery against you." The eagle was calm, almost detached.

"Let them send what they will send," said Kalanin grimly. "We will cut them if we can, and if we cannot cut them, we will bind them and cast them from great heights, and if they do not smash or shatter, we will find deep places and seal them away forever."

"'The Mid-World is rich,'" quoted the eagle. "We shall see."

Chapter Five
The Tarnished Sword

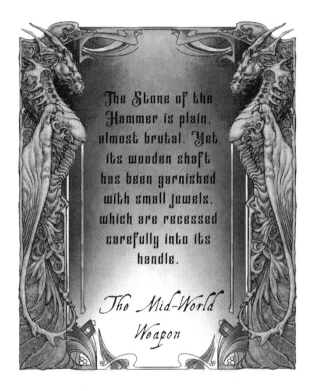

The Stone of the Hammer is plain, almost brutal. Yet its wooden shaft has been garnished with small jewels, which are recessed carefully into its handle.

The Mid-World Weapon

GALAD LAY BACK ON THE floor of the old tower and tried to sleep. His body was tired, while his mind still churned: in one day they had encountered a Gogra that was some kind of giant Troll, an enchanted storm, the death of Julian's small confidant, then a pack of wolves — and Kalanin was injured. It would take time for him to heal, but he would be whole, and dangerous again. Years ago, Galad had watched as Orlan gradually lost a step, a fraction of his strength, began to stoop a little, and finally ceased to travel with Kalanin. This same slippage would happen first to Kalanin, then to himself, but with any fortune, that time of weakness would be far away. In the meantime, they might win through and heal.

Beside the fire, Julian was whispering to his small Familiar; like a low, background noise, it lulled Galad into slumber. He thought of himself casually relating their adventures to Orlan, standing by the hearth fire in the Halls of Merlin at Sea's Edge. He drifted from the tower into sleep, his hand, some strange instinct, coming to rest on the hilt of his broken sword.

In the night, the first tentacles of the Great Spell sent shudders of cold through Galad's body: he still slept, but his hand tightened on his sword handle. Rumbles of sound shook the tower. His eyes flashed open. With a terrible wrenching sound, the roof of the tower was ripped away. Galad tried to leap to his feet, but no floor was left beneath him — he was being torn from the tower, hurtling through the night like a meteor.

Great waves of icy air struck at his body as he sped through the night sky, and his breathing stopped. He spun out of control, face whirling between ground and sky. Like a tumbler, Galad rolled into a ball, and with both hands, he forced the hilt of his broken sword into his belt. His fingers became numb from the cold, so he clasped them to his body, closing his eyes as he hurtled through the night. A second blast of wind struck at him, but less strongly — at least now he could breathe.

Somehow, the strength of the Great Spell was being checked — a powerful counter spell rose out of the darkness to contest the power of the Great Spell. Then, strangely, a second counter spell surged from the tower, so that there was war in the air all about his body. His speed slowed, and his body righted itself, with his feet pointing to the ground. Yet as he looked down, the ground seemed a distant, dark mass. Great Spell and counter spells would exhaust one another, then he would drop like a stone. Perhaps the counter spells would aid Julian or Kalanin, but he was beyond help. He was a dead man. His life was over; there had not even been time for panic. Strangely, his greatest regret was that he would never be able to tell Orlan of their battle with the Gogra.

The struggle about him rose and fell. At least Merlin had not sent them away unprotected. It was tragic that all the Wizard's efforts had been wasted. He began to sink, slowly gathering speed.

It was then, thousands of feet above earth, that he saw in the upper skies of the night the first glimpse of that which no man had viewed before: the Network, the Grid of Power, the great carnival of energy that fueled the Mid-World: here a river of golden light surged to the far horizon; and a little farther, a great pillar of light pulsed violet in the night sky. Now, he could see that green flickers leaped continually into the golden river and emerged blue and focused amid many other lights. And he could feel dark energies pulsing, radiating heat. He was sinking, but he was drifting closer to the lights. The ground was reaching for him as was the Network, but the ground was winning — he would be smashed by stone instead of being ripped apart by the Network's grid of power. *Maker, my Maker,* his mind whispered, *I am so sorry for all the things I've left undone.*

But then a great hand — the skeletal hand of some giant creature — loomed out of the night, smashing him backhanded into the grid, the Network. Galad cried out, once, into the night, just as he was sucked into the Field of the Powers and vanished.

· ⋊ ·

"You weren't *really* going to try that," said a soft voice.

"Well, I didn't, anyway." The second voice was more harsh and rapid. "Haven't you ever wanted to try a mortal?" There was a pause.

"I think I was tempted, a long time ago," said the soft voice slowly. "But I didn't. I remembered that I wasn't supposed to — though now I can't remember why we were barred."

"It's a stupid rule, anyway — Old Baldy will eat him for dinner."

Galad lay on the ground, listening. It was ridiculous, but he was alive — taken, no doubt to become a plaything or victim of one of the Mid-World Powers. He lay sprawled face down on what appeared to be sand, and though his eyes were closed, light penetrated: rays of distant sunlight. Cool breezes blew across his back. The voices seemed to come from far away, or they were aged and feeble creatures. He had to focus to hear what the soft voice was saying:

"He's larger than the other mortals, and he's armed. Perhaps the Bald One will have difficulty with this mortal."

"Don't forget our wager over the bear — you were wrong then, too."

The soft voice laughed. "Yes, but think how well we fared. After the Bald One overindulged in bear meat, then *we* feasted from his dark forces. I remember how the energy surged through me — it was like waking from a dream and finding my old strength renewed. Now if we could only persuade the Power guarding the Portal to make a similar donation."

"Not for me, thanks," said the harsh voice with a shudder. "Big Ghoul hungers after Her Highness, but I'm fairly sure that you and I would be eaten for dessert. I always wondered why Big Ghoul didn't blast his way here."

"We both wondered about that, long ago," said the soft voice, "and then we could think more clearly. But listen, now. This human's awake and listening, I think. Let's tell him about the Bald One and the Lady. Give him a better chance, perhaps."

"We tried that, long ago, with the other mortals, didn't we?"

"That was a troubled time," said the soft voice. "We were just beginning to fade from view, and it seemed to bother the humans. See, he's waking...."

Galad stretched carefully, testing each part of his body. He was sore, but nothing seemed broken. He lay on a sandy clearing, a little distance from a stream; on the other bank of the stream, a densely wooded forest began. It seemed as though the sandy area had once been a part of the stream bed, but some time ago the stream had changed course.

Slowly, so as not to disturb the distant voices, he stood and looked about him. There were no signs of the speakers, just a few birds swooping over the water, and two lizards sunning on rocks in midstream. He walked carefully to the stream, searching for footprints along the sandy banks. The birds flew away, the sun shone in the clearing, the lizards tensed to flee, but still he had no one to talk with. Then a voice spoke to Galad, distantly, from no obvious direction.

"You may hunt for us if you wish," said the soft voice, "but you will have trouble finding us. We've become somewhat insubstantial in our latter years."

"And it's a waste of your last hours," added the grating voice. "In just a little while, Old Baldy will come sniffing for you." Galad sat by the stream bed, not quite certain how to begin a conversation with disembodied voices.

"I come from the Wizards' League in the southern portion of Alantéa, and my name is Galad. How are you named? And what part of the Mid-World have I entered?" These questions were greeted by a little silence, with only the murmur of the stream breaking the afternoon quiet.

"Names?" said the soft voice. "Once we were named, so long ago. and when you said 'Mid-World,' there was a quivering feeling within me, as though the word was something I should know, or did know. Tell me more about this Mid-World."

"We were taught that the Mid-World came after the Truce," Galad said, "when the Powers, both good and evil, gave up their struggles and joined together to preserve their energies."

"He's talking about Fat City!" exclaimed the harsh voice.

"Yes, the Land of Energy," added the soft voice. "No, I'm sorry to say that we are beyond the Mid-World, as you call it. There the energies are so lush and varied, while here we have faded as the many years passed, and we can no longer recall what we were named, or what we were created to do. All we know about is the Lady of the Hill, the Bald One, the stream, the meadows, the forest, and the Power at the Portal. As you may have gathered, my associate has a different name for each."

"What is this 'Bald One' that you speak of, that you feel may be a danger to me?" asked Galad.

"Now *there* is a name I should remember...," said the soft voice.

"The humans called it a Manticore," added the harsh voice.

"What!" cried Galad, stumbling to his feet. "That's monster enough for fifty well-armed men! What am I supposed to do, alone?"

"You are armed, are you not?" asked the soft voice. Galad drew his broken half of a sword.

"Ah..." said the soft voice, with a little sadness, a little disappointment. "Ah...all in all, it might be well for you to flee, to live a little while longer."

"Don't forget the nose of Old Baldy," said the grating voice. "He hasn't had a human in a long time, but he's sure to remember the smell." Galad tried to calm himself, sitting once again, forcing himself to think. Had he been sent to this land as a snack for the pet monster of some Power? And yet there was no sense in leaping to conclusions; there might even be some straightforward way out.

"Tell me more about this creature," he said. "All that I know of the monster is its fearsome reputation as a devourer of men."

"At one time, the humans would say of the Manticore: 'Man's head, lion's body, snake's tail, ape's hands, but only one life,'" said the grating voice, and the soft voice added:

"I suppose they said that to reassure themselves."

"Not that it helped much," continued the grating voice. "When the last human perished, and their contest with the monster ended, the humans could claim no Manticore, but Old Baldy had eaten three hundred and more humans."

"Then, if it feasts on men," said Galad, "surely it would have starved and died with the passing of humans."

"It seems to *prefer* humans," said the soft voice, "but any warm meat will do. You heard us mention the bear, did you not? I thought that the bear would give a good account of itself, but the Bald One stepped up, and bit it once or twice, stinging it with its tail, and then it was over." Galad shook his head, wishing for a hundred men, armed with reinforced bows.

"You mentioned the Lady of the Hill," he said. "She alone seems to have prevailed against the monster. Was she not able to help the other humans?"

"She wears the form of a human," the soft voice said thoughtfully, "but I believe she is something other. And she did not help the mortals. Many, at the last, were devoured outside her walls, for she would not give them shelter. If you wish to seek her aid, the Lady of the Hill lives on your side of the stream, beyond the far hill. As for the last being that I mentioned, the Power at the Portal, he does not truly inhabit this land, but seems to seek entry and has been denied."

Galad stood. Turning from the stream, he saw that a meadow, still lit by the afternoon sun, ran up the hillside. He gathered that the dwelling of the Lady was somewhere in that direction, but she seemed to offer little help. On the other side of the stream, a deep forest began; it looked dark and uninviting even in the sunlit afternoon. He checked his pocket for flint. Here, where he stood now, was as good a place as any to face the thing.

"Does the creature hunt at night, or in daylight?" he asked.

"If the Bald One holds to his schedule, he will come thrashing through the forest in an hour or two, just before sunset," said the soft voice. "Best you were gone now — though it *is* a keen hunter."

Galad said nothing, but he began to gather bits and pieces of wood for a fire. Within a few paces lay enough dry deadfall to create a good watch fire. If the Manticore were kin to its component parts, it would not like being burned. His flint started some of the dry leaves, then the twigs took, and finally, the larger branches. Just beyond his hearing, the two voices were engaged in animated conversation.

"Are you really going to face Old Baldy today?" asked the harsh voice. Galad nodded, pushing larger pieces of wood into his fire.

"Will you shriek?" asked the soft voice, and its voice quivered a little with excitement.

"What?!?" said Galad.

"Shriek," said the soft voice. "It comes back to me now, with the fire. The humans used to leap out at the Manticore, with fire and metal, shrieking and calling on the Powers." The voice calmed a little, then continued. "Yes... if it's any help to you, I *do* recommend shrieking — it's very traditional." In spite of himself, Galad laughed.

"I'm glad I can provide a little entertainment for the two of you — what would you have done without me?" A brief pause ensued.

"You are right, human, and it saddens me. We should take no pleasure in such an unequal contest," said the soft voice. "But think: you are likely to go into the darkness at the peak of your strength, while we, who have lived so many ages, can no longer even remember what we were at the time of our strength, or why we have diminished, or know what we will become. Do not judge us too harshly."

"I will not judge you," said Galad. "Instead, I should thank you for your aid. But is there anything else you might do to help me deal with this monster? Despite its reputation, I intend to prevail, and even a distraction would help. Is there something you might do, at little risk to yourselves?"

"I don't think —" the harsh voice started, but the soft voice interrupted:

"Wait...this may be our last chance. It comes to me that once we were helpers. We will try, but it will be only a distraction and a brief one at that. Call out when you wish to have the Manticore distracted."

Galad bowed low to his unseen counselors. "If I survive, I will ask the League to aid you, to help you recover your strength."

· ⋊ ·

The day passed into the long shadows of late afternoon. Only a brief time remained before the Manticore's hunt, but Galad's hunger had begun to gnaw at him. The stream held several small fishes, no larger than the length of his hand, but by trapping a few of them in the shallows, he was able to ease his hunger. The smell of cooked fish might well make it easier for the Manticore to find him, and yet it seemed better to face the creature while there was still light.

Galad sat by his fire, feeding it until there was a wall of heat before him. In addition to his shattered sword, he chose a long thick bough, placing one end in the flames. From the stream bed, he chose a stone that could be heaved with both hands — he couldn't hurl rocks with the Gogra's strength, but he might bounce a stone off the thing's skull and slow it down.

Evening approached. Galad tried to reassure himself. Perhaps the humans had been weakened by illnesses. And how were all those varied parts creating a stronger creature? It had to be confusing to be part of this and part of that. What did it need with the head of a man? That didn't seem too horrible; maybe its neck was its weak spot.

From the depths of the forest came a deep, low growl.

"Ah...," said the soft voice. "Perhaps if you are ready."

"I will call out, 'Now!' when the time comes for you to distract it," Galad said quietly. He stood, and looked himself over, as he always did before a contest of arms. He was clad only in light leather and cloth — there was no armor to check, and no certainty that mail would help.... The growl in the forest turned into a loud bellow.

"That's the first smell of human in many years!" said the soft voice, and again the voice quivered with excitement. The sweat began to run down Galad's arms and sides. Maybe it had been a mistake to make a stand here, with invisible allies of doubtful reliability.

The tops of the trees in the distant forest began to thrash and bend as the heavy creature swung through its upper branches. Leaves flashed green against a red skyline. Now, he could hear snorts and grunts as the Manticore smelled him.

Then the creature reached the forest's edge and dropped to the ground. From across the stream, it looked straight into the eyes of Galad. His sword nearly slipped from his hand. The thing was huge! There was almost no neck, but what was incredible was the hairless head — who had called it a human head? It was three times the size of a man's, with great gapped yellow teeth. Its body was shaped like a lion' but it bulked larger than any lion, while behind it, the great snake tail whipped back and forth, lashing the underbrush.

This monster, this Manticore, couldn't be fought with a broken half sword! Galad shook himself from his fear, and cried out at the top of his lungs, "Now!" Then he turned and ran from the monster with every bit of speed that remained to him. A moment of confusion and delay came as the "distraction" held the Manticore for a brief moment, but then it roared and raced in pursuit.

Galad ran, his heart and lungs shuddering with the effort, as he sped from clearing to clearing, trying always to keep the creature away from any possible path in the upper branches, and on the ground. He changed direction again…it seemed not far behind…there was no place to make a stand, to take a cut at it before the end. The thing seemed to snort and gurgle with the chase — and it was getting closer. Galad dodged again.

There, at the top of the hill, in the last night of dusk, Galad saw stone walls: his only chance for refuge. He was down to his last strength. He sped up the slope, the Manticore bellowing behind him. He reached the wall. There were spaces in the rock for handholds — he could climb if he had time. The touch of the wall sent a wave of shock through him. No entry! He raced to the end of the wall, the Manticore just behind him. Again, the stones sent shocks through his body.

"Sanctuary! I call for refuge in the Maker's Name!" The Manticore pursued, though more slowly, as though sure of its prey. No answer came from within. Galad again sprinted to the edge of a wall, around a corner. The Manticore raced past, its great bulk carrying it beyond the edge, and Galad slashed at it, missing by a hand's breadth. The creature's tail swept by him, but the hind foot caught Galad and sent him sprawling. He spun, and turned rolling toward the wall, calling out, "I call for refuge in the Maker's Name, and by Merlin of the Wizards' League!"

As the Manticore stalked him, Galad felt the resistance of the walls subside. He hurled his broken sword at the creature, and scrambled up the wall, collapsing on the other side. The bellowing of the Manticore grew frantic as it tried to follow. Forces radiating from the wall seemed to repel the uninvited — and from the sounds coming from the Manticore, the creature was completely unwelcome. Galad lay on the ground listening, face turned to the twilight sky, chest heaving as his lungs struggled for air. The Manticore's sounds continued as it cried out in pain and hunger.

He was alive, against all odds, and he was somewhere beyond the Mid-World of the Truce if such a thing were possible. Where were Julian and Kalanin, and where were the little servants of the Apprentice? The sky of early evening was incredibly clear and peaceful, but it held no answers to his questions — he couldn't recognize any of the star patterns.

He stumbled to his feet and began to walk, slowly, toward the central hall. Like the outside walls, the great manor had been built with stones, yet it was more finished, with tall, polished pillars in the front supporting a massive, sloped roof. In the dimness of twilight, it seemed that the area within the walls was grassy and trim, unlike the fields and meadows of the hillside.

Galad peered into the stone hall — no light greeted him. He entered in the dark, tired, and disheveled, feeling naked without his sword. The only sounds in the darkness were those made by his shuffling feet and the cries of the Manticore as it struggled with the outside walls. The voices had referred to the Lady as other than human; perhaps she was the Power who had drawn him to this place and would now explain her reasons. He spoke softly into the darkness:

"Madam, I thank you for your aid, and ask pardon for my intrusion." There was no answer. He stood for a while, feeling foolish, then found a wall and sat, leaning against cool stone. Outside, the Manticore seemed to have lost interest in further pain. Galad rested in the darkness, but sleep was far from his mind. As his eyes became used to the absence of light, he could see that he was not far from the center of a large chamber, and a little distance from him was a table, one that might comfortably seat ten or more. Now, a muffled sound came out of the stillness, as though someone had shifted in a chair. Galad sat up.

"Why do you trouble me, mortal?" It was the voice of a woman, and it seemed to come from everywhere, and nowhere.

"There was little choice, my lady," he said softly. "It was sanctuary or death. I've backed away from wielders of magic, and from armed groups of many men, but this is the first time I've run for my life. The Manticore is monster enough for many men." Another silence ensued.

"When you called upon me, mortal, you used certain names. What are the meanings of these names?" Galad let the silence settle again before replying.

"I called upon you in the name of the Maker, and I was taught that the Maker was the source of all earth's life and life beyond this planet. To this name, you did not respond. But when I called out in the name of Merlin and his Wizards' League, you aided me. Are you a distant ally of the League?"

"Who is this Merlin person and what is this League, that I should be concerned with it?" said the woman's voice. To Galad, sitting in the darkness, it was the voice of one seeking to avoid obligations, listening to each phrase to see if one key word might offer escape. He spoke carefully:

"The Wizards' League led by Merlin counts itself as an heir to the Servants of the Maker, and the League has set aside a small portion of Alantéa as a haven for humans. Under the three Wizards — Merlin, and Balardi, and Thorian — the League has successfully shielded itself from the Powers of the Mid-World." He said nothing of the conflict within the League, nor of the disaster at Sea's Edge. The voice gave a soft laugh and seemed to relax.

"So, this Merlin is no Power, but only a mortal conjurer. Has he sent you to ask for help from me?" Galad had been overtaken by a Great Spell, his sword had been broken by one creature, and he had fled from another, but at last, pride flickered inside him.

"No, madam, I was not sent, nor did I choose to come here," he said, and he told her of their journey to Gravengate, though not the reason for it. He spoke about the Apprentice, of Kath and the Gogra, the storm, the fight in the tower, of the Great Spell, and how the counterspells had cast him into the Network of the Powers.

When he had finished, there was another long silence, and Galad considered that the Lady, for all her regal tones, was a poor conversationalist, and he wondered if she also was a fading, disembodied spirit. Finally, the voice murmured:

"So, it seems that mortals are gaining real power — after so many ages." Then, without a sound of flint or match, a candle flickered to life on a broad table. Sitting at the table was a lady, not young, with the regal beauty of middle years, though her eyes were those of an immortal.

"Come closer and let me look at you," she said. "Today, I saw the best race ever run by a mortal against the Manticore. How did you come by such speed?" Galad was tempted to ask how many races she had watched, while the humans perished, but he held back.

"It was terror, Madam, fear of the creature." She considered this neutral answer as carefully as she had listened to Galad's other responses, then spoke again:

"It comes to mind that both the swift and the slow might thirst after the race. Is this so with you?" Not waiting for a response, she drew a silver goblet from beneath her table and passed it to Galad. The water in the goblet tasted flavorless, like the distilled aqua preferred by Apprentices. She drew another goblet for herself, saying, "I will join you, though neither water nor wine will truly pass my lips," and she smiled the benevolent smile that the wise waste upon the ignorant. Clearly, she was not comfortable with him; Galad changed the subject.

"I saw only a little of the fields and meadows in the sunlight, but it seems a fair land. Have you lived here long?" She laughed.

"How long have I lived here? How do those of your League measure time? I have seen the sun rise and set over my lands many, many thousands of times, yet in my life, that is only a small part." Galad felt embarrassed by his few years; the Lady looked on him with amusement. "And how many years has this Merlin lived, the one that you serve, and call upon with such reverence?"

"Merlin was old when I was born," said Galad. "The Wizards seem able to hold back their aging, but they will eventually pass, like other mortals. Old age and death disturb us less, now that we are separate from the immortal Powers." Another long silence followed his answer; the candle began to melt down. Galad finally asked the question that had been uppermost in his mind.

"Madam, what of the Manticore? Has it been with you for long in this land?" Another silence ensued; at last, the Lady replied:

"Yes, the Manticore...perhaps tomorrow. You may rest here tonight." The candle burned low, sputtered, and went out. The Lady of the Hill vanished as quietly as she had appeared. Galad was left standing alone in a dark, dreary silence. He considered his strange hostess of mysterious origin and decided that she, in all her thousands of years, had never ventured into an inn, or entertained human guests. He stumbled about in the darkness and eventually found a cushioned place in one corner.

As he thought about his strange conversation with the mistress of the house, it seemed to Galad that she had been even more ill at ease than he had, and that she had not spoken many of her own thoughts. After a long dark quiet, sleep came to him bringing dreams of long evenings at inns with tankards of ale, and the casual laughter of friends.

· X ·

He woke with a start. A second roar came from the Manticore as it again attacked the walls. Galad leaped to his feet, striking his head against a wall ornament made of stone, then he sank back to the floor. Lightning flickered over the horizon, revealing a broad window at the side of the stone manor. Little could be done without a weapon; the Lady of the Hill would surely continue to protect herself. Yet there might be something to be learned, and so he stumbled to the window and peered out. The monster's cries halted briefly, then they were renewed as the wall was attacked from a different side. In the darkness, the walls gleamed with power as they repelled the creature. With an effort, he forced himself back to his makeshift couch. As the sounds of conflict died down, his weary body drifted back to sleep.

When he woke in the morning, he left the inner shadows of the manor hall and looked in the yard for a well or a spring of water. Neither could be found, but one of the trees in the courtyard bore fruit, as though by accident, and with a few pieces Galad eased his hunger and thirst. From several places outside the hall, it was possible to see over the outside barrier and view the far hillside. He sat in one of these places, watching the sunlight spill over the meadow. Butterflies flew carelessly about, as though nothing evil had ever been born, and their brief lives would go on forever.

He felt certain that if he wandered through the dark manor in search of its mistress, he would find nothing. Later in the morning, his patience was rewarded when the Lady of the Hill sought him out.

"So, you have been watching my butterflies," she said softly. "They, and all the small creatures of the fields and meadows, have been my lifelong interest. They are so unlike the Dominion of Man for —" and she cut herself off. "Forgive me. I have dealt with so few humans in all my many years — it was not my intention to offend you."

"There's no offense taken," said Galad. "I know nothing of this Dominion; I serve only the League. Yet it would seem that we have a common enemy in the Manticore. Is there anything we might do together to destroy the creature?"

"I have *nothing* to do with this Manticore," she said bitterly. "In its mindlessness and power, it pursues me endlessly, and I have the strength to protect myself, but barely. There is no justice to its pursuit! Had I created it, or injured it, then there would be a fine, moral lesson in its hunger for me. But it is a Creature of the Darkness, a child of the Dragons, and of the Demons, at the Left Hand, side sinister of creation. *I have nothing to do with it.* Now, I ask of you — what do you wish from me? *I* am not responsible for that monster." She looked hard at Galad, and she was tall so that her eyes were almost on a level with those of the Knight.

"All that I wish is to return to my own people," he said. "In the service of the League, there's enough challenges and danger, so that I've no wish to seek adventure in your land. Can you return me to the south of Alantéa?"

She shook her head. "I have little enough power as it is. Will Merlin or one of the other conjurors seek you here?"

"They may in time," he said, "if I can survive for a while."

"Then the Manticore is a double problem for you; it is a being of considerable power. It guards the entrance to this land and would surely block any attempt to reach you." Galad noted that she described the monster as "his" problem, and he considered that the Lady of the hill would be of little assistance.

"If I'd had a full sword with me last evening," Galad muttered, "I would have stood my ground; I would not have run."

"A sword, that is all?" she asked and seemed to brighten. "I will look in my armory to see if there is something suitable for you." Relief showed in her face, and she added, "I must also find water for you, and some food. It has been a long time since I dealt with mortals, but I can recall their habits — washing, eating, sleeping, working, and little time for contemplation in their short, busy lives." With this, she drifted away. Galad watched her depart, feeling that he had overlooked something. A night's rest, a bit of metal — these seemed easy for her to supply; why had they not been given to the other humans?

He spent the next few hours watching the sunlit meadows. It seemed likely to be the last full day of his life, and he felt that he should try to enjoy it. In the afternoon, the Lady of the Hill again came for him, leading him to her table, showing him proudly a loaf of bread, a cup of milk, and a small dish of honey.

"It was not easy to come by these," she said and waved him to a seat. Galad sat, pulling the loaf apart, eating it carefully: she watched him intently as he ate, as though she were studying the habits of some exotic creature.

"Yes," she said as he finished. "Yes, I remember. That's how it was done, so many years ago.... But now come with me and see what I have polished for you in my armory." She led him to a small room that was set in a far corner of her stone manor. Dust lay over much of the room. A small window let in just enough light so that an ancient anvil was visible in the gloomy partial light, resting on a block of stone in the center of the room. On the wall were six great swords, hung by their handles on a wooden frame. Each sword was beautifully crafted, sharp, and polished, with jewels set within the hilts of each. It seemed to Galad that each was the product of a different style and a different craftsman. He looked questioningly to the Lady.

"Choose one," she said easily. "Test each for balance and weight, if you like." Galad felt his confidence rise: with a full sword, he might have a chance; at least he could hack the thing before it killed him. He lifted the closest blade from the rack, and a faint tremor of warning ran through his body. He gave no sign but continued to test each of the weapons. As an emissary of the League, he was protected against illusion, and he was warned — none of these weapons would fade or vanish in the sunlight — they were not complete illusions, but there was a falseness woven into them, and into the Lady of the Hill. He finished testing each blade and chose the one most like his old sword.

"Madam, I will choose this one, and I thank you, for it is a great gift," he said, filling his voice with gratitude. "Few of the lords of men have a weapon such as this." He drew his sword arm back. "But there is one test," and he swung a half stroke at the anvil. There was a tinkling sound, and the sword shattered into many pieces, its blade breaking up to the hilt. He looked at her coldly. "They will all do that, will they not, madam?"

A wave of grief and anguish swept over her face.

"Why did you come here?" Tears began to seep from her eyes, though she held herself erect. "You know not what you require of me — this will be my end." Galad shook his head.

"I will ask nothing more of you. Let down your barrier, and I will take my own broken sword and depart."

"No," she murmured, holding his arm in her soft hands. "I will struggle no more. You do not understand what you require of me but go now and find your broken sword. Bring it to me and I will heal it. Go now, and there will be no more deceit, no more evasions. But go before darkness comes with the monster's return." She released his arm, pushing him gently toward the door.

Galad found his broken sword in the brush beyond the outside walls. Only a few marks had been left by the Manticore — broken bushes, torn ground — but these were nothing in comparison to the ferocity of the thing. He looked over the meadows: in the distance, the afternoon sun was leaning far over the horizon and would soon set. It was hard to believe that a land of such beauty could contain both the violence of the monster and the deceit of the Lady. He picked up his blade and considered walking away from the hill, but in the end, he returned to the manor's inner hall, though without great hope.

He handed the blade to the Lady of the Hill but said nothing. She held the broken sword up to the afternoon sun.

"I should be able to heal this," she said softly, "but first, no more lies." She shimmered in the light, and grew taller, shining in the afternoon sun. "I looked something like this in the beginning," she said gently. "Is this a form you recognize?"

"You are one of the Spirit Lords," said Galad, and he bowed. "We were told that all the Spirit Lords had departed or had entered into the Mid-World of the Truce, but you are kin to the statue of Llara that stands before the Halls of Merlin at Sea's Edge."

"Llara was great among us, with a part in the creation of humankind, and for an age, she instructed the mortal magicians. I was never as potent as she, and now I am no longer even holy, so do not bow to me. But if you would hear my story, come and sit with me and watch the last rays of sunlight pass over my hill." Galad followed, and they sat in silence, watching the first streaks of red reach out over the afternoon sky.

Ancient lore was not one of Galad's strengths, and he strongly wished that a Wizard or one of the Keepers of Records was here in his place.

"I will not speak of the left side of creation, of the Demons and Dragons, and the Creatures of the Darkness, for all of those beings fill me with anger. Why did the Maker choose to wake the Demons? Yet the Maker brought forth the Seraphs, the First Servants, and the Seraphs dreamed many dreams of Alantéa and the Lands Beyond, and when it was time to bring these dreams to fruition, the Spirit Lords were created, the Second Servants of the Maker; and these assisted the Seraphs in the fashioning of all things. I and others ushered forth the small, winged things, the butterflies, the finches, and the larks, things of great beauty for the long meadows of Alantéa. But when the Spirit Lords brought humankind into being, to become Third Servants, many of us were puzzled, for men seemed inelegant, peculiar, only a step higher than beasts, and we wondered if the fashioners had been corrupted by the Demons, or if the shapers of humans had been shaken by the emergence of the Dragons.

"Then the great, confused struggles of the Servants and the Adversaries of the Maker began, and each sought to subdue to the other. There were many betrayals, yet most of the Seraphs and Spirit Lords and Men fought on the Servant's side. I watched as great numbers of mortals were massed and armed against their foes. They always fled in panic at the first test, yet it seemed to me that much of the struggle was fought on their behalf, for their protection.

"As for me, I wished only to be left alone among the beings of my own fashioning, so I founded this distant place and withdrew from the struggle. I did this before the Truce, and outside of any pact so that later the Powers of the Mid-World felt free to torment me. My powers also lessened over the ages, for the energies of the Mid-World were not available to me. But there were many of your short lifetimes that I watched the sun rise and set over my hillside before my enemies discovered me. A group of humans was sent first as bait for the monster, with the Manticore following — yet the Manticore was my salvation, for I was able to preserve myself against the monster; while now it blocks the Portal, so that another Power, more dangerous to me, cannot enter."

The sun had now set, but the horizon still blazed red.

"I was warned that there was a Power at the Portal," said Galad, "but I was concerned only with the Manticore — there was no time to worry about the other."

"This 'warning,' was it given by two beings of little substance?" Galad nodded. "Once they were beings of some power," she said sadly, "perhaps strong enough to defy the monster. Now, they lessen with each setting of the sun, and will soon fade into whispers. Yet perhaps that is the fate of all of us, even the mighty Powers of the Mid-World, that we will someday decline, and diminish, to become ghosts, quaint and perverse whispers in the night."

"Some humans also grow dim and witless in their old age," said Galad, "but the Healers now seem able to prevent this. What of the humans and the Manticore? Why were you not able to help them?"

"I should have helped them, but I did not. My powers are limited, and if I had used them to aid the humans, the Manticore would have been able to overcome me. Had the humans prevailed and destroyed the monster, then the Dark Lord who waits at the Portal would have overwhelmed me. So, I thought of watching the sun rise and set over my hillside for another age, and I let the short lived humans perish.

"With the death of the last human, I was warned of your coming, that one other mortal would come and call upon me for aid in the name of the Maker, and of Merlin and his League. If I failed to help you, a great doom would be set for me. From that warning, I judged that some of the great Servants remained outside of the Truce and had the power to fulfill their oaths.

"So, you see why I have not been of significant help to you: whether you are victorious or defeated, my days on this hill have ended. But now, at the last, I will put forth my full strength to aid you. On this night, we will renew your sword."

All traces of day had vanished, but the moon was shining brightly over the hills, covering the ground with pale light. The Spirit Lord rose, gleaming with moonlight.

"By my Farsight, I know that the monster hunts elsewhere. Tonight, I will walk about my hillside, probably for the last time. Come, walk with me."

She led Galad beyond the walls and walked with him through the meadows and moonbeams, telling him of the wildflowers and birds, and butterflies with so many varied colors. Galad felt the tension ease from his body. Whatever happened later, the feeling of falseness and deceit had ended. He would take whatever help was given to him, then face the monster like a simple warrior of the League. For the moment, he let the charm of the hillside sweep over him. At the end of his short life, at least he could say that he had spent one day with the Lady of the Hill, in the splendor of sunlight and moonlight.

It was late at night when they returned to the stone manor. Galad followed the Lady back to the armory, and found it changed; all traces of the false swords had vanished, and, as many candles were being lit, he saw that layers of dust had also been cleared away. Only the anvil and stone remained, and these had been moved to one side.

"I have called this place my armory, but in reality, it has served as my place of power — look closely at the floor." The floor was carved with runes and symbols, with each carving carefully positioned within a complex form that spread over most of the room. "Once I begin, you may not touch these lines without harm...I will take the sword, now." Galad passed the sword to the Spirit Lord, and stood back, not knowing what might be required of him.

She began by kneeling and tracing her hand over each of the different shapes of many runes, moving from the outer edges of the diagram to the centermost portion. As she passed over each carving, the lines of all the runes lit, each with a different light, so that there were many, varied colors gleaming in the darkness. The Spirit Lord, too, began to glow with a dull light.

Now, all the carved runes were lit — more than a hundred glowing inscriptions, shimmering in patterns around the great diagram. She knelt in the center of the great form, sword in one hand, while with her other hand she traced a small oval about her own form and the sword, as though sealing herself from the outer rune.

Then it seemed to Galad that a great congress of Powers had been called, with the Spirit Lord addressing each one. Candles began to flicker, as mist or smoke surged from the diagram. As though they came from a great distance, a murmur of many voices rose, calling to one another, and to the Spirit Lord. Some voices were brief, some remote; others were cold, and a few burned with hatred. Lastly, there came a wave of moaning voices, sobbing with grief or pain.

This Congress of Powers continued for a long while, and its discussions were not peaceful.

At last, the voice of the Spirit Lord grew louder, rising above the others, calling out words of command in a language unknown to Galad. A moment of silent hesitation followed, as though the Powers would not be compelled; then came a flash, and a tremor, a shock that rattled through the stone hall. Lights within the great diagram faded, and a few of the candles flickered back to life. In the center stood the Spirit Lord, bent and weary. She spoke with a small, weak voice.

"It is safe, now. Come forward and light the other lights. Then we shall see what our combined strength has wrought." Galad used one candle to light the rest; his hand was steady, but his heart still hammered.

Willing himself calm, he walked across the barrier toward the Spirit Lord — she was insubstantial, almost like a wraith. In her hands, she held a full sword, not the broken half blade that Galad had given her. Without a word, she handed it to him. He looked closely at it; even by candlelight, the sword was strange: it seemed to be formed of mixed metals, some clear and bright, others tarnished and dull. No smith of Alantéa could have cast a sword of such varied metals — it would not even hold together to be cured.

The Spirit Lord looked at him and smiled sadly. "It has some of my own power in it, mixed with the strength of other Powers, both good and evil. It is a strange weapon, yet it should still have some strength. Test it!"

Galad swung the sword about the chamber, with motion in the air causing candle lights to slant about, forming shadow movements on the walls. The sword was light, and it seemed to move of itself, as though it knew Galad's mind, anticipating the motion of his arm. He looked doubtfully at the anvil, then back to the shimmering figure.

"Test it!" she said again, and Galad swung the sword in a high arc, and swept it down on the anvil. There was a crashing sound, and a flash of light illumined the chamber for a moment. Galad drew back the blade, looking at it under candlelight: it was unmarked. But when he looked at the anvil, there was a deep slash in it, and the top was bent from its base, as though an extremely powerful force or pressure had been exerted on it; and the top of the anvil still smoked from the heat.

"Take care with that blade — it will cut both the Servants and the Adversaries," she murmured, and she laughed a strange laugh. "Had I known what would happen, I would not have summoned my old Circle for aid in the creation of this weapon. Some were transformed by the Mid-World of the Truce, and it was painful for them to be called by their old natures. Others were dead and complained bitterly when called from the Temple of Waiting. I have become a Necromancer! How should I have known they were dead and would come when called?" She laughed again, then slumped in weariness. "I must rest, even as a mortal does, for now I am spent. We shall speak again in the morning."

Galad was left alone. He walked silently back to the main chamber, a candle in one hand, sword in the other. Before sleep, he looked carefully at the strange sword: its glittering portion was less shiny now, and the tarnished areas seemed flecked with rust. It no longer seemed alive in his hand, so perhaps its power was fading. He hoped the metal would hold together long enough to cut the monster.

· ※ ·

It was late morning when the first rays of sunlight reached his sleeping corner and woke him. He was alone, but a place had been set for him at the table, and again there was milk, and bread with honey. As he finished eating, the Lady of the Hill came into the chamber, still appearing as one of the Spirit Lords, tall and shimmering in the morning light. But she seemed much thinner and less substantial; the sun's rays seemed to pass through her. She set a leather pouch upon the table and stood beside Galad.

"This morning I will test our futures if you agree. There are times when knowledge of all possibilities is helpful. First, have you something small, of metal, that has been with you for some time?" Galad, somewhat reluctantly, passed over his ring that showed the insignia of the League, given to him by Orlan some four years ago. She examined the ring with some curiosity.

"This will be of little help against the Manticore, but you should not part with it — there are subtle spells of protection woven into this band that seems so simple." She dropped the ring into the leather pouch, where it made a slight tinkling sound as it struck other metal objects. She was silent for a moment, then rose and cast the contents of the pouch over the table. Scores of small metal figures of many shapes and sizes spilled out, spreading in a wide pattern over the table's surface. Among the metal shapes was Galad's ring.

She studied the pattern for some time, walking around the table, examining the formation from each angle; Galad drew his chair back to allow her room. After a while, she gathered up the pieces, sweeping them into her leather pouch, then sat beside Galad.

"Perhaps I will be permitted to depart with a little dignity," she murmured. "I have been wheezing and sighing, and weeping like an aging mortal, but now I will hold my head up. What I cast on the table was the ancient Pattern of the Powers. Ages ago, the Pattern would show the movements of the Ancient Powers and reveal something of the future. The Pattern shows my future, but not yours; it seems that much has changed. How do your Wizards now test these things?"

"Sometimes, a thing called *The Game of the Masters* is used," Galad said, uncertainly. "It shows some of the forces moving within Alantéa and the Mid-World."

"Describe this to me," she said, and Galad spoke of the Field and described the first rank of pieces, and told how *The Man at Arms, The Illusion,* and *The Mid-World Spy* were not as powerful as *The Apprentice,* or *The Charmed Knight.*

"In this, you seem to be shown clearly as a *Charmed Knight,*" she said, "a protected, skilled warrior, and your friend the young Magician as an Apprentice. Go on." Galad told her of the second rank that ranged from *The Princess* to *The Archers.*

"These are more varied and subtle, but I will guess that you now hold *The Mid-World Weapon.* The Manticore is perhaps equal in strength to

The Sending. Continue." Galad then described the last rank: *The Armed Host, The Great Spell, The Wizard, The Master, The Mid-World Power, The Ancient Secret, The Sorcerer,* and *The Fortress.*

She was quiet then, murmuring after a long pause, "So...your Wizards and some of your Sorcerers have become Powers. Who could have foreseen it? Perhaps the struggles of the Ancient Servants were not in vain.... But let me be for a while, and I will try to perceive your own destiny amidst this confusion."

Galad sat for a long while, listening to the birds of the hillside sing and flutter in the sunlight. At last, the Spirit Lord sat back and looked at Galad with a face filled with pity.

"What a grim fate! And I have been feeling sorrow for myself only. Yet your end is not certain; for many strange reasons, you might even survive. If my divination is correct, you will encounter the Manticore, and there is a chance you may prevail — with your sword. Then, the Dark Power at the Portal bars your way, and will not permit you to leave. If somehow, you are able to return to Alantéa, you will contend with one of the Mid-World, a Creature of the Darkness who has become a Power. At last, in the end, if you survive these, I see you being struck down by a Seraph! One of the First Servants! And I believed that I alone of the Ancient Powers remained on Earth, outside of the Truce. It is amazing!"

Galad looked downcast, saying nothing, but his heart surged inside his body—To the Pit Fiends with the other dangers! He might survive the Manticore!

"Against these forces you have allies — some have grown in strength — others are not yet revealed...and your sword will aid you." She leaned back and looked away from Galad. "For myself, I do not need your *Game.* The old Pattern shows my fate: I die today, or tonight." Galad came suddenly alert.

"How is this certain?" he asked. "You are a Power. Surely there's something you can do." She shook her head.

"I *was* a Power, long ago. Now I am a victim of Powers — if you die, the Manticore will come to destroy me. If you master the Manticore, then the Dark Power at the Portal will be free to seek me. I cannot survive. Once I was a Servant of the Maker, then only the Lady of the Hill, and tonight I will take my forever rest in the Temple of Waiting."

"There must be some way," mused Galad. "You say that I may survive my battle with the Manticore — let me return after, to aid you with your enemy." She smiled and touched Galad's arm with her fingers. Her hand seemed translucent, faded, cool.

"You may do that if you wish, but first you will need to deal with the Manticore. If daylight will aid you in your contest, you should go now."

Galad rose, searching for words of thanks for the Lady, and she felt his hesitation.

"Do not thank me, for I should have aided the other humans, long ago. Do not even feel pity for me — your own fate is more deserving of sorrow. Farewell! I was called Délea, in the days of the Great Fashioning; you may tell Merlin this."

· ⋈ ·

He passed out of the shadows of the hall and into bright sunlight. It would be best to face the thing on the hillside, a little distance from the stone manor so that he might return swiftly afterward. Touching the outside walls, he shook his head in dismay: the Lady of the Hill was spent. Little force was left in her walls, certainly not enough to stop the Manticore.

He was up and over the walls in a second. After walking a few paces from the barrier, he turned back: the sun was shining over the stone manor, and all seemed at peace. He drew his sword, examining the tarnished blade in the sunlight. Neither his flint nor other stones were able to remove the rust marks. But it was too late, anyway.

Galad stood, hesitating in the afternoon sun. The Manticore was a creature of sorcery, a sensitive, and it seemed almost certain that his defiance would bring the monster. Also, it was best to face the thing in the daylight. The problem was that he still wished to live, and it took an effort to summon the monster. Neither Orlan nor Kalanin would have hesitated, and each would have planned some clever strategy for dealing with the creature.

And in this land, he was fighting only for his own safety. Could he challenge in the name of the League? Merlin's alliance seemed a broken, far away thing. For the Lady? She had helped him, but, no. He would make his challenge in honor of the humans who had died at the monster's hands, men, women, children, the old, the frail, the weak. Today, they would be avenged. He said quietly:

"There is a day of reckoning for all evil beings — today is the day of reckoning for the Manticore." No sound came, except for the breezes blowing over the hillside, and the calling of birds in the meadow. He said in a louder voice:

"Today is a day of revenge, for the mortals who died in horror at the monster's hands." The hillside grew quieter, and there was a sense of listening. The sword seemed light and restless in his hands. In a loud voice, Galad called out:

"In the Maker's Name, I call upon the Manticore, a Creature of the Darkness, to come forward for judgment!"

This time, the challenge was answered. From far away came an echo of the monster's cry. In his mind's eye, an image formed of the Manticore bellowing as it swung through the branches...now it would reach the edge of the forest, then leap across the stream...his invisible allies might now be scurrying behind it, chattering with excitement. The sounds grew louder, and all the small creatures began to vanish from the hillside. Silence hung over the stone manor — he imagined the Lady of the Hill viewing the struggle, from her place of power. Galad turned from the manor and wiped his hands on his leather tunic.

The Manticore reached the top of the hill across from Galad. Only a few hundred feet separated them, and they stood nearly at eye level. Galad could see every detail — even the movements of its snake's mouth, as it opened and closed at the end of the thrashing tail. There was something vastly obscene about a nightmare leaping so boldly through broad daylight.

The Manticore stood staring at Galad and at the stone manor behind him. Then, with a bellow of hunger, it raced down through the valley that lay between the two hills, and up toward Galad. The Tarnished Sword began to vibrate as the creature sped through the brush on four legs, pushing down saplings and small trees in its hunger. Galad circled, paused, then raced down to meet it. At the last second, he leaped to one side, aiming a cut at the monster. The blade twisted in his hand, striking at the creature's back. The tail! The snake's body filled with venom! Galad picked himself up, watching the tail as it lay, still thrashing, on broken earth. The sword had known!

The Manticore was turning, shrieking with pain, trying to feel its severed tail. Nothing, not fire, nor steel, nor poisoned dart, had ever hurt it so much! Galad edged forward; the Manticore stopped and stared at Galad, as though regarding him for the first time. It watched the sword too, as the blade vibrated and twitched in Galad's hand. The monster began to circle warily, the stump of its tail flicking back and forth. Sword extended,

Galad circled away from it.... The blade tugged in his hand: a foot away, the severed snake's tail was ready to spring!

The blade's edge slashed the life from the tail, but before he could recover, the monster had pinned his sword arm to his body, rising on its hind legs to bear him backward. The sword leaped to his left hand, reaching around to slice and carve the creature's back. The Manticore cried out in pain but tightened its hold on him. The stench from its mouth was incredible — and its enormous face was leaning down with gaping, rotten yellow teeth. He jerked his right arm under its neck and locked it. Sobs of pain began to rack Galad; the pressure from its massive neck was slowly tearing his arm from its socket. The sword whined and vibrated, carving great slices from the monster's back. The creature shrieked and gasped, spurts of blood rippling over its matted fur.

They swayed back and forth in agony. At last, the Manticore put aside its pain and began to lean forward, to fall on Galad and crush him. As they tottered, Galad used his last strength to drive the point of his sword into the base of the creature's huge skull.

It stiffened...and died, pushing itself over on Galad in its last agony. He lay buried, gasping for breath, as the monster writhed in its death spasms. Only the incredible stench of the thing kept him conscious. With a convulsion, he pushed himself from under the dead hulk of the monster.

Every part of his body seemed torn and bruised. Above him, dark clouds were surging overhead. He lay, gasping for breath, face turned to the darkening sky, but the stench of the thing hit his nostrils again, and he rolled to his hands and knees, retching. He tried to force himself to his feet, but his body continued to try to rid itself of the terrible smell.

He began to crawl, still retching, on his hands and knees. A great crash of thunder forced him to look up: over the hillside, a huge, dark cloud loomed, blocking the sun. Thunder boomed again. He struggled to his feet and began to stagger toward the stone manor.

Bright bolts of light began to leap from the cloud, and smash into the hall of the Spirit Lord. And the dark cloud was sorcerous, unnatural — within the wisps of cloudy matter, turrets and bulwarks of black towers could be seen. He hurried forward in a lurching run, as the hillside began to shake. Against the great bolts of power, small flickers of force sped from the manor into the dark clouds overhead. He ran, gasping for breath...and then the hill exploded, casting a curtain of dust over his body and his mind.

· X ·

It was the stench that finally woke him; his hand had been drawn close to his face, and the blood of the Manticore rose once more to his nostrils. He was sick again. A light shroud of dust and rubble covered him, but he was able to pull himself up. The top of the hill had been blown away, with the body of the Manticore buried in the rubble. It would be a light burial, and the first heavy rains would wash the carcass free. He wondered if even the carrion birds could stomach the smell of the monster.

Galad turned and studied the destruction of the hillside. The stone manor had vanished; the Lady of the Hill had foreseen her doom, and she was gone. No butterflies were in sight, and the day was damp and overcast. The Tarnished Sword was covered with the dried blood of its enemy, and it seemed heavy and lifeless in his hand. He had won, though this distant and darkening land still held him in its grasp.

But now he had an overwhelming desire to get clean. He moved slowly down the hillside, over the meadow, and back to the stream. Voices no longer called to him as the neared the stream, and he was not surprised. A grey gloom was settling over the low, rolling hills, and it seemed unlikely that any speech would be heard again in this distant land for a long, long, time.

Interlude

The Mind of Merlin

The image is obscured, its power concealed.

—Unknown

MERLIN WALKED DOWN THE *long corridor, testing the doors on each side. They were always locked — and were not truly doors, but images of lost knowledge, things he had once known and had now forgotten.*

Merlin understood that there was little left of him; he was a tiny fragment trapped in the mind of his unknown host. As his host slept, he was free to roam the endless corridors. If he could discover the nature of his host, whether it was human or not — there was something he should remember, but it would not come to him. The next door was also locked, and Merlin shuffled on down the corridor.

During the day, when his host was awake, he could almost see out of the host's eyes; he was like a child whose eyes almost reached to the window's edge. Soon, he might be tall enough to peer into the wide outside world, to view whatever that reality might be. He hoped that he would see his old world, the one that he knew, and not some dark kingdom of death.

Now, as his host slept, Merlin was free to explore. He turned left, passing into another passageway. Perhaps he should have taken the Long Sleep, but there had been something surprising, a shock, and a sense that all his plots and devices would be ruined...there was still much he could do if only if he could remember....

And so, the dreaming last strands of the mind of Merlin shuffled down the endless corridors, testing each of the always-locked doors.

Chapter Six
The Raiders

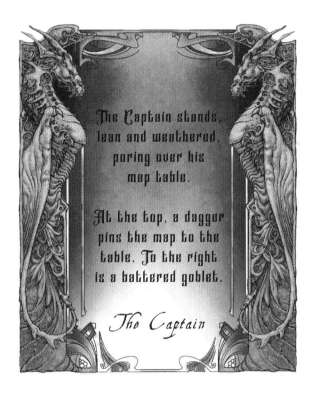

The Captain stands, lean and weathered, poring over his map table.

At the top, a dagger pins the map to the table. To the right is a battered goblet.

The Captain

HARLOND AND RURAK LEANED ON their shovels, staring up at Dargas.

"How did Envar manage to get out of this?" asked Rurak. It was midday, and warm. Sheets of perspiration were running down their chests, and both were already tired of the digging.

"Envar's out with the tiers," Dargas grunted. "You know someone has to keep an eye on the boy genius, no matter what the General here says," and he nodded his head at Kalanin. Before the old argument could be continued, Kalanin changed the subject.

"Right now, this 'General' thinks it's time for you two to get out of the hole, and rest a while." Kalanin leaned over and pulled first one, then the other out of the hole. His mind thinking all the while: *What are we to do? Dargas is so hostile to Rostov and all the other new men of the League. How do I change that?*

Harlond and Rurak had dug down about chest high. While the two helped themselves to water, Kalanin took off his shirt, dropped easily into the hole, and began to dig. His chest and arms were powerfully formed, and, as with his beard, there was a touch of grey in Kalanin's chest hair. Thin white lines on his arms and sides showed wounds that healers had treated, but not erased. Dargas frowned at the sight of Kalanin digging in the hot sun.

"You'd never have seen the Baron mucking about in a hole."

"I need the exercise," Kalanin replied. "You three won't let me use a weapon any longer, so I'm getting soft." Rurak took a second shovel and dropped down beside Kalanin.

"I'll work some more on your mysterious hole," he said, "We owe you that, and more."

Kalanin laughed. "Here's one mystery, at least, that will be soon cleared." He reached down to haul a small boulder from the pit. "Soon we'll have become large enough to be a real nuisance — then our enemies will be after us in force. We'll need to move more quickly. Things we can't abandon, we should set aside for later use." He pointed to the small, graven chest. "What did you think we've been saving in there, gold and jewels?"

"We did wonder why there was such a heavy guard on it," Harlond admitted.

"You told me at the start you were bringing weapons to Balardi," said Dargas, "and they were in the chest, but I said nothing to the lads."

Rurak stopped digging. "If it's 'weapons,' why bury them? Why not use them?"

Kalanin climbed out of the hole, passing his spade to Harlond. "These are tools, powerful ones in the hands of Merlin or Balardi, but one Wizard gone, and the other besieged. Right now, it seems more likely that our enemies would capture and use these, rather than the League. Yet I didn't want to take them too far from us...."

Kalanin paused, somewhat unwilling to share his hopes with them. "When we first began our journey to Gravengate, we were joined by an Apprentice named Julian. Our passage was challenged by powerful forces, and Julian showed a measure of strength beyond that of a lower-level Apprentice. It was my hope that he might find a way to employ these weapons or tools. But Julian is gone, and Merlin is gone, and Balardi is locked away from us. It's best now to bury the chest and go back to our swords, or spades as the case may be."

Conversation flagged; only the panting sounds of the diggers could be heard in the still air. After a brief time, Kalanin again reached down and pulled Rurak out of the pit, once more taking his place. The hole was getting steadily deeper now, nearly head high.

"You're also telling us," Dargas commented, "that you have no hope of breaking through to Gravengate in the near future. Otherwise, you would have held these out for Balardi's use." Kalanin nodded, and Dargas laughed. "Now that this strange digging is so nicely explained, I'd like to help you, but I fear that if I were to jump in the hole now, you'd never be able to haul me out. I'll serve as your water bearer, instead." He passed cups of water to the three of them, but for himself, he pulled a leather wine flask from his saddle, and took a long drink, saying, "That's better. I know something of wine and soldiering, and feeding a mass of men, but Sorcery's not been my study. How far down did you say we had to dig, to get your trinkets hidden?"

"Seven feet of earth will break the scent of almost all magic seekers," Kalanin replied, "but for safety, we'll go down ten feet, perhaps more." He switched places again with Rurak and began to tie ropes to the handles of two copper buckets. "It's bucket work now, and a good job for four men." He lowered buckets to Harlond and Rurak, keeping one rope for himself, and passing the other to Dargas. Soon they were all sweating in the heat of the late afternoon.

"By the Maker," muttered Dargas, "I don't mean to complain, but why are we doing this so far from our own camp, in this swampy, low ground, with plagues all around us, and thousands of insects?"

"Hold on for just a little longer," said Kalanin. "We're almost done... running water breaks the trail of sorcery. That's one of the first things I learned in the service of the League. There's a lot of moving water about this hill." After a few more moments, he stopped and smashed a biting insect with his hand. "That should do it," he called down to Harlond and Rurak. Now, the pit was so deep that the two were unable to climb out without assistance. Ropes were used to lower the chest to the base of the pit, then both men were pulled out.

"I'm glad to be out of there," Rurak said, smiling. "In all my grandfather's tales of treasure seekers in the Mid-World, there was this nasty habit of burying the last seeker in the dig — less for the others to share."

Dargas laughed. "I'm sure the General's been tempted to bury the lot of us from time to time."

"Not so," said Kalanin. "I have been tempted to go out and cut down a few of our enemies myself, rather than plotting against them. Let's finish this." With buckets and spades, the four men worked to fill the pit. Dust blew back at them, caking the sweat on their bodies.

"This is certainly easier than the dig," said Kalanin. "With luck, there'll be time to wash the muck off before evening."

At last, the pit was filled, and they finished by replacing the original sod, and scattering rubble about the area, disguising their work.

"Can each of us find his way back to this place, if it's needed?" asked Kalanin, and they nodded. "I could have done this work myself, if necessary, but treasures are easily lost if they're buried deep, and only one knows the hiding place. Five of us will know of this location, and one of us, at least, should survive even the worst disaster."

"Who's the fifth?" Dargas asked quickly. "Envar or the boy wonder?" Kalanin held up his hand in a gesture of peace.

"Neither — the Eye of Merlin will be the fifth. With his wings, he's the most likely to escape a losing battle." Kalanin scanned the afternoon skies, searching for the eagle. There was no sign of their winged ally, and so maybe the day's struggle had not gone well.

"There's still a short time left to us," he said, and he sat, lighting his hardwood pipe. In a moment, he was blowing puffs of smoke at the insects hovering about them, while the others cursed and slapped at the tiny intruders.

Harlond, perhaps the clearest sighted of the four, was the first to see the eagle's shape against distant blue skies. But there were none of the graceful spirals in this flight — the eagle came out of the south like a missile, speeding toward them, then sinking rapidly. At the end of his flight, the Eye of Merlin came down in a great power dive, letting up only as the last moment, striking the soft earth where the chest had been buried.

"I would not have known this place save for the presence of you humans. I will not forget this part of the marsh — if there is ever a cause to remember." Tension flickered through the eagle's form; Kalanin judged from his manner that their raiding party had survived, though the day's struggle had not gone well. He glanced to the others to see if they had drawn the same conclusion.

"There is a good weight of soil between you and the gifts sent by Merlin," Kalanin said, watching the Eye carefully. "Can you sense anything of what's hidden?" The eagle stalked about for a few minutes, beak, and head darting from place to place.

"It is well hidden from any sense of mine," said the Eye of Merlin. "There is no feel of it from the air, nor any down here. But any beast of Alantéa could easily find you! You humans smell of sweat, and wine, and burning weed." Tension and irritation flared from the eagle.

"We'll leave now," Kalanin said mildly. "In a few days, the rains will have washed our scent and tracks from here."

"And before we go," added Dargas, "has the Great Spirit of the Upper Reaches any further criticisms of these lowly humans?" The eagle looked at them with some disdain.

"Merlin warned me that humans could not be judged by their appearances, but surely I have never seen a more bedraggled lot of erstwhile captains than the four of you." Harlond and Rurak tried to brush themselves off; Dargas only smiled.

"Merlin, of course, was right," he murmured.

As they collected their gear, Kalanin again considered their conflicts — it was probably best to deal with them now. As always, he wished that the even tempered Galad was with them. He lashed his saddle pouch tighter, then turned to the Eye of Merlin.

"We're assuming that there is still a camp to return to?" The eagle did not respond; Kalanin nodded. "This isn't a good place to listen to battle reports, yet it will also be a poor time when we return late to our camp tonight. A few hours' ride from here, there's a good place for a few dusty men to wash and rest. Will you tell Envar and Rostov that we'll return tomorrow? Tell them, and then return yourself — look for us where the streams intersect."

The Eye of Merlin hesitated, showing a rare uncertainty, staring into the impassive face of Kalanin. Then, without speaking, the eagle turned and lifted into the late afternoon skies.

It was late in the day as they walked their horses through the swamps. It took a long time, and a small cloud of insects hovered around them until they reached the swamp's edge. When Harlond looked back at their passage, he saw that they had taken a long, circuitous route, and had passed through many swampy areas. Kalanin watched a puzzled expression form on Harlond's face.

"It's another way of protecting the Wizard's tools," Kalanin explained. "Let them try to trace our path by divination. Running water will foul their spells, and our route will confuse them — they will wish they had never tried."

They emerged from the swamp and rode down the horse track, glad to be free of the swampland insects and midday heat. The road was even and well kept; the villages and townships had shared in the spring work of fixing potholes in the road, cutting the brush, and moving stones that had been pushed up by winter frosts. By late fall and early winter, cartwheels and ground heaves would again mar the surface, but now as they rode with the setting sun at their backs, it seemed as though the earth had cast a fair green carpet before them.

They halted before nightfall, although they were only a few hours from their camp. Where they stopped, several streams intersected, forming a small river that would later merge with the great Bariloch. All the water passing from the swamplands to the north had been filled with debris and silt, but now the streams were purged and ran clear. Horses were left to browse along the green track, while the four men washed the dust and sweat from themselves, bathing in the swift waters, with cool evening breezes speeding their bath. After a brief meal, they gathered in a rough circle around a fire, waiting for the Eye of Merlin. Kalanin sat against a tree stump, drawing on his pipe. Dargas lay with his hands behind his head, watching star patterns form. Harlond and Rurak stood with their backs to the flames, swords still at their sides, ready to deal with any intruder as they watched the night sky for any sign of the eagle.

A long whinny broke the stillness, and the horses shuffled in response to some movement. Rurak's hand drifted to his sword hilt.

"At least you are wary," came a voice from above them, and the Eye of Merlin dropped from the tree above down to their circle that was lit by flickering firewood. The eagle looked at Kalanin and Dargas, one seated, one sprawled, and the eyes of the eagle glinted in the firelight.

"But it's a fine night," croaked the eagle, "to camp carefree under the stars. And indeed, what worries have you?"

"It's your feeling that we should be back among the tiers," Kalanin said, drawing on his pipe. "Is this the case?"

"I know more of eagles than of men," said the Eye, "and I will not say where or when you should act. But it seems to me that you are on a knife's edge: either you will forge a new force, or you will create nothing but a mass of brigands who will strike from the hills and fade away — a nuisance only and no challenge to our foes."

"There is some truth to what you say," said Kalanin. "It may be that we're at a turning point. At this council, each should speak his mind, without rancor, but openly — for a beginning, I will guess that news of this day's battle will not be much to our liking. But let the Eye of Merlin tell us openly of the events, even though fault be assigned to one of us or all of us." Dargas twitched in irritation, but he kept silent. The Eye of Merlin looked at each of them for a moment, as though finding them wanting.

"Very well," said the eagle. "I will tell the tale and let show the rights and wrongs of each portion." Dargas groaned to himself — this might take all night!

"From the beginning of this struggle, it was clear that you had not the strength to break the siege of Gravengate, and you chose to check the movement of men and supplies to the besiegers. Thus, in a lesser way, the besiegers would also become isolated, and worn down. In fairness, you have done this, and the pressure on Gravengate has been lessened.

"It was the judgment of this captain," and the eagle looked to Kalanin, "that your adversaries would assemble a mass of men and supplies to break through the barrier formed by your raiding parties. Here, you also judged correctly. But from this point, I have trouble stating fairly what transpired, for it seemed that there was muffled disagreement among you, opposition that was not openly stated, so I cannot say which of you chose one course, and which another. Yet, I will say that if you continue with this confusion, you are doomed.

"At the end of your discussion, three tiers, with fully fifteen hundred men were assembled and sent out under Envar and Rostov. The four of you went off on your long-postponed errand —why you chose this time was not known to me." Kalanin hesitated but did not speak. "Envar was given the captaincy of your force," continued the eagle, "and Rostov was sent as his aide and second. I know that between the two there was some disagreement as to the ease of bringing such a force of men to battle, undetected. So, you were off on your errand, and three tiers were sent under the command of Envar and Rostov. I was with the tiers, as their eyes and ears, or so they imagined...." Dargas admired the eagle, but he felt an enormous urge to leap to his feet and confess to whatever he was being accused of — anything to speed up this business.

"After riding the better part of a day, your tiers were in position in the hills above the valley of Kharadan, and this is a land with so many hills, that if you are in control of one hill above a valley, there will still be heights around and above you.

"That night was clear, with a threequarters moon, and Rostov, with two aides, rode out to a bluff from which they planned to attack the next day. When he returned, he was strangely uneasy and sought me out. 'What was the strength of our enemies when their forces left Stone Mountain?' he asked. I said that there were somewhat over two thousand, with fifty great wagons, and many fresh horses. 'And these last days,' he asked, 'have they made any attempt to screen the way before them, or send out a vanguard?' I said that they had done neither. Lastly, he asked, 'Have you any sense of other movements of men or sorcery about us?'" At this point, Dargas snorted.

"The boy wonder had a clear case of cold feet. Nothing new in that."

"To all these things," continued the eagle, "I replied in the negative, and I thought no more about it, for the ways of men are not always clear to me. But now there is some portion of the Gift in this young captain, and it might we well to heed his fears in the future.

"At the first light of morning, Rostov again went out in advance of the others. As we moved the tiers toward the bluff, he was just returning for the second time, and he called Envar aside for a last discussion. The tiers were halted; men milled about, asking what had occurred. To their parlay, I was asked, perhaps so that neither would be judged by the other's word alone.

"Rostov spoke first, counseling that the attack should be halted, that the area was too exposed, that our own force might be ensnared and destroyed. He urged us to break again into Sub-tiers and strike many times at the flanks of our foes in other places of our choosing. At this, Envar asked me patiently whether there were any other forces set to oppose us. I gave my sure answer: that there were none. Then Rostov asked that the better part of a tier should be left as a rearguard, to protect our exit from the gorges of the hillsides. At this, Envar struggled to restrain his impatience, and indeed, Rostov seemed least convincing at that moment, tired and anxious. Envar refused, saying again that the attack would go forward.

"At this, the shoulders of Rostov slumped a little, as though a great weight pressed down on him. 'Envar,' he said, 'it's clear that I'm miscast, and when we return, I will rid myself of this foolish captaincy. But for this one time, will you not accept my counsel on the matter of a rearguard?' Envar looked to me for some support, but he had no real choice but to accept the advice of his aide. He chose three hundred, more than half a tier, as the rearguard, and most of these had served with Baron Cadmon. As the rest of your force rode forward, there were many loud mutters of complaint from the rearguard, with glares at Rostov, and the shoulders of the young human drooped even more.

"I viewed the battle from above, in the blue skies of Alantéa, and from the heights, it looked as though one mass of ants had hurled itself upon another. But even from above, it was clear that your enemies were not surprised. There were distant trumpet calls and the men of Thorian wheeled and milled, seeming tiny to me, but in perfect formation. And there were more of them than raiders, yet I was not alarmed, for we held the high ground, and were able to break off if necessary. I can say that your captains led your men well because they were bringing great pressure to bear on your foes.

"As I watched from above, a chill shot through me, as if a cold veil had suddenly been pulled from my eyes. I wheeled in the sky and saw that the rearguard had been challenged by a force more than twice its size. How they had been hidden from me, I cannot say. Perhaps the sorcery of our enemies blocked my sight, or maybe they were sped by Mid-World Portal Spells. We were in deadly peril though, and I raced down to Envar's side — it was clear then, that all our plans and practices were known, for there were many arrows and darts cast at me, forcing me away. Had they not been forewarned, they would not have bothered with a lone eagle."

Kalanin and Dargas were leaning forward, red firelight gleaming over their grim faces. Harlond and Rurak were standing, facing the eagle, bodies tight with tension.

"It was the rearguard that saved us," continued the eagle, "and mainly the men who served with Baron Cadmon. A chant went up among them, repeated over and over: 'We fled once — never again!' and each time, they would lash out against their foes.

"Then a messenger reached Envar, and he began to pull back from the massed convoy in the valley. But the men of Thorian were not about to let him off; they meant to break the raiders and end the harassment forever. Men faltered as they understood the trap that had been set. Nearly a score fled, all, I think, young men, new to battle. Others were halted by their sergeants. Envar himself slew two men, and the rout was broken. Men rallied and fought again and again as they made their way back up the slope. They were fortunate, for the men of Thorian who were massed in the valley were not as mobile as the attackers. At last, Envar and Rostov reached the heights, and after a short, bitter fight, pushed their way past those who had ambushed them, and escaped. They wait for you now, grim but unbroken, except that there are some three hundred who will never fight again."

Kalanin let out a deep breath. The others stirred but said nothing. There was silence for a moment, then the Eye of Merlin continued.

"As to blame, I will assign it, though not as willingly as you might think.... Blame to you, Kalanin — how could you let the first large force go forward with such weak generalship? Blame to you, Dargas — why have you encouraged the older warriors once led by the Baron to keep apart from Rostov, and others who have come to aid them? Blame to me — how could I forget our weakness in this contest? Our adversaries are masters of sorcery, and it should not be a great challenge to deceive me. Blame to all of us for thinking our struggle would be easy." Then the Eye of Merlin was silent, staring into the distance.

Kalanin shook his head in dismay. "I expected some difficulty today — I thought we would never achieve surprise with a force of three tiers. But I never guessed that the Eye could be deceived, that we were courting disaster. I knew that we were confusing raids with open warfare. As for the generalship, we've had problems, and I had hoped to bring them out and resolve them...but I never guessed.... Let me put down this general's badge and take up a sword. Let's begin by choosing another to lead us."

"No. Hold it; wait just a moment," Dargas said, shaking his head. "You're three times, maybe ten times the leader of any of us. Now, here's something I never told you: the Baron admired you from a distance, and twice when he was in his cups, he muttered stuff about your sense of warcraft. All that mumbling stuff didn't make me love you more, but the Baron was a good judge of men. I know I've been a pain with all my talk about old tiers and the Baron's men, that's just the way I am. But now you should tell us what to do, and we'll do it. What do you say, lads?" He turned to Harlond and Rurak.

"I'll do whatever's needed," said Harlond. "Maybe I've been thinking too much about making a name for myself. Our struggle to save the League is our biggest challenge, and maybe to get some revenge against the rotten buggers who stabbed the Baron as he lay helpless on the ground. Let's get it right, even if the keepers of records spell our names wrong."

Rurak laughed. "I wasn't thinking about a name, I hoped for a piece of land, a fine house, and a lady who would greet me each day with bright, shining eyes. A bit of gold from Balardi would be nice, too. But I agree: let's get it right."

"Then let's make a fresh start," said Kalanin. "Perhaps this time we'll do better. First, it seems to me that experience in raiding parties is no substitute for proper training; if they're taught to cut at their foes, and then run, that's what they'll do in open battle." He paused, his mind racing.

"I will begin to equip and retrain the tiers for battle. Harlond and Rurak will be my captains. Dargas will take the tiers and lead them in all their movements. Soon we'll be moving from raids to open attacks on larger sections of our enemies. Envar and Rostov will be your captains. Men who served under the Baron will be divided between us, or perhaps we can even rotate them between the training and subtier leadership."

The name of Rostov made Dargas hesitate, but he could not refuse in good grace. "Are you sure you don't want to keep the boy wonder under your wing?"

Kalanin shook his head. "You'll teach him to organize, move and strike with always larger groups of men. In truth, each of you needs the other. Also, we need to find some way to persuade the old soldiers of the Baron that they can't win this struggle on their own. Unless they are willing to join with the young men of the League, then all our efforts will be wasted." The others nodded their heads in agreement. Kalanin stretched and tried to lessen his tension.

"Now let's try to sleep," he said. "Tomorrow, we'll make a new start. If you're asked where we've been, be as mysterious as you like — it may take their minds off our defeat at the hillside gorges of Kharadan."

Kalanin lay still, with his eyes shut, taking deep breaths as though sleeping, but his mind still churned. After more than an hour, when the sounds of the men about him indicated sleep, he drew his blanket over his shoulders and moved to sit closer to the fire. In a few moments, the eagle joined him.

"How could I have been so blind?" Kalanin murmured. "The loss of three tiers might have ruined us. And men, good men, are dead because of my stupidity."

"No need to reproach yourself again," said the Eye of Merlin. "We were all at fault. Yet this defeat does point up again our lack of sorcerous power, and soon the attention of our enemies will be turned more fully against us. I think that we have seen an end to the lull, the end of the aftermath, and so it seems likely that a great force of sorcery will soon be thrown against us."

Kalanin shook his head ruefully. "Do you remember my little speech at Amalric? 'Let them send who they will send,' — empty words, idle boasts."

"I would rather call them 'strong' words rather than 'boastful,'" said the eagle, "and I have given much thought to transforming those strong words into reality. Some tools are about you even now: in the woodlands nearby there are herbs and growths that will protect the wearers against many spells, and there are extracts from other plants that will ward away sorcery. In the hills, there are veins of metal that may be treated to impede magic. In every village and town, there are amulets and charms that were gifts of

Sorcerers and Adepts over many ages. All these things will assist you. I will show you where to seek and will advise which are potent protections and which are feeble."

Kalanin looked up from the fire into the eagle's glittering eyes. "You are suggesting that we attempt to build a host of *Charmed Knights*, a completely new type of force."

"Perhaps *The Game of the Masters* will change again," said the eagle. "It is said that in the past, the *Game* has changed, seemingly without warning, and the Powers have flocked to their fields, struggling to determine the significance of the changes."

"And in the end," said Kalanin, "will a host of *Charmed Knights* prevail against Thorian and Nergal?"

"They will not," replied the eagle. "Yet your struggles may not be in vain, for there are many things I do not understand about the forces at work."

"You are more soft-spoken tonight," Kalanin said with a smile. "Have you become more tolerant of men?"

"I am learning more of men, it is true. But do not misunderstand me. A hunter, as I am, is not a serene being like your songbirds. Merlin provided solace for me, but when I reach for the mind of Merlin, it is no longer there. For more than a score of years, I have served as an emissary of Merlin. All my brothers and sisters lived as brutes, floating on the winds, crying their rough calls, stalking prey, sleeping — they are all dead now. When I was troubled, I would reach to the mind of Merlin for assurance, and that would always comfort me. Merlin, in service to his Maker, had a mind that was like the surface of an incredible jewel, with many facets, a thousand ways for a thought to enter, and each refraction of the thought, a new and beautiful thing."

"I understand you now, a little better, perhaps," Kalanin said. "I hope that Merlin returns for your sake, and for the Leagues. For my part I miss Galad. He was clearly the man destined to become the finest master of weapons in the League if he had not already reached that peak. He was foolish seeming sometimes, but I could trust my life to him without hesitation. Can you tell me anything further about Galad or Julian, or the small ones?"

"Nothing further," said the eagle. "They are like pieces struck from the Field of the Masters. They may be alive, but they will have to fight their way back into the *Game*. But heed me: there should be no more fighting for you this night; you need rest. Sleep, and I will watch in the darkness." Kalanin felt a great weariness seep over him.

"Wake me if anything stirs," he murmured and lay down again. This time he was asleep in seconds.

· ⋊⋉ ·

In the darkest part of the night, when the moon had set and the woodlands were at their most quiet, Kalanin's sleep grew troubled. His mind was filled with weary dreams.... He was telling the people of Sea's Edge that the Halls of Merlin had been destroyed.... Then counseling Galad that Galad's shoulder was damaged and would never fully heal.... Now advising Dargas that the remnants of their broken tiers should seek the mountains above North Haven, though few would survive its grim winters. And as he thought of winter, his own body grew cold, and a chill settled over him.

In the middle of his cold dreams, it seemed to Kalanin that fingers of frozen ice were reaching over his chest to rob him of his last warmth. But as the fingers touched the seal of the League that he wore about his neck, the icy fingers drew back with a start, jerking him from his cold sleep. He sat bolt upright, beginning to shiver.

This was no dream! He struggled to his feet. The cold was everywhere around him, but it was the haunted silence that sent fear through his whole being. He took a heavy step and reached down to wake Dargas, but shaking did not seem to move or stir the sleeping soldier. Over the horizon, fingers of strange light were reaching out from the ground as though grasping at dark stars. He felt the ground shudder as if silent thunder rolled over them. Like a man wading slowly against great pressure, he began moving toward the light.

Their watch fire still burned, but its flames were like coils of dark fire that rose only a few inches, then collapsed back upon the embers. Beside the fire, the Eye of Merlin still stood guard, eyes open, but his body was frozen, like a statue's. He stared again at the pale lights flickering on the horizon — now they seemed to be drifting, vaguely, in their direction.

Trapped by this enchantment, Kalanin felt fear, the old fear that the child has for the ancient Creatures of the Darkness. With an effort of will, he forced his chilled body to stop shaking. He reached slowly for his sword — but his fingers burned at the coldness of its steel. Slowly, and grimly, he drew on a pair of leather gloves, then pulled out his sword, lifting it with both hands, with a great effort: it was incredibly heavy. He straightened and faced the flickering night sky.

His courage and defiance began to lessen the pressure for a moment. A throat cleared to one side of him; he turned and saw the Eye of Merlin, his head darting about, watching the pattern of lights play upon the night sky.

"One of the beings of the Mid-World has been seeking us," croaked the eagle, "but from a long way off, just as an icy hand might reach for us from a distance...yet, we seem to have eluded it." The eagle looked at the drawn sword of Kalanin. "Rather *you* have eluded it, by virtue of the charms of the League, or by your own strength."

"Something of both," said Kalanin. The cold was lessening, and the watch fire began to throw out real flames and warmth. Kalanin sheathed his sword. Night sounds were returning: the rush of water over stone, murmurs of insects, and breezes through the branches; but over on the horizon, the strange fingers of light still crept up into a dark night sky.

"This cold spell is strange to me," mused the eagle, "and I have never seen a pattern of lights like those before me. Almost —" A low rumble of thunder interrupted the eagle. Lights leaped from the ground, forming a great arch, framed against the night sky.

"Now *that* I recognize!" cried the eagle. "A battle of the Portals begins! We must flee!" Lightning began to flash in the sky above them as dark clouds massed.

"Wait," said Kalanin. "Tell me what's happening."

"Has Merlin taught you nothing?" croaked the eagle. "The one who sought you from afar now seeks entry from the Mid-World. Some force opposes it. A battle ensues — and so we must be gone!" The eagle's talons pulled at the leather sleeve of Dargas. Dark rain began pelting down on their fire. Kalanin ran to wake Rurak and Harlond. Strange lights were flashing within the great archway as a crash of thunder rattled the ground about them.

"But shouldn't we wait here," asked Kalanin, "to face either foe or ally?"

"We have no time!" cried the eagle. Harlond and Rurak were staring up at the sky with their mouths hanging open. Their hair, stringy from rain, was matted over their faces. Thunder again shook the ground. They raced to their horses, leaving everything except their weapons behind. The storm burst over the Portal as they sped away, and rain was hurled at their backs as they fled to the safety of their camp.

Chapter Seven
The End of All Magic

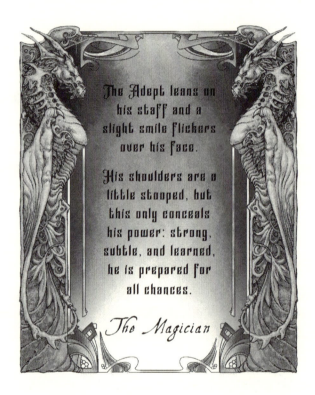

The Adept leans on his staff and a slight smile flickers over his face.

His shoulders are a little stooped, but this only conceals his power: strong, subtle, and learned, he is prepared for all chances.

The Magician

AT THE END OF THE alley, the trash lay piled: garbage cans, cartons of rubbish, and a few odd castoff toys thrown loosely on the top of the heap. Daylight was just coming to the city, but even now its great factories were sending soot and ash skyward, and in the early morning light, it was possible to see that the trash was beginning to coat with cinders. Not far away, ships moved through the harbor in the morning fog, deep horns booming at one another like leviathans moaning in pain.

At the end of the alley, on the top of the trash, were what seemed to be the discarded toys of children: a monkey with ridiculous feathered wings, and a small ragged, stuffed fox. Both toys looked as though they had been dragged through dust and dirt before being discarded. The haulers of trash could easily imagine a parent gingerly handling the toys before discarding the grimy things. But if the trashman watched more closely, he would have seen that the chests of both small figures rose and fell, as though they breathed. From the mouth of the fox came a trickle of blood, running down its chin onto the metal garbage cans.

At the end of the alley, in the first hours of the Last Magic, Sebastian stirred. He drew a deep breath and sat up. A coughing spasm shook his small body — there was something wrong with the air! He wiped film and dirt from his eyes and peered out: they were surrounded by walls on three sides, and there was no roof overhead. If this were a trap or a cage, he could fly or even walk out.

Peering closely at the walls, he saw that they were made of some strange stone and mortar, though they seemed corroded, as though ash had eaten away at them. His eyes were drawn to the red thing on the trash heap. The fox was with him, but was he still alive? Sebastian stirred Rafir gently, taking care not to place his hand too close to the fox's sharp teeth. Rafir woke with a start, rolling from the trash pile. A small cascade of trash followed him to the cement surface below, making only soft, shuffling sounds, drowned out by the horns of ships as they boomed their way through the morning fog.

"What's going on?" the fox muttered, shaking himself awake. "What's happened to us?"

"Hush," Sebastian whispered. "I don't know. From the sounds it's some sort of city, but where in the Mid-World...?" He trailed off, as the foghorns boomed again in the harbor. Rafir sniffed at the walls, then examined the trash pile carefully.

"There's the smell of man," said the fox, sniffing "and I'm pretty certain that sack is filled with cat's waste. But the other smells are much different — some even nastier." Rafir began to lick the black dust from his body. One of his paws was a little tender, and his body was bruised, but he thought he would survive if he could breathe — the air was terrible! "Are any of the others around?" asked the fox. "Julian might know where we are."

"They're not close at all," Sebastian whispered. "I can usually tell if Julian's within a few hundred paces — now that's what's bothering me! In the League, the feel of magic goes on and on, but here there's nothing, not a trace. Maybe though, these huge buildings are blocking me. Just a moment."

Sebastian flew to the top of the building and peered carefully over the roof's low walls. The sun was just beginning to warm the day. To one side, rows of buildings seemed to go on forever. On the other side, only a few hundred paces away, he could see the expanse of a huge river, with enormous boats shifting up and down. These ships had no sails, but cones in their tops pushed columns of black smoke into the morning sky. Sebastian turned in each direction, letting the Sight search for any trace of his master. In a few minutes, he flew back to the fox.

"It's a huge city," Sebastian said slowly, shaking his head, "bigger than anything I ever imagined. I can't sense any of the others, and it feels as though all magic is dead and has been dead for a long time."

"There's a city called the City of the Truce," said Rafir. "I remember Granny telling me about it."

"That's a place of great power," said Sebastian. "This is the opposite — like the end of all magic. What are we supposed to do? Why were we sent here?" Sebastian was silent for a moment, thinking hard.

Something had gone wrong — again! Julian might be dead. Balardi and Baron Cadmon might have been overwhelmed. It could be that he and the fox were the last of the League, alive in a far land, only by accident. And yet, images were coming into his mind, of men drawing swords in the forests of Alantéa, or hiding in the hills, waiting to strike; or townspeople planning revolt in the dead of night. The Wizards' League might be put down, but it would not be so easily overcome. He would try to survive and return to help them. And maybe Julian lived. He would need to work with the fox.

"We won't be able to learn much about this place right away. Our first step is to try to stay alive. Look — when you first joined us, it made me unhappy. Maybe, though, it was intended that we would help one another. Let's stay together. What do you say?"

Rafir studied Sebastian for a moment. "That's fair, I guess. Staying alive means that we need food and a place to hide. Just a moment." The fox vanished and returned quickly. "I can still disappear, but maybe not for a long time, certainly not while I'm asleep. Where can we hide?"

"Where can we hide, and what can we eat?" asked Sebastian. "One thing is certain — this feels like a city of people who don't have any experience with magic. We can't let ourselves be seen." He paused, looking at the sky overhead. It was getting lighter, and the sounds of men and machines were getting louder. "Nobody seems to be using the tops of these stone buildings," he continued. "I can stay there during the day, and at night, I'll return, and we can both look for a safer place. If you'll look for food, I'll return at nightfall." It seemed to Rafir that he was left with a harder task, but no better plan came to his mind.

"Be certain to return at night," he said, and he vanished.

It was full daylight then, and Rafir watched Sebastian slowly flap to the top of the building. No humans seemed to notice, but a few pigeons called out, fluttering away in surprise. For a while, Rafir stood by the trash, licking his fur. Then his fox senses began to stir, and he moved quickly out of the alley into the street. There were smells of humans and smells of machines, and just a hint of pollen in the early morning air. The street beside the alley led to a larger street, and on the main street, he found huge machines rolling noisily over stone roads, spreading clouds of poisoned air. Rafir stood at the street's edge, surprised, and distracted, and he failed to notice a large dog that was padding down the avenue, tied to his master by a cord. The dog, smelling Rafir, leaped forward, tugging at his leash; its owner cursed, pulling the dog away, but neither dog nor fox understood his words. Rafir shrank back, thinking that the dogs and this horrible city deserved each another.

The fox turned and padded up the main street. Despite storms and spells and the end of all magic, he was hungry, and it was time for a little theft. The greatest challenge was to avoid being crushed by one of those huge machines. He found that if he remained on either side of the avenue, the machines, despite rumbling noises and vapors, stayed in the middle of the street.

And food was left out in stalls — it was ridiculously easy! Only once was the theft noticed, as a shawled woman watched a small piece of fruit vanish when the jaws of Rafir closed over it. As she rubbed her eyes, Rafir slipped away to another stall.

More than an hour later, Rafir stared down at the small pile of fruits and nuts he had carried back to the alley. It had taken so many trips to get those little piles, and here by the trash his appetite sagged, but he nibbled slowly at some of the small fruits. The nuts were pushed aside for Sebastian.

Gradually, his hunger lessened, but he no longer felt quite as pleased with himself.

For the first time since morning, he thought about his companions and the old Sorceress who had cared for him with so much love — there seemed to be little chance that he would ever see them again. In the late afternoon, he slipped off to sleep, dreaming about the lush fields and forests of Alantéa that had seemed to go on forever.

He woke suddenly. A small hand was shaking him.

"Wake up! You're too exposed — anyone can see you!" Sebastian took his hand away as the fox came awake. The little Familiar looked better, but part of his fur was still singed, and his wings seemed darkened from the ash. Rafir retreated into a dark corner. It was dusk now, and shadows were all around them.

"I'm sorry if I startled you," Sebastian said, "but you could be seen so easily. This place is too exposed. Tonight, with luck, we'll find a better place to hide. Did you find food?" Rafir nodded at the small pile of nuts he had stolen during the day. To Sebastian, these smelled strongly of fox saliva, but he broke them open and nibbled, testing each one. He was able to eat most of them, chewing with his small jaws, as he glanced up every now and again into the darkening sky. Only a few stars could be seen overhead, as most of the streaked sky was covered by clouds. No moon was shining either, so it should be a good night for travel.

The city had grown quieter, but down by the wide river, boats still moved and huge machines were rattling through the darkness over metal tracks.

"So, food first, then shelter," said Sebastian, putting down the last nutshell. "This may take me a little while. I'll find a tall building first, then have a look around. I'll be back." Rafir waited in his dark, silent corner, thinking about their journey. He had certainly fallen into the wrong sort of adventure: in the stories told by the old Sorceress, the Powers were always providing magical tools, arming, and counseling the hero so he only had to obey a few simple instructions in order to succeed. Here, they were in the wrong place, with no tools or Powers…Sebastian was taking a long time… at the edge of his thoughts was a regret that he had joined Julian, but he knew that if he let those ideas fester in his mind, he would become more and more unhappy. More time passed. Sebastian was taking an awfully long time; something must have gone wrong — again!

Sebastian flew with an effort through the thick night air, searching for the tallest nearby building. Even now, he was nearly as high as the castle of Thorian at Stone Mountain, and there were many buildings still higher. He chose one of these and flew toward it. A red glow remained from sunset, but lights were already shining from thousands of windows, and it was an even, unblinking light, so unlike the flickering candles and torches of Sea's Edge. Sebastian reached his goal and sat breathing heavily at the building's peak. Beside him was a huge wooden tank; thin lines of water were seeping from its siding. As he looked over the city in the light of sunset, he saw that these water towers were perched on the tops of many buildings, stretching out in front of him like fields of fat, sinister mushrooms.

In the last light of day, Sebastian saw that the city had no end, except where it bordered the river, but there were several large green areas. In one of those, they might survive a little while. The red glow of sunset finally passed, and at that moment, the Last Magic came fully awake. The heart of the small Familiar hammered at his chest wall, filled with excitement.

To the west, beside the river, something stirred, and began to form.

To the south, a being powerful with the Gift began to wake and search for them…. Could he help them to return to Alantéa?

And finally, by one of the wooded areas, magic called out to Sebastian, strong and vibrant, like a beacon in the night.

They would not need the being with the Gift! Julian had not forgotten them! Sebastian lifted his wings, and with a drifting glide, flew back to Rafir.

"We're going to get out of here!" he said to Rafir in a hoarse whisper. "At least we have a chance, a good chance."

"Why — have they sent someone for us?"

"No," said Sebastian, "it won't work that way. It's probably a guide to a portal, or a way of tapping the last bit of magic, a talisman or incantation. I don't know."

"No chance it's a trap, is there?" asked Rafir. "I mean, our enemies have been a step ahead of us every time."

"I don't think so. You're not a sensitive, so it's hard to describe. But there's a feel or smell to magic. This thing is clearly calling to us. Other bits and pieces of magic were waking — I couldn't sense much about those, but this one's calling to us and it's a force for good." Sebastian, with an effort, calmed himself. "This Talisman or Portal Spell is near a wooded, grassy area. We should try to reach the grasslands tonight, even if we can't get away from this city right away."

"I can try to follow you," said Rafir, "if you go slowly."

"How will I know that you're still with me?" asked Sebastian.

"If you like I can call out at the end of each street. It's a city filled with noise. Who would notice?"

Sebastian thought for a moment, then touched the fox carefully on the back. His small brown fingers looked strange against the red fur of the fox. "We should make certain we stay together," he said. "If we're separated, we'll meet again back here. I think we should get away from this city as quickly as we can, and I think we may need each other. Are you ready? Let's hope that Julian has done his part!"

They made good progress at first, as Rafir padded quickly and quietly along dark streets, and Sebastian flew in front of him. Yet their path grew lighter with each street. Ahead of them were large lamps, not only above the street, but also beaming from building tops. Within the lighted area, there were many humans, some walking dogs, others talking loudly on street corners. Sebastian turned in midflight and began to fly back toward the river.

He halted by one of the dark street corners, hoping that Rafir would see him and not return to their starting point. In a moment, the fox appeared, slipping silently out of dark shadows.

"Did you see those dogs?" asked Sebastian. "If we're caught, they'll chain us, too. We can't let that happen."

"They'll never catch me if they keep those stupid dogs tied," said Rafir. "Where do we go now?" Sebastian pointed to their right.

"Up first to the left, then over to the grassy area — the streets up there are darker. Are you ready?" Rafir nodded, though the roughness of the pavement was wearing down his feet.

They moved again quickly and quietly, Sebastian fluttering from dark street to dark street, while Rafir avoided the few humans who walked or sat on stairways in the darkness. Once, Rafir halted as the ground trembled beneath him, as though some great engine rumbled underground beneath his feet. After the sound passed the fox raced to catch up with Sebastian.

Hours later when they reached the woodlands' edge, they felt tired, but some of the tension had left them. Sebastian's wings drooped with fatigue as he watched the fox roll in the grasses. Rafir could still smell dirt and filth from the great city, but grass was much better than garbage. The fox rolled one more time then turned to his companion. Sebastian was staring along the side of the grasslands. In the distance, they could see the outline of a huge building that lay just inside the grassy area.

"There's a thing," Sebastian said slowly, "an amulet or a talisman. I don't think that it's a creature or a spell scroll. It's an object, and it's in that building."

"Some sort of temple?" asked Rafir, focusing his night vision on the building. "Or is it a palace?"

"We'll have to see," said Sebastian. "I'll walk with you to the building — my shoulders are so tired."

They moved slowly through the park, squirrels scattering as Rafir's strange smell reached them. Along the way, they found a small brook, and drank deeply, although the water seemed tainted by the ashes that had spread all over the city. Before them stood the massive building, looming dark and silent against the City's strange lights. By the time they reached it the night was far gone, with daylight growing near.

"It's in there," Sebastian said quietly, "but what sort of building is it?" They made several circles around the building's edges, finding each entrance sealed. In the distance, the horizon was growing brighter.

"If it were a palace or even a temple there would be guards protecting it," Sebastian muttered. "I don't know — maybe we can have a look at it in the light. For now, we'll have to find shelter — the burrow of a fox, I suppose."

"A foxhole!" said Rafir. "I've never dug one in my life."

In spite of their circumstances, Sebastian had to smile. "I'll help you," he said, "maybe your instincts will come back to you." They found a grove of trees with patches of ivy that covered soft earth. Here, Rafir dug, and Sebastian moved handfuls of soil away from the entrance. As dawn began to light the park, and many hundreds of birds began their morning songs, Sebastian and Rafir had completed their shelter and lay inside. The hole was shallow, with its mouth covered by ivy woven with fallen leaves. It seemed to Sebastian that they were well on their way out: they were close to the Last Magic, a force that had clearly been sent to help them get back to Julian. He dozed, dreaming of the Halls of Merlin at Sea's Edge.

· ⋈ ·

In the night, beside the riverbank, the Seeker began to stir. Slowly, across many thousands of years, bits and pieces of the Seeker had been deposited on the riverside: here, a bit of soil carried by the tides; in another place, some dust from Alantéa, carried for an age by air currents, then dropped at last on the river bank; and a bit of cloth, some rotting leaves — all in place for just this one time, when the Last Magic began to bring power to the Last Sending.

Now aware, the Seeker slowly drew itself together piece by piece. At daybreak, the Seeker was still incomplete, and it collapsed back into its components. Yet it was satisfied. The next night it would be strong enough to rise and destroy both the Last Magic and the small servants of its enemies.

· ⋈ ·

The Last Magician pushed himself away from the chess problem that lay spread over his coffee table. He read the headlines again, considering how the news might affect him. The paper, dated June 25, 1941, told of Soviet armies reeling under massive German onslaughts. German victory was the current expectation, but he suspended judgment; Soviet military quality was an unknown. The fall of France had not surprised him, though he recalled with some amusement how reporters had spoken so seriously about the power and quality of France's military. He had traveled in France just a few years ago, and the smell of decay was powerful even then. Would America be drawn in? It seemed likely. Astrologers would benefit from war; he would probably be forced to relearn that nonsense.

The Last Magician had names, several of them, depending on circumstances, and he had several characters: to neighbors, he was simply a quiet man with many interests; to the skeptics who learned of his work, an investigator on the fringes of science; to the unwary and the ignorant — a predator, feeding on fear and superstition. And he was not aware that he was the last human born with a powerful measure of the Gift. Like a sighted man born into an almost lightless universe, he was not aware that anything was lacking; but his dreams were troubled.

Abruptly, he pushed himself away from the newspapers and chess puzzles. Back to work. He placed his cup in the sink and returned to his studies. The book on telepathy was too dry, too abstract; he put it aside and chose instead *The Occult: Science of the Mystics*. This was a wonderful book, written by one of the most gullible of fools. If he had a few more clients like this author, he would again become wealthy. Vastly amused, he read until sunset, then drowsed off.

That night he dreamed again, the old dream, the one that had come to him so many times in his life. He was on the surface of a great underground sea, one shrouded in darkness. Far above him, the roof of the great cavern glistened with moisture. The dark sea supported him, high above the waters, awaiting his words; he understood that if he could speak those words of power, the sea would obey him — heed his commands, rise, and fall with his words, carry him over his dark kingdom. As always in his dream, he would rise above the waves, ready to speak the words of power, but never had the words come to him...often he would wake drenched with sweat, as though he had been engaged in some great confrontation.

On this night he struggled again to speak the words, and again they would not come — they formed in his mind, but his mouth could not speak them — and suddenly, so differently from any of the other dreams, a great ringing sound echoed over dark waters, shaking the cavern's roof. Dark seas rose against him, waves splashed his body, winds sprang up in the stillness and swept him over the dark ocean. He tried again to say the words of power, but the ringing sound filled his mind with fear and wonder.

The Last Magician woke suddenly — he had thrown himself from his bed and was lying, shivering on the ground. But the ringing sound was still with him! Where had it come from? It was different now, a new sound, like tiny chimes, ringing in the distance, but always more clear and real than any sound he had ever heard before.

It was dark night. At the moment the ringing had begun, Sebastian had felt the power at the park's edge, and then the Seeker had come awake. And now, a third force, the Last Magician rose from the floor and began to search for the Last Magic.

He dressed quickly, fearing that the sound would vanish. He hesitated at the door, then, for a reason he could only vaguely explain, he drew a heavy cane from his closet, then raced down the stairs and out into the street. How to find the source? Under the shadows of the leaves made by the treelined street, he turned, facing in each direction.

He was alone — so there was no need to explain his actions. He closed his eyes, feeling for the source of the vibrations. Like a blind man seeking the source of sunlight...it seemed to come from the north...after walking a little more than a mile, he grew certain. He stepped up his pace. Lean, agile, muscled like a tumbler, the Last Magician stalked forward like a predator scenting prey. By early morning, he had come to the edge of the waters that separated his portion of the city with its heartland. But the sound became fainter with the growing light, and at daybreak, it vanished.

The Last Magician refused to be discouraged: all his senses told him that daylight had ended the sounds of magic and that nightfall would revive it. Tomorrow afternoon, he would be on a train to the other side, and begin his quest again at dusk. The thought of using a train to find magic might seem ridiculous, but whatever he had to do, wherever he had to go, however difficult it became, he would seek out and control the Last Magic.

· X ·

Rafir woke in the darkness, in a musty hole, thinking for a moment that he was back in the domain of the old Sorceress, that everything since had been a very, very bad dream. Then he sniffed at the air; the soil was strange, unclean, and there was a smell of monkey. After a few moments, he asked quietly, "Are you awake?"

Sebastian nodded in the darkness, whispering, "I can't sleep for too long in a dark hole...you should be quieter, though. A few humans went by, just a short time ago."

Rafir lowered his voice. "Is there still light out? Should we leave now?"

"It's just a little after midday — I don't think we can just sneak into that building without knowing more about it. And we'll both need food before we start...don't you think?"

"Time for the hidden thief of a fox to do some more sneaking," asked Rafir, then added quickly, "but I don't mind — I'm hungry too."

Rafir edged to the opening of their hole, then peered out: there were only a few humans close by, and no dogs. Not far away he found some bits of stale bread, then, some distance into the park, a few leafy plants. Now, food for Sebastian. He let his nose explore for him. Strangely, there were smells of many animals and their droppings. All the smells seemed from the same place, and he wondered why they would wish to be so close together. When he reached the first series of cages, he saw that their fate was worse than that of the chained dogs: these creatures were imprisoned for life in close quarters. One section even held monkeys, though their faces were so different from the grave, wise face of Sebastian.

It was simple to pull bits of food from around the monkey cages, then slip them into Sebastian's hole. He said nothing about the cages; Sebastian had enough to worry about, and besides, there were probably foxes locked away in other sections of this prison for animals. Rafir and Sebastian had a whispered conversation, then Rafir was off to spy out the building.

It was late afternoon, and already fewer people strolled over the grasslands. Rafir stepped up his pace, speeding across the grass, invisible to all eyes, but a surprise to the noses and ears of small animals when he crossed their paths. In the distance, he could see the huge building, with its stone sides and high windows. As he drew closer, he was surprised to see people climbing up and down the steps, apparently moving in and out of the building with ease. Rafir watched them from a distance, then crept slowly to the door, hugging the wall...the door was propped open! It wasn't even barred, or chained, or protected by legions of sentries, as were the palaces of the Mid-World Powers — there were just glass and metal doors, fastened open.

As he watched more carefully, it seemed that there were people who casually watched the doors, different in dress from those going in and out, but these watchers were relaxed, even bored, and could be passed with ease. The fox began to edge toward the doors, then hesitated. This entrance would serve for himself as he could vanish from the guards' sight, but Sebastian would have difficulty. The winged Familiar might fly by the guards...Rafir had an image of many men pursuing Sebastian inside the building, casting stones and shooting arrows until the Familiar was brought down. The thought filled his mind with sorrow and Rafir moved away from the front entrance.

He searched the ground for places where they might slip in on foot, or for entry points that the Familiar would be able to fly through. Rafir had just decided that the open windows would provide a night entry for Sebastian when those windows began to close. People were no longer entering, either. As it grew darker, a last trickle of humans walked out from side doors, then all movement halted except for the shimmer of the last rays of sunlight against the building's high windows.

So, there was an entrance for himself, but not for Sebastian. The fox began trotting back to their hiding place. Although the sun was setting, it had grown warmer, and the air was moist. Not far away, Rafir could hear thunder rumbling, moving toward them. By the time he reached Sebastian, both rainfall and darkness were upon him. He pushed easily into their hiding place, and Sebastian quickly replaced the covering of ivy and leaf, trying to keep the rain from their shelter.

"I didn't think it would be that easy," Sebastian muttered after Rafir had told him of the closing of the doors and windows at nightfall. "We'll have to go again this evening…it probably means that we'll be here another night, or maybe forever."

"We should be able to get in somehow," said Rafir. "It's like a puzzle — very different from Granny's stories. In her tales, the hero would be given some impossible task, then one Power would appear and give him a magical weapon, and another would show him a secret Portal, and still another would explain how to do the job. By the time they were done, the impossible became simple. This is different; we don't need those magical forces — we just have to get into a building."

In spite of his fatigue, Sebastian laughed. "I hope it's as simple as that. Some other strange things were happening that first night, but they probably have nothing to do with us." He trailed off for a moment, thinking. "But you're right. As I think about it, when Julian traveled he used his wits more than his Gift," and he told Rafir a few of the adventures of Julian as an emissary of the League, speaking of Alantéa as though it were only a little distance from them. But Alantéa lay several thousand leagues from their grassland burrow, and it was buried under mountains of dark water, lost forever.

· ⋈ ·

When daylight began to dim, the Last Magician reached out from his dreaming and woke. By nightfall, when the sounds of the Last Magic reached him again, he was already on the other side of the water, walking steadily up the island. As he neared the park at midnight, the harmonic sounds of chimes grew steadily clearer. At last, he was growing closer to his heart's desire.

· ⋈ ·

At nightfall, on the banks of the river, the Seeker drew itself together again. It was more powerful the second night, and able to weave an illusion for itself. An ordinary creature, one without the Sight, would now see only a normal, though largish human in the jumble of rags and dust and old leaves from which the Seeker was drawn. The Last Sending moved in the darkness toward the park. It had other powers, and these would be used to destroy the Last Magic. Only a few dogs stopped and whined as the Seeker passed, and even the dogs could not understand why they cried.

· ⋈ ·

As darkness settled over the wet grasslands, Sebastian and Rafir crawled out of their hiding place. Despite the steamy dampness, the sky was beginning to clear, and a few stars were out. They were parched with thirst and turned first to drink from the winding stream, moving quickly in and out of wet shadows. Already, the beacon of the Last Magic was calling to Sebastian, and he hurried on foot back to the building, with Rafir trotting easily alongside him. The doors opening onto the grasslands were so dark that they were dim even to Rafir's night vision. They crept toward the entranceway, seeking some partial opening, or place to slip through. None could be found. Sebastian peered through the glass...he could see nothing, but the feel of sorcery inside pulsed harder as though calling out to him.

Sebastian flew to a high window, searching for an opening for his small body. He tried the next level, then the lower ones, and there at the side, he felt strongly drawn to one set of glass panels. He pressed up against them, his wings flapping to hold himself aloft: there inside, and beneath him, in a glass case, were the Seeking Stones given to Julian! Around the Stones were trinkets and bits of stone and old amulets and charms that had saved no one, but beside these were the green jade Seeking Stones. As Sebastian watched, the stones began to glow, on and off, almost to the beat of his own small heart. He cried out into the darkness, "Julian! You have not forgotten us!"

· ※ ·

The Last Magician felt the pulse of the Seeking Stones beat harder and his desire for the Last Magic intensified, beginning to consume him. He saw now, as he moved closer, that it must be in the museum. How could he get in? Then he heard a cry in the night, a clear speech filled with melody, but in an unknown language. It seemed to come from one of the windows. He peered carefully from a little distance — there by the windows was some animal — and it was winged! Perhaps the Last Magic was sought by others too. He backed into the shadows of the trees, watching the winged creature... it was coming away from the window, onto the grass, and it was whispering to another small figure. He edged forward toward shapes that darkness and distance had made indistinct.

"We were not forgotten!" whispered Sebastian. "The Seeking Stones your old patroness gave to Julian are in there." He calmed himself, letting his wings fold back to his small body. "Think again. Isn't there some way for us to get in now, and leave this place?"

Rafir looked again at the side of the building. The bottom windows were all carefully locked and reinforced. "I can enter tomorrow in the daytime, but not now. Tomorrow night I might be able to open a window or a door for you."

Sebastian looked sadly at Rafir's paws which were made for running, not handling latches. "You should enter in the daylight. At nighttime, when the guards are gone, I'll break one of these thin high windows, with a stone maybe. Meet me at this corner of the building when you hear breaking glass." He sniffed a little in the direction of the fox. "I suppose that means another night in the hole." The smell of monkey was becoming a little strong for Rafir, but he held his tongue, anxious not to quarrel. The two began walking quietly over dark grasses, back to their hiding place.

The Seeker paused for a moment at the edge of the building. Joy and hatred filled his being. He had found both — the Last Magic within the building, and the tiny allies of his enemies, outside in the grass. The rest was easy. A word of power would halt his small prey, then he would burst in and destroy the Last Magic. He needed only to get a little closer...he edged forward toward the little creatures. Then the Seeker stopped. The winged creature was moving away from the building. For the first time, the Seeker hesitated — which should be done first, seizing the Last Magic, or crushing the Magician's creatures? After a moment, the Seeker's hulking form turned and began following Sebastian and Rafir.

· ⚹ ·

The Last Magician felt the sound of the Last Magic lessen as the small creatures moved away from the building. Perhaps the creatures and the object in the building were needed together! The pulse of magic continued to diminish as the small ones moved from the building. But the awakened Gift within him remained completely alert: when the body of the Seeker began to follow the small creatures, the Last Magician saw at once through its disguise — it was not human, it was another part of the magic! He needed to find some way to control all of it! He moved forward quickly, hunched, and predatory, walking in parallel with the two small creatures, and the huge bulky one. In a lurid, silent parade, the four strolled through the soft darkness of the park.

· ⚹ ·

Sebastian and Rafir found their hiding place again and crept quietly inside, saying nothing to each other. Sebastian thought that he might have offended the fox, but he kept silent, concerned that further words might lead to a quarrel. It was almost over; they just needed a little more time.

Rafir had begun to drowse when he felt the ground shake from the weight of some massive foot. Sebastian, for the first time, felt the Seeker's presence and he leaped to the base of the hole, trying to dig deeper, as his small body shook with fear. Rafir felt the panic and pushed Sebastian out of the way, beginning to burrow with all his energy. A large hand, or something, began to clear brush from the mouth of their hole. After thousands of years of waiting, the Seeker finally groped for his prey. His fingers began to feel around the inside of the hole, then stopped: some human was running toward him, shouting words of command to control the Seeker; but the powers invoked had no effect upon him.

The Seeker straightened, perceiving the Last Magician. It was some Sorcerer's son — but ignorant. The Seeker spoke a *word* of power; the Last Magician froze. Reaching into the hole once more, the Seeker ripped the roof of the hiding place away. Below him, the two terrified creatures continued to scrabble deeper into the soil. But before the Seeker could destroy them, a heavy cane came smashing down on his back.

Ignorant or not, the Last Magician had broken the Seeker's spell and was raining blow after blow on his back. The Seeker recoiled. The little Familiars darted out into the night. Thousands of years of waiting lost!! The little creatures were free again!! In a great rage, the Seeker turned and grasped the Last Magician, hurling him far, and deep into the bushes. The Seeker left the Sorcerer's son for dead and turned again to the pursuit of his small foes. This time he would not fail.

· ⋈ ·

Rafir ran the terrified race of the pursued fox, over hills, past running water, but when he reached the edge of the grasslands, he turned quickly to one side, unable to think clearly. At last, his terror began to ease, and he started to wonder about Sebastian. The night was overcast, but moonlight and the lights of the city gave the night sky a strange glow. How was he supposed to find Sebastian? It would be light again in a while. He could return to the lane, but the thought of being trapped by that *thing*. The fox slowed, thinking hard. In the end, he found a large open field in the grasslands, stood in the center, and let himself become visible. Filled with uncertainty,

Rafir turned every few seconds to see if their enemy approached, hoping that Sebastian would find him first.

Night was ending and the birds were beginning their morning songs when Sebastian settled down beside Rafir. The little Familiar was still shaken, gasping from his long flight.

"It's still after us. I don't know what it is," he panted. "I wish Julian were here...but I should have been warned — there were other things that woke beside the Seeking Stones."

"But what happened?" asked Rafir. "They *seemed* to fight, or at least the man tried to."

Sebastian shook his head, trying to understand. "That man had the Gift. He should have been able to stop the other thing...but let's not try to understand this land. Let's just get *away*. Can you still slip into the building?" The fox nodded. "Then be inside at nightfall. When you hear a window breaking, that will be me."

"I can hide in the building," said Rafir, "but where will you stay?"

"I'm going to find a high place," Sebastian said grimly. "No more holes in the ground with *things* after me. If it can fly, maybe *then* it will catch me." Sebastian's wings opened, stretching for flight. "Remember, when you hear glass breaking, that will be me!" and Sebastian was gone, racing to be hidden before sunrise.

The fox, now tired almost beyond fear, waited, hidden in bushes. Shortly after sunrise, the doors of the great building opened. Then, vanishing from sight, he crept past the guards, and paced through the first two floors of the building, until he was familiar with its corridors and rooms. On the second floor, he found a little used and dusty chamber with cases covered in cloth. Here, Rafir hid, drifting off to sleep. When he woke, it was late afternoon, and everything seemed quiet — maybe they were coming to the end of their adventure. He began to drowse again.

· 𝕏 ·

Dawn was returning, and the Seeker was filled with hatred for all living things. He was following the fox, but several times he almost stopped to take his revenge on the small animals he encountered in the park. Tomorrow night, he would begin at the building. Then, he would find and destroy them all...the sun came up, and the Seeker collapsed to the ground, to become leaves and dust in the forested park, once again.

· 𝕏 ·

The Last Magician stumbled to his feet, blinking in the sunrise. His strength and agility had helped, yet it was the brush that had saved him, though not without a price. His body was a mass of scratches and bruises; blood from the cuts on his face and hands still seeped out as he staggered from the park. Onlookers saw a man who had barely survived a party that had lasted more than a week, but the Last Magician paid no attention when people backed away from him: he was preparing for the next night, the next round in his struggle.

He reached home and examined himself carefully. His side was sore, one rib might be cracked, but he could tape it. His face and hands were a mess; there would be no consultations for at least a month. Later, he would blame the marks on a failed experiment. But those concerns were as nothing compared to his fantastic opportunity. He bathed, bandaged himself, and sat in his study considering his problem. That bulky creature had to die, not because it was evil, but because it could not be controlled. How to destroy it? It would be an interesting test to hurl fire at it or use a highpressure hose, yet those things were not available, nor were they appropriate. For evil supernatural entities, there were ancient remedies. He had not believed in those remedies before, but...from a locked cupboard, he drew a vial of water, consecrated water, stolen from one of the great, consecrated churches in Europe.

Gingerly, he tested his left wrist: he had a slight sprain; he would have to use his right hand to douse and destroy the monster. His confidence in this remedy was considerable, but in case another option was needed, he took the pistol out of his secretary, and dropped it into his coat pocket. At sunset, he was off again, limping, but filled with a grim determination.

· 𝕏 ·

Rafir woke with a start. Was that breaking glass he had heard? The fox ran out of the corridor, and down a flight of stairs. He was about to pass through the largest of the huge chambers with their high ceilings when he heard a sound near the outside doors. Rafir darted behind a low display case and peered out. It was that bulky monstrosity — again! It was feeling around the doors, seeking a way inside!

From another direction, he heard Sebastian's voice: "Rafir...Rafir...I'm inside — let's get away from this place!" Sebastian came around the corner. The green jade Seeking Stones were in his hands, shining brightly in the darkness. The Seeker saw the Last Magic, too, and put forth its greatest strength to burst the doors. Sebastian and Rafir watched in horror as the doors began to buckle.

But the Last Magician had not given up his struggle. He had watched the monster from a distance as the creature approached the museum. Now, as it began to press on the doors, the Magician leaped forward and splashed holy water over it: nothing happened. He fired his pistol into the place where its heart should have been, then twice into its huge shaggy head, and finally into its spine. The creature wasn't even distracted. The glass of the doors fractured; metal began to buckle.

"It's too stupid to die!" shrieked the Magician, and he struck again with his cane at the Seeker, forgetting his last encounter. Sebastian and Rafir woke from their terror. There were Portal Spells — what would those words be? The creature was turning on his human adversary. Sebastian yelled out the only words that would come to his mind:

"JULIAN! GET US OUT OF HERE!"

The stones, shining green in the darkness, rolled from Sebastian's hand, joining together on the floor to form a single ring. The circle grew larger, pulsing green light. Magician and monster stopped their battle at the doors, watching stunned at the spell of the Last Magic. The conjoined, single stone formed a Portal, radiating green light. Sebastian, grasping the fur around Rafir's neck, leaped with the fox through the circle of light and disappeared. The Jade Portal vanished, and the Last Magic was gone. At the doors, the Last Sending collapsed into a pile of rubbish. All traces of the music of the Last Magic vanished from the Magician's mind. But he could hear in the distance, the sounds of police sirens, racing toward the museum.

Chapter Eight
The Dark Emissary

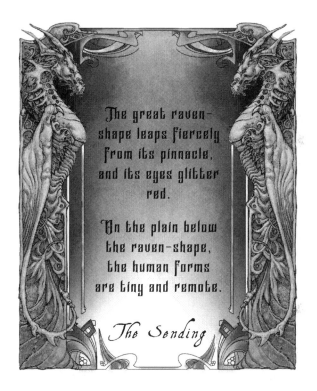

> The great raven-
> shape leaps fiercely
> from its pinnacle,
> and its eyes glitter
> red.
>
> On the plain below
> the raven-shape,
> the human forms
> are tiny and remote.
>
> *The Sending*

TINY STREAMS OF RAINWATER WERE flowing underneath the side of his tent. Kalanin was slumped down in a wooden armchair, watching the streams with a combination of interest and disgust. He sipped a little more of his wine. First, the water had run cleanly over the grass, then it had turned muddy, and now he had a few of his own tiny, dark rivers. Rain had lasted for more than three days, without a break, and it brought the ugly side of soldiering: rust, bad tempers, and deserters who slipped away in search of warmth, wine, and women.

The tent flap slipped open and Harlond pushed his way in, shaking some of the rain from his cloak. He sat down on a chair beside Kalanin, regarding his leader carefully, from the corner of his eyes: Kalanin's face seemed even more tense, and his eyes were red, with dark, unhealthy circles beneath them. Kalanin stood, bringing out another goblet, pouring a measure of wine for his captain.

"So, what tidings?" he asked.

"The rain's letting up a bit," said Harlond, "and even with the rain, we've managed to fit nearly two hundred men each day with mail. We still need more swords, but that shortage has forced us to arm a goodly number of pikemen." Harlond sipped his wine. "And your own day?"

Kalanin hesitated. "Not good — every night there's a struggle inside my mind, and in the morning, it's so hard to get up. No need to repeat this to the others — but you can tell Rurak if you like." He changed the subject. "How's Rurak doing with the new men of the League?"

Harlond laughed. "We lost a few again today, but it's just as well. Every farmer's son drifts to us, dreaming of glory. When they're given wooden swords and wooden shields for training, and after they bash each other in the rain for a while, then the farm doesn't seem so bad."

"Any more friction?" asked Kalanin.

"Wets and Grunts are at peace for the time being. The officers of the guard forced out the worst of the troublemakers." Kalanin nodded in agreement — "Wets" and "Grunts" were the personal names given one another by the new soldiers and the veterans of Baron Cadmon. Old loyalties were fading, but friction still flared on occasion. Silence fell over the two men while Harlond finished his wine.

Finally, Harlond stretched and stood. "We've told everyone that you're wrestling with a weighty decision. That's what they expect from a general. Still, it might be a good thing if they could see you make the rounds, tonight, before nightfall." Kalanin rose, without a word, and drew his campaigning cloak over his broad shoulders. The only emblem of his generalship was the symbol of the Wizards' League, a white emblem on his dark cloak.

The two walked together out into the early evening rain. Many of the men had just finished their evening meal, sitting, or standing silently as the rain drizzled over their food. Smoke rose from scores of campfires; rain and mist mixed with the smoke as it curled and lifted into the evening sky. Iron cauldrons were set in the embers of watch fires, with chunks of meat and tubers hissing and bubbling in thickening broth. Here and there, a few men were rolling dice listlessly over wet gaming boards.

"How's the work going on the outer boundary?" Kalanin asked.

"There's been a crew out for each of the past three days," Harlond replied. "A little more goes up each day." Kalanin nodded: walls of wood now shielded the camp on three sides, but on the fourth side there was only a makeshift barrier of brambles and light fencing, supported by a series of wooden stakes driven into the ground.

As they stood by the barrier, watching as smoke and steam rose from the encampment, a murmur of laughter passed through the camp, moving slowly from one side to the other.

"That's the wine going around," said Harlond. "We thought that after three days the lads could use a break. I've doubled the guard, but it would be bad fortune to have our enemies upon us tonight."

As Kalanin and Harlond walked from the perimeter, the drizzle deepened into rain. Yet the sounds from the watch fires were becoming louder and more boisterous. Rowdy singing had begun, and bursts of laughter greeted returning patrols. In spite of his weariness, Kalanin's mind flashed an old image: he had returned, in the rain, to Stone Mountain, more than six years ago, joining the tier leaders serving Thorian. They had laughed as they cleansed themselves, then feasted, and the wine had flowed freely in a long night where they spoke of their struggles along the northern and eastern borders of the League.

Kalanin returned to their council tent, alone, and set his campaigning cloak over a chair to dry. He sat at the table and picked at bits of bread and cheese. Outside, the rain beat down a little harder as dusk passed into darkness. He lit a candle, beginning to think of the long night ahead. Perhaps the Eye of Merlin would return tonight to share the struggle with him.

His candle burned lower. A chill crept over him as he felt the beginnings of pressure against his mind. Each night the pressure seemed to begin earlier. He felt like an insect, hiding in a clump of grass, knowing that something large and hungry was searching for his small body. As he sat, the first tiny beads of perspiration began forming on his forehead. To his disgust, the nerves in his right hand began to twitch, as though the hand was being tested by some other creature. From the corner of his eye, he saw the tent flap begin to move. Kalanin came quickly to his feet, drawing his sword. A face peered into the tent and Dargas spoke.

"If you stick me with that, you'll have to find another tier leader." Dargas let himself in; then he sat, placing a lantern on the table beside the small candle. The movement in Kalanin's hand subsided, and the pressure on his mind seemed to let up for the moment.

"Since everyone's having a party, I thought me and the lads would join you for a bit of wine," Dargas continued. "They'll be here in a moment, but I just thought I'd come a bit ahead of them — you know, I think you might want to tell the lads a little of what's going on. They know about the stinking Mid-World and all its dirty games. Nobody's surprised anymore after listening to all the old stories. Let them know."

Moments later the tent flap opened, and out of the rain came Harlond and Rurak, with a small cask of wine. Envar and Rostov followed, each dragging two more chairs into the tent. They sat cautiously, as chair legs tended to sink into the soft ground. Kalanin leaned back trying to relax. Dargas cheerfully tipped the cask, spilling wine into pewter goblets.

"You all know that white wine clears the body," he said. "It's red that mixes and fouls the blood — and the beer you drink, Rurak, that's what swells the gills and rots them." Dargas joined the others with a brimming goblet. "So, here's to white wine! If the devil thing that's after us comes near, why I'll give it a splash of white wine! That'll clear it out quickly enough!"

Kalanin shook his head, joining in the laughter. Dargas pulled up a chair, staring at Kalanin, saying in a somewhat different tone, "And it's my way of leading up to a question that me and the lads have been asking — what is this 'Devil Thing'? What's going on?" Kalanin drew a deep breath, looking unhappily at the faces of his captains.

"The Eye of Merlin knows far more of matters of magic than I do," he said slowly. "But it seems that our enemies have called some new power out of the Mid-World. Its way was blocked a week ago — the Eye named this contest 'a battle of the Portals' — but now it's fought through. The Eye said little about its nature." Dargas turned and nodded to Rostov.

"We think it's interested in us, as well as you," Rostov said. "Last night as I slept — dreaming pleasant old dreams, I suppose — a dark thing, far larger than a man, strode through my night visions like a man kicking over the sandcastles of a child. I woke suddenly. Its contempt for me was complete, and it wasn't human."

Kalanin looked around the table. "Have each of you experienced this?" he asked.

"None of us as strongly or as clearly," said Harlond. "But each of us, in some way, has been watched, or touched from afar."

"So, if it breaks you," added Dargas, "it will turn to each of us until the tiers are left leaderless. What are we going to do about it?"

"Resist," replied Kalanin. "Hold on, resolve not to give in." He shrugged and threw a few more coals on the campaign stove that served to heat food and warm the tent. "Are each of you protected in some way?"

"The Eye picked out this geegaw for me, and I wear it," said Dargas, touching the amulet that hung about his neck. "Will it protect me in the end?"

"In the end, this powerful thing, probably a Creature of the Darkness, will break you, just as it's breaking me now," said Kalanin, "but I sense its impatience. It does not regard us highly."

"This is a filthy business!" Dargas said, banging his goblet down on the table. "A Wizard, a Sorcerer, a Seraph, and now some creature of the Mid-World — it's as snarled and stinking as a Pit Demon's hairy armpit. Listen! There are good lads out there — give them something to cut, and they'll do it, but this filthy mumbling sorcery is a rotten business."

"You're right," said Kalanin. "Let's talk about something else. The Eye has gone to view the siege of Gravengate; there's no doubt that when he returns, he'll have an earful for us. For the moment, let's forget our long struggle." He went to the tent flap and opened it. From the tier camp came the sounds of a vast party, as the wine flowed freely. The night rain had eased somewhat and had become no more than a light drizzle. Kalanin took a deep breath of night air; the tension inside him had eased, and it seemed that the pressure on his mind lessened when others were around him. He turned back to his captains.

"Let's have one more round of wine while we wait for the Eye to return. But plug the cask after that — there's enough wine being swilled tonight." For the rest of the evening, Kalanin listened, leaning back in his chair as the others spoke of the Mid-World and its hold over Alantéa, and each had a story that was new to the others. He even felt himself nodding to sleep as the strain of the last few days slipped from him.

· ⅄ ·

Just after midnight, their conversation was interrupted by a scratching sound from the lower tent flap. They sat up and fell silent. Rostov peered outside, then opened the flap with an extravagant gesture.

"Behold the great eagle, the Eye of Merlin," he said pontifically, "who is studying to become a duck." The eagle entered, shaking water from his feathers, glancing at Rostov with very little affection. Harlond pushed a few more bits of wood into the small stove, and the eagle approached the fire, with wings extended to expose them to the drying warmth. As the chill passed, the Eye turned to Kalanin.

"Of all the Maker's jests you humans are surely the greatest! The air about you on all sides is thick with the stench of a black, evil emissary. I expected to return to an armed camp, one ready for desperate battle. But what do I find? A drunken party! Listen to it!" They were silent for a moment, as the sounds of singing and laughter seeped through the tent.

Dargas shook his head, then spoke in reasonable tones. "You speak often of the teachings of Merlin. I ask: Has Merlin taught you how to raise and train a force of men? If so, perhaps you should be leading us."

"I learned something of men," said the eagle, "but most of my lessons were much more concerned with sorcery and the many forces ruling the Mid-World of the Truce."

"Then," said Dargas, "while you were learning of those things, Kalanin and Cadmon, and others were learning how to train and lead a force of men."

"Don't judge us so harshly," added Envar. "We're building a force of men that will stand together in victory or defeat, and it's not done solely by making rules and issuing orders."

"So be it," said the Eye of Merlin. "I am in the wrong." His head darted again to Kalanin. "Even if I were right, we cannot afford to disagree, for we are beset by many foes. I journeyed to Gravengate, hoping to find that the Sorcerer Nergal had left the siege, that he and this Dark Emissary were one and the same. But Nergal presses at Gravengate with incredible strength, and the Dark Emissary presses here — it seems as though all the evil beings flourish, while all the good and decent ones have been swept away." The eagle stepped closer to the coals and lowered his voice. "Yet Balardi holds, against enormous power, and this, too, is a mystery." The eagle trailed off, peering into the coals as though lost in thought.

"What of Balardi?" asked Kalanin. Were you able to reach him?" The eagle croaked a harsh laugh.

"You almost lost your lone, winged spy today — and danger came far from the fortress of Balardi, far, far above it. Who would think to be concerned with a lone eagle, so high as to seem only a speck from the ground?

"At the top of my climb, as though from a mountain peak, the land about Gravengate seems remote, tiny, but even at that height, the din of battle echoes into the sky, and turmoils of vapor billow up to the heavens. With my Farsight, I saw all the wreckage of war, to the slightest marks upon the fortress walls. Two great armies commanded by Powers assail Balardi, and yet he stands. The forces expended against Gravengate could tear hillsides apart, and yet its towers are unbroken. Tunnels have been dug beneath its ramparts, then filled with blasting powder, and yet its bulwarks remain untouched. Great siege towers are drawn up to the walls of Gravengate, but men of the League have beaten back their assailants. Around the perimeter of the fortress lie the rotting bodies of monstrous beings called upon to attack or defend the fortress, while the emblem of the League still flies, untouched, from its topmost tower.

"I beheld all of this in wonder, from afar, believing myself secure due to my height and distance from the struggle. My enemies were waiting, though. In the calm of the upper skies, and without sound, I was struck from above and hurled downward. I was enraged and turned to destroy it, but driving me was no flyer born in Alantéa, but a creature of the Mid-World, a winged serpent. It was larger than I, and nearly clear-skinned so that I could see the red heart of that being pushing blood through its pulsing organs.

"I turned in the air, wheeling, circling to get higher, to rip at its back, but another stroke from above pushed me farther down. The first serpent was not alone; there were two of them, now laughing and calling out in malice, as I slipped downward. 'So long! We waited so long! What held you back, spy of a dead Wizard?'

"Then it was time to dive, to escape, speeding downward with the wind rushing against me. They followed, still laughing and mocking: 'Lord of the Skies — now you are the prey!' But they waited too long, for I reached a massive bank of clouds, and leveled into it, letting them pass beyond me, as I hid for a moment, flapping slowly through wet mists. When I emerged, they were a little below me, within man's sight of the fortress. They called out to me to turn and face them, but their sounds only served to arouse Balardi. Out from Gravengate, a bolt of force flashed, rippling with many colors, leaping as lightning might. That force swept them away. I turned from the castle then, for I was within bowshot of the battlefield." The eagle halted, letting his mind return from his struggle in the sky, back to the tent, where candlelight twisted shadows over canvas walls.

"So Balardi holds," continued the eagle, "against all odds. And this is not the only mystery. The mysteries began at the very start of this struggle and seem to go on endlessly."

"The first riddle," said Kalanin, "is why Thorian began this war."

"And the second," said the eagle, "who is this Nergal, and what is his interest? And there are more: What befell Merlin? How has Balardi managed to hold on?"

"Add to those: What of Julian, and what of Galad?" said Kalanin. "And here is the last question: what kind of creature attacks us now?"

"That last question is likely to be first answered," said the Eye. "There is an impatience to the Power that hovers nearby: it will not waste much more time leaning and pushing against your minds. It will want to break your bodies soon enough."

Harlond had listened somewhat remotely to the discussion, but with the eagle's last warning, he seemed to come awake. "We'd best look to the guard then," he said, and he rose and left the tent. Rostov followed a few paces behind him.

Outside the air was cooler and clearer. The rain had passed but the watch fires still smoldered, still struggling with damp wood. Dark clouds passed overhead so that every few moments, moonlight would surge over their sodden campgrounds. Harlond and Rostov walked to their central watch fire, seeking the officer of the guard. The night watch was composed of seventy five men, with another one hundred and fifty prepared to be woken for their shifts; and these had weapons near at hand. Of the rest of their tier camp, more than half of the men lay in a deep stupor from the wine, with snores pouring from their tents. Harlond called up the next watch, doubling the guard from seventy five to one hundred and fifty. Dry wood was added to the watch fires, and the darkness about them lifted a little.

Harlond returned to their council tent, while Rostov slipped back to his own quarters, seeking a brief sleep before the next watch. He slipped his boots off and rolled up with several blankets. It had not been complicated to keep dampness away from his sleeping gear, just a matter of a few poles, some leather thongs, and he was suspended over the dampness. Though, on this night, many men would be lying on damp grounds, filled with wine. There would be some bad tempers out on the wall works tomorrow; he would need to be careful not to make matters worse. He drifted off into a half sleep...

...matters in my own lands. Nothing of power, to conquer or possess... Like mumblings from a distant room, thoughts were slipping into Rostov's mind. He came awake instantly, and the thoughts receded. With an effort, he calmed himself, closing his eyes, forcing his breathing to slow, to become more like a sleeping human, until murmuring thoughts began to return. *...power to call beyond the Truce...would be of use...and again, who among us has not desired power over Alantéa, all these many ages...? RISE AND LISTEN, MORTAL!*

Rostov was up, his feet dampening on the wet ground, body shivering with fear.

Come out. You will live if you obey. Rostov pulled his boots on, lashing his scabbard to his waist, and stumbled out into the darkness. As an afterthought, he reached to the amulet that was fastened about his neck. It was gone. *A simple matter, to take that from you. How powerful were the ancient Servants! How feeble you mortals are....* Rostov took a deep breath, and looked over the campgrounds, seeking some sign of movement outside their borders. A few tree leaves rustled in the moonlight, but their adversary remained motionless, concealed. He took a few steps toward the council tent.

I am here, small one. Rostov stopped and stared again at their camp's edge. Three barriers seemed clear...but beyond the lightly fortified side, a tall, black shape, like a dark tree trunk stood at the outermost edge of the flickering firelight. Was that it? Rostov peered forward — it was more than twice the height of a man, standing motionless at the edge. He took a step forward.

Tell your master that I have come for him. Do not delay, or I will take you as well, small one.

Moonlight flashed again from beneath dark clouds, and Rostov could now see clearly the true shape and size of the Dark Emissary. He edged toward the council tent, unwilling to turn his back on the creature. When he fumbled aside the tent flap, the others were on their feet, as though the alarm had already been given.

"It's here," said Rostov, voice shaking. "It calls for Kalanin." Kalanin drew his sword, moving to the exit, but Dargas and Rurak barred his way.

"I'm not going to deal with it by myself," said Kalanin; his face still showed strain, but his voice was even. "The guard is armed with sword and shield — we'll need a force of pikemen as well. I'll speak with it while you raise the pike." They gave way before him.

"Tell them to wear spell wards, or they're lost," said the Eye of Merlin, and he leaped to Kalanin's shoulder. "Come, let us see what manner of being now confronts us!"

Kalanin walked out into the moonlight. The camp was quiet except for the hiss and crackle of their watchfires, and the low hum of insects from the nearby woodlands. The night seemed peaceful, but beneath the dark quiet surface lurked a violent riptide.

Kalanin's eyes were drawn across the expanse of tents and watch fires to the dark figure at the camp's edge. The two stood, regarding one another for a moment, as dark clouds swept beneath the moon.

The Dark Emissary seemed huge but lithe: it retained limbs and proportions that were almost human, and yet its features were remote, indistinguishable, while something in its swaying movements suggested an ancestry of insects.

Behind Kalanin came the muffled sounds of men being roused quietly. He stood far from the Dark Emissary, but he was certain that the distance between them could be covered rapidly. Insect sounds lessened, as tension built in the air.

I was sent for you, mortal. The being spoke into Kalanin's mind, softly and without sound. *Why you are wanted, I know not, but I was drawn from my own kingdom for this task.* Neighing came from the stockade as horses were lashed to the sides of the horse pens.

"You have no hold over me — I have offered no service to you," Kalanin said softly into the night. "I am an ally of the Wizards' League, and we count ourselves among the Maker's Servants. Who is your Master?" There came a pause; Kalanin's question was not answered.

Here alone are your choices: to come with me this moment, and let the other puny humans live out their short, brutal lives...or you may all die now....

Kalanin shook his head and drew his sword. "We are of the League — we will cut you if we are able to." Then the creature perceived that companies of men were forming behind Kalanin, scurrying about, some slipping on the wet grass. The Dark Emissary raised its head into the night sky and laughed: it had no mouth, but deep gurgling sounds came from a damp opening in its throat.

"Now for the drums!" cried Kalanin. "Raise the camp!"

The creature threw back its immense shoulders, hefting a huge metal staff in its hands. Rurak, leading two dozen of the guard raced toward it with torch and sword. The Dark Emissary stepped forward, crushing the wooden barricade. Men fell upon it with sword and flame, crying out in the name of the League and the dead Baron. The being stood to its full height, more than twice the height of the men assailing it, and the great metal staff swept the swordsmen away, crushing the first rank. It stood like a god among mortals, and it leaned back and laughed like a god.

The rest of the guard fell back, leaving broken men shattered on the ground. Drums began their low rumble...doom...doom...doom.

Dargas cried out: "Bring the pikes, you fools! But shoot its eyes out first. We'll blind it then burn it!" Doom...doom...doom, the drums beat louder. More men were spilling from their tents, many staggering from wine. A ragged volley of arrows and javelins spewed about the creature, but only a few struck, bouncing off its armored hide. But now Harlond and Rostov led two hundred pikemen, surging forward against the Dark Emissary. As they streamed over wet ground, black clouds boiled beneath the moon.

Again, the creature drew back its head, spreading its huge arms out into the night, calling an invocation to the ancient Adversaries. Vapor curled from the palms of the being...and the sounds of soft sucking and gibbering seeped over the camp.

Suddenly, the air was filled with a multitude of dark things, headless black floppy seekers of warm blood, spilling over men, fastening suckers to bare skin, and grasping with claws that clutched in a deathly grip until they were severed or torn away. Men fled shrieking into the darkness. Pikemen fell back, crying with pain and fear, dropping weapons, and drawing daggers to hack and stab at the bloodsuckers. Kalanin raced toward the archers, his dagger slashing at the dark things.

"Shoot now!" he cried out to them. "Don't wait for a volley!" The eagle too struck among the archers, shredding the dark skin of floppy attackers with its talons. A stream of arrows began to flow toward the Dark Emissary as it strode into the camp seeking Kalanin.

Now, many others, waking to noises of fear and dying, drew knives or daggers and staggered from their tents, throwing themselves against the dark, headless things, hacking and stabbing them to death. Others, with gloved hands, seized the floppy creatures and hurled them into the flames, where they crackled and shriveled like enormous leeches.

Drums began to beat again...doom...doom...doom. A vast anger boiled to the surface. To the drumbeat, the drummers began to chant, "Death!...Death!...Death!..." and others picked up the chant, "Death!...Death!...Death!..." so that many hundreds of voices called out their challenge to the Dark Emissary. Pikemen reformed their ranks. In the middle of their camp, the creature halted. Hatred burned brighter.

"Death! Death!" they cried. "Death to the Monsters of the Mid-World! Death to the Enemies of man!" and many hundreds of pikemen pushed forward, pressing against the creature's armored skin, some seeking to pierce the throat mouth that lay under its armored features. Enraged, the creature swept its metal staff around, shattering the first line of pikes, but another row of pikes surged forward, men all the time chanting, "Death! Death! Death!"

Now the great weight of men against it began to force the Dark Emissary back so that the creature was forced to shield itself with its great staff. Under intense pressure, the creature staggered back toward the barrier. More men joined the press. At a call from Dargas, the pikemen dropped to their knees, and a volley of arrows was fired, again bouncing from the creature's armored skin.

"Get the reinforced bows!" Kalanin shouted to the archers.

Pikemen pressed forward again, pushing the Dark Emissary to the barrier. But now it took one sweep at the pikes, again crushing the front rank, and it leaped backward, bringing its staff smashing to the ground, calling a spell out into the night: the ground heaved and shook, casting hundreds of men from their feet. Yet, spell wards and amulets held back the worst of the destruction, while other pikemen pressed forward, again crowding the Dark Emissary.

Now, even the most drunken of men were awake at last, staggering onto the moonlit battlefield, watching open mouthed as the Dark Emissary towered above the pikemen, standing amid blood and carnage. Some emerged to fall upon the ground vomiting, but others drew weapons, weaving and lurching toward the intruder.

At a signal from Kalanin, the pikemen again dropped to one knee, and the archers fired a volley at the creature, this time with powerfully reinforced bows. Many arrows went wide, others struck the armored hide and fell back, but six or seven stuck in the creature's skin.

Drumbeats halted, then silence swept over the battlefield as the Dark Emissary stood bewildered, pulling an arrow from its hide, then staring first at the weapon, then at the men who were on their knees, vomiting and sobbing in the moonlight. Finally, it turned to the grim faced legion opposing it.

The Dark Emissary paused, its head bobbing in confusion, and it backed from the light of the watchfires to the field beyond the armed camp. A vast set of wings unsheathed from its back. Turning from the bloody battlefield, the Dark Emissary lifted into the night air and began to glide away, soaring always higher as it passed over a countryside that was bathed in moonlight.

A cheer rose from the battlefield, first raggedly, then fully voiced, mixed with shouts of defiance against their foes. Kalanin looked down at his sword: this was the first battle in which he had not used it, and the weapon glittered, unscathed, in the moonlight. All about the battlefield men lay broken and dying.

"This was a grim victory," he muttered. "It's a cold thing to order men to their deaths."

Dargas looked at him somberly. "The dead won't blame you," he said. "Envar's dead, never to laugh, or speak again — but it's better than running from it and being hunted in the darkness." Dargas left Kalanin and began to organize the tending of the wounded.

Morning was just a short while away. Kalanin walked slowly back towards his tent, a swirl of emotions and weariness washing over him. Rurak, moving quickly, intercepted him.

"There's one among the wounded you should look at," Rurak said. "There's not a mark on him, and none of us know him. Young looking, maybe even a spy slipping into our ranks in the middle of all this confusion. He's over here...."

Wearily, Kalanin trudged over to one of the perimeter's watch fires. On the ground lay a youth, his face shining with peace and contentment. Kalanin blinked, and for a moment he did not recognize him; he looked again — and he saw that it was Julian, but the mind of the Apprentice seemed remote, distant, perhaps even destroyed.

"Call for the Eye of Merlin," Kalanin said quickly, and he knelt beside the Apprentice. Julian's pulse seemed even; no wounds were visible, but he lay as though in a trance. He shook the figure, gently, murmuring, "Julian..." but the Apprentice would not wake. With a flurry of movement in the air, the Eye of Merlin swooped down beside them.

"It's Julian," said Kalanin. A small knot of men had begun to cluster about them, and Rurak began to herd these away, just as the first light of day reached over the horizon. The eagle reached out, talons curled, and gently touched the forehead of the Apprentice. There was a long silence, then the Eye of Merlin turned to Kalanin and spoke almost in a whisper.

"I cannot tell — here is something I have not seen before. His body is here, and yet his mind, and his Gift are far removed. Has he been returned, mindless, so that our foes may mock us? It does not feel like the triumph of evil. Has he fought his way back onto the Field of the Masters to renew the *Game*? I cannot tell. Care for him and perhaps he will be well. I am no judge of these things." The eagle drew away from the Apprentice and stared again at the battlefield. "I have seen Man the Buffoon before, but on this night, I watched Man the Hero — and so I will no longer attempt to judge men or their doings."

Chapter Nine
The Hall of the Dreamers

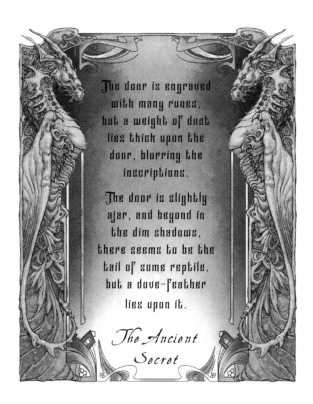

The door is engraved with many runes, but a weight of dust lies thick upon the door, blurring the inscriptions.

The door is slightly ajar, and beyond in the dim shadows, there seems to be the tail of some reptile, but a dove-feather lies upon it.

The Ancient Secret

THE GIFT LAY RUINED WITHIN Julian, broken by the power of the Great Spell. As the Gift lay dying, his mind and body were beginning to fade. Death was coming.

Sebastian! Julian's mind called out. *Sebastian, if you live, try to hold on. Try to help Kalanin and Galad and Rafir. You and I may well meet again at the Awakening at the End of Time when the Maker calls to us.*

And those were the last thoughts that the mind of Julian could gasp as he drifted into the oncoming darkness. With death near, the Gift was bringing Julian one last vision: the dream of peace that comes to the dying wielder of magic when all hope is lost.

In his dream, Julian lay in a sunlit valley, and on each side of the valley, a snowcapped mountain peak reached into blue skies. This was the last moment before forever, and Julian knew that he had no power to command anything, not even a blade of grass, or a leaf; and there was not the slightest reason to command anything. As he lay in the valley, he knew that if he closed his eyes, the sun would hover above, mountain peaks would glisten in the distance, and the last dream, the dream of peace would go on forever. He closed his eyes, to let the fading peace settle over him....

A light wind blew through his dreaming valley, making only the slightest whisper of sound. He imagined a stray leaf tumbling slowly over the grasses, seeking a resting place...but now the breeze blew a little harder, and the whisper was more distinct. It said, "Julian."

All sense of contentment left him. Why was he lying here? The Gift stirred inside him, thrashing around like a beast with a broken back. More was needed from him, much more — he tried to open his eyes, but could not. He tried to pull himself to his feet, but there was no strength left in his body. Now, as the wind blew through the valley, it was no longer a whisper, but a strong, clear voice and the voice called out, "Julian — rise and wake!" With a supreme effort, he pulled himself from his dream of death, forced his eyes open and struggled to his feet.

He stood, hunched, and shaking like a young man dying of the plague, in the middle of a cloudless wooded land, with sunlight pouring down through leafy trees. A voice spoke from behind him.

"Welcome, Julian, to the Land of the Dreamers! Welcome, Servant of the Maker!" It was a woman's voice, the same voice that had brought him from his trance. When he turned and stared up, he saw clearly that he was in the presence of a great Spirit Lord. Astonished, he realized that he recognized her features.

"Llara," he mumbled, still hunched, and shaken. If she resembled the statue at Sea's Edge, the marble form had failed to capture the power and light radiating from her living form. A gentle, but musical laugh came rippling from the ancient Spirit Lord.

"So, I am remembered after so many ages!" she said. "Merlin has taught you well." She looked down at Julian for a moment, her tall figure shimmering in the sunlight. The face of the Apprentice was bloodied, and his body was bruised and battered, but she understood that the real wound was to the broken Gift inside of Julian. Her hand reached forward, taking him gently by the arm, leading him slowly through the forest.

"In this land, known as the Hall of the Dreamers, our service to the Maker is at an end. We watch, but we are no longer permitted to intervene. However," she smiled down at Julian, "since you have been cast upon our doorstep, surely we can seek to refresh you."

She led Julian to the base of a hillside, where a long set of marble steps were set into the slope. The hillside was wooded, so in the bright sunlight green-leaf shadows fell over white marble stairs. They began to climb, but Julian was forced to halt after only a dozen steps, leaning on his staff like an old man. And within Julian, the Gift continued its slow painful process toward death. Unbidden tears streaked the face of the Apprentice; it was time to pass, to take the Long Sleep. He looked into the shining face of the Spirit Lord, and it was filled with compassion and understanding. He took one step, then another, until he stood gasping for breath at the top of the marble stairs.

There, at the top of the hillside, Julian beheld a great wonder, a sight that aroused the Gift within him, and would refresh him again every day of his future life. The top of the mountain was shaped like an enormous basin, half a league wide, flowing with sparkling waters, like a small sea. But this sea was lighter than water, heavier than air, clearer than foam; and the crystal sea surged back and forth over a vast marble plain, sparkling in the sunlight, shooting to great heights, dancing with delight. Llara raised her arms in celebration.

"Julian, behold the Cup of the Maker! Rejoice! It is said that when the Maker returns, He will drink from His Cup, and then this world will be renewed." She led Julian to the edge of the sparkling sea. "Be glad, Julian, and wash away your weariness and your wounds." Julian's staff toppled to one side, and he threw himself into the crystal waters.

The waters reached up and embraced the Apprentice, surrounding him, cleansing the dirt and harm from his body. From within the sea, he saw that the waters broke sunlight into patterns of red and blue, green, and orange, like a prism that revealed many hues. Now, Julian felt himself sinking, as the waters calmed and no longer held him suspended. His feet touched the surface of the great marble plain, and the waters parted, pulling away from Julian so that he was left dry at the center of the mountain sea. He stood still for a moment, watching the crystal sea as it swept over the mountain top, and the Gift within Julian was healed, and even strengthened.

Waters filled with light again lapped at his feet and he leaped forward into the shimmering waves, speeding like a porpoise away from the center, shooting high up a column of sparkling foam, then racing to the side, leaping in and out of the waters with easy motions. He passed around the edges three times in wide circles, then he turned back to the shallows where he stood for a moment, watching the sparkle and delight of the Cup of the Maker. The first red touch of sunset was beginning to spread out over the horizon, and the Gift reached out to Julian, telling him that it was time to emerge from the crystal waters.

He lifted himself easily from the waters, gathering his staff and walking to the edge of the stairs where Llara stood gleaming in the closing light of day. As they walked down the first steps, Julian turned back for a moment, watching as the high columns of crystal waters became red and gold under the rays of the setting sun. Nothing could equal the delight of the Cup of the Maker; no sorcery, or magic herb, or enchantment seemed likely to ever bring such pleasure to him.

Down in the forest, it was still light, though as they walked through forest paths, flocks of birds were beginning songs of dusk and early evening. With the onset of darkness, Llara's form brightened, beginning to radiate light.

"Your coming was foretold, Julian, but not the time of your arrival, nor the forces that would send you here. We watched you confront the Great Spell and understood that there were many counterspells woven about your journey, while other forces were intervening, so that spell and counterspell and other strange magics warred over your fate and those of your allies." Julian listened in silence as they passed through the forest. "The forces and stresses of that struggle were so great that the very fabric of power was stretched so that you and your allies were hurled to the uttermost edges of sorcery, to the borders of all enchantments. They survive, but they are pursued and must either escape or prevail. You also will be hunted, yet we have sought a moment of solace for you."

She looked down at the Apprentice and smiled. Julian stared down at his cloak and saw that his garments had changed — where they had been torn and dirtied, they were now restored, as though new.

"Shall a Servant of the Maker visit the Land of the Dreamers and not behold the Cup of the Maker? Should we turn aside a Servant without counsel or refreshment?" They came to the end of the forest, to the edge of a field where slight grasses and wildflowers flourished. At the far edge of the clearing, a massive hall stood, shining in the last light of day, and this great hall was formed mostly with panels of glass so that burning vat-candles within the hall could be seen from across the field.

"Behold the Hall of the Dreamers," Llara said. "Those who have given great service to the Maker find rest in this place. They dream through days and nights, choosing things of the past or present that they wish to view, and they dwell at their Hall in the greatest peace. You will be the first of living mortals to enter the Hall of the Dreamers. But your time at the Hall will be short, for your opponent is hunting you, and we are no longer permitted to intervene against the Ancient Adversaries." Julian nodded as they crossed the field, yet he could not believe that the great ones in the service of the Maker would abandon him to the pursuit of his foes. Still, the Gift was reawakened within him, and he was armed with his staff and with many potent spells.

They reached the entrance to the Great Hall. Outside, Julian could see an incredibly clear night sky, with stars so bright that they gleamed like tiny suns. Within the glass Hall, many candles were lit, and Julian saw that the figures were seated at a long table, set at a dais above the floor. Llara opened the portal, and led the Apprentice in, saying,

"Welcome, Julian, to the Hall of the Dreamers...O Dreamers, behold the first living mortal to enter our Hall." As Julian bowed low, the Dreamers rose from their seats in greeting. Llara led Julian forward.

"Some of us you know by reputation, while others will be new to you," she said. "Here is Voll, ElfLord, mighty with the Gift. When the ElfKindreds were born into the Mid-World, the Maker had long departed, and the Powers of the Mid-World were claiming Godhood. But Voll raised the Maker's standard, and led many of the Kindreds — Elves, Tanu, and Sidhe — away from those who proclaimed themselves as Gods and their corruption." The ElfLord stood nearly as tall as Llara, with white hair outlining ageless features.

"Here is Orissa, High Priestess of the Maker. Her people turned from the priests who were filled with the deceit of the Mid-World Powers. The Dark Lords of the Mid-World brought about her destruction, but at her death they found her transported to the Hall of the Dreamers, and the Mid-World was astonished. The Sight is powerful within Orissa, and among us, she alone has glimpsed the Maker, where he sits at the heart of the universe, at the center of all understanding.

"Here is my place," said Llara, waving to an empty chair, "and next to me is the greatest of the Dreamers. Behold Voritar, Prince of Demons, fashioner of Dragons, and great Servant of the Maker." The Demon stood higher than the others, fully five times the bulk of a man, and his head was as large as that of an ox. Yet his face held a look of complete peace and tranquility. Julian bowed low.

"Greetings, Lord," he murmured. "It is amazing to see you in this holy place, yet it brings to mind the Maker's instructions — 'Prepare to be surprised'." Llara passed to the next figure, who seemed tiny beside the Prince of Demons; he was hunched, an old man with twinkling eyes.

"Here is Hestaur, one of the most powerful of Sorcerers, explorer of the Mid-World, subtle student of *The Game of the Masters*, and forerunner of the Wizards. He has watched Merlin closely these many years and will give counsel about your master.

"Here is Nablus, a being born into the Mid-World, who gave great service to the Maker, long after the Maker had departed. For an age, Nablus was a seeker and binder of the fearsome Creatures of the Darkness, who lurked at the borders of the Mid-World, preying upon the unwary inhabitants of Alantéa the Forerunner." The features of Nablus were subtle, like those of a lizard, and his skin was scaled, patchy. "Among the Dreamers, only Nablus changes," said Llara, smiling. "Each year he grows taller, and the Dragonskin slips from him. Here is room for another Dreamer," Llara pointed to an empty chair. "We believe that this place has been set aside for Merlin, and at his passing Merlin will join us. Yet Merlin is now beyond our sight and has not yet joined us. Hestaur will tell you more of Merlin, but first, we should seat you, and refresh you."

Llara pulled out a small table and chair for Julian, and he sat facing the high table of the Dreamers. A goblet filled with light, sparkling waters appeared before the Apprentice, together with a small tray of cakes. Llara again smiled down at Julian.

"The water is drawn from the Cup of the Maker," she said, "and the cakes from the table of a lord of men. They will not be missed."

"I will speak while you eat," said Hestaur, "for your time here is short. Your enemies have sent one of their most powerful, resourceful servants in pursuit of you, and already he draws near." Julian sat and ate. He was beyond surprise now; anything might happen.

"I have watched Merlin from a distance over these many years," continued Hestaur. "I judge that there are few equal in wisdom to Merlin, even among the Powers of the Mid-World. Yet I feared for Merlin, great as he had become, for he had begun to explore hidden ways. There are matters that are concealed, even from the Dreamers, even from the Powers of the Mid-World, and Merlin had begun to seek these. It seems that some new Power has arisen that is able to block our sight; some of us believe that the Mid-World has given birth to a being greater than any of the Powers, but we are not certain. Has Merlin said anything of this to you?" Julian shook his head.

"He told Kalanin that he was close to naming the author of our troubles, and then he was gone."

"He attempted to wrest the answer from the ocean at Sea's Edge," said Hestaur, "and now he is beyond our sight." The old Sorcerer was silent for a moment, staring beyond Julian, out into the starlit night. "Merlin's fate is a strange one: I believe that many ages will pass before Merlin comes to the Hall of the Dreamers. Images have come to me, dream visions, of a long, enchanted sleep for Merlin, and some tasks set for him in the Far Lands, beyond Alantéa, beyond the Mid-World of the Truce. But if Merlin were destroyed before his enchanted sleep, he would be here, among us…and he is not yet in this, his final resting place. Therefore, he lives, captured or hidden." Hestaur fixed his eyes again upon Julian. "In the struggle of your League, you may learn more. If you reach Balardi, tell him that Merlin lives. Also, he should watch the Sorcerer Nergal with care — some shrouded mystery hovers about him, some secret enchantment."

Hestaur paused before continuing. "Some matters are better shown than described. Let us all look more closely at the warfare in the night skies created by the Great Spell."

Hestaur opened both hands slowly, and from his hands images flowed, showing the storm beating down upon the tower where Julian and his allies had sheltered such a short time ago. In that stormy night, an enormous dark cloud shaped like a dagger was surging toward the tower: the Great Spell had been cast, ready to destroy Julian and his allies and bring an end to the Wizards and their League. Lightning flashed over the horizon followed by a muffled concussion of thunder, but the storm's menace was overshadowed by the power of the Great Spell.

"Watch now," Hestaur murmured, "how the Great Spell is countered by other forces." Merlin's counter spells raced up into the stormy night radiating blue, and violet, and green, with surges of gold. Other forces leaped up into the night, a mix of different forces and power. Julian's own, slender force of gleaming white light was overshadowed by the others.

"We see your own strength, that of a young Magician," Hestaur said, almost whispering, "yet other forces are most difficult to identify. Here, however, is what we most wished you to see."

They watched on as the tower burst open, and the tiny image of Galad was sent hurtling into the storm, surging high over Alantéa and to certain death.

"A dying Charmed Knight, of no use to *The Game of the Masters*," Hestaur whispered, "but now watch this!"

A Wraith-like form swept up into the night sky, as dark as the cloudy matter of the Great Spell. A dark cloak hid its form, and a hood obscured its features, but one hand was that of a skeleton, fleshless, while the other hand was like that of a beast, choked with fur. As Galad hurtled through the darkness, the beast hand reached out, shoving Galad, so that the Knight's body changed direction and was sent hurtling into some unknown direction, with his fate changed.

"Such an intervention has never happened before," Hestaur said softly. "I can only guess that *The Game of the Masters* felt that its own fate, its own existence was challenged, and so it intervened to preserve Galad."

"Julian," Orissa murmured, "the fate of the Wizards and their League is uppermost in your mind. Yet what we have seen suggests that greater events are in play. So self-absorbed are the Great Gods, that none of them — Wotan or Ahriman or Set or Ra or Ahuramazda — has any idea that their own destinies might be involved."

"Those are names of several Great Gods," Julian said, shaking his head, "names that I am not even supposed to whisper when speaking to the Wizards."

"Yet the Great Gods have been involved in the long history of the League," Hestaur added, "and some of them were hidden allies of the League. A truce now prevails, so you cannot count on aid from the Powers of the Mid-World. But you must warn the Wizards that they are dealing with momentous events, far greater than the future of their League. Now I am done. Is there still time?"

"A short while, only," said Llara.

"Then Julian should hear the first story, the story of the Beginning," said Hestaur. "So many histories are twisted by the self-serving fables of the Powers, but Voritar was present at the Beginning. Listen, Julian, one of the Firsts will tell you the tale."

"I will recall for you the story, the old story, the sad story if you wish," said the Demon Prince. His voice was low, rumbling throughout the Hall, and the glass of the great Hall trembled somewhat. "Though I was not present at the Beginning, only the Maker knows truly what went through His mind when he began the great Fashioning. And I cannot remember these events, I must relive them....

"I imagine the Maker come to Earth to breathe life over its dead surfaces, and I see Him hesitate as he perceives the Demons, asleep in the Earth's crust, some echo or ghost of an earlier creation. The Maker ponders whether to wake the sleeping Demons, whether they will prosper in the future gardens of earth. After an age, He wakes them, but first He fashions the Seraphs, to be fosterbrothers to them, Lords of the co-dominion of Earth.

"Now I am awake, and the Maker is teaching us about the Earth, and all the many, potent energies that surround it. He takes shape as He wishes, neither Seraph nor Demon, and I perceive that the Maker is careful not to overawe us. We begin to fashion and tame the Earth, great labors shared by

Demons and Seraphs. But I and the other great ones of the Demon Princes begin to hold ourselves a little apart, for we come to understand that our power is unequaled, except by a few of the mightiest Seraphs. The Maker does not put forth his own strength but advises and counsels in an utterly soft voice.

"Now Earth's gardens are tilled, and ready for seed. The Seraphs begin the fashioning of the Spirit Lords to aid in the creation of Earth's life. The Maker counsels the Demons to obtain his aid before further creative efforts, but my brethren have begun to mock the Maker, referring to him, in his absence, as 'Elder Brother.'

"The Demon Princes have come to believe that the Maker is not greater than they, only the firstborn, wise and powerful due to time. In secret, I and my brothers begin the creation of the Lords of Dragons. In this, we have the help of Adonai, the great Seraph, who has compassion for us and is deceived. Now, the Dragons burst forth in splendor, sparkling and gleaming with power, so that Seraph, Demon and Spirit Lord are dazzled. But the Maker is silent, for He alone perceives the flaws within the Dragons. A brief time later, the Seraphs and Spirit Lords bring forth humankind, and these seem pale and feeble beside the Dragons. Though now, others begin to understand the corruption of the Dragons. Adonai repents and the Maker forgives him. I see within the Dragons, the Creatures of the Darkness waiting to be born, and great sorrow fills my being. My brothers turn against the Maker, claiming that He alone brought about the corruption of the Dragons' seed.

"Now the Maker stands forth and casts aside his guise as advisor and elder, showing himself as Lord of the Universe. In a quiet voice he says only, 'You will need to seek Me,' and He is gone. All the Powers hear those words, and at that moment, I put aside my kinship with the Demon Princes and declare for the Maker. Five of the wisest of the Dragons understand their flaws and leave Earth to seek the Maker in the starry universe. Here, in the Hall of the Dreamers, I often watch my children, as they leap from star to star in their quest for the Maker, and the dross burns away from them....

"The War of the Servants and the Adversaries of the Maker begins. I stand with a few of the Dragons for the Maker. A handful of Seraphs and Spirit Lords are corrupted by the Demons and stand with the Adversaries. With my foster brothers and my children, the Dragons, we fashion a great work, and three of the most fell of the Demon Princes are chained forever. Lucifrage is destroyed, but two of the most powerful Spirit Lords perish in the aftermath of that battle.

"I hesitate, pondering the death of the immortals. But now, the Dragons give birth to the Creatures of the Darkness, and these bring immense power against the Servants. The humans aid us, but they are feeble, fleeing or dying harmlessly. Some of the Dragons perceive their own corruption and seek to leave Earth, but they no longer have the strength.

"Now, in the depths, the Nameless one stirs; the greatest of the Creatures of the Darkness begins its rule over Earth's oceans so that all the Servants flee salt waters, but great billows of vapor pursue them, and they are dismayed.

"I stand for the Servants, yet I am filled with loathing and anguish, for the Creatures of the Darkness are the first truly evil beings born to Earth. I descend into the depths to give battle with the Nameless. In the darkness of the waters, our struggle shakes the ocean floor and boiling rock surges from seething waters. New lands are formed, and old ones cast down. In the end, I am mastered by the Nameless and pinned to the ocean floor, with all power lost to me. Yet, in that hour, Adonai, greatest of Seraphs, rescues me, drawing me from the depths.

"I stand on the shore, weary and filled with despair. The land about me is dark and grim; already the Nameless has begun to poison Earth's gardens. Adonai stands beside me and says, gently, 'The Maker will forgive us if we fail, yet He would wish us to try once again.' Then I and my foster brother return to the depths, and all the fear and loathing and anguish depart from me, and my vision clears. We break the Nameless utterly so that only the Maker might renew that being when He returns."

"Our time is ending," said Llara gently, almost in a whisper.

"Here, then is the Table of Creation," said the Demon, and in letters of fire, an inscription was traced on the floor of the Hall. "You will see that men survive, after the Adversaries, Servants, and Mid-World Powers are but confused legends." Julian walked about the floor, reading the inscription carefully. So, men would also be borne in the Far Lands, emerging perhaps from the small creatures that dwelt among the Great Lizards! And what was this event, the Pantheonic Alliances? He opened his mouth to ask, but Llara spoke first.

"Now, the time has come to prepare yourself. Julian, your enemy approaches! We are not permitted to aid you, but I will say only one thing: the Land is good; it was created for the Servants, not for the Adversaries. Farewell!"

Julian gripped his staff, standing before the high table of the Dreamers. Candles burned brightly, and starlight shone through the glass dome. Fiery letters vanished from the floor.

Across from Julian, near the entrance, a swirl of shadows began to spin around, then to take shape. First, it seemed a wolf, then a man, and strength from its Gift radiated out...it was that of the werewolf creature, the Adept who had led the wolf pack, and transformed into man's shape after.

It took shape as a man, grey and dark and powerful, standing in the light of many candles. Silence prevailed in the Hall of the Dreamers as they beheld the first of the Adversaries to enter their Hall. The wereman returned their stares, looking scornfully at the Dreamers.

"So, a tiny heaven for a few fools," and it turned to Julian. "For you, my Master has a gift," and the wereman raised its arm and cast a massive bolt of force at the Apprentice.

Julian raised his staff to counter it, but to his surprise, the bolt crashed to the ground, lurching along the floor, blasting a huge hole through the glass.

Julian looked open mouthed at the Dreamers: they had turned their faces and were staring at the night sky. The werebeing regarded its own arm with astonishment. Julian pointed his staff at the creature, calling out a spell to hold it in man's form. His staff vanished in flames; only its handle remained. Julian gazed at the Dreamers in amazement...their faces were turned to the stars, faces filled with complete serenity.

Julian hurled the handle of his staff at the werebeing, and raced from the Hall, leaping through the gap blasted by the spell of his enemy. He sped through the fields, and as he crashed down the hillside, he could hear behind him the baying of a great wolf.

· 𝕏 ·

Like an animal pursued by a larger beast, Julian ran for his life. Speeding down one slope, and up another, he expected to feel wolf fangs at any moment. His breath grew shorter. The pace was too fast...a fallen branch sent him sprawling, skidding over the forest floor: the race was over. He lay on the ground drawing great gulps of air, expecting wolf fangs at any moment; but he was alone.

Julian picked himself up, listening intently. In the distance, he could hear a faint whine, as though the were-being had grown confused. The Gift began to reach out, to explore — great power lay over the land, the solemn and majestic power of the Dreamers, and was overwhelming both the senses of the Apprentice and his foe. All the sounds and smells that lingered over and about the Land of the Dreamers were completely different from those of Alantéa and stronger. No wonder the werebeing was confused!

And there was running water, not far from where he stood. Above him, Julian saw the stars still shining huge over the forest canopy, filling the woodlands with an eerie half light. He began to move, quickly and deliberately, toward the flowing water.

From a distance, Julian heard the wolf's cry as it picked up his scent. He broke into a run. With fortune, he might escape for this one night....

He reached the stream, and crossed it, then doubled back, then crossed again, now wading down the stream, until, in midwater, he found a large overhanging tree limb. He leaped for the limb, climbed, then rested while his dripping clothes spilled more water into the stream. As he relaxed for a moment, he understood another reason for the wolf's confusion: every tree seemed to be in flower in the Land of the Dreamers, and a vast unseen tide of many fragrances was surging over the land. He let his clothes dry for a while, then climbed to a higher branch of the tree. With his belt, he lashed himself to an intersection of tree limbs and began to doze under a brilliant canopy of stars.

In the morning Julian woke, stiff from his awkward sleep, but refreshed. He stretched then sat high above the rushing water. A few puff clouds rolled across the horizon, but the sky seemed incredibly blue. Julian sat and considered his future: he could flee from his enemy, for a time, yet in the end, he would be overtaken and destroyed. He might confront his enemy, but then his own destruction seemed certain. No help could be found at the Hall of the Dreamers — apparently, they had foresworn interference, and anyway, his adversary would certainly be prowling around the Hall. Perhaps he might surprise it, catch it while it slept.

As Julian pondered, the sun rose over his perch, huge and golden. If the wolf creature hunted at night, did it sleep during the day? Where would it sleep? Julian climbed back over the stream carefully, and lowered himself into the water, wading upstream. At the end of his search, he found a large, flat rock in midstream, one large enough to hold a divination pattern. From the bank of the stream, he took several handfuls of soil, then used these to form a pattern on the rock, carefully positioning each particle. He prepared the field slowly, running his fingers over the rune shapes several times, repeating the divination spell twice; without his staff, the Gift was unfocused but still potent.

He stepped from the rock. In a moment, he would learn more of his adversary, for if the creature slept, or kept its wolf's form, it would not be able to ward off his divination. Placing his hands on the rock, he added a last surge of power to the spell. Pale light flickered over the runes, but where he looked for wolf's form or man's image, there were only tiny clouds moving over his design, rolling aimlessly back and forth as they bumped into the spell's edge.

Julian laughed ruefully, shaking his head with dismay, then he broke off the divination. So, sorcery was confounded in the Land of the Dreamers. His contest with the wereman would be one of strength and wits. How could he become the hunter rather than the hunted? He lay back on the rock for a while, searching for a way to change his fate, and listening always for the sounds of a wolf or human passing over the woodland floor.

He sat up. As the werebeing changed from man to beast and back again, shifting between the two forms, it could not carry a weapon; it would rely on its sorcery, and in the Land of the Dreamers, its power would be diminished. So, if he had even a simple weapon, his chances would be considerably improved. Along the banks of the stream were many saplings, and Julian tested several before he found one that had begun to thicken, hardening into wood while still pliant.

After a little more than an hour of work, Julian had made himself a rough, clumsy spear, one that a leaping wolf might impale itself upon. Now, he needed food, shelter, and a plan....

· ⋊ ·

During the many days that followed, Julian became cunning, like a forest creature that had been hunted since its birth, never sleeping twice in the same place, brushing through patches of wild garlic and goblinrush to confuse the wolf's pursuit. He crossed streams and springs when he could, resting at midday in the reeds. Sorcery was a thing that was used in another world, at a different time; here, speed and strength and cunning were all important. Sometimes in the evenings, as he dried in cool breezes, he wondered about his strength and health; in Alantéa, the wetness and cold would likely have brought sickness, but in the Land of the Dreamers, living only on fruits and berries, he had become stronger. Llara had said, 'The Land is good.' Perhaps it would favor his own body and not that of his adversary. Again, he considered his ambush.

While Julian sat, planning the death of his adversary, banks of clouds began rolling out from the hillsides. They were dark and swollen with rain, but so intent was Julian that he only noticed when the first raindrops began to break the stream's surface: each drop made a light musical sound as it touched the stream. Overhead, in the forest's upper reaches, the rain pattered and swept against soft leaves, trailing music, and moisture in its path. Julian put down his spear and stood on the rock, hearing the music of fresh waters.

Was there no way of avoiding a confrontation? In this peaceful land, would he be forced to destroy his adversary to survive? Many conflicts within the Mid-World were resolved when each party returned to its domain. Perhaps his adversary could be persuaded to return, in peace....

The cloud cover began to roll to the west, taking its concert of rain into distant hills. Julian sat, deep in thought. Could he and his adversary withdraw? It seemed unlikely; the creature had pursued him, moving beyond the farthest reaches of the Mid-World in order to destroy him. And all the actions of his enemies had been grim, and unrelenting — so, his only hope was to attempt to overcome the creature, then seek the Dreamer's aid in returning to Alantéa. And to meet the creature on even terms, he would need a trap or a surprise.

It was midday, and the sun's heat began to lift warm moisture from the forest floor. Julian waded further upstream, searching for higher ground. From the stream bed, he saw several hills that were crowned by rocks, treeless at the top, ones that might only be climbed hand over hand, surely not by a wolf. Julian walked to the closest of these, stopping to listen every few minutes for any sign of his adversary. The birds of the forest were in full song after the rain, and Julian hoped that the wolf's presence would silence them and provide him with some warning.

He began the climb, reaching the hilltop after half an hour, and he saw quickly that the hill was not suitable — on one side, was a gentle slope covered with trees and brush that might easily be climbed by a four footed adversary. But here at least the land about him could easily be viewed. To his left was the great hill, almost a mountain that dominated the countryside: the Cup of the Maker at its peak, with the Hall of the Dreamers just a little beneath. The surrounding land was rolling countryside — forests, valleys, hilltops, and small streams. Above the treetops swallows swooped and circled, then disappeared into high branches and leafy shade.

To his right, a craggy hilltop loomed above him. The peak was nearly all rock, with only a few stunted trees growing out from its scarred rock face. He leaned on his makeshift spear and squinted into the distance. There seemed to be enough loose rubble at the top — if only he could see the other side! A movement below Julian caught his eye and he froze. He moved his head carefully, and saw flashes of movement, as many small birds dove at some object that was obscured by forest cover. Julian sank to his hands and knees and peered forward, watching as the flock of birds dove again, and again, like a swarm of angry insects.

The wolf's figure surged into a clearing, leaping, and snapping at its small assailants. Julian pressed his body against the ground. The wolf creature snarled at its small foes, then, with a shudder, changed again to man form. It stood, leaning against a tree, spasms shaking it like an aftershock: so, even the shapeshifter was troubled by the land. The birds paused a moment in confusion, then began to swarm again. The wereman raised its arms, and its Adept's voice shook with anger as it called out spell words. Julian held his breath. Tiny flickers of light darted about the hands of the wereman — barely enough to tickle a dragonfly, and not nearly enough to blast a flock of birds. The wereman seemed grey and gaunt, and the sense of physical power radiating from his body had grown less. Julian watched closely as the wereman cursed his small enemies once again, and stumbled back into the forest, vanishing from view. Birds followed at a distance, as though to keep watch.

Julian turned over and lay on the ground for a moment, hands clasped behind his head, eyes fixed on the sky. The hunter was now being hunted, or at least followed. What would the wereman do? Probably shelter during daylight and use his night senses for hunting in the dark. At this thought, he looked to the sky's edge where the sun had begun to sink. He decided quickly. For one more night, he would be the hunted; then tomorrow in the Land of the Dreamers, beneath the Cup of the Maker, he would turn and face his adversary.

· ✴ ·

Julian woke with a start. It was night. He was lashed to a perch above the stream, and he lay without moving, straining to listen above the noise of the stream...then on the stream bank came a shuffling sound, followed by a low growl. Julian's hand, like a creature beyond his control, began to creep slowly toward his crude spear. With an effort, he stopped it. Against a wolf, his tree shelter and spear might help, but the wereman could easily tear him from his hiding place. He kept still, though drops of sweat poured down his face. In other lands, the beast would easily pick out his scent, but here in the flowering forests of the Dreamers, perhaps his smell would be masked. After a few minutes, he heard the creature move downstream, sniffing at the stream bank. A while later, the flow of the stream changed a little, as the wolf creature crossed to the other side, prowling along the opposite bank. At last, the sounds faded into the night.

Julian calmed himself, turning on his side, letting his hand finally grasp his spear. He closed his eyes, but no sleep came, and after a while he lay again on his back, staring into the brilliant night sky, searching for the star patterns he had learned as a child.

Where was the Great Worm? The Sorcerer's Hand? Where was the Breaking Wave? On some nights, it had seemed to flash and roll, but here there was no sign of it. Julian gave a deep sigh. Although the stars were not familiar, they brought back memories of nighttime studies as an Apprentice. For ten years, he had been taught to solve most problems by use of sorcery, yet here his mortal contest with the wereman could be solved only by force. All his sorcery and training had become nothing. Kalanin or Galad, even without weapons, would have easily tracked and destroyed the wereman. Was it possible that the warriors were now facing problems that needed sorcery, where all their strength and speed and skill with weapons were useless? He was not greatly comforted by that thought.

Gradually, the night sky gave way to shades of grey, then to blue as morning arrived. All around Julian, birds burst into song, and some began to sweep through the forest in search of food. Julian watched the bird flocks carefully for a few moments, hoping that they would reveal his antagonist if the wereman were close. Satisfied that he was alone, Julian climbed down from his perch and moved rapidly through the forest. One small errand had to be performed first: a little grove of trees lay a few minutes away, but he had stayed away from them for fear of leaving his scent. Now he gathered a small pile of fruit, using his shirt as a sack.

Walking quickly, shirtless, with a sack in one hand and a crude spear in the other, Julian saw himself more like a young savage, rather than an Apprentice. He laughed as he thought of meeting Merlin or Balardi — they would be so disappointed!

It was still morning when he reached the base of the hill he had chosen. Halfway to the top, the forest faltered as the hillside grew steeper, with only a few trees straggling parched and stunted from the rock face. He climbed higher. Near the top was a level area, a small clearing with mosses and brush, and only a few blades of grass pushing from the rocky surface. From this clearing to the top, there was only one pathway, and it was a ragged, rough trail.

At the top, he rested for a moment, then laid out his possessions carefully, so as not to spill them over the sides: a rough spear, enough fruit for a day or two, a few small pieces of flint from the stream bed — fire starters, he hoped. He began to pile the hill's debris into two great mounds, mixing jagged boulders with gnarled chunks of wood. Each of the mounds was held to the slope by a dam made of smaller branches and stones. After an hour, Julian's face was covered with sweat, as the hot sun began to beat down on him. Stopping for a moment, he watched birds circle about the forests that lay beneath his hill. A few pieces of fruit slaked his thirst, though he still wished for water. Through the afternoon, Julian gathered many stones, enough to create a small avalanche, and in each of the mounds, he placed broken branches and wood debris, so that a fire once started in the mounds would burn for several hours. At the very top of the hill, he readied a larger fire, one that would be at his back.

By late afternoon, Julian was tired, not with the spell weariness of the Magician, but with the aching muscles of a field laborer. He sat for a moment and looked ruefully at his scratched and blistered hands. It took an effort to focus on his last preparation — a javelin, or short spear, one that could be thrown, heavy enough to damage his powerful opponent.

At sunset, his preparations were complete. He watched the sun slipping down beyond the far hills; it had never looked more gigantic and redder…and peaceful, as the forest sank into twilight. Yet, out there on the woodland floor, under a canopy of leaves, his enemy would begin to stir, to begin the hunt anew.

· Ⅹ ·

Dusk passed into darkness, and the hilltop was filled with starlight. Julian worked the bits of flint together until a few dry grass strands caught and began to ignite dry bits of wood. Within a short time, he had two small fires smoldering in his rock piles, and a large watch fire blazing at his back.

He stood, leaning on his heavy spear, looking to the forest below. His fires hissed and crackled, though the night itself had never seemed quieter. Julian's heart began to beat faster. Down to his left, he heard a faint sound, as small pebbles trickled down the hillside. With an effort, Julian turned from the sound and placed the last wood on his fire. Battle was coming! The wolf creature was closer...to his right Julian heard a soft sound, like a dog panting in the distance.

With a howl, the wolf creature leaped into the clearing. It paused for a moment, powerful, menacing, gaunt, mouth open, staring at Julian. Firelight flickered over its greyish, black eyes. Then, with a spasm, the creature shook and reached human form once again. As a man, it was even more gaunt, yet still powerful and dangerous. A little grimace ran across the face of the wereman.

"What is your beacon for, Apprentice? The dreaming fools care nothing for you...but I have found you, and your death will free me from this accursed land."

"Exit from this land lies through the Hall of the Dreamers," Julian said quietly. "Your Master has no power here. It is not too late to seek exit through the Dreamers." Light from the watch fire flickered over the gaunt form. The wereman said nothing but reached forward to begin the climb to Julian's peak.

Julian cried, "Now it *is* too late!" and he kicked aside the supports from the base of the mounds. Showers of sparks and boulders and smoldering wood came cascading down the hill. Julian hurled his makeshift javelin at the creature; it leaped to one side, but as it dodged, a heavy stone came bounding out of the night, striking the lower leg of the wereman. With a gasp of pain and surprise, it fell on its back, hands trying to brush bits of fire from its body.

In the middle of smoke and burning rubble, it took wolf form again, turning to Julian on three legs, growling deep in its throat. But Julian caught the wolf form as it changed, heaving down a heavy stone with both hands, smashing the creature's ribs. It gave a wild whine, falling back, then it limped away, seeking refuge in the dark forest. Julian called out:

"Tomorrow, *you* will be the hunted!"

· ⟩⟨ ·

The next morning, Julian returned to the stream, kneeling beside it, and drinking great gulps of water. For the first time, he noticed that his left hand was burned, in addition to being scraped and blistered. Hesitating for a moment at the stream, he began to wash the grime and charcoal from himself. It was ridiculous to wash before hunting a wounded enemy, but habits were hard to break.

When he returned to the trail of his enemy, he found that the bloody trail of the creature ended about five hundred paces from the hill. At the end of this trail came a stretch of mossy ground; it was easy for Julian to imagine the wolf, lying on the moss, burning with hatred, licking its seeping leg in the darkness.

From this place, Julian had neither sorcery nor good woodcraft to aid him, though maybe the bird swarms would once again pursue the creature, and after, he would need to be higher to see them. He mounted a hillock. Only a few bee-larks and wind-finches fluttered around; somehow the larger flocks had vanished. Where had they gone? He walked with increasing speed along the floor of the forest, seeking higher ground. Far from the Hall of the Dreamers, the land continued its sequence of hills and valleys. He began to walk uphill again, climbing as the way grew steeper.

At the top was a nearly complete view of the countryside. The Mountain of the Dreamers loomed in the distance, but it seemed far away, remote, and strangely lacking in winged or climbing creatures. Perhaps his search for the wereman would take a longer time. Julian turned from the Hall and saw in the distance an astonishing sight: a great column of birds was hovering over the forest, like a winged cyclone, shaped like a funnel, with larger birds at higher levels. Shocks of alarm ran through him. His adversary was attracting enormous attention — the wereman was going to use sorcery to strike back at him! He hurried down the hill. His opponent was an Adept; he might succeed where an Apprentice failed. He broke into a run. The column of birds disappeared from view as Julian plunged through the forest.

Without warning, the ground heaved in front of Julian, casting him from his feet. The forest was filled with the sounds of shattering tree trunks. He struggled to his knees, but again the ground buckled. Above him, masses of birds called out as they fled from the tremors. What was happening? The ground stopped shaking, but the air grew suddenly cool, and sharp with tension — the Adept was calling on another Great Spell! But this was madness — in the Land of the Dreamers that collision of power could destroy them all! Julian raced forward as the forest began to darken. It was probably too late to stop it. All the bird-flocks had vanished, but now the Gift within him was drawn by the power of the Great Spell.

He found his enemy in a clearing, where only a few stunted trees grew. On the ground about the wereman, the grass had been carved with runes of power, and covered with ashes. A Talisman of great power lay in the center of the wereman's design. Flecks of cinder fell from the air like a small, black frost. Julian halted, panting for breath. He was too late; the Great Spell was complete.

Silence hung over the clearing, but Julian sensed the surge of power as the Great Spell took shape. Then his mouth sagged open in surprise. The wereman stared in utter disbelief. A brown figure, knee-high, emerged from the Talisman's surface and bowed to the wereman, saying in a small, squeaky voice,

"Command me, Master."

"Command *you?*" shrieked the wereman. "Look at you! You were supposed to be a huge Dragon-slaying monster!" The wereman hobbled forward, and demolished the creature with one kick, transforming it into a cloud of brown dust. Enraged and crippled, the wereman turned and stared at Julian. The Apprentice approached warily, his spear held before him. His opponent held his hands outstretched and called out to the heavens.

"I have had enough! I can take no more...in the Name of the Maker, I renounce his Adversaries! In the Name of the Maker, I call upon his Servants to preserve me!" At that moment, it seemed to Julian that all light and sound slowly shut down, as though the universe was being rolled up, softly and gently, like a quilt at daybreak.

· ⳩ ·

Julian's eyes blinked: before him, candles flickered on the high table of the Hall of the Dreamers. The Dreamers sat and stared at a space beside the Apprentice. He turned and saw that his adversary stood beside him. The wereman was shivering with sickness and self-loathing; his leg wound had reopened, and a thin stream of blood ran over polished marble floors. The Dreamers watched the wereman for several long moments, but he was unable to lift his eyes to meet theirs. At last, Llara spoke.

"Many of the Adversaries have learned that invocation, hoping to ward off death should the Servants prevail. Yet that invocation has been spoken rarely, for those who are deeply corrupt are not easily able to mouth those words. How were you able to speak them?"

The wereman looked away, still unwilling to meet the eyes of the Dreamers. "This land has poisoned me," he murmured. "Perhaps it has changed me in other ways." Hestaur laughed. He sat, hunched, with his grey beard, dwarfed by the great bulk of the Prince of Demons who sat beside him, but his eyes sparkled.

"Here, again, is the Maker's great lesson: 'Prepare to be surprised.' Well, we are surprised. We never expected that you would survive. But that's not a good reason for us to let you collapse upon our floors. You have become our second visitor, and if Julian will bring a chair for you, we will speak more comfortably." Julian was beyond wonder; he moved as though dazed, gently pushing a chair under his crippled adversary, then he stood behind the wereman, as though he had become no more than an attendant to some highly regarded visitor.

"Now, that's better," said the Old Sorcerer, and he leaned forward. "My name, given to me so many ages ago, was Hestaur." He looked carefully at the wereman. "How were you named?" The wereman looked up for the first time, and the pupils of his eyes shone darkly in the candlelight.

"I was called Merodach, like you so many years ago."

"Good! Good! That wasn't so difficult," said Hestaur. His palms flashed, and two goblets appeared on the table. "The waters of the Maker's Cup would be difficult for you at this time...but a light wine shouldn't hurt you." He pushed the goblets forward so that they came gliding across the table's surface, one to Julian, and one to the wereman. Merodach sat in silence, sipped then drank deeply.

"And when you were given the name of Merodach," the Sorcerer continued, "was this given to you as human, or as wolfbeing?"

"I was Merodach before I was ever a man or wolf — I came into the Mid-World soft, and half-formed. The wolfform was chosen for its speed and strength, while the manform was selected for the Gift, and the powers of Adepts and Sorcerers. I see now that the wolfportion was easy, but these human thoughts...." The wereman was beaten, yet his voice was tinged with bitterness.

"So, you were not altogether happy with your dark service," said Hestaur, "even before you were altered by the Land of the Dreamers."

"I will not try to deceive you," said Merodach, and he looked away from the eyes of the Dreamers. "Had I been successful in my service, I would have returned to my Master. And yet...the stench of evil had begun to choke me. I could no longer sleep as a human, for my night visions had become so grim. Long ago, in my Apprenticeship, my Familiar foretold this fate for me and taught me how to call upon the Servants. After, my Familiar fled into the Mid-World, and I was left alone to deal with my dark Master. Later, when a dark spell passed through my lips, the invocation to the Servants would pass through my mind." Hestaur nodded thoughtfully.

"He must have great power to have held you so strongly and to have given you so many potent weapons. In the Hall of the Dreamers, we should see all that passes in Alantéa and in the Mid-World. Yet this lord of yours is hidden behind a cloak of darkness. Can you tell us of this lord of yours? Can you name this Master?" Merodach nodded.

"Yes, of course," he replied. "He is —" Here, the wereman cried out in agony, and pitched forward to the floor, like a dead thing. The goblet bounced from his hand, and the wereman's form shook and changed, half man, half wolf, shaking in spasms on the marble floor. Hestaur darted around the edge of the table, and touched the werecreature, tracing spell wards over the creature's chest; and the shaking stopped.

"I didn't think he would be permitted to tell us," Hestaur spoke softly, almost to himself, then he turned to the table of the Dreamers. "Before us lies a dying creature who might have become human, like Julian or me, but he is trapped by his service to his dark Master. He wished to be free, and whole — can we grant this wish?"

"In me, there is power to heal all Earthborn forms." The voice of Voritar rumbled through the Hall. "Yet we have seen that his spirit is bound to his Master's will. How shall this hold be broken?"

"You will heal his mind and body," said Llara, "and I shall place his spirit beyond his master's reach. Until his Master is discovered or declares himself, the spirit of Merodach will rest upon the foothills of the Mountains of the Moon." She turned to Julian. "As a sign that we wish no evil to Merodach, Julian, a Servant of the Maker, shall accompany him." Hestaur, nodding, leaned over and touched the arm of the Apprentice.

"But for a short while only. Julian's friends will need him." And he added quietly to Julian, "Seek Merlin — he is the greatest of the mortal wielders of magic. Find him if you can."

Julian stood, astonished. The Moon! The Moon was an airless void. What were the Dreamers doing? Merodach's mouth opened with a half-formed protest. But now it was too late. The Dreamers stood behind their great high table, radiating light as they put forth their power.

· ⋈ ·

And Julian was gone, moved like a stream of light through an airless void.

Then he was at rest, and he saw the outline of his old adversary, lying with his back against a mound of soft grey matter. The figure of Merodach was ghostly, insubstantial. Through his own form, Julian could see particles of a dead, lifeless world. His own spirit was translucent, without feeling, resting like that of his former foe.

But now, for the first time in the moon's starlit evening, they felt their faces turn to the great cup of the heavens…and they beheld with wonder the constellations moving rank upon rank: the incredible splendor of the starry universe.

Chapter Ten
The Many Portals

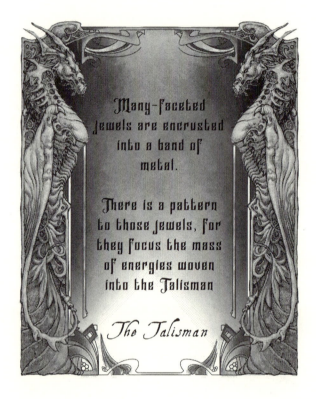

Many-faceted jewels are encrusted into a band of metal.

There is a pattern to those jewels, for they focus the mass of energies woven into the Talisman

The Talisman

K**ALANIN OPENED HIS EYES, STRUGGLING** to stay awake. Some distance from his tent the wounded were calling for water and an end to pain. So, it had not been a dream. They had withstood the Dark Emissary. Envar was dead. Julian had been returned, mindless or enchanted. If the Apprentice lived, at least they would have a Healer. Groggily he pulled himself to his feet.

Outside the day was overcast, but the high mass of clouds above them seemed distant and moisture less. Kalanin drew a fresh roll from the provision master and walked to the tent where the Apprentice lay sleeping. The Eye of Merlin was outside, standing guard.

"Your Magician still sleeps," said the eagle. "He is returning from a far place, slowly. I think now that all will be well, but he should not be woken."

"I'm sure he'll be able to help us," Kalanin said, breathing a sigh of relief, "though the wounded need him now." Out of the corner of his eye, he saw Dargas, moving slowly, heavily towards them.

"The wounded will have to wait," said the eagle, and he turned his head toward Dargas. The face of the old soldier was strained and heavy with grief.

"How's your Apprentice?" asked Dargas.

"We think he'll be well," said Kalanin, "but some enchantment still lies over him. It's easing, though slowly." Dargas nodded.

"The dying will have to wait then, but we should attend to the dead. Envar's gone, along with many others. We'll bury them and pass a measure of wine around — only a bit, though."

"I'll walk with you," said Kalanin.

The burial party began to collect the bodies of the slain, carrying them in wooden carts or litters. Outside the camp walls, they found the corpses of many who had fled and had been taken by the black drinkers of warm blood. The bodies of these men were pale and bloodless, while the black creatures attached to them were gorged with blood and unable to move. Men of the burial party slashed the black things with daggers and left them to writhe and die in the open air, but their victims were carried with reverence to be buried with those who had fallen in battle.

Hundreds worked, digging a vast pit, and others gently lowered the bodies of the fallen into the ground. At the end though, men hesitated before casting dirt over their comrades. Dargas stepped forward.

"There's no cleric about to speak for these men," he said, "and anyway, the preachers all dream and guess at man's fate — not one of them has ever talked to the Maker. But I'll speak for Envar, a good man, a loss to us, who died a warrior's death in a brave stand. If we hadn't held, he might be out there now, chased like a rabbit through the hills. When the Maker returns to wake us from the Long Sleep, he'll have a pat on the back for Envar and the others, for a brave stand in a just cause. But for now, we'll say farewell, and the earth will close over them, and they'll not be seen again in this life. Let's not forget them, and let's not forget that our enemies are without mercy, and they are evil." For all his measured words, the teeth of Dargas were clenched as he struggled to control his emotions.

After the burial, they returned to their tier camp. Dargas sat on a long bench, nursing his goblet of wine, staring into the distance.

"I'll have to send word to his lady," Dargas said, shaking his head. "She'll take the news hard." Kalanin looked at him in surprise. The old warrior met his glance. "I told you he had a lady and two small ones, but you were thinking about too many other things at the time. No blame to you — you're not perfect. Best you should see to the wounded and to your Apprentice now." Kalanin walked slowly back to the center of the camp where Julian slept. The Eye of Merlin said nothing but pulled back the tent flap for him. Cupbearers stood by ready to provide food.

Julian was awake, eyes staring at the tent's peak, his face still shining with peace. Kalanin hesitated, considering what to say. The eyes of the Apprentice turned to him.

"There's no need to fear me," he said. "I'm not mad or bewitched by clouds of dark sorcery." He sat up. "Right now, I'm only a starving Apprentice.

Bring your food forward." Cupbearers hurried with bread and slices of meat, and one poured a goblet of light wine.

"I never thought I'd see you again," Kalanin said quietly, "and when we found you last night, I was sure that you were in the deepest of trances and that your mind was ruined." Julian laughed.

"I was elsewhere," he said, wolfing down another slab of meat and bread.

"Were Sebastian and Rafir with you?" asked Kalanin. "And what of Galad?" Julian rose, gulping down the last of his goblet.

"I was alone. I would guess that the others were also hurled into distant lands, there to undergo trials of wit and strength, as I have had." Julian looked up into the weary face of Kalanin. "And you, you have been through a test of strength, have you not?"

"It might have broken me," said Kalanin. "I'm still weak from the encounters."

"Then I haven't come too soon — I was a healer first, before learning other magic."

"Treat me last," said Kalanin, trying to shake off his weariness. "So many others are struggling with grave wounds and broken bodies. I'll tell you of the battle, later. You should do what you can now, for those outside." Julian's hand gripped his staff, and he realized with a start that the Dreamers must have replaced his old staff. Hestaur probably....

Outside the tent, Julian stared up into layers of high clouds. Beyond those clouds were blue skies, and beyond the skies were masses of sparkling, distant stars. He would never see anything the same way after the Hall of the Dreamers. He looked around him to the array of tents, sentries, and milling men. The field all around was torn and ripped, not just by mailed feet, but the ground had been burst apart by magic and spell shock still lingered.

Julian's eyes were drawn to the Eye of Merlin. The Gift stirred within him; Julian turned and bowed to the eagle.

"You were only a rumor to those of us at Sea's Edge," he said. "There were whispers that Merlin had a Farsighted ally."

"Servant, not ally," replied the eagle. "Apprentice, it is a very good thing to have you with us again; though you are tangled in an astonishing *Web of Fate*."

"I'm a Healer for the moment. Later the Web will test me." Without waiting for introductions or assistance, Julian began to go among the wounded. For those in pain, there were charms to ease their stress, and for bodies that were hurt or damaged, there were spells that knit bone and sinew together. Harlond sent two aides to bring Julian's saddle pouch to the Apprentice — all his potions and sorcerous herbs had been kept intact. Julian worked on, and slowly the low moans of the wounded began to die down, with silence and slumber settling over the camp once again.

Dargas watched Julian closely as the youth went about his tasks: the Apprentice seemed altogether too young and gentle.

"Perhaps of value as a Healer," muttered Dargas, "but this is no great Magician to stand in battle with us." The eagle stood nearby and snapped at the old soldier.

"And if I were to look at you, without really understanding, I would see a fat Sergeant useful only for flogging the cooks." The eagle shook his head several times, as though trying to control himself. "Wait!" he croaked. "I must learn not to overreact — you are a strong captain and leader of men. The Apprentice is untested, but there is a powerful measure of the Gift in him." Dargas smiled, his first smile since the grim battle of the night before.

Evening approached, and the camp began its cycle of fires and cooked meals. Julian finished his work with the sick, except for two who were beyond his help, with spines so shattered that no sorcery could aid them. For these two, there were charms that eased the pain and fear, but certain death lay before them. Julian waved others aside, and spoke to these two privately, telling them about the Hall of the Dreamers.

"It's easy to feel that the Maker has abandoned us," he said gently, "but I believe, now, that He will draw us all from the Long Sleep, and then there will be new tasks for us." The two nodded at his words, only partly aware of his message, for at the last, charms and potions were more helpful than any reassurances.

At nightfall, Julian stood among the tier camp watching as masses of men milled about the weapon racks and kitchens. The ground was still scarred by the shock of many spells and the night air still touched by the Dark Emissary's aura. As the Gift explored about him, Julian felt the Eye of Merlin approach.

"It was no simple battle of men against men, was it?" asked Julian. The eagle was at his side, and even in the pale light, the Apprentice could see how large and fierce the great raptor was — several times Sebastian's bulk.

"It was an ancient Creature of the Darkness," said the eagle, "called from the Mid-World to strike at us." Julian was silent for a moment, awaiting more information, but the eagle seemed reluctant to say more.

"I've one last act of healing," said Julian, "then I'm done. Will you join Kalanin and myself in a moment?" The eagle shook his head.

"You should consult with Kalanin first, Apprentice," said the Eye. "He leads these men, yet he does not rule them."

Julian picked his way among the tents, letting the Gift seek for Kalanin. At the entrance to the council tent, the guards stood back, letting the Apprentice pass. Kalanin was lying back on his couch, bleary eyes trying to concentrate on a scroll that showed a map. Julian took a battered goblet from a side table, mixing water with a potion of herbs, then cast a slight charm over the beverage. Kalanin drank, then lay back with his eyes closed. In a few moments, he rose refreshed.

"So much for my life as an invalid. How are the others?"

"Most will be well in a while, but there are two who will not live out the night. Also..." Julian hesitated, "there's a slight sickness in the camp, with heavy heads, red eyes, and nasty odors. It seems familiar, but I've forgotten what it is." Kalanin laughed.

"Think of the feast days at the Halls of Merlin — or rather the next morning. This sickness was caused by too much wine. It will pass soon enough, with the next march." Julian nodded thoughtfully.

"There's much I should know if I'm to be of use. Is this the time to talk? Perhaps the eagle could join us."

"We should talk," said Kalanin. "But the other captains should be with us. These are men that I lead but don't command. The League is rising again, not just as a Wizard's tool, but as a band of many free men."

Messengers were sent out into the dark camp, and the four Captains, together with the Eye of Merlin, were called to the council tent to join Kalanin and Julian. The sunless day had passed, leaving a chilled evening, and Kalanin had heated cups of steaming broth for them.

"Best to save the wine," Kalanin said. Dargas sniffed at the broth, then made a sour face at it. Julian sat, sipping his broth, and the Gift reached out, showing that he sat at the place of a fallen Captain. He stirred uneasily.

Kalanin introduced each of the Captains, adding a few words of what each had accomplished. Then he spoke of the death of Baron Cadmon, of the broken army, of their regrouping, their raids, the trap that had been set for them, and lastly of their fight against the Dark Emissary, a battle where Envar had perished.

"That Power would surely have prevailed," added the eagle, "but it knew little of men. Perhaps its knowledge of men came from ages ago when mortals lived in fear of the Creatures of the Darkness."

"But we did prevail," Kalanin continued, "and now we'll grow stronger every day. Not powerful enough to break the siege about Gravengate, but strong enough to challenge those supporting the siege."

"Everything the Baron might have achieved, we've done," Dargas commented.

"You haven't mentioned the gifts sent by Merlin," said Julian. "I tried to protect them, but they might easily have been destroyed."

"They're safe, and well hidden, in a half day's ride from here," said Kalanin. "We'll go tomorrow if you choose. But now, tell us if you will, of yourself — and what you can of our other companions." Julian's eyes passed over the circle of faces; the Gift showed him the doubts of Dargas. He began slowly, haltingly:

"In the ruined tower, while you slept, our foes struck what should have been a deathblow. Their leading wolf was no beast, but a werewolf, and also an Adept and powerful Magician. It was he, I think, who launched that Great Spell against us." Julian looked to their faces to see if they understood.

"We know of Great Spells and Sendings," said Kalanin gently, "the Eye has taught us a little." Julian went on to tell them of the Hall of the Dreamers, his pursuit by the wolf creature, and how the Dreamers had intervened when called by Julian's adversary. The mouth of Dargas hung open in disbelief, but the Eye silenced him with a rustle of his wings.

"That was bold of our foes to send this *thing* to a Servant's haven," said the eagle. "What was the fate of this Adept?"

"At the end, they sought to heal him," said Julian. Dargas' mouth began to slip open again in surprise. Julian laughed, a roll of pure humor that had seldom been heard in any tier camp.

"There will be more surprises for all of us," Julian continued, then he grew more solemn. "The Dreamers told us to seek for Merlin, that he was not dead, but captured or hidden." He turned to the Eye. "Do you know anything about this?"

"Merlin passed from my sight after the disaster at Sea's Edge," said the eagle, neck bristling in surprise. "It is a shock to learn that he lives, while cut off from me.... How has this happened?" The Eye of Merlin trailed off, and the small, enchanted mind of the eagle raced in thought. Harlond leaned forward to question Julian, but Kalanin waved him to silence. Julian leaned back, watching their faces: Kalanin and Dargas were both strong willed, yet seemed able to defer to the emissary of Merlin. The eagle came out of his trance, his beak and neck turning to Julian.

"Why do they continue to call you an Apprentice?" asked the eagle.

"That has been my true level among the wielders of magic," Julian replied. "Of some matters of sorcery, I know much, while of other matters — like *The Game of the Masters*— I know less than Kalanin."

"There's some device here," the eagle said softly. "It may be that your true powers have been masked, or perhaps the Gift has grown within you.... You did not know the mind of Merlin, none of you watched as Merlin played the role of Master, thinking levels even deeper than those of his brilliant Mid-World opponents. He may be gone or captured, but it was no sloppy, poorly conceived move that sent you forward followed by the gifts of Merlin. Do you understand these matters?"

Kalanin nodded. "I'm no student of the *Game*, but I wondered if Merlin had intended those gifts for Julian's use."

"Just a moment," said Dargas. "Not only am I not a student of this *Game*, but I don't have the slightest idea what you're talking about. Are you talking of Merlin, or of this lad's powers or of the trinkets? Or of all three?"

"The Eye thinks that the devices we buried might help us, perhaps even to find Merlin," explained Kalanin. "He wonders if Julian has the power to wield them."

Dargas grunted. "So, no harm in sending a little party out to dig in the swamp," he said. "In the meantime, we can mount another raid."

Rostov shook his head. "If I understand all of what's been said, Thorian and Nergal will not wish Julian to intersect with these things." Rostov turned to the eagle. "Is this correct?"

"Not only will they try to prevent this junction," said the eagle, "but if you divide your forces, then the Dark Emissary will again fall upon you. If we go in any direction, we should all go, even the smiths and cooks."

"And it may all be for nothing," said Julian, "but I should examine these devices if the Eye suggests it. So, first the tools of Merlin, then a search for Merlin and our friends, then last, the testing of the siege of Gravengate."

Dargas sat upright. "The last is a matter for considerable debate," he muttered. "That's how the Baron was broken — going straight up against them. But otherwise, it may do us all good to get away from here."

·))((·

They massed early the next morning, taking their force of more than twelve tiers — more than six thousand fighting men — along the winding pathways that led to the swamps. Morning winds had blown the sky clear, except for a few billowy clouds that floated over the distant horizon. For Julian, with the light of the universe fresh in his eyes, everything was new and full of wonder — the feel of Bluescent under him, with the wind in his face, blue skies, and drooping grasses about him — like a child, he discovered them and was amazed. When they halted at late morning, many of their fighters lay in the sun drowsing, but Julian walked through the fields among the wildflowers, viewing them in wonder. Dargas snorted, watching the Apprentice from beneath a tree.

"If he had wings, he would be flitting away among the buttercups," Dargas muttered. "Look at him! He's got a mind like fresh Dragon's turd — sorcerous maybe, but still mushy." Kalanin, nearby, moved to Dargas' side.

"That's how it seemed at the ford," said Kalanin. "Then —"

"Wait!" Dargas interrupted. "I was only muttering to myself — I've nothing against your Apprentice. Indeed, I've been to the eagle's school for humble diplomats."

Kalanin laughed. "I'd have given a small sack of gold to have been at your lesson." They remounted and rode slowly forward behind the tier mass.

"Is this all just for exercise?" asked Dargas. "Or will they truly move to stop us?"

"Have they not challenged every step we've taken?" Kalanin replied. "Keep those around you alert; there's likely to be some counterstrike." Tier forces moved forward again, their pace growing swifter as noon approached.

The masses of men that rode beside Julian tended to drift away from the Apprentice — the youth was strange, distant, otherworldly. As for Julian, the hard warriors about him were only a small distraction. His mind wandered through the waters of the Cup of the Maker, into the Hall of the Dreamers, or it reached to the moon's surface, watching the clear splendor of the starry universe.

Yet even as he rode, distractions seemed to mount, and at last Julian understood: a warning was being given by his Gift. His eyes focused on the men walking or riding about them; they seemed to be most at ease when they were far away from him. Long columns of men were astride the road, but many others trampled over nearby fields and meadows. Kalanin and Dargas rode together, talking easily together. The Gift reached out; Julian slowed as he concentrated. Men passed, giving the Apprentice a wide berth, staring at him curiously.

About Julian, there were many small eyes, eyes of small creatures that should have fled at their coming: the eyes of the Mid-World. He looked up into the blue skies of Alantéa — only the eagle shape was distinct, but other flying creatures watched them from a distance. As he stared about him, the eagle began to descend, in a spiral, coming to rest on Julian's shoulder — and the eagle was much heavier than Sebastian.

"Are you back now, Apprentice?" asked the eagle. "Do you feel the Watchers?"

"They were never this bold when Merlin held power," Julian murmured. "Hundreds of them — the many eyes of the Mid-World. Are they around at all times?" The eagle croaked a harsh laugh.

"They have not bothered with us to this extent before, for we were only a small matter, while the clash of power at Gravengate drew thousands of Mid-World eyes. But now we have attracted their attention, perhaps because of the Dark Emissary, perhaps because of some new danger. Welcome back to Alantéa, Apprentice! Polish your staff! Scramble your spells! As for the Mid-World Spies, they had best stay clear of me." The eagle leaped back into the skies, jarring Julian's shoulder.

A sense of menace began to develop around their many tiers. Men began to slow as growls of thunder rolled in from distant hills. The air grew tight with tension, as though readying for discharges of power. The stench of dark sorcery hovered about them. Julian's mouth opened in surprise, and he slowed.

"The League has faltered, but what is this?" Those about him paid no attention. Messengers were beginning to pass among the tiers. The Eye came to rest on Kalanin's shoulder. Men began to form tier lines, muttering curses at the brush and boulders around them. Julian pushed forward.

"Is it the same one?" Kalanin was asking the Eye.

"No, it's not the Dark Emissary — it's another, perhaps worse, perhaps more easily opposed."

"Do you mean that they've done this before?" asked Julian. Thunder grew louder as the disturbance neared.

"Yes!" muttered Dargas, with a grim face. "But now we're mounted. Let's see it hold against two hundred mailed men and horses. We'll leave it dying in the dust!"

"Pikemen," Kalanin said to Rurak. "I'll lead the archers." The captain nodded and raced away.

The first flickers of the Portal appeared in the sky. Again, a storm lurked beyond it. Julian edged toward the Portal, his hand fumbling in Bluescent's pouch.

Suddenly, the great arch of power flickered into life, with sounds of warfare within and beyond it.

"A battle of the Portals — again!" cried the eagle.

"We'll ride the filthy thing down!" Dargas yelled to the mounted force. Julian slipped from Bluescent, taking a handful of powder in his hand, racing toward the Portal. Rain swept over him.

"He's crazier than a rabid rat!" Dargas called out. Julian closed the distance. Light and power flashed from the Portal. He hurled the dust into the great arch. A great concussion destroyed the Portal, hurling Julian backward. The great arch vanished, tremors of aftershock rattling the ground where it had stood.

The massed tiers stood frozen in their ranks. Julian, the Apprentice, stood up and began dusting himself off. Dargas, sword in hand, rode slowly toward the Apprentice, an unhappy look of disbelief clouding his face.

"You mean, that's all there is to it?"

Julian nodded. "They would not even have dared such a Portal had a Wizard been among us." He remounted Bluescent. "Also, I could not have stopped the Creature, if others had not fought it." He looked for the Eye of Merlin.

"If it's that easy," muttered Dargas, shaking his head, "then I and my warriors are in the wrong Maker cursed business." The Eye of Merlin came forward, riding on Kalanin's shoulder.

"Who of the Mid-World would help us?" asked Kalanin.

"They battled before," the eagle replied, "but they were forced to give way. I believe that there were two of them."

"An old Sorceress helped us at the beginning," Julian said uncertainly.

"They were both mortals," said the eagle. "One, at least, was a woman. But we should proceed with our tasks. Kalanin tells me that this journey is an unwieldy, tiring exercise for the tiers."

It was early afternoon as they reached the edges of the bog. Men looked askance at the masses of grey water that were seeping from dreary marshlands. Kalanin turned to Julian and the Eye of Merlin.

"Bad ground to fight on," he noted. "Do we need the tiers?"

"We're alone," Julian said, watching the marshlands carefully, "except for the eyes of the Mid-World."

"Our enemies have had their turn," added the eagle. "We will make the next move." Twenty men with spades were chosen to accompany their captains. As their party rode through the bog, Harlond noted the looks of distaste passing over the faces of the digging party, and he laughed.

"You've joined the noble order of swamp creatures," he told them. "Rurak, Kalanin and I are cofounders. Dargas is an honorary member."

"We've an emblem too," Rurak added. "Dried but still stinking muckworms pinned to our cloaks."

"It was their finest moment, down there in the pits," Dargas murmured with a smile.

Julian was at the rear of the digging party, watching Bluescent struggle through the mire. He patted her flanks to encourage her, and soon they were climbing up toward higher ground, then up to the top of a low hill. As yet there was no scent of sorcery: the chest had been well concealed. The winged eyes of the Mid-World hovered from a distance, with no clear idea of their quarry's destination.

On the hilltop, Rurak and Harlond slipped from their horses and began to trace an outline in the sand. The eagle nodded in agreement: no visible signs could be seen, but this was the place. To Julian, no strength or power of sorcery could be sensed. Teams of men, six at a time, began to move mounds of earth, each team giving way to a fresh one as it tired. The chest sent by Merlin was quickly unearthed. Kalanin shook his head, recalling their previous effort.

"I only wish you had been here before," he said softly.

Now the chest was out of the ground, dripping mud on a patch of green grass. Julian knelt beside it, clearing wet soil carefully from its carefully inscribed surface. Rostov brought forward a bowl of clear water and a clean cloth, handing them reverentially to Julian, as an acolyte might to a priest.

In a few minutes, the chest stood openly in the sunlight, now mostly clean, with all its intricate inscriptions clear and distinct. Julian felt the force of the spell that sealed the chest but could think of no counter. Gravely, and carefully, Kalanin took a slight double chain from his neck, and on it was linked a lone bronze key. He passed it to Julian. The Apprentice held it up to the sunlight, then turned back to Kalanin.

"This may be the real reason that the Dark Emissary was sent for you," he said softly. "With this, the location of the chest might have been discovered." Kalanin nodded but said nothing. Julian opened the chest carefully: inside were four velvet pouches, dark blue in color, each of them strongly sealed. Only one of the pouches was of any size, and this was as large as a small sack of grain, one that might be held with one hand.

With a cry, the Eye of Merlin leaped into the air. Julian looked up: the eyes of the Mid-World had become overly curious, drawing closer to the chest. Now, they fled from the great eagle's talons.

"Is it wise to show these so openly?" asked Kalanin.

"They are hidden devices, masked by sorcery," Julian replied. "If one with the Sight were to touch them, that being might learn more than we would like him to know. Now, give me a few moments to study these." Julian took a clean blanket from Harlond and set each of the four pouches out on it. It would be foolhardy to open them, but the Gift might show him a little of the nature of these devices. He knelt on the carpet, putting both hands out to touch the first pouch...

...a device for Portals...perhaps an escape hatch for the trapped magic wielder...not a Great Spell...but a subtle one that might be used for several purposes...

...the second was sorcery, powerful sorcery created by a Lord of Dragons! In thousands of tiny parts, assembled in the largest pouch... Dragon seed mixed with Wizard's magic stirred with metal...

...the third was cold and dark, as empty as an airless void with no stars...his hands could not touch it for long, or he would be drawn into nothingness...

...in the fourth pouch, a Power stirred, ready to wake and serve if called properly...Julian's hand drew back quickly....

His eyes opened, and he stood so he could wipe the beads of sweat that formed on his forehead. No wonder the Magicians looked old before their time! Silently, he repacked the pouches. Then, he cleared a patch in the loose dry earth, and knelt beside it, lost in thought, placing pebbles in patterns over the loose ground. After a few moments, he cleared the patterns of the stones from the soil and stood, looking up at many faces. The eagle was highest, perched again on Kalanin's shoulder.

"The first is a lesser spell and may be of some use to us," Julian said quietly. "The second spell I might use as a last, desperate measure. Use of the last two spells would probably result in our destruction. None of these instruments points to Merlin."

The eagle broke the silence that followed. "Then we will not overwhelm our enemies, nor can you be expected to do everything, Apprentice. *The Game of the Masters* has far too many pieces moving over its enormous Field." Kalanin looked up at the sky: it was early afternoon and overcast. It was unfortunate that their expectations had been so high.

"We're still so much better off," he said easily. "We've built a force of arms and held off the Dark Emissary. Now, we have an Apprentice with an Adept's power. It would be tedious, even boring if Julian could solve all our problems so easily. Let's return to camp."

Those on horseback rode back to their camp at a good pace, letting those on foot journey more slowly. Kalanin and the Eye of Merlin rode beside Julian, talking every now and again as the rough parts of their journey evened out.

"Will you seek for Merlin tonight?" asked the eagle.

"A brief test, perhaps," Julian replied. "And yet I'm more likely to be able to reach Sebastian and Rafir, or Galad." Kalanin's face eased at this comment. They reached level roads and increased their pace so that they reached their camp well before sunset.

Through the last hours of sunlight, and into the evening, a party of men worked with Julian, clearing, and leveling a great oval patch of ground. Sub-tiers were still returning at nightfall, and they called out in jest to those who were hacking away at the brush. With the fall of night, a perimeter guard began to clear men from the area, and the sounds around those working groups lessened. They finished by torchlight, long after the last rays of sun had passed. The oval clearing was seventy five paces at its longest width, and fifty at its shortest diameter. All the trees and small brush and rocks were gone, but green grasses still flourished in patches.

Julian drew back, examining his work. All was well — in theory; he had never tried this spell before. He thanked his helpers and dismissed them. With his staff, he traced the oval's edge, sealing the field. Now would come the first test; everyone was back far enough. He stood outside the oval and cast a mix of goblinrush and dried kobold blood into the center — and the great oval burst into flames. The fire drove Julian back, and he shielded his face with a cloaked arm. In a moment, the fire had burned out, and the green grasses within the oval were replaced by grey ash. Darkness surged back over the campground.

A critical time had come: if he had judged rightly, the Portal Talisman would be the focus of his energy field. Carefully, reverently, he drew the first of the velvet pouches from the chest sent by Merlin. Men were beginning to drift toward the oval; the few guards were not able to keep them away. Kalanin called out the second watch of seventy five, and Julian waited as grumbling guards moved into place.

Then the Apprentice carried the gifts of Merlin into the oval's center. From the velvet pouch, he drew a shape of metalwork and set it down in the grey dust: it was small, not higher than the hand of a child, but even in dim light, Julian could see that it glittered, and was intricate in design and craft. Like a tiny temple, the figure had a single, round dome, but it was eight sided with each metal side showing a different door.

Julian knelt, examining the Portal Talisman. No doubt it had been intended to permit easy access to the many kingdoms of the Mid-World. But he would put it to a different use — if his strength of magic was great enough. Cautiously, Julian carved a small rune of power in front of each of the eight tiny doors, then he stood back as he finished the last of them.

The edges of the great oval began to light where Julian's staff had traced the ground. His footprints vanished from the dust of the oval. The air grew sharp with the pull of energy; it would work.

"See if the Eye of Merlin will join me," he called out to Kalanin. "Warn everyone — *do not cross the lines of the oval.*" He began to inscribe the oval with diagrams of power...these lit as soon as Julian's staff lifted from them. The eagle came forward and paused at the oval's edge. Julian walked over quickly and extended his staff beyond the barrier. The eagle grasped the staff with his powerful talons and was drawn through to Julian's shoulder. Magician and Familiar conferred for a moment; within the oval a distant hum had started as though many energies were drawing closer. Kalanin called the officer of the guard to his side.

"We should keep everyone well back," he said quietly. "It's bad for soldiers to see too much of sorcery — and the Apprentice is not sure what he's doing. Best to be far back." Kalanin stood with the guard, watching the great oval glow. For a time, the figure of the Apprentice could be seen with the eagle on his shoulder. But later, these images became less clear as a hazy glow grew within the circle so that those who looked on imagined that they were watching a far seascape, with no sight of land. Though the images of the oval became dimmer, the sounds from within were much clearer; men in the camp could now hear murmurings and mutterings, and groans of many forces that had been summoned against their will. Some of the warriors began to slip back to their tents, while others moved toward weapon racks.

Within the oval, Julian stood uncertainly, at an intersection of power, wondering whether to attempt his most challenging task first, or whether to try the easiest.

"Do what you must, Apprentice," murmured the eagle. "I will guard your back." Julian wiped his brow with his sleeve.

"We'll test for Merlin, then," he said, raising his voice over the hum of power and the cries of unwilling spirits. "But I can't imagine that it will be easy." Julian closed his eyes, letting the Gift search for him. Every now and again, he called out the Wizard's name in a faint voice...but no answer came. He opened his eyes and began to pull free.

"I'm afraid there's noth —" he broke off, for to his amazement, a Portal was opening before him. *"I* could not have called this!" he cried. The Portal was as high as a tall man, and it opened into nothing but blue sky, with a flourish of clouds rolling in the distance. Julian took a step forward.

"Watch, Apprentice!" snarled the eagle. The Portal vanished. Another Portal leaped into being beside the first, but this one showed swirling dark, turbulent waters.

"Stand back!" cried the eagle. Julian stepped back to his original place. The second Portal vanished; another Portal formed, again to one side, and this showed the starlit night skies of Alantéa. The eagle's talons were dug deep into Julian's shoulder, but now they began to ease their grip.

"Best to break this off," murmured the eagle. Julian's staff flickered, and the third Portal vanished. The Apprentice leaned on his staff, breathing hard.

"Merlin's too far from us," whispered Julian. "Or he's separated, dispersed...what's next?"

"Try for the warrior," replied the eagle, "if you have the strength."

Outside the oval, Kalanin waited in silence, staring at the night sky. The oval field was still a hazy mass, with surges of power and tension flashing at intervals. Just after midnight, there came a lull, and the lights of the oval dimmed, with voice sound fading to a low hum. The Eye of Merlin stepped out of the haze, and walked slowly, warily toward Kalanin.

"The Apprentice has failed twice," said the eagle, "though his efforts were valiant." Kalanin drew a deep breath.

"It was too much to hope for. What happened?"

"We tested for Merlin, and found only mystery," said the eagle. "We sought Galad and found him...but the way is blocked. The warrior lives, at the farthest reaches of the Mid-World. A Power stands astride the Portal, and it will not be moved. It might yield to Merlin, or Balardi — it is not one of the great Dark Lords — but it will not yield to the Apprentice." The eagle looked back into the spell haze. "I, even I, am afraid of that collision of magics. We are moving into the sorcerous unknown, and the Apprentice is risking himself. We will try once again, this time for the small ones, but you should stand farther back, for events might easily turn against us." The eagle walked slowly back to the oval, and the staff of Julian appeared at the edge, drawing the eagle back into the sorcerous haze.

Now, Julian stood once again in the center of the great oval. His face was grey with fatigue, and he took deep breaths of air, readying himself for a final effort. At the spell's edge, the haze formed walls, creating a vast oval chamber, while above, a cup of stars covered it like a vast dome. Behind Julian, the Eye of Merlin watched warily as the Apprentice straightened.

Julian leaned forward, shaping a new rune at the side of the Portal mechanism. Lights within the oval flickered as energies once again flowed to the Apprentice. The hum deepened. He bent his mind to Sebastian and Rafir...their Seeking Stones were calling to him.

From a great distance of time and space, Julian watched the dim images of Magician and Monster as they moved toward the strange, stony museum. The next second, the Gift within Julian flashed to the Seeking Stones...they were glowing in the darkness, green and bright. The staff in his hand surged with power. Julian reached across the years. In the museum, the Seeking Stones dropped to the floor. A Portal formed. His small friends were at the other end. He reached with his staff, drawing them — but then the eagle gave a great cry of warning — and surprise!

A powerful hand gently but firmly grasped Julian's arm, then another hand reached into the Jade Portal. The images of Sebastian and Rafir disappeared. The oval spell collapsed, leaving Julian kneeling on grey dust, gasping in surprise. He rose and staggered to the edge. Kalanin stepped quickly toward him.

"It was madness to test the Portal Spell!" Julian cried. "Nothing went right — they were taken from me! But I had them!" There was something in his staff's hand. He looked down, peering into his open palm — in it was the signet ring of their ally, Balardi. He looked up into the stress filled face of Kalanin.

"Balardi has taken them, but why? What's the purpose? Why should he do this?"

Chapter Eleven
The Siege

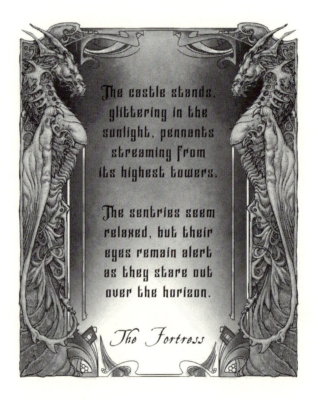

The castle stands, glittering in the sunlight, pennants streaming from its highest towers.

The sentries seem relaxed, but their eyes remain alert as they stare out over the horizon.

—*The Fortress*

SEBASTIAN CLUTCHED RAFIR'S FUR, WATCHING as the Portal grew, shining green and inviting in the darkness of the museum. Before him, the vague figure of Julian loomed at the Portal's end. And Julian's staff was extended, reaching for him. Sebastian glanced back. Magician and Monster were facing him, as though willing him to stop. But no power in Alantéa would stop him now! He tensed, as did Rafir. Julian was reaching, calling to them — and they leaped through the green Jade Portal, racing as though through a tunnel toward the Apprentice.

Suddenly, the Portal groaned and wrenched. Sebastian cried out in fear — their enemies had struck again!

"Julian!" he cried and let go of Rafir. The fox vanished as quickly as a firefly on a dark night. Sebastian sprang to one side, ready to flee for his life again.

Before them, massive and powerful, stood a great bearded man, with gold and grey hair flying in all directions, eyes red, his face strained. But when he spoke, it was in a calm, clear voice.

"I do not know your friend the fox, but I remember...." The voice paused for a moment, for the walls were trembling around them. "I remember you from years ago when you first journeyed with Julian. You were young then and liked to glide around the upper beams of our fortress, peering out from its highest windows," and he pointed above them to the upper reaches of the great chamber where the windows glinted black in the darkness. The little Familiar looked about him, eyes still wide; yet he no longer drew away from the Wizard.

"Balardi...." Sebastian breathed the name out slowly. "But it was Julian who searched for us."

"It *was* Julian," said the Wizard, moving to the chamber's entrance. "These and other things I will begin to explain if you will walk with me for a brief time." He turned back to the empty chamber adding quietly, "You should join us, sir fox." The walls had stopped shaking, and after a second, the soft feet of the fox came padding warily after the forms of Wizard and Familiar.

They passed through corridors lit dimly by a few torches fastened against stone walls. At each intersection, a man at arms stood, tapping the butt of his spear to the ground as they passed. Along the corridors, and about the fortress hung a smell of burning and decay. The fox, sniffing the air, hesitated in confusion — beyond the strong smells of death and destruction, and the presence of many men, there were other, even stranger smells. He padded quickly to catch up with Balardi and Sebastian.

The castle seemed huge, holding many scores of men camped in a warren of chambers on either side of the passageways. Men quieted as the Wizard passed, lowering, or stilling their voices. Those casting dice threw cloths over them until the Wizard had passed.

Sebastian and Rafir followed the Wizard out of the tower's base into a vast keep. Within the walls of the fortress were many hundreds of other warriors camped on the ground under open skies. It was night, and only a few torches lessened the darkness, but sentries saluted Balardi as he passed. It was several hundred paces from the tower to the outer walls, but the distance seemed much longer as they picked their way through weapon racks, and tent ropes, and large casting engines of war.

At the foot of Gravengate's outer walls, Balardi began to climb, Sebastian and Rafir following slowly, feeling their way in the darkness. At the top, armed guards made no move to salute, but kept their nightly vigil in motionless silence. In a few places, the walls were just high enough for a man's head and shoulders to rise over the top and see beyond the fortress walls. Balardi stood by one of these gaps, and he looked out, saying nothing.

Rafir and Sebastian climbed to the top of the walls, peering out over the Plain of Gravengate. What they saw left them openmouthed with amazement: before them on all sides were a series of vast circles, surrounding the fortress walls. The Plain was choked with their enemies, and in the darkness, thousands of torches lit the tent cities of the besieging armies. Torches, sentries, and tents were set back a distance from the walls, beyond the reach of bowshot or rock-casting machines. Sebastian found his breath, at last, drawing in musty night air before he spoke.

"This was a beautiful land, filled with gardens, and small farms and orchards. What has happened?" Rafir looked up at the face of Balardi — it was filled with a rage so that the Wizard's hand clenched and tightened. Now, as Sebastian's eyes became fully attuned to the darkness, he saw that many huge shapes were lying just outside the fortress walls. All these enormous bodies lay still, and lifeless.

Rafir whispered to Sebastian: "Look down below. There's a thing with two heads...and the one next to it has horns — on both ends!" Beneath them was a great jumble of wings and scales, and horns and talons, lying still in the darkness. No scavenger was yet bold enough to approach them, and the great bodies lay drying and rotting in the moonlight. At last, Balardi broke his silence.

"Yes, it has been monster against monster and man against man, and sorcery against sorcery. And the land has suffered." His voice rose. "Curse them! Curse Thorian who was a brother Wizard! Curse this Nergal who is an evil Adversary of the Maker!" Balardi stood in the moonlight, his hair, and eyes fierce and wild, his hands resting on the ramparts. His voice lowered for a moment. "Nergal called me woman slayer and stealer of the young, while Thorian accused me of holding his child, in my deepest dungeons. These things I denied, astonished, but in no friendly manner, for they marched upon me with all their weapons of war, forcing my people to flee or seek refuge in my fortress.

"I asked, 'What is this madness to me? I know of no child. I have slain no being that did not assail me first. Come alone, singly, and all that I have can be seen by you.' But they did not respond; instead, they sent images to me, images created by divinations, showing that I had done these evil things.

How did their divination, which is compelled to show the truth, become so perverted? It seems to me now that it was this Nergal, this evil corrupter!" His voice rose again. "Curse him for an Adversary of the Maker, and curse Thorian for a fool!" His voice rose so that it filled the night sky.

"*Curse and blast them for what they have done to my people!! Curse and blast them for what they have done to the land!!*" Shaking with rage, Balardi's hand twitched and drew something out of the night air, and he hurled it at his enemies.

In the dark stillness came the sounds of a distant explosion, followed by shouts and curses, then a hail of arrows sped toward the Wizard. Sebastian and Rafir leaped to the walkway, but Balardi stood facing his adversaries, with arrows falling away from him harmlessly.

When they moved on, Balardi seemed calmer. "No power have I, nor can I muster greater force from within these walls, to break this siege. First, I hoped that the League would come, with Merlin arriving in a chariot of fire, but Merlin is gone, perhaps subdued by some Power of the Mid-World. Then, I hoped that Baron Cadmon would end the siege, but the Seraph broke his forces." The Wizard paused, shaking his head. "How might I have known that our adversaries had such powerful servants? Alas for Baron Cadmon! Alas for the Wizards and their League when there is no Merlin! But do not say, 'Alas for Balardi,' for I am not yet done!"

He looked down at Sebastian and Rafir as though remembering his audience for the first time. "No, they will never say, 'Alas for Balardi,' they will say, 'Beware of the Mad Wizard.' And mad or not, I forget common courtesy in my ramblings." He smiled down at them for a moment. "How can you tell Servants from Adversaries if the Servants are not, at least, considerate? You have returned from a grave peril of your own, and I've offered you neither food nor rest. Let's at least provide food." They began to descend from the upper walls, walking back through tangles of sleeping men and stationary guards. Despite all the new smells and sounds, Rafir wondered if they had not been better off back at the museum.

It was now well beyond midnight. In the long storage rooms of the kitchens of Gravengate, Sebastian picked among the canisters, drawing fruit for Rafir and a bowl of shelled nuts for himself. The Wizard sat on a stool while they ate, his eyes staring into the distance. After finishing, the fox nosed about the kitchen areas, as he might have explored a new burrow. Massive quantities of food were stored ceiling high, enough to feed guards and servants of the fortress for many months, but hardly enough to provision the army that now lay within the fortress walls. Rafir hesitated, seeking some way to ask the Wizard without offending him, but Balardi perceived the thought of Julian's small companion, and he smiled.

"There are great storerooms beneath us, and if these become exhausted, there are other ways, through sorcery, to provide for the soldiery. No, I may lose this war, sometime, but not by famine." The Wizard paused for a moment, watching Sebastian and Rafir closely.

"Now, watch. You must remember all that I tell you and all that you will see — you *must* remember, for one of you may be telling Julian what I cannot." Rising, Balardi cleared one of the larger cutting boards of the kitchen.

"Let us begin with the Siege," he said, and from a pouch at his side, he took a handful of fine powder and cast it over the table. After a moment, the dust began to glow, then a clear image formed, showing Balardi's fortress, and a portion of the vast plain of Gravengate. For a few moments, the castle stood shining in the sunlight, then quickly there came a flurry of motion, activity of the guard, as the gates opened, then first scores, then hundreds of armed men pressed their way through the gates, followed by many wagons bearing provisions.

Then the image of the castle faded, and a picture of the south edge of the plain formed. There, pouring over the hilled edge of the Plain were tier forces many times larger than the ones seeking refuge in the castle. Then the image of the fortress was renewed: before the great carved gates of the castle, two figures stood, inviting parlay. Sebastian recognized one.

"That is the image of Thorian," he murmured.

"Yes," Balardi murmured. "Mark the other beside him." Thorian seemed taller than Balardi, yet slimmer, with a long dark cloak and a beard of shining silver. The one beside him had the bearing of a powerful noble, with dark hair, tall as Thorian, but his face peered forward, like that of a hawk.

"Behold Nergal, the dark Sorcerer," said Balardi. In a moment, the images of Wizard and Sorcerer were joined by the figure of Balardi, splendid, golden looking, less haggard then, and there was far less grey in his beard. Rafir looked carefully at the three wielders of magic: three princes of sorcery stood before the walls, radiating power, but each was very different from the others. Balardi spoke again in a low voice.

"I judge either of these to be my equal in power, perhaps greater than I am." The image of the three powers faded and that of the fortress formed once again. "I will not show you the ruin of the land, for it would only move me to anger once again. Here is the story of the Siege. Watch closely."

As Sebastian and Rafir watched in astonishment, the images of battle formed and reformed, with great siege towers mounted in warfare against the walls, Monsters struggling before the gates, sheets of arrows clouding the skies, engines of war catapulting boulders, war in the air with clouds of fire and storm and hacking, stabbing, and bleeding. Men lay dead around broken siege towers while wounded creatures crawled away, bellowing through sunset and into darkness before death took them away, forever. But through the many days of the struggle, the lines of the fortress reformed its damaged walls and towers restored. At last, the lines began to fade, but Balardi held his hands over the image.

"There is one more thing that perhaps you should know." Then the image formed of an eagle, flying serenely in the upper air; but suddenly the image was shaken as a massive, winged serpent struck at it. "Did you know about the eagle?" asked Balardi. Sebastian hesitated.

"Merlin was supposed to have some Farsighted winged servant...."

"Yes," said Balardi, keeping his voice low. "This war has forced the Eye of Merlin from his hidden errands. But he is overmatched." They watched as the eagle fled from the plumed serpents. Sebastian felt a knot of fear form in his own small stomach.

"These others are the Watchers," whispered Balardi, "the greatest of many small sentinels. These hold the Siege so tightly that I am unable to call upon messengers from the Mid-World." They saw the winged serpents dive and strike at a dark shadow that sped over the grass. "The eyes of the Mid-World are blinded now, and they hover at the edge of the plain, seeking to learn of this mortal contest from afar, for none may depart or enter the walls of Gravengate."

Rafir felt a sudden flash race across his small, enchanted mind — so this was the reason they had been summoned! The images of the eagle and winged serpents faded, and light began to seep back into the room.

"You have seen that the power raised against me, of men, and Mid-World servants and sorcery, is far greater than my own. Many are asking, 'how has Balardi held?' Perhaps my enemies believe that Merlin is hidden here, aiding me, but he is not. An *Ancient Secret* lies hidden within Gravengate, one that goes back to its beginning. I have told no one, yet I believe that Merlin knew. At the beginning when I first considered the foundations of Gravengate —"

A sudden knock at the door interrupted the Wizard. Balardi strode swiftly to the entrance and jerked the door open. "What's happened?" he asked quickly. The captain of the guard was a woman, tall and mailed. Water ran down her long, dark hair.

"Lord, it rains," she said.

"Follow!" said Balardi, and he strode swiftly out, through the passageway, down a flight of stairs, and out into the night air. He stared up into the streaming night sky, water running down his grim face, then the Wizard relaxed, and began to laugh. He turned to the captain, still laughing.

"Tell the others to fear the water — but only for the rust that it brings." The captain looked down at the small guests of Balardi for a moment, and then she saluted and was gone. Balardi turned to Sebastian and Rafir. "I have struggled with my enemies over the weather, and so we entered a long stalemate, a dry hesitation. Now comes the rain, but from no outside intervention. It is the ancient hand of the First Fashioners that has at last broken the stalemate. It should be a lesson to all the fancy Powers who claim lordship over the world!" The Wizard laughed again, letting the water run through his grey and gold hair.

Sebastian sneezed from the dampness and the cold. Balardi looked down at him.

"There's more to tell you of the Siege, but rather than mumbling to you in the dampness, I'll let another tell the tale, in a place where it's dry."

Balardi returned to the tower, gathering a torch from a standard on the wall, leading them through a series of passageways and stairs, always downward and deeper into the base of the fortress. Down at the deepest level, the Wizard drew a key from about his neck; Sebastian noted that the key's metal was ancient, flecked with rust. The oaken door creaked open, and Balardi led them through. They entered a chamber that was barren of furnishings except for one wooden chair with a high back that stood alone in the center. Against one wall was a great support pillar of the fortress, and at the base of the pillar was a massive cornerstone, carved with many runes. Sebastian peered at the inscriptions closely, as they were unlike any he had seen in the service of the League.

With a start, the little Familiar felt the presence of a great Power within the chamber. The fox also halted, as though he had smelled something strange. Balardi sat on the chair, stretching his legs out, as though settling down to speak with an old friend.

"Hail, Ancient One," said the Wizard. "I have brought two guests to meet with you. Will you greet them?" A voice spoke to Rafir and Sebastian gently, into their minds, a clear whisper, with an echo of wind chimes.

Greetings, little Servants of the Maker. It was well done to escape the Last Magician and the Last Sending.

"Thank you, Lord," murmured Sebastian.

"I thank you also," added Rafir, looking about, "and I would attempt a bow if I knew where you were — or what you were." The Wizard laughed, sitting in his chair, but he said nothing. The voice came back into their minds.

I am...Gravengate, and before that I was one with the stone that lies before you. In the beginning, I was of the Spirit Lords, a Fashioner, and Servant of the Maker. But many Servants and Adversaries fell in the early struggles. A triple strength of mighty Demon Princes struck me down, and I sank slowly, gravely wounded, toward the Temple of Waiting, where the Immortals gather, dreaming of the Maker's Return. Yet, a fraction of my strength remained, and I sought refuge, here in the stone, healing slowly over the many ages.

"The Ancient One is near his full strength," added Balardi, "and in the fullness of his power, I believe he was among the most potent of Spirit Lords. Here at Gravengate neither Wizard nor Sorcerer nor corrupted Seraph has proved able to master him."

Soon I must assume my old form. Even now, I yearn to be gone, to depart Earth, and seek the Maker in the starry universe. Yet I hold for a little while longer, so that the Adversaries may not triumph. Also, I am troubled by what I see in your minds. You were cast to the uttermost edge of time when the First

Energies have run down to a feeble force. Tell me of this time, and this strange land.

Sebastian spoke for a little while, telling in a faltering voice of the great engines, and air that was filled with ash, and the absence of sorcerous energies. A time of silence followed as the Ancient One considered Sebastian's tale.

Is this the design of the Maker? It does not seem right. Might this be the final resolution of the early conflicts? I pity mankind, born into confusion, and fear of the Creatures of the Darkness. It is no wonder that they have learned such violence, and this violence will haunt them after their assailants have passed from Earth. After, they will fall upon one another with their sharp weapons and complex machineries. I pity mankind, born onto a battlefield. If I reach the Maker, I will ask him to send aid or counselors.

"It is good that the Ancient One can see beyond our current struggles, and to the future of all humans," said Balardi. "But for myself, I can grasp only the needs of Gravengate and the League. I see that we will be overwhelmed after the Ancient One departs. That is why we must break the Siege. That is why you were summoned."

"You called *us* to break the Siege?" Rafir exclaimed.

It was I who urged Balardi to bring you. From its beginning, the Siege has been so tightly reinforced that no messengers can be sent, and we cannot reach beyond our walls, no matter how great our power.

"Yet there are things that can be seen if one has the Sight," said Balardi. "Of your company, only Kalanin remained after the attack, and over time he has forged a potent force of many tiers. Of you, we knew little except that the fabric of power was stretched, and you were cast to the end of all magic, to the very last moments of sorcerous energies. Of Julian, we foresaw his return from a Servant's haven. But Galad remains sealed off from us, locked away in a far land."

You cannot triumph without the other warrior, for a tale of power surrounds him. But his way is blocked by a lesser Dark Lord of the Mid-World. We cannot reach Galad because of the Siege, while Julian cannot reach Galad, as he has not the power.

"Here it is," added Balardi, "as simply as it can be put: we need a messenger to reach Julian. The Apprentice needs to know how to retrieve Galad, and he needs instructions as to the use of the Dragon's Teeth. We need a messenger. And specifically, we need you, Rafir. If you fail, we shall be defeated."

"Who, me?" Rafir blurted. "What am I supposed to do?" Rafir's mind had an image of a winged serpent hovering overhead, then sweeping down on his small body.

"We shall see," Balardi said, smiling. "Sometimes those who set out looking for adventure find more hazards than they wished. But first, you must show the Ancient One your talent." Rafir looked first to Sebastian, then to the Wizard. With some reluctance, he vanished. After a moment, Balardi spoke again, "Please return," and the fox reappeared.

It is as though the small one had never been.

"Those who cannot be seen can often be perceived by those with the Gift," Balardi explained. "But when the fox disappears, he is gone. Yet there is more to it. Come to me for a moment, sir fox." Rafir was uneasy about being touched by the Wizard, but he held still while Balardi fastened a strap of leather about his neck and shoulders. At another request, the fox again disappeared, but this time, even to Sebastian, there was a hint of Rafir in the deep chamber.

He will not escape the Watchers. An unhappy silence followed, while slowly, a feeling of determination was building in Sebastian's mind.

"Then I'll take it," said Sebastian. "If it needs to get to Julian, then I'll take it."

The Watchers would also trap you, though you might escape if the Watchers were distracted. Rafir had begun to droop, and an immense feeling of fatigue was coming over him.

"I will do the distracting," he said. "Make your plans but let me sleep now — we are really just at the end of a different adventure, and I'm very, very tired."

· ⵋ ·

It was morning; Sebastian and Rafir could see beams of light shining through the upper windows of their chamber. Rafir, tired and drowsing, still found that all the details of their adventure were bouncing around in his mind.

"Nergal," he muttered, "the Watchers, Baron Cadmon, the Eye of Merlin — who could keep all this stuff straight?" He shook himself awake for a moment, looking at the monkey-shaped Familiar beside him. "Listen, this is confusing. I can't remember all those things Balardi told us."

Sebastian nodded his head. "It's like some of the early wars of the Servants and the Adversaries — confusing, complicated, and bloody."

"Well, maybe," said the fox, drifting to sleep. "Maybe tomorrow there'll be two dead spies — that will make it less complicated." Rafir's eyes closed, and he slept. Sebastian stayed awake another moment, staring at the sunbeams passing through the upper windows. As he thought about their chances, he could not agree with the fox about the two dead spies: he thought that the fox would escape, and there would be only one dead spy.

· ⵋ ·

At midday, Rafir and Sebastian were jarred awake by the cries of many men, as shouts of command followed cries of agony and shock. After many short, brutal sounds, the noises stopped, and they slept again until sunset.

At sunset, the Captain of the Guard opened their chamber door, calling to them gently.

"Sirs, Balardi awaits you." She stood tall, beauty masked by armor and long dark hair; and unlike the maidens of Rafir's legends, she was dangerous looking. The little Familiar watched her, filled with his usual curiosity.

"You are very courteous," Rafir said, staring up. "I have a question, one that's perhaps not as considerate." Gravely, the Captain nodded down at the small figure.

"Are all of the women of Gravengate armed like you…I mean?"

"I am not of Gravengate," she said gently. "Those women and the small ones of Gravengate were transported, long ago, to the coast. We were sent by the Mistress of Illusions to aid the League, and number only three hundred. Didn't the Wizard tell you about us?" Sebastian shook his head. "He should have told you about us and about other matters, but he is preoccupied. My name is Géla, and I know yours, Rafir, and yours, Sebastian. The Wizard is still preoccupied — we should go to him now, for he expects you."

They followed Géla to the Wizard's great council chamber. A half dozen guards stood alertly in front of tall doors that were engraved with many runes. The guards bowed gravely to the two small creatures, admitting them, then closing the massive doors behind them. Balardi was sitting at a great oaken table, writing on a thin scroll. They waited in silence for a moment, then Balardi's face lifted to greet them.

"Did you sleep well?" he asked.

"Yes, Lord," Sebastian replied, "except for the disturbance at midday. What was happening?" Balardi looked grim.

"I'll speak of it later — if there's time." He drew a long, rolled map from its cylinder, and spread it over the table. "Can you find your place on this?" he asked Sebastian. The Familiar pulled himself up to the table and traced his fingers over the map.

"It seems so long ago," Sebastian hesitated, "but here's Gravengate, and here's the Greenway, leading to Sea's Edge."

"That is the road over which Merlin should have ridden, surging with all his great power to renew the League," said Balardi, "but that is by the by.... You, sir fox, should also view this," and he lifted Rafir gently to the tabletop, using only one great hand. The fox ran his nose over the map, sniffing the treated fiber. It was strange to view the world that he knew as ups and downs, easy running, and hard going — to see it all laid out on flat paper. But after a moment, he found the image of the fortress, and the road leading away from it. One road seemed to meet another, more winding road.

"I think that this is the castle, and this is the Greenway," he said. "But what is this other winding road? Do they meet?"

"That is a river, called the Saugus," said Balardi. "To the west of the Greenway lies Sea's Edge, or what's left of it. To the north Kalanin and his allies harass the besiegers, but they cannot break through. Julian has joined them.... You, Sebastian, must deliver this to Julian," and Balardi fastened a leather pouch with a small harness to the neck and shoulders of Sebastian. "This contains instructions concerning the Dragon's Teeth and a word of command that should aid in freeing Galad. The moon will set to the west this night, away from the fortress. Do not become lost. Remember, *flee the setting moon.*" The Wizard turned to Rafir. "Sometime before Sebastian leaves, you will speed down the road to the west — you need only to draw the Watchers for a while, then circle around, and follow the river to the north. After about fifteen leagues, there should be some sign of our allies —

they will lead you to Julian. Now, each of you will repeat these instructions." For almost an hour, Balardi reviewed his directions with each of them. At last, he halted.

"I don't mean to make little of your understanding, but so much now depends on reaching Julian and Kalanin. Come! Before your evening meal, you will see what has happened on this day of the Siege." Balardi led them to the outside of the keep, still within the great walls of the fortress. Before them, in the early moonlight, lay the dead hulk of a gigantic lizard, with an enormous head.

"This is no creature of magic, summoned from the Mid-World," the Wizard explained, "but rather an ancient creature from the past of the Lands Beyond, where the rule of the Great Lizards has passed. It was brought upon us by sorcery, passing our defenses because it was not itself magical — it hopped about here this afternoon like some mindless, gigantic hippy-hoppity rabbit, until it was felled by three darkish, chilled cold drakes I summoned. In the meantime, the north wall of Gravengate was almost overthrown! The Ancient One saved us again. But our struggle was nearly lost in one afternoon."

The Wizard drew a deep breath, calming himself. "Now the time has come. We will reach Julian, or we will not. Julian and Kalanin will break the Siege, or they will not. Let the Maker witness that I have done all that is within my power." Balardi looked again to Sebastian and Rafir. "Take food now, though only small portions, for you cannot race with full stomachs."

Sebastian watched Rafir pick at a little food. For himself, he took nothing. Despite his determination, the feeling had grown in Sebastian that he was a small creature caught in great events, easily ground into nothingness. He patted Rafir lightly on his soft fox fur.

"Before you go, I want to thank you for your help — and your company. I'm glad you were with me, and I hope we'll do more together. I wasn't happy at the beginning, you know, but I am now. Tell Julian what I said if you reach him, and I don't."

"We are friends and companions," said the fox. "Even if we weren't, we should stay together around all of these large and powerful folks. Anyway, don't worry about reaching Julian. Tonight, I will lead a great chase!"

Out in the night again, Sebastian noted the moon and its position: the sky was hazy, dimming the moon's glow, but it was still clear enough. Sebastian walked at the fox's side, wings folded, resting for the long flight. They met Balardi by the north wall of the fortress: he seemed less grim, more at peace with himself, and he waved the guard away gently, as though shooing a flock of geese. In his hand, he held a thing of leather encrusted with an assortment of jewels. Even in the shadowed moonlight, those jewels seemed to radiate a range of powers.

"This is a lure for the Sensitives, the magic smellers," he explained. "In truth, it was never of real power, but more a Wizard's toy, an extravagance of my youth, so long ago." He smiled as he said this. "You need only let this thing fall from you, and you will vanish, even from the Watchers. But let them seek you for a while, as a distraction. Sebastian will then escape, perhaps to reach Julian's shoulder by early morning. I bid you farewell! The Ancient One also bids farewell, and tonight he will put forth his power to spread confusion among our foes. Ghostly creatures of the Mid-World will stalk the encampment of our foes on this night. Fear them not! Farewell! We will meet again at the breaking of the Siege!"

"Goodbye, Rafir," Sebastian murmured. "Maybe we'll be seeing Julian again after tonight." But his voice was not convincing.

Rafir was lowered to the outside of the walls, and he stood in the gloomy moonlight for a moment, looking out over the Plain of Gravengate. Around his slender body were the carcasses of giant beasts and strange creatures of sorcery that had fought and died outside the walls of the fortress. Their bodies lay still; some were rotting into the dust of the plain, while others were curiously preserved. Almost against his will, Rafir padded around the dead creatures, sniffing their strange smells. For some reason, the decay of death had been delayed; maybe some magic was still left in the dead bodies of the creatures.

Rafir turned away, clearing his thoughts. Then the fox was off, picking his way in the moonlight toward the garrison holding the west side. In a way he was happy — after all, this was what a fox should be doing in an adventure, trotting through the moonlight, not locked away in a castle, or sent to an ugly, stone, nasty-smelling future land with strange machines that belched poison.

In the distance, the camp of their adversaries was beginning to stir, with guards and more soldiers shuffling about. Then, the night began to shake with shrieks and cries of terror. Men were spilling from their tents in fear, as the shapes of many, dead Mid-World creatures prowled among them. Rafir slowed, muttering softly to himself: some fool could easily trample him. He paused as he neared the campsites, then began to spurt, bit by bit, through the confusion. He was partway through when he heard the first alarm given by the Watchers.

"Spy! Spy! Beware spy!" called a piercing voice, then a lower one like a groan, "Thief among us! Wizard's tool!" Rafir sped up. He was nearly halfway through the camp. A voice of command penetrated the chorus of cries and warnings. "Leave the phantasms! Seek the spy!" Rafir was still not in great danger — it would take them a few minutes to organize the pursuit, then he would be through the camp...he looked up, checking the moon for direction. And he nearly dropped Balardi's charm from his mouth: above him, fluttering in the moonlight, were the winged serpents! The two were hovering overhead, sensing, but not seeing him.

He sped under a wagon, halting, and letting them carry beyond. His heart was pounding, shaking his small body. He dropped the charm from his mouth, catching his breath. In a second, the Watchers began to cry out in confusion. They were all around him now, searching in the darkness — he had to keep them in pursuit! Rafir picked the charm up again and began to run for the road. In a few moments, the voices were again hovering overhead, and they were closing in.... On the moonlit ground in front of him, he saw the shadow of a winged serpent, moving closer, swooping, ready to strike.... At the very last moment, he darted to one side, letting the charm slip from his mouth. Then he stood, panting in the shadows.

"That should do it," he whispered to himself.

It was then that he heard clearly, for the first time, a sound that had been troubling the most distant corner of his mind. It was the sound of many dogs barking, of hounds tracking him by his smell. He began to run again, this time in a race for his life.

Chapter Twelve
The Council of the League

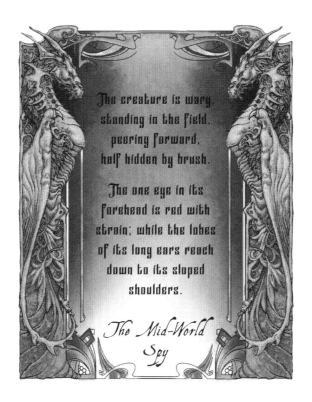

The creature is wary, standing in the field, peering forward, half hidden by brush.

The one eye in its forehead is red with strain; while the lobes of its long ears reach down to its sloped shoulders.

— *The Mid-World Spy*

IN THE FIRST LIGHT OF DAY, Sebastian was clinging to the upper branches of a tall poplar, looking down over a broad meadow. His whole body was exhausted from a long dark flight, but he had flown farther than he had ever thought possible. Now, his wings and shoulders were numb with fatigue, good only for short flights, or longer glides.

Wearily he climbed to the top of the tree, again casting himself off, flapping his wings a few times, then gliding to the next meadow. He looked down: the land was becoming more level and viewable now, with tall trees harder to find.

Drifting beyond the meadow and into the next field, he found himself coming down short of the far trees. In a way, it was restful to walk through the fields, but Sebastian's eyes scanned the horizon, watching for signs of pursuit. Far away, nearly beyond his vision, he thought he could see the outline of hawk wings or some large bird of prey. It would be madness to come all this way, only to become a meal for some brute predator!

He started to climb at the base of a huge tree, so shaggy that its grey bark crumbled in his hands. Soon, if he traveled in the right direction, he might begin to sense Julian. He launched himself, gliding over the next field, thinking how wonderful it would be to see Julian again.

All those nice thoughts were interrupted by a cry of malice and triumph: overhead, a winged serpent was surging toward him, a Watcher, and as powerful a flyer as Sebastian was weak. The little Familiar dropped to the ground, darting over the field, looking for shelter, and there was none.

The serpent cried out again in triumph — but from above it, like a meteor, the Eye of Merlin hurtled downward, striking the serpent's wing, raking it with powerful talons. While the creature struggled to stay in the air, the eagle circled, struggling to get higher — then the Eye struck again, completely shredding the injured wing.

The winged serpent cried out in rage, tumbling to the ground beside Sebastian. The little Familiar leaped away from its striking range, but the serpent had no time for Sebastian, for the eagle was upon it. Thin blood seeped from beneath the serpent's pale skin as the eagle struck repeatedly at the creature. Sebastian watched from behind a bush; the serpent was larger and stronger than the fierce eagle, but now it was crippled, and death was coming for it. At the end, the winged serpent sought only to destroy its opponent, but the eagle was striking, then leaping out of reach — then striking again in the rage of its killing lust. At last, the serpent's head began to droop, collapsing to the ground beside its crippled wing. It turned then to Sebastian.

"I go now," it whispered, hissing, "but I will greet you in the Master's place after he has destroyed you." With that, the serpent died. Sebastian could see its reddish heart pulsing underneath translucent skin as it beat slower and finally stopped. In death, the creature's skin became even more transparent and strange. The Eye of Merlin stood beside the fading figure, his beak, feathers, and talons still flared in his killing fever so that Sebastian was afraid to approach him. After a few moments, the eagle settled back and looked away from its fading enemy, turning to Sebastian.

"It is over," said the eagle, "and you need no longer fear me." Sebastian peered at the ground where the serpent had died — all that was left of the creature were a few strands of blood and bits of its translucent skin. Sebastian bowed to the Eye of Merlin.

"Thank you," he said, "you saved both my life and my errand."

"You need not thank me," rasped the eagle. "This thing mocked me when I could not respond, and it angered me. Also, you need not bow to me — we are of the same order, the servants of Magicians." The eagle was silent for a moment, studying the horizon, where the sky was clear and blue except for a few high clouds that were sliding slowly to the southern seas. Sebastian felt his tired body begin to stiffen, but his mind was surprised and relieved: he would live, at least for a while longer. The eagle looked doubtfully at Sebastian's wings.

"Take the harness and packet to Julian," said Sebastian. "I will follow in a little while — the packet is important, and it's supposed to reach Julian soon." The eagle touched Sebastian's harness with his claws.

"This thing need only support you, and I will take you with me," said the Eye, and before Sebastian could disagree, the eagle grasped him by his harness, and after a moment of heavy, beating wings, carried the little Familiar into the air. As they climbed higher, the Eye of Merlin called to Sebastian.

"Be satisfied that few other winged creatures could carry you this far, but strength was given to me for such a purpose." Sebastian glanced down: beneath them, the ground was growing more distant. They were flying at a great pace, and so the danger was over. He relaxed and began to drowse.

· ☩ ·

When he woke again, he was inside a tent lit by several candles. Julian was seated beside his bed, with eyes the color of a grey sea watching over his Familiar. Julian's eyes were filled with sorrow and understanding, as though he had followed Sebastian's adventures while the little Familiar slept. Sebastian reached out to touch Julian the Apprentice, Julian the grave, Julian the good, the wise and compassionate, and his small eyes filled with tears for a moment, then became clear.

"Well met, Sebastian, my friend, and companion," Julian murmured. "So many leagues and dangers have separated us, but we're together again." Behind Julian, Kalanin rose, almost a head taller than the Apprentice, and he reached over to touch Sebastian's other hand.

"Greetings, Familiar," said Kalanin. "We're beginning to come together again, and there are more of us, many more. With the aid you brought from Balardi, we will free Galad. Our adversaries had best learn to fear us."

"Is Rafir still with Balardi?" asked Julian. "The Eye had not thought to ask." Sebastian sat up quickly.

"No, I forgot! He's by the river, on the west bank, or should be if he still lives — he should live, he's a brave companion and my friend. Can you help him?" Kalanin was up in a flash.

"We'll send a search party right away," he said and was out into the night.

"Don't be too worried," Julian said, smiling. "I foresaw a wet future for Rafir, and I wondered. You've explained it. I also saw that Rafir would survive to investigate the moonlight once again. It's a good thing though, to have a task for these warriors. Soon the struggle may be less exciting — fewer raids, more marches, and countermarches, or perhaps it will be overly exciting with one last battle." Sebastian lay back, confused but relaxed. It seemed that Kalanin was somehow in charge. How that came about was a mystery, but for now, it didn't matter.

"Tonight," continued Julian, "with these words of command, we will try to draw back Galad from his imprisonment. On this night, the Eye of Merlin will aid me, but after, you will help me, as before." Julian smiled again at the little Familiar. "And later, there will be a great telling of tales, so that each of us will know the other's part in this struggle." Julian began to leave, then leaned back into the tent. "While you rested, dinner was set before you," and he pointed to a table, winked at Sebastian, and was gone. Sebastian breathed a sigh of relief.

"That's better," he murmured. "He was beginning to sound like Balardi."

· ☿ ·

Once again Julian stood in his great oval with rune carvings throughout its surfaces, and starshine streaming overhead. In his right hand, he held his staff, while in his left was a scroll, sent from the Ancient One who dwelt still at Gravengate. Behind Julian was the Eye of Merlin, watching the flickering shapes of runes, guarding the back of the Apprentice.

The spell and the strength of the Gift inside Julian again sought the return of Galad, and as before the way was blocked, though gently, as if a small child was denied entrance to a room filled with dangerous devices; lights within the oval began to dim, as its web of power struggled with resistance.

Julian put forward a second, more powerful spell, of one who would avoid conflict, but who would not be denied. Slowly, before Julian there appeared a figure, menacing, more than four times the height of the Apprentice, dark and cloaked, a being of the Mid-World, a Dark Lord, ruler of its own domain, origin ancient, wreathed in mystery.

"Lord, I seek a friend," Julian said in soft tones, "one who belongs to this place. Neither I nor that mortal would wish to quarrel with you." The Mid-World Power said nothing; its attitude seemed easy and amused, but scorn lurked behind its countenance. It gave no answer. Julian beckoned the eagle to his side.

"Beside me is the Eye of Merlin," said Julian. "I will ask him to witness that I sought to avoid confrontation with a Power of the Mid-World."

"I will bear witness," said the eagle. Julian nodded then opened the Ancient One's scroll, showing in words of power, the secret name held by the Mid-World being, before the Truce.

"Then I call upon you by my own spell.... By the power of the order of Wizards.... By the inscription of your ancient Name.... By the right of a man to live in his own land.... That you should depart or pass from the Mid-World!"

The Dark Lord moved back a pace, showing surprise and dismay, as though a child had been given a dangerous weapon. Yet it would not give way: drawing itself together, in the fullness of its own strength, the Dark Lord began a low chant, a rolling mumble of power and mastery, of racing free and unchained through the skies. Scorn for lesser beings was woven through its melody. The letters on the scroll began to blur, and the walls of the oval flickered, and Julian's staff grew heavy and cold in his hand so that it nearly slipped from his grasp.

But then Julian raised his voice in counterspell, nearly singing, telling of the natural order of things, of joy in service to the Maker, of compassion for all things, and hope for mortal humans.

Now, as the spells of Julian and the Dark Lord struggled for mastery, power surged through the diagram, but destruction hovered: the air about Julian was filled with the smell of burning. Men began to break away from the edges of the oval, moving to their weapons.

Then Julian had the mastery, and the figure of the Dark Lord began to fail: bits of its body, falling like grey ash, drifted slowly to the ground. In great fear, the Mid-World being withdrew, vanishing and leaving the path to Galad unguarded.

Julian stood, breathing deeply in the middle of the great oval.

"I was worried for you, Apprentice," said the eagle. "On neutral ground, that Mid-World Power might have been a match for several Adepts. Are you weary?" Julian nodded.

"We are almost done, and I can rest later." He closed his eyes, letting the Gift search for the presence of Galad. Gloom still lay over the land taken by the Dark Lord, and the Gift by itself was not enough. Julian began chanting in a muffled voice, murmuring a seeking spell, weaving Galad's name through his chant, He seemed to hear the sounds of a brook flowing beside him. Julian opened his eyes; a Portal was forming, and through it he saw the dim figure of Galad lying with his hands behind his head, staring into an overcast night sky.

But now, Galad was aware of Julian's spell work, for his hand was drifting toward his sword, as though not to be taken by surprise in the darkness. Julian leaned toward the Portal, and whispered, "Galad…." The knight did not respond, but pushed himself easily to his feet, holding his sword with his right hand. Then, peering forward, he looked for the first time into the oval field.

"Julian!" he murmured, but he made no move to come forward. Julian could see that Galad was whole, though thinner, and much more cautious. The spell grew stronger as the Portals meshed; Julian and Galad could now see each other clearly, as though standing only fifteen paces apart. Yet Galad would still not step forward.

"You are free, Galad," said Julian, standing under the starry skies of Alantéa. "You need only walk forward a few paces." Galad looked at Julian uncertainly.

"It's true that you're not like the other phantasms," he said slowly. "But perhaps there's some other deception in this." Julian shook his head.

"Those ghosts will no longer trouble you, Galad. Their master has removed himself. But you should come now, or be left in this distant land, alone, perhaps for a long time. And the League needs you now, not later." Galad smiled, a flicker of his old easy manner.

"Say no more. It's become boring here, anyway." He stepped forward to the Portal's edge. At the border, something seemed to block him, to hold him back — the sword would not pass. Galad stepped through the Portal, both hands tugging at the Tarnished Sword. At last, he jerked it through; the sword whined a keening ring, as though in pain.

Now Galad stood beside Julian and the Eye of Merlin, in the center of the great oval field where lights from carved runes shimmered over the ground. Above Galad, the stars began to form a clear dome over hazy, sorcerous walls. He opened his mouth to speak, but Julian motioned him to silence and began to close down the elements of his spell.

At the spell's end, nothing but grey ash was left on the campground. Julian took Galad by the arm and led him out into the starry night. Kalanin stepped quickly forward, clasping Galad's shoulders with both hands.

"You live!" he cried. "You've returned! Now let our adversaries beware!" Galad laughed.

"They had better all beware if they come between me and a plate of food. Is there a cook about? If not, you had best lash your horses from me, or they're gone." Dargas pulled the provision master from his sleep, and in a brief time, a platter of steaming red meat was set before Galad. Kalanin, Julian, and the other captains sat in silence as Galad finished first one, then a second heaping platter. Then Kalanin introduced each of the captains to Galad, as the young knight lay sprawled on the ground before a watch fire.

"It's not a good night for storytelling," said Kalanin. "Tomorrow, we'll have the first great gathering to discuss the nature of our struggle." Galad nodded, his eyes a little sleepy, but he saw that he was in the middle of a vast warlike camp.

"It seems that the tale has grown in my absence," Galad said, nodding. "But two of our small members are missing."

"Tomorrow," said Julian, "Sebastian should be well enough to join us, and I think we'll have a small, wet fox nearby."

"I was afraid that the little ones wouldn't survive." Galad smiled. "That's even more reason to celebrate." He stood, placing an arm around Dargas' shoulder. "This captain looks like a seasoned campaigner. Odds are that he knows a reasonably reliable source of wine."

Dargas chuckled. "Lad, you've come to the right place. Let's go now, before night ends and daybreak crowds in on us." He began to lead Galad away, but a few paces from the fire, Galad halted with an afterthought, and he took the Tarnished Sword from his side, tossing it to the ground in front of Julian and Kalanin.

"That's something you might want to look at," he said, "even before tomorrow," then he turned back to join Dargas.

Julian picked up the sword and examined it carefully, holding it close to the firelight. "It's a weapon of power," Julian said softly to Kalanin, "of very strange origin, though we should take great care with it, for it will cut both Servants and Adversaries."

· ⚜ ·

When Sebastian woke, he moved gingerly from his bed, testing each part of his small body. He was still stiff and sore but wonderfully rested. Sebastian pushed aside the tent's flap, walking into a bright morning sunlight, stretching, and rubbing until the soreness eased. He tried his wings gently, then lifted to the peak of the tent, searching for some sign of Julian.

All around him, the tier camp was buzzing with activity — tents were being shifted, wagons loaded, horses shod, armorers were hammering mail, and men were capping wooden pikes with sharp metal. At the camp's edge, Julian was standing, staring out over the woodlands. Sebastian flew to his master, settling down on the shoulder of the Apprentice. Julian waved at the meadow's edge.

"Have you noticed our visitors?" he asked. Sebastian saw nothing but a few ravens, and a flock of blackbirds, with a lone seagull floating far from the ocean. Then he felt the probes of many watchers all about them.

"These aren't simple bird flocks," Sebastian said slowly. "Are these spies sent by Thorian and Nergal?"

"Those have come and gone. Before us are the eyes of the Mid-World. The Powers understand that great matters are afoot, and they send their Farsighted onlookers. But enough of them." Julian moved away from the forest's edge. "We have some two pieces of good news. First, we've retrieved Galad, and secondly, Rafir's made it safely to our camp. He's damp but safe."

"That's a relief," said Sebastian. "I know that you said he would come through safely, but somehow I was certain that one of us wouldn't survive — we are such small creatures and the forces at work seem so huge and powerful."

Julian shook his head grimly. "They sought to strike you down. How has Thorian become so evil? But the Eye of Merlin saved you, and the peculiar powers of the fox saved him."

"Peculiar indeed!" Sebastian exclaimed. "I'm used to Rafir now — I even miss him. Is he awake?" Julian smiled.

"He'll be awake soon, no doubt. We may need to carry him to our conference."

"You mentioned a gathering before. What's being planned?"

"Let's find Rafir," said Julian, "then I'll tell both of you."

Most of the camp was now packed, moving toward the roadside. A few of the wagons with broken wheels or axles had been left behind, and it was under one of these that they found Rafir. The fox was alone, except for a single burly guard who stood watch over him. Rafir looked wet and bedraggled from the water — his fur was still damp, matted with burrs from the meadows and muck from wet riverbanks.

"You look terrible!" blurted Sebastian, but he added quickly, "though it's great to see you alive, and Julian will have you in good shape again in no time." The fox yawned with fatigue, but his eyes twinkled with relief and pleasure.

Julian knelt beside Rafir. "We certainly owe you a good grooming — and much more, but you might want to do the grooming yourself, while you listen to the rest of us talk."

"There's some sort of meeting to be held soon," added Sebastian. "Can you join us? We'll probably need to tell them about Balardi and the Siege." The fox rose to his feet, still unsteady.

"Is it far?" he asked. "I don't think I'm up to much traveling."

"Ride with me again," said Julian, "as you did just a little while ago. But I should warn you that many other things have changed in a short time. The Wizards' League was wounded, terribly wounded, but it wasn't broken. Today's a day when the captains and key figures of the League will draw together. We'll meet, just a few hours from here, and I'll tell you more, as we travel."

Julian walked toward Bluescent, and the Mare raised her head in recognition. It was good to have Sebastian and Rafir back, but he would be spending a lot of time in explanations. He mounted Bluescent and began to ride back to his small companions. The Gift stirred within him: spies of the Mid-World wheeled skyward, far from hearing, but motions were stirring in the corner of his eyes.

Julian slipped swiftly from his horse, and his staff flashed: bands of sparks sped knee high over the grasslands. Yelping sounds were followed by the swift motions of hidden spies as they raced from Julian and his small allies.

"I'm sorry you had to see that, Rafir," Julian said.

"A spy's hazard," said Rafir, "and anyway you might not have chased all of them." The fox thought that as a spy, he could have ducked down, rolled once to extinguish any fire on his singed fur, then turned back to follow Julian.

Julian nodded. "One or more spies might still be lingering nearby." He watched the bird flocks as they scattered, drifting over the horizon. "Our struggle is coming to a great test, and the focus of the Powers will be on us. We should be careful what we say."

Gingerly, Julian took Rafir and set him back into his old saddle pouch. The fox seemed lighter than before, and his fur was coarse and ragged; but time and rest should heal him. Bluescent began to pace, slowly, toward the road.

"Here we are just as we were at the beginning," said Sebastian, "perhaps a little more worn, but at least we're back together. Now, what of this conference?"

"We're moving toward Gravengate," said Julian. "Perhaps on our way to challenge the Siege. Who can tell? A massive raid? Possibly a movement toward the fortress of Thorian at Stone Mountain? We'll talk of these things after we find a place that can be sealed off. As you saw, Sebastian, there are those wishing knowledge of our plans and weapons — it's clear that much has happened of a surprising nature, and new forces are moving over Alantéa, forces that may challenge the balance of the Powers in the Mid-World. Who can tell?"

Julian sounded vague and expansive to Sebastian, though perhaps the words of the Apprentice were really meant for the host of spies that were hovering around them. Sebastian fell silent as Bluescent began to move more quickly toward their destination; Rafir drifted back to sleep despite all the jostling motions.

·) (·

They met at a somber, dark, abandoned inn, where several of Dargas' veterans stood guard, taking Bluescent as Julian dismounted. Rafir was eased carefully to the ground. His fur was still caked and matted, but he moved more easily, eyes bright with life. Kalanin met Julian at the door.

"We're set," he said, "except for the Eye of Merlin."

"We'll wait for a few moments," said Julian. "A few things should be done before we start, anyway." He looked up into Kalanin's grim face. "But don't look so stern. You and I disagree now, but perhaps we'll find a united purpose here." Kalanin smiled at the Apprentice but did not seem convinced. Inside the inn, they found the others gathered in what had been the main dining hall. Julian greeted each briefly, then turned to Sebastian and Rafir.

"Let's have a look around," he said, "then we'll begin to seal ourselves off." They walked through the lower floor, finding mostly rooms covered with layers of dust. The inn had long been abandoned, as the new road from Amalric to Khiva ran more than a league away from it. A few years ago, the local villagers and the men of Baron Cadmon had sat and talked over tankards of ale — at separate tables, no doubt; but it was easy to imagine the young men of the villages overhearing Dargas, as he entertained a few cronies with some spicy story. Now, everything was dark and silent.

In the old cloakroom, beneath wooden pegs, Julian found the old, weathered sign that had once hung outside. On the sign was the image of an armed man, upper body slumped on a table, clutching a battered goblet. Beneath the portrait was the old name of the inn: *The Last Stand* — it had certainly been a gathering place for soldiers.

But now the inn was silent and empty — and it was important to make certain that it remained empty, free of watcher or intruders. Julian left the cloakroom and led Sebastian and Rafir to the upper floor. He began to seal the building against all outsiders, both their foes and other beings of the Mid-World. Every now and again he paused, asking Sebastian and Rafir if the spell was sufficient. Rafir was asked as a courtesy, but Sebastian had the Sight and was sensitive to acts of sorcery. Several times the little Familiar called on Julian to reseal or change a portion of his spell. The fox nosed about, calling Julian to places in walls or ceilings where drafts of air entered. These were sealed doubly against Air Elementals, though Julian doubted their use as spies, as Elementals were not known for their powers of concentration.

They finished and returned to the main floor, doing as they had done above. The main hall of the inn was the last room sealed, and the captains watched in silence as the Apprentice ran his staff over the edges of cracked, grimy windows. At last Julian's work was done and he turned to the others.

"We're being watched very closely," he explained, "but the task of Mid-World Spies should now be more difficult, if not impossible." The Apprentice sat and looked to Kalanin to begin.

Kalanin sat at the far end of the table, with Galad at his right, and Dargas at his left. Harlond, Rurak, and Rostov sat along the table sides, though closer to Kalanin and Dargas. Julian sat at the other far end, with Sebastian and Rafir curled on the table in front of him. The Eye of Merlin perched on a chair's back some distance from the table. Kalanin's face was troubled as he spoke.

"At this council, I encourage each person to speak freely, but also to be prepared to hear freely and change opinions if warranted. I won't hide from you that Julian encourages one course, while I lean to another." Kalanin paused, wondering where to begin.

"I'm no fountain of wisdom," Dargas broke in, "to make a judgment between a general and a magician. But here's what I say: the lads and I don't know much about Merlin and you of Sea's Edge, even though the Baron was his ally. And this young warrior," he nodded to Galad, "knows little about this war. Let's begin at the beginning, and maybe a clear course will come from the telling of the whole tale." Kalanin nodded.

"I'll agree to that if the rest concur." Each of them agreed; even Rafir stopped licking his fur to bob his head in agreement.

"Then Julian should begin," Galad said. "He was the first of those sent by Merlin."

"There's not much to tell of my errand," said Julian. "I'm apprenticed to Merlin, and also used as an emissary of the League, sent sometimes just to make certain that the Greenway remains open. I've been to Stone Mountain before, and to Gravengate many times because Balardi was also my mentor, my second Master after Merlin. I was sent by Merlin to learn more of Balardi's troubles with Thorian, but I was sent too late."

"How did Merlin seem when you last spoke with him?" asked Galad.

"Nothing seemed wrong, though in retrospect it seems to me that he was more than a little distracted."

"He was more than distracted when we forced our way in," added Galad. "It's the only time I ever saw the Wizard when he wasn't in complete control." Galad shook his head and let the Apprentice continue. Julian went on to tell of finding the fox, the arrival of Kalanin and Galad with news of the disaster at Sea's Edge. Then Julian told of the fight at the ford, of the shapeshifting Adept, and his Great Spell. At last, he spoke of the Hall of the Dreamers. "These were great majesties, powerful Servants of the Maker, yet when they spoke of Merlin, they knew nothing of where he might have gone. Merlin, they said, had pursued some dangerous path, and was alive, although beyond their sight. Where should we seek for him?"

"Perhaps the Eye can help us," said Kalanin, turning to the eagle. "You were close to Merlin, in contact with him more than any other. What of Merlin? What was he doing? What did he anticipate?" The eagle moved forward out of the shadows.

"I was closest to Merlin, nearly a part of him, so that today, without Merlin, I still feel injured and only partly alive. Yet I did not know the greater part of the mind of Merlin, but only that he feared a great danger from over the western ocean beyond Sea's Edge."

"Yes, that's what the Dreamers told me," Julian added. "Merlin tried to take something from the ocean at Sea's Edge. But Merlin said nothing of this to anyone else."

"I knew of it!" rasped the eagle. "For at Merlin's command I hunted both in the day and through the long night. In the waters beneath the seas, in the valleys and mountains of the ocean, a turmoil seethes, as though the world prepares to be transformed. Powers of sorcery are moving in the depths, beyond Alantéa, beyond the Mid-World of the Truce. Their aims are still hidden, but I believe that they have taken or destroyed Merlin."

"You said nothing of this before," Kalanin said doubtfully.

The Eye of Merlin responded with scorn: "What would you have done? Lashed the water with your bright swords? Shot arrows into the depths? The Apprentice and I tried and failed with a power of mongrel magic behind us. With all your men, you cannot free even one beleaguered Wizard."

"And if we free Balardi?" asked Kalanin. "What then?"

"Then, perhaps Balardi might force the issue," replied the eagle. "At least that would be my hope. At the last, before Merlin contested the waters off Sea's Edge, I was instructed to seek Balardi. Yet when I sought to do so, my path was blocked." Silence held sway over the chamber for a moment; in the late afternoon, the sky had become overcast, and gloom seemed to seep into the abandoned inn.

"Hold on for a moment," said Harlond. "The mind of Merlin must have been tuned, in part, to Balardi: first Julian was sent, and that cannot have been solely by chance. Then Kalanin and Galad were sent, and they with sorcerous devices and weapons. So, despite his preoccupation with events under the seas, Merlin also gave some focused thought to our own struggles. What of the sending of Kalanin and Galad?"

"It was done in haste," said Kalanin, "like a desperate afterthought.... What about the contents of the chest, Julian? Were these also prepared in haste?"

"To the contrary," said the Apprentice, "they were prepared for this very purpose, crafted over many years."

"What then of these mysterious trinkets?" asked Dargas. "What are they going to accomplish?"

"Let's return to them later," Julian replied. "We should first hear from Galad, then call on Sebastian and Rafir for their part." Galad picked up the story, telling of the Manticore, the Lady of the Hill, and the Tarnished Sword.

"All my days I have cheerfully served the League, as the only right thing to do, but it seems to me now that in the struggle between light and darkness, there are many who face more difficult choices." He held up the Tarnished Sword; it was heavy and dull in his hand. "The Mistress of this blade was one of those and I pity her."

"Save some pity for the rest of us," said Kalanin. "We also face difficult choices. But let's continue — what of our small friends?" Sebastian began speaking in a faint voice so that those around the table leaned forward to hear him. Gradually, the Familiar relaxed and began speaking more easily.

"We knew nothing of that Great Spell, we only found ourselves tossed like discarded trash to a far land, to a time when all sorcery seemed exhausted. It was an ugly place, made of soiled stone and lifeless matter. We were glad to get away." Sebastian described the Sending and the Last Magician, then told of the Seeking Stones, and their escape.

"If I understand this properly," said Rostov, "these two were passed into a far time, a grim, unhappy time. Does this mean that our adversaries have triumphed? That, at the end of time, they rule over a dark kingdom?"

"No, not so," Julian replied. "The Dreamers showed that the Powers of the Mid-World would fade after many ages. But the struggle between the light and the dark will go on even then, in a different form. But there's more from Sebastian and Rafir, for they have news of Balardi, the first message brought since the Siege began." Julian nodded to Sebastian, and the little Familiar began to tell of the Siege, of the anger of Balardi, and the claims of Thorian and Nergal, and lastly of the Ancient One.

Rafir had said nothing, but at this point, he lifted his head from his grooming. "Down at the base of Gravengate, I felt that I was in the presence of the oldest, wisest thing alive, and he seemed gentle, too."

"With this tale," said Kalanin, "comes the answer to one of our many mysteries. Balardi and Gravengate hold because of the great ancient power of a Spirit Lord. It seems likely that our enemies do not completely understand how strongly they are opposed. But now, for Julian, Galad, and the small ones, I will tell our part of this struggle." Kalanin spoke of the Seraph, of the broken army of Baron Cadmon, of the Raiders and their newly forged force of arms. "We now have seven thousand, massed in fourteen tiers. These are too many for a raiding party, yet too few to assail the besiegers who have at least four times our strength." Galad was puzzled, staring into the distance, and he heard little of what Kalanin said.

"It seems that ghosts from the ancient wars are waking," Galad said softly. "A Demon Prince, one of the First Adversaries aided Julian. A Spirit Lord, a Second Servant, aids Balardi. You fought an ancient Creature of the Darkness. A Seraph, a First Servant, aids our foes — this last event troubles me. And if he is indeed a Seraph, he should be able to command the Spirit Lord, should he not?"

"There seems to be a hierarchy," Julian replied. "For the ancient Servants: Seraphs, Spirit Lords, Mankind. For the ancient Adversaries:

Demons, Dragons, Creatures of the Darkness. Yet within each category, there are different levels of power, greater and lesser beings. So, a Greater Seraph might command a Greater Spirit Lord; a Prince of Demons would command a Lord of Dragons; a Lord of Dragons would call upon its own offspring, the Creatures of the Darkness. Yet, from what we've heard, this Seraph is a lesser First Servant, who has been further diminished by his evil service."

"I was there when the Seraph appeared," added Dargas, "and I can tell you that he was not pleased to have been called. Also, he did not seem as powerful as the others described in all our stories. Perhaps we've seen the last of him."

"More surprises are waiting for us," said Julian. "This is the one consistent story in this struggle. The League has survived an amazing series of disasters; and so, we will confront more difficulties. So far, we've survived only by a narrow margin. If we make the wrong choices now, we shall fail completely."

Julian took a deep breath before continuing. "We should now ask Kalanin, the chief of our captains to tell us more of the choices before us." Kalanin looked about him, to the faces around the table, and then into the deep gloom of the abandoned inn.

"I like none of these choices," he said, "but let me go through each of them and tell what I like least about it." He sighed. "I wish we could call for wine or beer, to charm this dreary place."

"Time for that later," Dargas grunted. "What's your first choice?"

"To go on as we have: to grow stronger while all the time, our foes become weaker. But against this thought, we have heard that Balardi will probably fail when his ally, the Ancient One departs. The second choice is to take what force we have and seek for Merlin at Sea's Edge. He was said to be at the heart of this struggle."

"You would not find him there," said the eagle.

"That would not surprise me," Kalanin replied, "and I care little for this choice, but...." He smiled at Julian. "If you are given instructions by Great Powers, as Julian has, it is best to consider them."

"And what is our next choice?" Julian asked.

"To attack the enemy as he has attacked us," said Kalanin with a fierce glint in his eyes. "Let us mass the tiers and move on Stone Mountain. Let us bring down Thorian's fortress."

Rostov stirred. "But even if we triumph, there would still be two Powers who would come against us, while our greatest strength would be lost when this Spirit Lord, the Ancient One departs and Balardi fails."

Kalanin nodded in agreement. "We might bring destruction down upon our enemies, but I too think we would fail. I mention this choice only to show that we have explored every possibility. And so, we come to the last choice: to go with whatever force we have to break the Siege and free Balardi."

"Are you insane?" said Dargas, starting in his chair. "They would destroy us in a few bitter hours! We've worked too hard to throw our lives away so casually!"

"Half a moment," said Harlond. "There's more to this, and perhaps we've come to the heart of our disagreement. It's best to bring matters out in the open." He nodded to Kalanin. "Which of these choices do you favor?"

"I like none of them, but the first seems least bad, to press the enemy on his flanks, growing stronger, while he weakens."

"And you, Julian, what course do you favor?" asked Harlond.

"I put forward the last of the choices, to break the Siege," Julian replied. "But there's a part of the matter that we haven't touched on yet."

"There's the chest sent by Merlin," said Kalanin. "Julian believes that there's something he might call to our aid."

"Now that's better," said Dargas. "What do we have? A tier-swallowing monster? A brace of trolls? A mass of invisible backstabbing fiends?" Julian smiled; Dargas was fond of his role as a rustic soldier.

"If those were summoned," Julian said, "they might just as easily be dismissed, even turned against us. There is a force that might be *invited* to join us, but they cannot be summoned — this is a portion of the message Balardi gave to me about using the Gifts of Merlin. And again, he warned me not to speak of them too openly, for if our enemies know our intentions, they might block this power before I can invoke it. I will say this to Dargas: the force that we will call upon is more potent than those that you mentioned but less dramatic, more worldly."

Kalanin shook his head doubtfully. "Too many chances for failure exist: *if* this thing comes, *if* it is not blocked, *if* it is powerful enough to aid us. While we wait, our tiers may be ground to dust."

"Hold for a moment, cousin," said Galad. "I've held back from these discussions — I've been a great distance from this contest for so long. But do I understand that Balardi sent directions about the use of this tool, that he expects us to use it to break the Siege?"

"This also occurred to me," said Kalanin, "but perhaps he credits us with more strength than we have, and perhaps he is desperate."

"I, too, like the first choice," said the Eye of Merlin, "to strike and strike again, while the enemy weakens. But should Gravengate fall, we have lost our war."

"And the attacks we make now are no longer easy," added Rostov. "Sorcery anticipates our every move, and we only succeed by keeping many plans, and choosing one of them at the very last moment." The face of Dargas now looked grim, and all trace of humor had left him.

"It seems that we must move to save Balardi before Gravengate collapses," he said, shaking his head, "and the test for all my young men comes so soon, and for the old soldiers, it is still only a short time since the Baron was killed."

"So, we drift to this choice," Kalanin murmured, "to hazard all in dubious battle. Yet, in each struggle there comes a moment when one side must choose swiftly — or be brushed away from the battlefield. I will agree to break the Siege, or to test it unless there are others who favor a different course." There was silence in the room. "Then, it's done. We should begin to plan for the passage tomorrow. Dargas, Rostov and I will stay to plan our order of battle. Harlond, Rurak, and Galad should ensure that we're ready to move tomorrow at first light. For all of us — say nothing of our destination yet. Let me have a word with Julian before he departs." Julian and Kalanin stepped away from the main tap room and stood speaking quietly in the shadows.

"You've won," said Kalanin. "Let's make certain we don't fail."

"I don't really believe that I won," Julian said, smiling. "I think that you also believe that the Siege has to be broken."

Kalanin nodded in response, but without a smile. "It's true that I let you convince me, and it's true that we have no choice except to test the Siege — you see, I understand that sorcery and the wielders of magic are the real Masters in this conflict. You will have your moment of truth before Gravengate. Do not fail me."

Julian looked away, staring into the grey gloom of the abandoned inn. "You know that I'm far beyond my depths — I can't give you any assurance of success." He glanced back into the grim face of Kalanin. "But if we fail, I will promise to stand and die beside you, at the last stand, if it comes to that."

Chapter Thirteen
The Dragon's Teeth

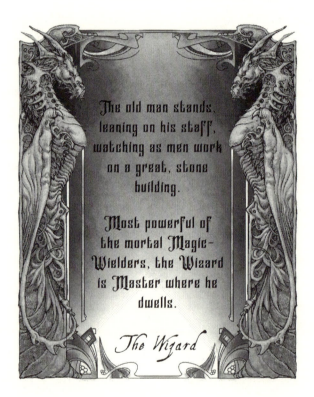

The old man stands, leaning on his staff, watching as men work on a great, stone building.

Most powerful of the mortal Magic-Wielders, the Wizard is Master where he dwells.

The Wizard

RAFIR RACED THROUGH THE NIGHT, running free over wet grasses with all the smells and creaking night sounds of the darkness around him. Only the guards were awake, with the rest of the camp asleep in tents under bright moonlight. But the guards, struggling to stay both warm and alert, couldn't feel as the fox felt, running wild and invisible with every sense focused on shifting night breezes and patterns of moonlight passing over tangled grasses.

The fox froze at the edge of the camp, just as a shadow over the meadow showed that some broad winged predator was passing overhead. Lifting his head cautiously, he watched the great wings of the Eye of Merlin floating over the fields. Did the eagle lack trust in their human guards or was he just as restless as the fox? Rafir watched the Eye for a moment, then he was up and running again, resting, walking, sniffing the night air with its wood smoke, and so many other mixed smells of humans, horses, and other beasts of burden. The fox investigated through the night until a grey daylight began to counter a fading still glowing moon, and then he slept in the back of a provision wagon, expecting to be carried with the tier forces in the morning.

In his dreams, Rafir could dimly feel a jostling movement as the wagon rumbled over rough roads...they were moving toward Gravengate...time for more sleep...and in his dreams, he raced again over the moonlit countryside, over ground that was always shifting under his feet as he ran. But now the shifting motions were changing, becoming a bobbing, up and down motion. With an effort, he forced his eyes to open and peered out.

His wagon was lashed to a broad, flat barge, and many men were on either side of the barge poling hard against the rushing water of a river that was trying to drag them downstream.

"It's the Saugus, sir fox," said a voice from behind him, "and it's nice of you to wake from your dainty nap." Rafir turned around and saw that he was guarded by a Herald — one of the young men who bore few weapons but traveled swiftly, carrying precise, direct orders.

"Does Julian know I'm here?" asked the fox. His head flashed downriver, watching as ducks, cranes, and seagulls called out loud as they flapped away from the humans' invasion of the Saugus.

"That's why I'm with you, rather than poling at the sides," said the Herald, cheerfully. "If we ever reach the other side, I'm supposed to take you to the Apprentice." Rafir stared again at the swirling waters. Men were poling hard, but they were being carried downriver — and several of the other barges on the wide river were not making much better progress. On the opposite bank, men were riding down the river's side, readying ropes to pass to the barges. After a struggle Rafir's barge finally reached the far shore, but it landed in the wrong place, in a tangle of brush and low trees. With the brute strength of many horses and men, Rafir's wagon was pulled free, and they moved toward a mass of men who were milling and sorting just up from the riverbank.

Rafir shook his head — it all seemed very messy. Rafir looked for Julian, but he wasn't nearby — only tangles of men, cursing and muttering as they tried to sort themselves out.

After more than an hour of ferrying and sorting, the tier masses again moved toward Gravengate, slowly gathering speed. Rafir's guard was now on horseback, and after lifting the fox from the wagon, he began jostling his way toward the central tier mass. Within a few minutes, Rafir could see Julian on Bluescent — the Apprentice was leaner and shorter than the larger, mailed warriors about him. Julian and Kalanin were riding together, speaking in low, intense voices. The Herald stayed back a few paces until Julian shifted away from Kalanin. As Julian left Kalanin, Dargas and the Eye of Merlin came quickly to Kalanin's side.

"Where are we?" asked Rafir after the Herald passed him to Julian. "What's happening?"

"We're coming to the last decision," Julian said. "After this, everything should fall into place."

"Is it this evening or tomorrow?" asked Sebastian. He sat, as always, on the right shoulder of the Apprentice.

"We rest one more night, then fight tomorrow," Julian said. "The river crossing took more time and more energy than we expected." In late morning, cloud masses had moved in from the west, and the day was now overcast and gloomy. Riders came and went, seeking Kalanin, or one of the other captains. As the message spread of the battle's delay, gloom seemed to deepen through the ranks of men. Julian let Bluescent drop slowly away from the captains, and the Apprentice began to speak with various groups of warriors. Some were in horse drawn wagons, some were on foot, while others rode on horseback. Rafir was let down from time to time to check with the rearguard. Sebastian was sent periodically to those who were guarding the chest sent by Merlin.

He's showing all three of us off, thought Sebastian, *to let them know that they have magical allies too. So even if we're not much, I guess that we're better than nothing.*

Sebastian watched the chest shift and bounce from the side of a pack horse; even from ten paces, he could feel the power of its magic, radiating from the chest's contents. *Now there's real power. I wonder if anyone, even Julian, really understands the strength of the things stored in the chest, or how to use them.*

It was late afternoon, and the tier masses slowed so that they were only a few leagues from Gravengate. Even from a distance, they were able to see the damage done by the forces led by Thorian and Nergal. Anger began to replace gloom, and men began to call for revenge against their enemies. Dargas rode among them, stoking their wrath.

"Don't forget the Baron," he called to them. "They cut the Baron to pieces when he lay helpless. And don't forget Envar, and the others — tomorrow brings a day of reckoning!"

Before evening Kalanin brought their many tiers to a halt, though many sentries were sent forward to form a screen against any sudden attack at night. Galad shook his head in disagreement.

"Our foes are going to meet us at Gravengate," he said. "They won't try to disperse us again — they'll want to destroy us."

"Of course," said Kalanin. "But would it not be unfortunate if Thorian and Nergal suddenly became irrational, while at the same time we became reckless? Also, would you not harass us if you stood in their place?"

"I suppose so," Galad said, concentrating, then he brightened and leaned back in his saddle, smiling. "But I'm not the General, and it's just as well. Soon this strange blade will test itself against our foes — you make plans and I'll hack away. Just point me towards them," and he pulled away, still smiling.

Nighttime slipped over them, bringing a mostly overcast, quiet darkness. Julian sat quietly with Rafir and Sebastian, as the three watched the camp prepare for its evening meal and then sleep. The staff of the Apprentice poked idly at the surrounding, dry ground then began outlining patterns. Sebastian peered forward, expecting runes made for divinations but found instead lines and strange shapes to help the Apprentice form his own thoughts.

"We've got to make certain you both stay alive," Julian said softly, still framing patterns. "Tomorrow will bring an enormous collision of forces: as in *The Game of the Masters*, one massed set of powers will meet another upon the Field. Either we'll fail, and lose forever, or we'll have new hope. But each of you has to be very careful — the Master of the Great Spell will have enormous malice for all of those who escaped his first Sending." As darkness gathered, Rafir began to stare with longing eyes to the evening meadows. Julian studied the ground before him for a while, deep in thought.

"I can't foresee the outcome of the struggle tomorrow," murmured Julian, "and I can't tell what might happen to you. But the Gift says this: watch out for arrows. Tomorrow, you may be called on to serve as messengers

— stay out of bowshot! Or if you must go near our adversaries, stay low. Particularly you, Sebastian. The archers will be looking for you."

"What about you, the Apprentice?" asked Sebastian. "Won't the archers look for you, too?"

"In *The Game of the Masters*," Julian said softly, "pieces that have made progress on the great Field begin to grow in power. So, you two are stronger and much wiser than at the beginning. Kalanin and Galad have grown much more powerful, and I have gained some strength — enough power so that weapons of wood, even steel, will pose little danger to me.

"But this is likely to be a mortal struggle for many of us. Listen, if you survive and I don't, stay together and search for Merlin, even if it takes years." Julian stood, then looked down at his small companions; his grey eyes were filled with compassion, and light from the Hall of the Dreamers still shone within them. "That's enough of grim warnings and grave counsel. We've come far, very far, against amazing odds, and tomorrow the enchanted dice will roll again. For this night we need to put aside our fears." Idly, he stroked the soft fox fur; with every passing day, the fox seemed healthier, less ragged.

"Rafir, you never knew us as Apprentice and Familiar in our early days when we first learned the weaving of illusions. The healing arts are taught first, then the creation of illusions to amuse others. Tonight, we'll become entertainers again." Sebastian sighed, but a brief smile flickered over his face.

The three of them began to go among the campfires, bringing relief to the solemn men who sat thinking thoughts of deep wounds and death. Sebastian drew on Julian's power, weaving a range of illusions, shaping clouds of colored smoke around the campsites, entering one cloud, then appearing out of another. Then there were illusions of attacks on Sebastian by his own monkey's tail, with the tail mastering the little Familiar after a stiff struggle. So many of the soldiers were new from the countryside, and in the early days of their struggle, they had often seen the sorcery of the

Mid-World used against them. But here, magic was entertainment, and they laughed in surprise and delight.

Kalanin was relieved that some amusement was offered, for much to the disgust of Dargas and others, all the wines and ales had been left behind. Kalanin caught up with Julian as the Apprentice moved with Sebastian and Rafir to another campfire.

"It can't be easy for you to do this," said Kalanin. "Thank you for your efforts."

"It's nothing," Julian replied with a smile. "Tomorrow we're taking our performance to Gravengate. Let us hope that our adversaries don't find us as entertaining as our own allies do."

· ⋈ ·

Evening passed into dark night, and one by one campfires died down, as more men rolled away from the flames and slept. Sleep came hard for Kalanin, as his mind struggled with a range of battle plans. At last, he rose to make certain, once again, that their screening party was properly relieved after midnight. Harlond was not surprised to see him, nor was he upset that Kalanin was watching over him.

"They tell me that the Baron was also a bad sleeper," Harlond noted. "But for me, sleep comes easy. I wake Rostov, and then I sleep. Good night! May you choose wisely tomorrow!" With that, Harlond left and Kalanin was alone for a moment, staring into the overcast night sky. After a few moments, the Eye of Merlin emerged from the dark night sky and settled at his side.

"I can see no sign of their remaining winged emissary," croaked the eagle, "though that flying serpent would be most difficult to sight in this accursed darkness."

Kalanin glanced up into the overcast night sky. "I wondered about your searches, but I gathered that you hunted something."

"They mocked me," said the eagle. "One now sleeps the Long Sleep, yet the other still lives — for a brief time."

"Watch that the serpent creature doesn't get higher in the sky than you again," said Kalanin. "It's a pity that there's no high ground for the humans. We'll all be on the level Plain of Gravengate tomorrow, and there will be many more of our adversaries than men of the League. Is there a chance for us?"

"The first test will fall to you and your captains," said the eagle. "Then, *if* you hold, we shall see how the Magician fares."

Kalanin laughed. "I'm sure that every Power of the Mid-World has a counselor like you — one who can say yes, no, and maybe in the same phrases that sound so wise." The eagle's beak would not permit a grin, but the eagle's eyes flashed with amusement.

"What I said was true, though vague," said the eagle. "Yet I will add this: You should think of yourselves as locked in *The Game of the Masters*. In the beginning, a tempest of power was hurled against you, and Julian, and Galad, and the companions of the Apprentice. You have survived the Ragged Passages, and you are all more dangerous than you were at the beginning. So, be heartened — and yet, our enemies will also have new moves that will surprise us." The Eye trailed off, looking now and again for a break in the bank of clouds that darkened the night sky. "I will also give you other advice," the eagle continued. "You should rest now, for all these things will come to pass as the Masters will ordain, and nothing that we say here in the darkness, will now change them." Kalanin nodded and returned to his sleeping roll. With a great effort of will, he forced his worries from his mind and slept.

· ℳ ·

Unable to follow his own advice, the sleepless Eye of Merlin rose in flight over the great Plain of Gravengate. In the cloudy darkness, the eagle could see only scattered watchfires and shifting shadows as sentries paced over the plain. It was so late at night that all the scent of burned meat and baking bread had passed far into the overcast night. Now reaching into the night skies came the delayed smells of decay and death — enchanted creatures that had been destroyed so many days ago were beginning to rot, and soon the beetles, and worms and rats and buzzards would begin to feast.

A subtle shift in the light overhead forced the eagle to swerve suddenly and dive into a bank of dark clouds. As the eagle hid, the winged serpent that hunted him overhead hissed in frustration.

Soon, thought the eagle, *very, very soon.*

· ℳ ·

Sebastian sat on Julian's shoulder, listening carefully to the conversation of the captains as they rode along, but the eyes of the Familiar scanned the horizon, looking for signs of the Eye of Merlin. Galad was speaking in low tones to Kalanin so as not to be heard by men marching nearby.

"I must have been asleep before," he murmured. "I'm just now absorbing a few key numbers: we're marching with little more than fourteen tiers — seven thousand men — against three times our number. It sounds brave, but it's not the battle plan of any sober general."

"The numbers are worse than that," Kalanin replied. "The Eye thinks that Thorian now has a few more than thirteen thousand, and this Nergal about sixteen thousand — twenty nine thousand in all. But a good portion of these must maintain the siege of Gravengate. If they're not careful, Balardi will sortie with forces numbering five thousand, and take them from behind."

"We've worked it out any number of times," Dargas added. "They can meet us with perhaps only two for every one of us."

"Yet that's a great weight of power against us," said Kalanin. "A force that great valor and generalship might not otherwise be able to overcome. But we shall see." He glanced at Julian, who rode silently alongside them. The eyes of the Apprentice stayed focused on the sky, but he had heard all.

"Often a Magician will know the likely outcome of an event through divination, or even contemplation," he said quietly. "I can tell you that the outcome of this event is hidden, obscured by clouds of uncertainty, although we seem overmatched on any plans printed on parchment." He smiled at them. "It's a good omen for us, and it must bring uncertainty to our foes, with vast interest flowing from the Mid-World. Yet we should say nothing openly of our plans for the eyes and ears of the Mid-World are all around us."

"Another Eye approaches," Sebastian added quietly, and he pointed upwards. The eagle had begun to circle above them, and the sky had grown blue and clear beyond the eagle's flight. A murmur of voices rose from the men of the League as the eagle settled on Kalanin's shoulder.

"Our foes have prepared well for you," said the Eye of Merlin. "Your path to Balardi is blocked by a force of perhaps twelve thousand. And I sense, too, that another five thousand of the men of Nergal are held for a killing stroke — which leaves but twelve thousand to block any sortie from Balardi. May the Maker curse their power! For the force that opposes you is captained, or led by the Dark Emissary, that same Creature of the Darkness that sought you before. Of that Ruined Angel, the Seraph, there is yet no sign." Galad shook his head grimly.

"But that is not all," Julian prompted.

"No," said the eagle drawing a deep breath, "indeed there is more. Balardi is prepared and awaits your coming. His forces will do battle from the walls of Gravengate, and they are ready to force battle onto the besiegers."

"Other forces are shifting," said Julian, looking beyond the Eye of Merlin. "Something like a sea change is sliding over us."

"The walls of the fortress put forth a vapor that radiates magic," said the eagle. "Tension builds in the air, as though a Power readies itself to do battle."

Julian nodded. "We will not name Balardi's ally, or speak too much of this being, but our opponents now understand that we do not fight alone. On this day, our hidden ally will put forth his utmost strength."

Far in the distance, the Plain of Gravengate began to slip into view. Reports of skirmishes came to Kalanin as outriders of Nergal and Thorian clashed with the vanguard of the League. Great flocks of ravens and blackbirds began to come closer. From the highest banks of clouds, batwinged serpent creatures swooped and darted overhead, then settled onto leafy branches.

"The eyes of the Mid-World have gathered to this place," Julian commented, "for they seem unwilling to come much closer to Gravengate."

The eagle's wings flared with tension. "All these Mid-World spies will reveal many surprises for their Masters. And I will astonish a few of them should they come too close to me." The pace of their tiers began to quicken as men saw the rim of the Plain of Gravengate loom closer.

"We have not yet come to the test," Julian said quietly. Kalanin felt the surge of men press about him and sent messengers out to slow their progress.

"A few moments remain to us," Kalanin said quietly, almost to himself. "It would not be wise to come to battle overtired." Now they could see the men of Thorian and Nergal, vast in numbers, awaiting them in battle tiers on the ruined Plain of Gravengate. The fortress of Balardi seemed remote and serene in the distance; only the eyes of the eagle were sharp enough to see that men were teeming along its battlements, drawing sharp swords and spears, and crying aloud in distant voices.

"Let me ask once more," said Galad. "Are you certain that you wish me to hold back — as a reserve?"

"Not a true reserve," Kalanin said softly, "but just hold back from the center at first. We'll keep two tiers in reserve. Our right is steady with four tiers, totaling two thousand men, under Dargas and Rurak. The left likewise with Harlond and Rostov — the greatest danger in such an unequal contest is that our flanks will be broken, but to strengthen them, we have greatly weakened our center. You, and perhaps Julian, will help to hold the center."

"Of course, General," Galad said lightly, but his face was grim as they came to the edge of the plain. They halted to see if their foes would give battle at the rim. Only silence met them as their foes held, massed and ready, halfway between the plain's edge and the fortress. Men of the League began pouring over the edge, setting foot on Gravengate with loud clashes of metal and shouts of defiance. From the fortress the battle trumpets of Gravengate began to echo, sounds made faint and dim by distance.

The last of their battle tiers reached the great Plain of Gravengate. Kalanin paused, letting silence settle again over the plain as he studied the sky and the ground before him.

Overhead, a high darkish grey roof of clouds blocked the sun. The weather magic of their foes ruled again, as all the moisture reported by Sebastian and Rafir had long since been absorbed by the dry dust of the plain. All Gravengate's rich soil had been reduced to brown dust, alternating with seams of yellow and grey sand. Kalanin took a deep breath of dry air and spoke.

Then came cries of command as the captains and tier leaders called out their orders; tiers of the right and left flanks began to form. Dust rose from the ruined plain. Galad noted with surprise that the masses of men formed without the traditional milling confusion. Center tiers hung back so that a movement of armored horse could precede them. A half league away, in the overcast gloom of noon, they watched the formations of their adversaries adjust, forming left, right, and center tier masses. Hot blood was rising now, stirred by many bitter memories. Men began to call out "*Death to the Destroyers!*" "*Revenge the Baron!*" Their enemies held, silent, waiting. Kalanin leaned forward in his saddle, with one last word for his captains.

"Listen to me — we'll do battle today, but not as they wish. We'll juggle them around for a while before we strike. But we are *not* leaving!" Julian was silent. At his side was the chest sent by Merlin, and on its contents so much depended — their own lives and the future of their peoples.

Tier ranks moved forward, men silent now with the sweat of heat and tension dripping from their bodies. Men of the League advanced a part of the way, then halted. From the stacked tiers of Nergal and Thorian came cries and taunts of defiance, but distance reduced their words to meaningless noise.

A moment of hesitation prevailed, as the two forces faced one another from a distance. Dust from the plain rose to a little height, drifted to the east, then fell back. Slowly, almost fearfully, Kalanin rode to the forefront as though to measure their opponents' numbers. A thin volley of arrows fell far short of him. He turned, rising in his saddle, and called out a series of commands that were swiftly echoed to sub-tiers: men of the League shifted, beginning to move back from their enemies, farther from the fortress, while Kalanin rode swiftly back to his position.

"They were too close to the siege," Kalanin explained to Julian. "We need to stretch them a little." Men serving Nergal and Thorian seemed frozen in surprise: the tiers before them had marched for so many leagues and were now seeking to escape from the Plain of Gravengate. Was their march only a maneuver to reduce pressure on the fortress?

After a pause, a mounted force was sent out to harass the left flank of the League. In a flash, Harlond and Rostov called out commands, and tiers halted with lines of archers drawing and firing at their mounted opponents. Their foes scattered, leaving only a few fallen steeds behind them. At this, the tiers of Thorian and Nergal turned, wheeling in formation, moving in pursuit to catch their opponents before they might escape. Every few score paces, the archers of the League would halt and fire a volley at long range, but each time the gap between the two forces narrowed.

Above the battle, the Eye of Merlin arced and turned, his eyes watching the forces of men about the plain. Enemy archers with powerfully reinforced bows shot volley after volley at the eagle, but the Eye hovered just out of reach, sometimes knocking aside a spent arrow that came too near; but the eagle's scorn was shattered as he felt the gaze of the Dark Emissary upon him. The eyes of Familiar and Sending locked together... the eagle struggled to avert his gaze, but he was drawn by the creature's power.

The Emissary shifted to the center of surrounding tier ranks, but a wide space bordered him, as men of Nergal and Thorian struggled to avoid their ally. And the dark being, in the fullness of its power, broke through the enchantments of Merlin, casting a spell over the eagle, one that nearly doubled the weight of the Familiar's body so that the eagle coasted heavily toward the earth, barely able to reach the lines of the League. A messenger hurried to bring the fallen eagle to Julian and Kalanin. Battle was almost upon them.

Julian touched the eagle's great wings, carefully soothing their spell sting. Throughout the plain, men were shifty with quick movements, amid shouts of defiance and command. As the eagle gasped, struggling with his new weight, Julian's Gift reached out and lifted the Dark Emissary's spell from the Eye.

It was then that the Dark Emissary perceived Julian and his Gift. Their eyes met for a moment over the battlefield…with an effort, Julian broke the spells of his adversary. He turned, seeing that the many tiers of two massed armies were almost colliding.

"We'll need to know what happens with the Siege," Julian murmured, and he held the eagle aloft. "You will not need to fear the spell that brings heavy weight again."

Then the eagle was in flight, calling back to Rafir and Sebastian: "Stay with our own tiers, and *keep from bowshot!* Be careful!"

Now with a great numbing sound, massed tiers crashed together. Kalanin sent the first charge of mailed horse against their foe's center; men and horses began to move forward, gradually picking up speed. But then they began to buck and cry in terror as the field about them became filled with rock and steaming fissures — until Julian broke the illusion magic sent by the Dark Emissary. Horses steadied, and their riders struck at the center with long spears, yet without their initial force. Both wings of the armies smashed together as the men of the League, called out, "Break the invaders!" "Remember the Baron, how they hacked at him!" Yet on the other side, men of Thorian and Nergal cried with equal bitterness, "Death to the backstabbers! Death to the killers of children!"

Rafir watched in horror as men fell upon one another with fierce hatred. Rows of pikemen clashed, thrusting cruelly at armor joints. Swordsmen pushed forward with their shields through walls of pike, hacking and stabbing where they found openings. Hails of darts and arrows swept from the center tiers. Wounded men fell, groaning and crying aloud;

but even some of the wounded maintained their hatred, crawling under the press towards their foes, slashing at their enemies with sharp daggers.

On the right, Dargas marched beside his tiers, calling, "Hold! Now, hold! Hold for the League!" Though they faced five men for every three of their own, their lines held and withstood the pressure. Men fell and were trampled in the milling press. Again, and again, massed cavalry charged from the center, covering its weakness. As men and horses regrouped, volleys of javelins and bow shot kept their foes from bringing full pressure against them.

Rafir hovered behind the left tier ranks, where some of the most bitter fighting took place. Here, their opponents had placed their greatest strength, with more than seven men for every three of the League, and no generalship or stratagem seemed able to counter that imbalance. Though Harlond and Rostov called and shifted, and men struck and fought, their lines were giving way, creaking, slowly at first, but nearly to the breaking point. Harlond looked around in desperation.

"Where's the fox?" he called out.

Rafir flickered into view. "What do you need?"

"Tell Kalanin that we're failing. In a few minutes, the other parts of the battle will be meaningless." Then the fox was gone, racing over dusty ground. Kalanin was back a few hundred paces from the center, looking grimly over the battle. Without hesitation, the two reserve tiers were sent swiftly to the left. Galad still stood back, waiting, watching as his sword flickered, glowed, and began to whine.

Battle lines steadied. Cries of anger and hatred passed, giving way to the moans of the wounded, and dying. Men of the League held but had no hope of breaking through, or of retreating. Nightfall was far away. In the center, Kalanin tried again to drive a wedge through their opponents, but their weight of horse and armor was not enough, and their steeds would not pass near the Creature of the Darkness as it loomed so much taller over its human allies. The Dark Emissary stood with scores of warriors a few paces from itself, like a shelf of granite in mid river, a bastion that would never be washed away. His metal staff remained sheathed; he sought instead to ensnare the eyes of the Apprentice.

Now, the weight of their foes began to be felt in the center, as the captains of their enemies perceived its weakness. Kalanin nodded. All his stratagems were coming to nothing; yet the outcome was not surprising considering the numbers of men facing him. He looked at Julian. The Apprentice shook his head. Galad drew his sword. Across the tarnished blade bright metals flickered, while dark metals glowed with a dull flame.

"Now?" he asked.

"Time to test your weapon," murmured Kalanin. "You and I are the last reserves."

In the center, tier lines were crumbling as fresh forces were hurled against the League. Galad sped forward and slipped from his horse. A great press of men was nearly through. He pushed his way to the front rank. The Tarnished Sword had begun a low, deep vibration, like a moan. Masses of spear points pressed at him — and the sword cut through them like a scythe through light grasses. His shield brushed aside the spear stumps. A second sweep of the sword cut through armor and men, leaving them smoking, dead on the ground. He slashed again. A second rank went down. Men of the League began to fight to his side, covering his flanks. Pikemen gave way before him, but a score of swordsmen pressed forward. Galad sprang, slashing at them; as the Tarnished Sword hammered against metal there came flashes of light, and explosions, as men were hurled back, swords were shattered, shields crushed. Galad stood above the mass of smoking metal and ruined bodies. He turned to rally the center tiers.

"For the League!" he cried in a great voice as the sword tugged in his hand. "Now, one stroke for the League!" Along the lines, tier groups rallied, hurling their foes back. Men gave way before Galad, diving out of reach as he neared. But to the right of Galad, not fifty paces away stood the Dark Emissary. Men began to gather closer to this Creature of the Darkness.

Galad pushed forward, with swords and shields scattering, smoking from him. But now a mass of pikemen began to press Galad, and though their pikes were struck down, others replaced them, so that their weight and mass began to force Galad back. The Tarnished Sword slashed wood, and more wood: Galad felt that he was reaping a great field with only one tool, while the stones and bolts of his enemies rained down over him like a hailstorm. Watching from a distance, Kalanin saw the battle again waver, and he pulled together a force of thirty mounted spearmen and sent their long lances against the side of the pikemen facing Galad.

The riders smashed at the flank of the pikemen and rode them down. Galad smote down the last of the pikemen — and he stood facing the Dark Emissary. The dark being was immense, powerful, towering over the humans. From over its shoulder, it drew its metal quarterstaff and stepped forward to face Galad. Julian moved quickly to the battle lines, on foot, with his staff in hand, a slight figure racing toward the armored warriors.

The Tarnished Sword flickered and glowed. All grew still around them, as both sides stared at this encounter. Human warrior and Creature of the Darkness edged toward one another. A low moan slipped from the sword, as it tugged forward; the Dark Emissary stared down at the blade, perceiving its nature.

The creature's head lifted, and its throat-mouth called out a spell of dissolution. Dark metals warred against light metals, and the sword fell, blazing hot, from Galad's blistering hands. The metal quarterstaff was lifted...but Julian called out three words of command, and the Dark Emissary halted, frozen in conflict with Julian. Galad hurled metal gauntlets from his hands. Underneath, his skin was blistered and burned, but he searched desperately on the ground for a glove, or cloth to shield his hands from the sword's heat.

Power began to radiate from the Dark Emissary and the Apprentice... men of both sides edged back from the encounter. Silence surged over the battlefield as Julian and the Dark Emissary swayed back and forth, spell against counter spell — and control began to slip from Julian, his Gift stretching and straining with effort. Slowly, like horror in a dream, the Dark Emissary raised its great metal staff and lurched toward the Apprentice.

Galad seized the sword, his hands wrapped in bloody rags, and he raced forward, slashing at the creature's weapon. Its metal staff exploded with a concussion that hurled both Galad and his opponent backward. Men woke from their trances. Julian sped forward and smote the ground before the Dark Emissary. Spell words burst from his lips.

A pit formed around the Dark Emissary.

And it was filled with slag and ash — and its own people. Men of Thorian and Nergal turned away in horror. Out from the pit, like hordes of dark insects, leaped the creations of the Dark Emissary: some were tiny, some were inches high, and a few were knee length, but each was made in the image of its Master.

Galad turned away, sickened. The mass of creatures leaped over their fallen Master, binding him with webs and cords. The Dark Emissary fought, bellowing through its throat-mouth. But its own creations swarmed over him, binding their Master like an army of spidery creatures, as the earth closed over the pit and the Portal vanished.

Julian then mounted Bluescent. Men of both sides were still backing away, as though the pit might reopen.

"Do you serve the Master of this one?" Julian cried out to his adversaries, but his voice wavered, and he remained pale and shaken. "It's time then, to free yourselves from these evil beings!" He took a deep breath and leaned over to Galad. "Rest for a moment — this is only the first test, with many more to come."

Julian stared out over the battlefield and beyond: with his Farsight he watched the walls of Gravengate, where the Ancient One and Balardi were locked in battle with Nergal and Thorian. At the fortress, men of both sides hung back, as powerful entities were called and checked, Portals flashed — then magic slammed them shut. Outrageous monsters surged from nothingness — and began slashing at one another. Julian's mind recoiled. *Maker's Touch! Nothing I've ever seen or done compares to this moment.*

He struggled to refocus on the battle around him. Sub-tiers loyal to Nergal and Thorian were falling back, regrouping, and sending to their Wizard and Sorcerer masters for more men. Kalanin was harassing them with mounted archers, but League tiers were too few and too worn to break their opponents. Yet now the captains were gathering around Kalanin. Julian joined them.

"If we'd had two more tiers, we might have broken them," Dargas muttered. Kalanin shook his head.

"If we'd had two more, they would have added four more."

Harlond's shoulder was cut above his shield line. As Julian bound it, Harlond asked, "Have we done enough to free Balardi?"

"I've summoned the eagle," Julian said. "It may be that they are breaking free, but I fear that we've only passed the first test." As they looked over the battlefield, their foes launched a great flight of arrows, but these were sent skyward, not at League lines.

"That's the Eye," said Kalanin. He called for a volley from their own archers to distract their opponents. Then, the Eye of Merlin was speeding down to them, moving in haste from powerful bow shots. The eagle was blazing with anger.

"Curse them forever!" he snarled. "May the pit fiends stir their dead bodies with barbed sticks! They strike at me when I cannot respond...what of the Dark One? I can no longer sense him."

"His people have come for their God and Master. He rules them once more," said Julian. "That's one score that's been settled. As for other scores, those will depend on Balardi. What of the Siege?"

"The Siege is shaken but not broken," replied the eagle. "The Ancient One has taken up his old form as mighty Spirit Lord, and battles openly at Balardi's side. With his power, neither Thorian nor Nergal may depart Gravengate, but they send a strength of men, perhaps twelve tiers more."

"Six thousand!" cried Dargas. "That's nearly three men for every one of ours! Can't the Wizard break free yet?"

"My friend, you forget your arithmetic," said Galad. "That leaves two tiers for each one serving Balardi. Truly this was no even contest."

"But I do not despair!" said Julian. "My greatest fear was that the Dark Sorcerer would be freed to come against us. Yet he is locked in a deadly struggle, shielded from us. Take heart!"

"Then let's move *now*," said Kalanin, "before their new strength is set."

Orders were given, and men massed in formation, drawing themselves together; and the tiers wheeled and struck, catching their opponents off guard. Galad pressed against the center, like a spear point, with men of Thorian and Nergal backing away from him. When the force of twelve tiers neared the battle, Azaric, captain general of Stone Mountain, was astonished, for men were giving way to a force that was no more than half its size. Azaric hung back, testing the battle until he understood that the Tarnished Sword would disrupt any mass of forces unless it was countered.

Gathering a tier of five hundred pikemen, Azaric sent them to attack Galad with orders to wear him down, to press him until their weapons were destroyed, then to let others take their place. After a time Galad was blocked: though he hacked and hewed, striking enemies down periodically, it seemed that he was fighting through an endless, impenetrable forest. As the center steadied, Azaric began to put pressure first on the right flank, then on the left flank, so that all the men of the League were drawn in.

Sebastian sat on Bluescent, watching Kalanin's grim face, listening to the cries of destruction and pain. Everywhere down the tier lines, men were calling, "Hold! Hold! Now, hold!" Revenge was a fleeting thought — men would stand now or be broken. But the weight on the right and left was enormous, and on each flank, men began to fall back, cursing and stabbing, some weeping or sobbing in frustration. Julian was on the ground, kneeling among the wounded, aiding those that he could. He glanced up to see the grim face of Kalanin staring down at him.

The wings of the army of the League were folding, like the closing of a book — and when the backs of the two wings were forced against one another, the book would close, and their story would end. Julian stood.

"Now, it *is* time," he murmured, and he ran to Bluescent, drawing the bulkiest of the pouches from the chest sent by Merlin. Racing like fire, he sped to the empty ground beyond the battle and the wounded, to a place where warfare had left only dust covered and deadened fields, with only a few, spent arrows and broken spears scattered around.

"Fly truly!" Julian cried, and with all his force he hurled the contents of the pouch into the air. Like tiny seeds of grain, thousands of white bits flew over the field. Sebastian peered down at a seed: each bit seemed white as ivory, jagged, like the fragment of a tooth — but as a seed, it had been sewn into dead, lifeless soil that would never again grow anything.

The Familiar looked up, expecting a spell or words of power, but Julian had put aside his staff; the Apprentice was holding his hands out, speaking an invocation.

"The firstborn of the Adversaries of the Maker, the Lords of Dragons... now seek the Maker among the countless stars...in their sorrow for their brethren's deeds of darkness...in hope for the new morning of the world... they ask that you aid the Servants of the Maker, freeing ourselves from our old waywardness. And see, we have no other help but you."

Sebastian's head darted back to the battle lines — they were folding, and the League had failed. Where he stood there was nothing, except one lone, massive warrior, standing before Julian. The warrior's mail was strange, with greyish hues, and he wore only a single emblem: a necklace of jagged teeth.

"There's no time!" cried Julian. "Come now or fail us forever!" The warrior looked into the mind of Julian, then beyond, to the battlefield.

"Come for what?" asked the Grey Captain. "Before me is civil strife, war among the Servants. You cannot..."

The Captain staggered backward — for in Julian's mind he saw images of the Hall of the Dreamers and understood suddenly that the conflict at Gravengate was far more than anything like a "civil war." He turned, and lifted mailed arms over barren fields, and cried out in a great voice: "My brethren, our time of service is at hand! We are released — and redeemed!"

Before the Captain, on barren fields, the seedlike teeth began to sprout. Sebastian clutched at Julian as the plain began filling with masses of grey clad, grim warriors, and row after row of mailed men, armed with short spears and shields, armored from head to toe.

As they formed from the earth, they moved without speech or hesitation, surging toward the flanks of the League.

Then they struck at the men serving Nergal and Thorian, with massed, inhuman, almost mechanical motions, pushing, stabbing with spear points, silent and grim. Men of the League shifted away from them, in fear and wonder, looking back to the place where Julian stood with their Grey Captain; the Apprentice was wiping the sweat of fear from his forehead.

"Where is your master?" asked the Grey Captain.

"Hidden, or taken by our foes," said Julian, and he knelt on one knee, struggling to collect himself. "But there is another powerful master we might free — with your aid." Julian stared back to the battlefield: the men of the League were standing back in amazement, while those serving Thorian and Nergal were falling back, dumbfounded. But captains on both sides were riding along tier lines, and in a moment the battle would be renewed.

The Grey Captain turned from the battlefield, looking around in every direction, with eyes that perceived more than any human.

"I have slept long, for the Mid-World of the Truce has come into being, and its many eyes are watching us, from afar." He turned back to Julian. "Now, what are your wishes?"

"Your aid in this war," said Julian, "first to force our foes to the uttermost extension of their strength." As they spoke, Kalanin rode up, pushing his way between Grey Captain and Apprentice.

"Will these depart as quickly as they came?" he asked Julian. The Apprentice shook his head.

"They can be destroyed, but not dispatched."

"Then let our opponents beware," Kalanin murmured, then he turned to the Grey Captain. "How do I order these grim men? I need to know quickly."

"They are ordered through me," said the Grey Captain. "Command me, and it shall be done."

"Hear me," said Kalanin, "there's no time for nice talk. These warriors of yours are fell and grim, yet maybe not as mobile as the tiers of the League. If you'll relieve my captains on the right and left, then we'll have one great thrust at the center."

"It is done," said the Grey Captain, and to Kalanin's wonder, grey warriors began to shift and reform, although no words had reached their ears.

Then there came a massive shift, a sea change in the battle, as Harlond and Dargas and Galad led a great press of men against their foes' center, and out of great weariness, the League found new strength. And the grey men fought beside them, somewhat mechanically, but powerfully. Rostov maintained pressure on their left tier-flanks, as did Rurak on the right. For the men of Thorian and Nergal, the day seemed filled with far too many surprises, even shocks, and they began to give back, looking to break off the battle. A few sought to flee but were shot down by hails of arrows, called down on them by their own tier leaders.

Dargas took a fresh spear from Harlond and readied for another strike. In front of him, the tier lines of their enemies were beginning to give way. He leaned back in his saddle and laughed a great laugh.

"One more push!" he called out to those around him. "There's a cask of ale for every man of you!" Turning to Rostov, he said in a lowered voice, "To think that I doubted the Apprentice! Although a brace of trolls would be more truly magical than these zombie men. Come, let's ride." They surged forward again, crashing against their foe's center ranks

Now at last in the middle of the long day's battle, came the event that Kalanin and Julian and Balardi had looked for. The tide of battle on the great plain of Gravengate had gone completely against their foes, and another eight tiers were released from the gates of the fortress so that the besiegers were stretched to their own breaking point.

Julian could feel the stretching of forces as Kalanin hurled men against their adversary's center, then at the right flank. In the din and tumult of battle, it seemed to Julian that a voice was speaking to him, just at the edge of his hearing. Sebastian's hand touched Julian, as the Familiar, too, became aware of the sound.

"Julian...," murmured Sebastian. A great crash echoed, as armored mounts struck again at the right flank of their foes.

Julian halted; closing his eyes he began to shut out all other sounds from his mind. A distant, deep, rich voice called out, "Julian." The Gift within the Apprentice stretched toward the sound.

"I stand here, Balardi," he said softly. The Gift brought him the image of Balardi, and the Wizard reached out to touch his mind so that full contact was made between Wizard and Apprentice.

Julian opened his eyes, and in the center of the ruined plain stood the ghostly image of Balardi, with the great, shimmering form of the Spirit Lord, the Ancient One, looming just behind him. Julian bowed to them.

"The siege is breaking," said Balardi. "They can no longer restrict us to these walls. Beyond all hope, you have come to our aid."

"It was the distant hand of Merlin," said Julian.

"Not all was Merlin's doing," said the Ancient One. "Other emissaries might well have failed."

"It was well done," said Balardi, speaking quickly. "But now we have come to the next great move in this *Game* — we cannot overcome them, but we can break this siege and unite our forces. The Ancient One takes up his old form, for the last time, and will test this Nergal before he departs."

"I will wrestle a fall with this Dark Sorcerer," said the Ancient One softly. "Yet win or lose, I must afterward depart; and I believe that no Power of Earth, Ancient or New, now has the strength to hold me to this globe. If I reach the Maker, I will seek aid for you mortals and for all of creation."

"Do you understand, lad?" asked Balardi. "In victory or defeat, the Ancient One is gone. But you, lad, you must turn the enemy a little, and make a path for us. Then hold, for a great darkness brewed by myself and the Ancient One will come over the Plain of Gravengate while I and my people break free. You must wait for me to lead you from the mists — otherwise, you will be lost in the same maze of dark mists that traps your foes. Do you understand?"

"I do," said Julian. "We shall await you."

"Good lad," said Balardi, and the spell was broken as he released Julian from their encounter. The Apprentice took a deep breath and rode to Kalanin.

"Did you hear much of that?" he asked Sebastian.

"All, I think."

"Then you should find the fox and join the captains." Sebastian flew off, still hovering low over the plain. As Julian reached Kalanin, he could see that mists were beginning to obscure the overcast skies above. A great darkness was gathering overhead. Quickly, Julian explained how the siege would be broken, and with the opening of a path, Balardi would come for them. A series of messengers rode from Kalanin, and the weight of battle shifted again to their left. Kalanin then turned and looked directly into the sea grey eyes of the Apprentice.

"So, it's done," he said, letting a flicker of a smile crease his face.

"It's the end of the beginning," Julian replied. Grey mists were swirling about him; Kalanin's image was still clear, but the tier masses were becoming lost in the darkness.

Surrounded by sorcerous fog, Balardi and all the men of Gravengate burst through the forces besieging them. Beacons of light shot through the fog as Thorian tried to pierce the darkness. Kalanin and Galad waited in the damp mist as the tiers reformed. Behind the two Charmed Knights stood Julian, Sebastian, and Rafir, with water droplets settling over them. All about them in the darkness came moans and calling sighs, as though the Earth was passing into its final darkness, and all its dying creatures cried out in agony one last time.

"We are standing in the middle of yet another Great Spell," Julian murmured to Sebastian and Rafir. A little distance before them in the fog they heard the padded steps of a horse, then more horses. Galad drew his blade: looking at it now, it seemed nothing more than a poorly made weapon, so badly maintained that it was spotted by rust. A figure appeared out of the mist: the Wizard, Balardi, riding forward, with moisture dripping from his golden, grey-flecked beard. Behind him was the vanguard of the men of Gravengate.

"Welcome to the Plain of Gravengate," Balardi said quietly. "Come, let's away." The Wizard led the men of the League away from Gravengate, weaving along sorcerous trails. Beacons of light still shot through the darkness, as Thorian struggled to master his adversary's Great Spell. The Siege was broken. As Julian picked his way through the darkness, he could hear sounds of battle in the distance, as Spirit Lord and Dark Sorcerer fought together in the groaning mists.

Chapter Fourteen
The Ruined Angel

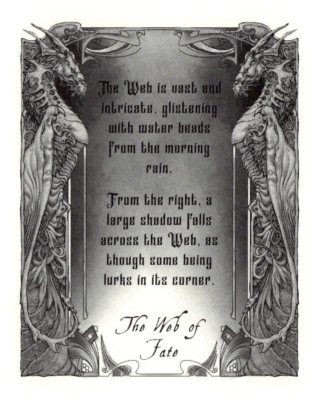

The Web is vast and intricate, glistening with water beads from the morning rain.

From the right, a large shadow falls across the Web, as though some being lurks in its corner.

The Web of Fate

OVERHEAD, THE SKY ALTERNATED BETWEEN cloud and sun, with masses of billowing white puffy clouds surging south toward the ocean. Weather magic still maintained its hold over the atmosphere above Gravengate, but to the southwest, the energies of the upper skies had been unleashed and wild weather ruled.

Kalanin's eyes drifted lower, back to the pack wagons pouring into their tier camps, and he sighed. Victory, even a temporary one, was making life more complicated as trades' people, bringers of gifts, wine merchants and young women serving in taverns drifted into their tier camps. They had moved southwest, closer to Khiva and the coast, where more towns and villages flourished — with more opportunities for trouble.

But their real difficulties were likely ahead: Balardi was a Power and leader of men, and Harmadast, a great captain in his own right. With Balardi was a sub-tier of archers, woman warriors sent by the Mistress of Illusions. Dargas and Harlond muttered how the Baron would never have permitted women archers in *his* camp and urged Kalanin to send them away. Rostov was tongue tied near their captain, Géla, while Rurak was openly intrigued by the tall, dark-haired women. Battle would resolve their conflicts, a struggle with a common foe — but when?

From the corner of his eye, he saw Dargas striding toward him, with Géla, Captain of the archers, walking serenely at his side. Kalanin drew a deep breath and stood straighter.

"Now listen," Dargas began, "I've put up with a lot, but this is the hairiest chunk of meat I've ever bitten into. I can't even get the day guard to listen to orders." He turned to Géla. "I don't want to offend you, but we've chased many town maidens from our camp because the lads were fighting over them. Now we've more trouble — my lads are following your ladies about, casting sleepless moony eyes at them. It's no good. It just won't work." Géla stood as tall as Dargas, meeting his eyes evenly. Kalanin readied for the explosion, but to his surprise, Géla leaned back and laughed softly.

"And?" Géla prompted.

"And what?" Dargas replied.

"Our leaders have taken wagers," Géla said, smiling, "as to which of your two issues you would bring forward first. We have three younglings as part of our force of archers, and each time Dargas sees them, he grunts in disgust. *That* is his second issue."

"Children brought to battle," Dargas muttered. "Maybe there's some history of arming women in emergencies, but none of children. What's next? Arming the village chickens with metal beaks?"

"Those 'children' are the core of our forces," Géla replied. "They are nearly adults, and we turn to them when we need an expert bowshot, or a change in strategy."

"I've seen them in conference with Julian," Kalanin added, "and judged that those three, Kayal, Naith and Issah had some awareness in matters of magic. So, perhaps we should let that issue pass. But what of the first issue that Dargas raised, that of fraternization.?"

Géla laughed again, this time with more humor. "Do you think we were sent out so poorly prepared? What would the Mistress of Illusions do with three hundred pregnant archers? We're charmed against lovemaking: you should tell your lads that we're fine and close companions, but shocking bedmates. But listen...." She put an arm around Dargas' shoulder. "I like soldiers. Something might be arranged for our victory celebration." She laughed again and walked away from the crimson-faced old soldier.

"You're in luck," Kalanin said. "I think she means it."

Dargas took a long deep breath, then exhaled slowly. "Laugh if you want — there are days when I'm like an old boar with bad eyes, rushing onto a mass of spear points. The Baron used to do that, but no one ever had the nerve to stick him."

"Don't be too hard on yourself," Kalanin said quietly. "She may mock you on the surface, but at a deeper level, she respects you. As for our 'victory celebration,' that's a good distance away." He waved at the mass of people streaming through their camp. "Can we use some of these new men?"

"A batch of fair-haired seekers of glory," Dargas snorted. "Cooking and smithing are beneath them. Although, just a minute...as I take a deep breath and consider things more carefully, some of these lads have come a long way, from the coast, and they started before we broke the Siege. We'll take those and let most of the others go back to their farms. Unless...." Dargas searched Kalanin's face. "Unless it's going to be a long war. What do you say?"

"We'll talk about it tonight," said Kalanin. "You should tell Rostov, Harlond and Rurak to join us. I'll ask the Grey Captain and Géla to come also."

Dargas stared up at Kalanin from under his bushy eyebrows. "Is this the Wizard talking, or is it you?"

"You'll be my guests, "said Kalanin. "We need to be allies of the Wizards and not just their pawns."

The old warrior stared up into the afternoon sky and finally muttered, "Maybe the Wizards, too, are being moved in *The Game of the Masters*, willy-nilly, without knowing what's really happening."

· ✵ ·

At nightfall, the Captains gathered in a clearing beside a great bonfire that shot sparks upwards, into a night sky filled with glittering stars. Several companies of Rangers were set out to screen onlookers, but few precautions were taken against the eyes and ears of the Mid-World.

"At this point," Balardi noted wryly, "they probably know more of our affairs than we do."

Balardi sat, hunched forward on a wooden stool, firelight dancing over his eyes and golden grey flecked beard. His right hand clenched his staff, while in his left he held a pipe. After a time, his eyes closed, as he drew in smoke and listened. Sebastian and Rafir were at the gathering with Julian and the Eye of Merlin, while Kalanin and Galad were joined by Dargas, Rurak, Harlond, and Rostov. With Balardi was Harmadast, Steward General of the Wizard, leader of the men of Gravengate. Géla came last to the gathering and sat next to the Grey Captain, master of the men of the Dragon's Teeth.

One by one, each recounted his share of the struggle, Balardi nodding, and puffing, measuring each word carefully. When they came to that portion told by the Grey Captain, Balardi straightened and interrupted gently.

"Captain, we've thanked you for your aid, but we know not what to call you. How are you named?"

"I have never been named," said the Grey Captain. "I was only a dream of power, now grown to reality."

"But then let us reward you!" Balardi said. "I will name you Baroda, which is in the early speech of Alantéa, 'earth seed'."

"A name may bind," said the Grey Captain, stepping closer to the fire. "I would not be so bound."

Balardi nodded. "I understand the choices faced by you and the ten thousand beings that you lead. Some of you will join the ranks of humans, to become like other men and take the Long Sleep, while others will join the masses of Mid-World beings in the long afternoon of Earth's Sorcery. I know these things! I will not bind you; I will lift your name from you when you wish." The Grey Captain bowed to the Wizard and stepped back from the flames.

"So, now we hold each of the strands of this tale in our hands, except for a few," said the Wizard, then turning to the eagle, "What did you find when you sought for Nergal and the Ancient One?"

"The Ancient One is gone," the eagle said evenly, "departed, I believe as he wished, leaving Earth to seek the Maker in the starry universe. Yet

Nergal remains, having avoided destruction at the hands of the Spirit Lord." Balardi shook his head, seeming very discouraged.

"That's not what I had hoped." He sat quietly for a moment, puffing on his pipe, and thinking, eyes still closed. "Well," he murmured, sitting up and looking around the circle. "It's not the point of this gathering. What should be done next? Of all the tales told at this assembly, that of Julian's is the most surprising, bringing news that Merlin lives — but if those who were greatest in Service to the Maker cannot find him, how can we seek for Merlin with any hope of success?" Silence slid over them for a moment, with only the sounds of heavy logs crackling in the bonfire's center; then Balardi continued.

"So, this is the first step in our decision, to learn what there is to know about Merlin and the events at Sea's Edge. Under siege from Thorian and Nergal, it was too dangerous to explore Merlin's fate, but now I believe we should try." Balardi rose, taking his staff, walking several paces from the bonfire where dark shadows began. There he traced a section in the air, from the ground to the highest reaches of his staff, over and down again, making the outline of a wall, as it might have been in the chamber of a lord of men. The Wizard whispered a little over the edges of his divination, then stepped back.

For a moment, his vision panel showed only the woodlands that lay beyond the clearing and the night sky above the woodlands. Then the panel became filled with a clear picture of a sandy beach with seagulls swooping overhead, and sunlight sparkling over rippling, foamy waters. Beyond, the ocean seemed to stretch out endlessly, pulling sand softly from the shore then sending waves crashing again and again onto the beach.

That image held for a moment, then a few men came straggling across the beach, porters carrying materials for a small, grey bearded man. Under the elder's direction, the assistants set up several small stands; on each of these, a slight instrument or device was carefully placed. When they were finished, the old man in the picture nodded and smiled at the porters, his eyes following them as they shuffled from the shore back toward the Halls of Merlin. As the porters retreated over soft sands, the figure turned and looked around the beach, and he seemed to gaze directly at the viewers, and he let a smile flash briefly over his face.

"Behold Merlin, as he was several months ago," Balardi murmured in a low voice. "It's no illusion. But what is he doing?" As if in response, the figure turned, and began tracing symbols in the beach sand. When he was done, he turned to his devices, adjusting them, but here the old man hesitated, as though stray thoughts troubled him. Then Merlin touched his staff, murmuring a few words. Quickly, the image blurred and did not form again for a few moments.

"Merlin wished no one to watch his work on the shore," Balardi said, "though I could not begin to guess the purpose of those sorcerous machineries." After a pause, the image cleared again, and they watched as Merlin stood on the shore, arms extended over the waters, as though invoking the ocean. The figure of the Wizard seemed casual and relaxed as if he performed an everyday chore.

After his invocation, Merlin stood back, waiting for a moment. Then, tumbling over the crests of sparkling waves came a white piece of marble, a statue, perhaps the figure of one of the early Spirit Lords. It dropped to the sand in front of the Wizard; Merlin bowed to the ocean and set the statue upright.

"That was a nice bit of work!" Balardi muttered. "The sea takes and buries things of power and beauty in its deep pools and would not normally release them. Yet it yields to Merlin." Again, Merlin invoked the sea, and again, the sea sent an object tumbling over its foamy surface: this was far smaller — an armband, with a single ruby set in it. Balardi rose in excitement.

"Behold, a tool of power!" he cried. "No other mortal wielder of magic would be able to retrieve such a thing!"

Now, the Wizard again summoned the ocean to do his bidding, but this time the waves along Sea's Edge hesitated and fell back; and the expanse of ocean surrounding the shoreline drew far back into the depths and grew still.

"Time for Merlin to make peace and depart!" Balardi muttered, but the image of Merlin continued to work on the shore in the long afternoon, while the sea, as though sullen and sulky, retreated beyond its deepest tideline.

At sunset, heavy winds began to blow along the beach, and the ocean seethed, though it no longer cast waves upon the beach. But at nightfall, a storm broke, with wild winds surging, and great waves smashing down on the shore. Now no more gifts were given; instead, great boulders and a tempest of waters were hurled against the shoreline of Sea's Edge.

Yet, as they watched, Merlin labored on, unmoved, unyielding, and the sea spray fell far from him, as though the Wizard stood behind some massive, invisible curtain. At last, the powers of the Wizard seemed to prevail, and the winds and storm died down, leaving a clear, moonlit sky. The sea returned to its normal pace, pounding at intervals against the shoreline of Alantéa the Forerunner. Balardi let out a deep breath.

"Merlin made that seem easy," he whispered, "yet it was far from simple."

They watched on as the Wizard repeated his invocation — in the same casual motions as in the afternoon. Shore waves continued their steady pace, but beyond, in the depths, came the sounds of a titanic struggle, as though the spells of Merlin were countered by forces that proved far greater. At last, the sea answered — with terrifying power — a great wall of water, fully a hundred feet high, came racing toward the Wizard as though to smash him away forever.

But Merlin smote the shoreline with his staff and walking to the water's edge, brought the great wall of water to a halt. Before them, in their vision spell, they watched a tiny figure standing in the moonlight in front of an immense wall of water. As the Wizard struggled to contend with the ocean, fish spilled out from the wall of water, to fall, flopping, onto the beach. An amazing tension held for a moment; then slowly, incredibly, the great wall of water collapsed down upon the Wizard.

"Get away!" Julian cried out. "Get back!" Balardi's hands tightened around his staff, but nothing could be done to change the past. Where Merlin had stood, only water and swirling foam existed. Where the devices of the Wizard had held the sea in check, only surging torrents remained. And now, under pressure from the ocean, the earth's crust broke, the ground heaved and shattered, sending a flood of lava bursting out, shooting flame and ash into stormy night skies.

The image flared — and then it was gone. The outlines of the vision screen began to fade. Where there had been a wall of water, the shoreline returned, with woodland images beyond the shore, and a normal night sky reappeared. Onlookers took deep breaths of night air, some standing and stretching to relieve their tension. Julian looked up into the starlit sky, struggling with his own emotions: Merlin had been his tutor, his master, nearly a father to him.

"Almost, almost I would rather not have known," Balardi said, shaking his head. "If Merlin lives, he is captured or lost to us. Yet this Divination has answered a portion of the mystery."

"What does it answer?" croaked the eagle. "Merlin sought a Power beneath the waves. That Power remains shielded, impenetrably masked."

"It's beyond my understanding too," Julian added, "though you seemed to recognize the Talismans that Merlin sought from the ocean. Do these things name Merlin's adversary?" Balardi looked at them sadly, somewhat warily, then sat, lighting his pipe once again.

"I'll tell you," he murmured, puffing, and he put his staff aside. "It seems that we are the last of the League — Merlin is gone, Thorian is a traitor. Old secrets no longer matter.

"In the beginning, you know, the Wizards were not much different from the Sorcerers in terms of pure power. Our instructions were left to us by the Ancient Servants, and we tried to keep close to them at first. On the other hand, the Sorcerers learned much of Dragon lore, and later, from the Mid-World Powers. Yet, on the whole, we were not that much different — it was Merlin who conceived of an alliance of magic wielders, a sharing of knowledge, and a departure from the lore of the Spirit Lords. There was much to learn, said Merlin, and three good men, acting together, could keep from the pitfalls of power and dark knowledge that compelled the Sorcerers to serve dark masters.

"Thorian and I counted ourselves as cofounders of the League, though it was Merlin's concept, and his name is often attached to it. At the beginning there were but three of us later joined by two Apprentices who were trained and raised to Magician's status. All this was long before your time, Julian, and yet this tale concerns you closely. Earlier Adepts came and went, but at crisis time, our Adepts were named Orantes and Wylar. Merlin had settled at Sea's Edge, and I, at Gravengate, while Thorian built his fortress upon Stone Mountain. Our Adepts acted as emissaries, a more mobile force that extended our reach far from our stone fortresses.

"Then our League was challenged. A time of great confusion ensued, called 'The Wild Time.' For me to speak openly of that time might well invoke the anger of the Gods, the undying Powers of the Mid-World; and so, I can say no more. But after that struggle, our Adepts, or Magicians as they are no called more frequently, chose a small island for themselves south of Sea's Edge, and there, many men labored to build a great fortress, in the likeness, perhaps, of Gravengate.

"A time of peace followed the Wild Time, and our growing strength must have alarmed several of the Powers, for a series of Great Spells struck at us. I endured, as did Merlin and Thorian, but the small island of Orantes and Wylar was struck down, and their fortress washed into the sea. Merlin and I and Thorian searched and struggled to find them, while at the same time we amassed knowledge and power so that the League would not be assaulted again.

"Over the years our power has grown so that none have sought to come against us openly. Yet our Apprentices and Adepts were always drawn to the Mid-World, taken from us. It seemed to Merlin that there was some design at work, some plot against the League. So, in the Apprenticeship of Julian, his real learning was obscured, even from himself." Balardi smiled at Julian. "You were made resourceful, rather than strong, and shielded from *The Game of the Masters*. For these reasons, we hoped that the Powers would not concern themselves with you."

"So, it was as I thought," said the Eye of Merlin. "The Apprentice knew too much of the Art, too little of the *Game*, and the Sight became quite powerful within him. But Merlin has said nothing to me of these ancient Adepts. How do they enter into this struggle?"

"We searched for them for many years, but the sea left no record," Balardi continued. "I knew nothing of our younger brethren until this evening. Just now I have seen the first traces of them, objects that Merlin raised from the ocean: the statue cast upon the beach was an oracular device favored by Wylar, while that armband was a *Talisman* of power fashioned by Orantes, a seeking device to find beings who were deeply hidden within the Mid-World.

"I can only guess that Merlin called upon the sea to deliver our old allies, or to name our adversaries, and neither was the sea permitted to yield. Further, I guess that Merlin now shares the fate of Wylar and Orantes. So now not only have we lost our Adepts to our hidden enemies, but Merlin is gone, and Thorian is a traitor, separated from me by an impenetrable wall of hatred and violence. We, then, are the last of the League." Balardi shook his head sadly. "I can only do my best."

"Yet Merlin may have foreseen his fate," Julian said. "Why else would he equip us with spells of power, except that he knew he might not be able to come himself? And if he had foreseen this, then perhaps he also anticipated his own rescue."

"You may be right," Balardi said after a pause. "I will go to Sea's Edge to contest the ocean and attempt the rescue of Merlin. But that's not something I can do with two such mighty foes at my back. First, we must deal with the dark alliance that now holds Gravengate." The Wizard looked about him, into the many firelit faces. "Our conduct of this struggle should be decided in a more private place, with a single commander for all the many tiers. My Steward General Harmadast is senior among the men at arms, and he has acquitted himself valiantly during the siege of Gravengate. I put him forward as commander. Is it agreed?" Galad looked sideways at Kalanin. It was as Kalanin had expected, and not unreasonable: the Steward General of Balardi was a noted tactician and a seasoned captain of men. Kalanin nodded in agreement, as did the Grey Captain. To their surprise, Julian spoke up.

"The Sight within me says otherwise. In this matter, I believe that it was intended that Kalanin should lead." Balardi stared at Julian with raised eyebrows.

"This is my counsel also," added the Eye of Merlin. "Many pieces have been transformed since the first moves of this *Game*."

Julian studied Balardi's face carefully, perceiving an unusual hesitation. "We shouldn't disagree," he said. "It's much easier to cast a future on it." Balardi frowned then nodded, and drew a leather pouch from his side, passing it to Julian. The Apprentice rose, casting the contents on the ground: from the pouch came a variety of many, multicolored pieces of varied shapes and sizes. Some fell flat, others spun like tops, but in a moment, all shapes had settled. Sebastian leaned forward: each piece held an image of a piece in *The Game of the Masters*.

"You must read," Julian said with a smile, "as we discussed, I've been shielded from the *Game* and its devices." Balardi walked about, studying the pattern from several angles. Finally, he swept the pieces up into his pouch and handed them to Julian.

"Again," said the Wizard, and Julian cast the shapes on the ground a second time. In a moment, Balardi looked up and searched Kalanin's face, as though understanding him for the first time. He put his arm around the shoulder of his Steward General.

"Old friend," he said softly, "this captain has grown to generalship in the service of the League. The message is clear. Will you serve under him?" Harmadast stood straight, looking at the many captains standing together under the starry skies of Alantéa.

"Come, it's not so bad," he said. "These leaders were chosen by Merlin or have surfaced in the fiery cauldron of war. A great force of arms has been forged from the ashes of a broken army, while a powerful feat of arms and sorcery has broken the siege. Yes, I will serve." Balardi seemed relieved.

"You will be my adjutant general," said Kalanin. "We'll decide matters together." Balardi sought Julian, Kalanin took Harmadast aside to go over the map board with him, while others drifted away to their separate quarters. Sebastian remained with Rafir, still close to the great bonfire that was finally beginning to fade.

"With all these proud men," said Rafir, "it's a wonder that they can agree on anything."

"The bonds of the League formed by Merlin still remain," said Sebastian, "though it seems that Merlin is gone, probably forever."

·)(·

Sounds of squeaking wagon wheels woke Rafir and he peered out into the early light of day. At least it wasn't raining, and the camp was stirring. The fox rose and stretched, then made the silent brief *shift* that left him invisible. Then Rafir began running through the camp, unseen both by humans and Mid-World Spies. Men were packing and loading, as though a march would be called soon. Even the Grey Men, the product of some Dragon Magic, were moving more quickly. Some of these men were becoming more animated, talking, and laughing with the men of the League. From what Rafir understood, those would become human, while others would eventually join the masses of Mid-World beings. Another campsite flashed by as the fox sped through the fields.

Where was Sebastian? Julian's Familiar always knew what was planned next. The nose of the fox, though burdened by all the smells of horses, humans, and their cooking fires and waste pits, began to pick up the smell of his small ally's monkey shape.

He found Sebastian seated just in front of the chest sent by Merlin. Armed guards were stationed in the area, but the eyes of the Familiar seemed to be watching the chest far more closely than any humans. Rafir flashed back into view.

"You seem worried," said Rafir. "Is there something wrong with the Wizard's stuff?"

"Nothing is *wrong* with it," said Sebastian. "It's just that if I knew more about what's inside that chest, then I'd have a better idea about what will happen next."

"Then you don't know more than I do," said Rafir. "Won't there be more talk, a conference or something?"

Sebastian smiled. "It's happening now, but only Balardi and Julian and Kalanin are present. They've sealed themselves off from the others. Julian told me that no one, either hidden foe or Mid-World Power, could approach." Rafir nodded in silence, but his eyes gleamed with the thought of adventure — could they really seal themselves against the invisible fox?

He raced off, hunting the screen of guards that usually surrounded these conferences. Rafir found them just a short distance away, in a thicket of forest — and slipping past the guards was easy as always; even a slight wind helped to mask any sounds. He scooted forward, a few steps at a time, but not thirty paces from the screen of men, he bumped into an unseen barrier. It seemed to be a wall —was it made of sky matter? He could see through it, but nothing could be seen beyond it but blue sky. It was very strange.

He circled the wall twice, and it seemed that the wall closed off a section of forest, roughly the size of a large chamber. Carefully, Rafir touched the wall with his paw. It felt as though the wall moved, like a barrier formed from streaming water. There was a force to it, but no pain. He looked around: the guards were far away. Greatly daring, he turned visible, extending his paw again into the force field. This time the wall was impenetrable, as though made of stone. Rafir smiled to himself: when he was visible, there was no give to the barrier, but when invisible, and if he pushed hard enough....

Aha, he thought to himself, *the invisible fox slips by again!* He vanished, rearing on his hind legs forcing a way through the enchanted barrier.

On the other side was forest, with three humans gathered in a little clearing. Julian was leaning against a tree, Kalanin was seated, but hunched forward on the ground, and the Wizard sat on an old stump, pipe in hand. From the expressions on their faces though, they seemed far from relaxed.

Rafir was close, but he wasn't close enough to hear...he padded forward....

"I have always looked," Kalanin was saying, "to the Wizards for guidance, to a force of magic to show us a path...." He halted, watching while Balardi stared into the distance with a troubled look on his face, suddenly intent on other matters. The Wizard held up his hand for silence, as though the sounds of some intrusion had disturbed him.

Balardi stood for a moment, taking his staff in his right hand. He spoke a few words that were just outside Rafir's hearing, but suddenly Rafir found that he was no longer able to breathe. With feet of quicksilver, the fox turned and raced back through the enchanted barrier and out into the woodlands. After taking a deep breath, Rafir muttered a little about his own stupidity, though in reality, he was pleased with himself.

· ⋊ ·

"I have to think that our intruder was Rafir," Julian said with a slight smile, "but I will make certain later. We are at the crux, Kalanin. Go on."

"I have always looked for clarity and understanding from the Wizards," Kalanin continued, "but we are having trouble seeing possible futures clearly. Tell me again what happens if we avoid battle at Gravengate."

"We lose this conflict," Balardi said, "either a swift defeat or a slow decay as we dwindle away in the hills — but we lose."

"So," Kalanin replied, "if we arm ourselves with all our weapons — both sorcerous and those borne by men — what happens then?"

"We have a chance to hold the day," Balardi said, looking away, "but do not dream of some total and complete victory that ends with us riding into Gravengate while happy maidens cast rose petals at our feet."

"My lord," Kalanin said, "since I have some responsibility for the lives of so many other simple humans, I must probe and search, hopefully without offending you."

Balardi smiled a brief, grim smile, nodded, and puffed on his pipe.

"When Galad and I spoke about the Wizards and their League," Kalanin continued, "we understood that Julian was slowly gaining power, moving from Apprentice to Adept level. But we also understood that the Sight was unusually powerful in Julian, that the Apprentice could see things beyond the vision of an Adept. So, Julian, what are you seeing when you look at our destinies?"

Julian laughed, a short bitter laugh. "That's the one question I feared you would ask. Different futures flash through my dreams, and almost none of them make any sense. For the men at arms before Gravengate, there seem to be two main futures: in defeat, you flee in disorder, likely signaling the end of the League; while in victory, you withdraw from Gravengate, still strong and resolute, with many of your Captains still alive.

"As for those of us contending with magic, we stand at the endgame on the pinnacle of Gravengate, struggling for the future of our peoples and the fate of Alantéa the Forerunner. Most of the time there are four of us, though our features are always distorted as though we have been transformed by dark magic. Balardi and Thorian are there, as are Nergal and this Apprentice. Sometimes we are joined by an unknown fifth person, and sometimes a sixth is also present. This sixth person is mysterious, appearing as a huge wraith, features cloaked and hidden, but one of its arms is that of a skeleton, fleshless, while the other arm is covered with beast's fur."

"That vision suggests *The Master* in *The Game of the Masters*," Kalanin breathed out.

"What can I say?" Julian said, lifting both hands in surrender. "None of this makes sense to me or to Balardi. To add to our confusion, the sky at the peak of Gravengate is strange and the light surrounding us is distorted. Lenses seem to float through the sky, as though many of the Great Gods are peering down at our complex and confused conflict through Vision Portals."

"This discussion has not been entirely reassuring," Kalanin murmured, shaking his head.

"Then let me restate the matter," Balardi said quietly. "We are choosing between two options, one with some hope and the other with no hope, so there really has not been much to choose from."

·))(·

Rafir paced through the woodlands. His curiosity was stirred, and he was even more restless than before his failed spying effort. He halted panting, letting his mind work rather than his feet.

The eagle is wiser than the rest of them, he decided, *but where to find him?* It seemed to Rafir that when the eagle was not in the air, or with Kalanin and Julian, the Eye was usually with the outer sentries. Rafir began to move, sniffing the ground toward the east, where a screen of sentries stood between the forces of the League and their adversaries. He sped on, panting shallow breaths from his half opened mouth.

He found the eagle perched on a low branch in a forest glade, with sunlight beaming over his folded wings. Rafir hesitated because the Eye of

Merlin was staring far into the distance: his usually grim look had faded, replaced by an appearance of wisdom and peace, radiating from the Familiar's face. The fox flashed into view — suddenly, the eagle was transformed into a menacing creature of the wild, prepared to strike with beak and talon. Rafir vanished again and began to edge away, but the eagle had seen that the intruder was his ally, Rafir.

"Wait!" the eagle called. "You do not need to flee. I was caught off guard and that is seldom done."

Rafir, though uncertain, flickered into view. "I didn't mean to surprise you," he said, hesitantly. "You looked so peaceful — I had never seen you like that before."

"I was dreaming of flight over the ocean at sunset," said the eagle after a pause, "when the day's heat brings drafts of air from the water, like warm winds rising from below. The rise of such air will carry a creature with broad wings far into the night. But you have not come for lessons on flowing winds. What did you wish?" Rafir told the story of his curiosity, how he had sought first Sebastian, finding news of Balardi's parley, and how he had penetrated through their barrier. The eagle raised his head and gave a great croak of laughter.

"A fine jest! They will be searching for their Mid-World adversary who came so far through their screens." The eagle looked down at Rafir. "I must tell them of your exploit, so they will be freed to worry over other matters. Yet you should not regret your actions — the Wizard should learn to be more careful with his spell work." The eagle was obviously pleased with Rafir. "Let me consider for a moment, then I will tell you what I believe will happen." Rafir was silent, watching the eagle stare over the horizon.

"Matters have become simple," the Eye continued. "We are as well armed and equal to them as we will ever be, without the presence of Merlin. We will have another strike at them, probably soon, and it will be our final strike, for in the next struggle we will win — or be defeated utterly. There will be no confusion and no stealing away under an enchanted fog." The eagle looked at Rafir. "Here is your answer: we attack, we win, or we lose."

"Is this really what we want?" asked Rafir. "All this is strange to me. In the stories of the old Sorceress, the good side always won in the end, but everything has been so different. Do we have a chance?"

"Now you pose a harder question," said the Eye of Merlin. "We barely escaped before when we had the Ancient One with us, and the Grey Men of Dragon Magic surprised them. Yet now they will know that we have the enchantments sent by Merlin, and they will know that the Ancient One has departed...and it is also possible that the reluctant Seraph will again be called to their side. Though that being is not one of the great First Servants, the latterday Servants have reason to fear him. Then, there are the Great Spells fashioned by Merlin and the unchecked, unbroken power of Nergal. But all these things will be tested again, in fearful and dubious battle." The eagle fell silent again, returning to his study of the late afternoon sky.

"Thank you for your answer," said Rafir. "I would rather ask you than the warriors. But it all seems a grim business."

· X ·

The next morning tier groups moved forward, horse, wagon, and foot, pressing toward Gravengate. Those groups assigned to Rostov were well ordered, but his mind was not. Men seemed in good spirits; a few were stiff with fear or anger, but many joked and laughed. Not much more could be done for the moment. Rostov slowly drifted from his tiers, seeking Dargas. When he reached Dargas' side, the old warrior anticipated his question.

"Don't ask me, lad. I only know what you've been told: that we're to take another crack at them."

"Then, what's this closely hidden mystery, this secrecy about?" asked Rostov.

"That's what I asked Kalanin, but not so nicely. What I said was: 'You've confused your allies more than you could possibly confuse your enemies.' To give him credit, he did look more than a little unhappy. 'It's Wizard stuff,' he said. 'Fair enough,' I said, 'but what are we supposed to do about this Wizard, Thorian?' 'Taken care of,' he muttered. 'What about this Sorcerer, Nergal?' 'That's Balardi and Julian's problem.' 'All right,' I said, 'what of the others like the big black insect thing, or the filthy, perverted angel that broke the Baron?' 'Those beings are our problems,' he said. So, stop worrying, lad. All we've got to fear is a force of better than fifty tiers, with whatever Power or Creature that comes stumbling about. Relax!"

Galad was riding beside Kalanin. Within his metal gauntlets were thick leather linings. Julian had healed the burns on his hands, but when he held the Tarnished Sword, even with padded gloves, traces of the old pain returned. Galad studied Kalanin's face carefully as they rode side by side: the knight's face was marked, though not by burns: more of his beard was turning grey and the lines on his face seemed to deepen each day.

"It was less complicated, wasn't it, when we were simple emissaries of the League," Galad said. "What was it like say two years ago?"

"The Mid-World was sending shielded emissaries against us, riders who were illusions for the most part — some of them were even amusing."

"Perhaps this time next year it will be easier, less grim," said Galad. Kalanin did not agree but rode on in silence.

The Captain of the Grey Men walked on foot, without fatigue, moving at the head of the men of the Dragon's Teeth. It seemed to him that the struggle would soon be over, one way or another, at day's end. Then he would be free.... What should he choose then? In a way it was simple, for the Mid-World was a dream world for all creatures born of magic: he would abandon his human form and become a being of undetermined strength, living for thousands of years within the Mid-World, pursuing his pleasures, building his strength. On the other hand, if he retained human form, he would live another thirty to fifty years, then die. What happened to humans when they died? They spoke of the Long Sleep, that their Maker would wake them at the end...it seemed so unlikely. Yet Kalanin was human as were Galad and Dargas — these three drew him like magnets: the inner intelligence and strength of Kalanin; Galad, powerful, supple, laughing at some great jest; or Dargas, weaving a tale over a flagon of wine. If he could be like them...his mind churned as he strode toward Gravengate.

As they marched, Julian picked his way among the tiers, seeking captains and tier leaders. To them, he passed healing potions: Dragon's Breath and Bindweed woven with Serpine.

"With these, the body will often repair itself," he said, "but you must staunch the blood flow, or life will slip away from your men." Dargas nodded, looking at him shrewdly. He spurred his horse to keep up with the Apprentice.

"And this means that you're likely to not be around at day's end," he said in a low voice. Julian's face was weary; he had been up much of the night preparing healing potions.

"So many uncertainties lie hidden in this contest," he murmured, setting more enchanted bindings into an aide's hands. "It's best to be prepared for all chances." He waved to those around him, but he caught the eye of the old soldier and nodded, telling Dargas that he had guessed correctly.

· ⋊ ·

The men of the League pressed forward toward Gravengate. Kalanin and Harmadast had judged that their foes would give battle on the Plain of

Gravengate, where they might apply the massive weight of their many tiers. Yet as the tier groups moved closer, they found that their advance parties and screens were coming under attack. Groups of mounted archers fired volley after volley, fleeing after the deaths of several of the League's scouts, while creating growing confusion. A company of rangers passed through a dark glade and were enveloped by a sudden cold spell. All would have frozen had Balardi not countered the enchantment.

Again, and again, the outer screen of their tiers was harassed and checked, and though the massed tiers pressed forward, a deep sense of menace built among them. Julian quietly began to move forward toward the vanguard. The Eye of Merlin lifted from Kalanin's shoulder, sweeping toward the forefront, but a stream of arrows sent him wheeling skyward.

Julian pushed Bluescent toward the vanguard, at times riding through fields when sections of road were clogged with soldiers.

"Are we joining the screening party?" asked Sebastian. Julian shook his head.

"Something's up there, on the road," he said softly, as they rode past a provision cart. "You should be able to sense it now." Sebastian closed his eyes and leaned forward. The feel of dark sorcery beat at his brow, mixed with the smell of decay.

Julian reached the edges of the main tier masses and spurred Bluescent over the last half league. As they sped forward, Sebastian saw that part of the vanguard had fallen back, with some left sitting, ashen faced, at the side of the road, not fleeing, but unable to press on.

They reached the vanguard. Many within its ranks faltered, while others were unable to control their horses. Julian said nothing as Bluescent pushed her way through the milling press. Harlond stood at the front, with only a few of his aides about him. With one hand, Harlond held the reins of his horse, and with the other was his sword, but it was pointed to the ground, hesitating with uncertainty.

Standing before Harlond were the slain men of the League, old companions, horribly scarred, bodies rotting, soiled by burial dirt. But they stood, calling out to the living.

"How do I know that you speak the truth?" Harlond was saying, struggling with his charger and his own doubts.

"We have come back to warn you," said a dead man in a dry voice. "No joy lies in the shadows. Go back to your farms and villages. Death lies before you and the end of all pleasure. Go back." Bluescent was calm beneath Julian, and she carried the Apprentice to Harlond's side. The Gift reached toward the dead man, and it touched a many layered mass of illusions. Julian turned to the men of the vanguard.

"Hear me!" he called out in a loud voice. "The dead have begun their Long Sleep. They will trouble us no more! I name these as phantasms, creatures of the Mid-World, filled with malice and deceit. Let them yield their shapes!" Julian's power flashed through his staff, and the illusions were stripped from the Mid-World creatures: large, winged creatures were revealed, with buzzard talons, and slight bald heads that held features that were almost human. But an enormous carrion stench hung over them so that both men and horses were sickened and fell back. Bluescent held.

"In the League's name, I bid you depart!" Julian cried. Harlond and others freed themselves from their fearful horses, and advanced to Julian's side; yet there were more than fifteen of the carrion seekers, and they began to laugh and jeer at the Apprentice.

"You are nothing but toys of the Mid-World," they mocked, "yet you think so much of yourselves." There were too many for Julian...his mind raced. Carrion creatures moved to menace both men and the horses around them. But in their malice and scorn, they had not marked a cloaked figure riding toward them. Balardi reached Julian's side and cast the hood from his greyish gold face. The Wizard rose in his saddle.

"If you will not yield, then you will perish!" he cried, and in that instant, the creatures were enveloped in sheets of flame and scalding steam; they leaped up in a rage of pain, struggling to take flight. Most were too damaged by the spell and crashed to the woodlands, where rangers put spears and swords to them, and so they died.

After a pause, Balardi murmured, "These were not truly a threat; perhaps I should not have become so angered."

"Don't judge yourself too harshly," said Julian. The two halted, letting the vanguard reform and push forward. "We've been careful not to provoke the many beings of the Mid-World, and so perhaps they should treat us with more care. Besides, these carrion seekers are not much loved in any place as they seek even the corpses of their allies."

Balardi took a deep breath. "I promised the Ancient One that I would put aside all rashness, and become more measured, but it's unpleasant to have the young people menaced or threatened. So Thorian must have felt in his own madness and self deception." Julian shook his head but kept silent.

· ℳ ·

Again, the men of the League pressed forward, and now their screens of scouts and rangers were no longer obstructed, as their adversaries slipped back toward Gravengate. Word was passed by messenger that the rim of the great plain was undefended, that the men of Thorian and Nergal were drawn up close to Gravengate, with the walls of the fortress anchoring their left flank.

"It's as I would have done," mused Kalanin, "to bring us before them, matching tier mass against tier mass, where their greater numbers might yet overwhelm us." Julian was beside him, deep in thought, and Kalanin watched as Julian ran his fingers over the runes of the chest sent by Merlin. The Apprentice shook his head in response to the unasked question.

"We can only hope to balance the forces of sorcery," Julian murmured. "You will win or lose based on the strength of your tiers and the skill of their leaders. May the Maker support us and forgive us, for now the killing and the dying begins."

Once again, the men of the League spilled over the rim of the Plain of Gravengate, and now there were more of them, many more. Their cries and shouts of defiance echoed over the ruined plain, as the Grey men of the Dragon's Teeth clashed spear and shield together, rocking the afternoon air. Kalanin watched as the tiers milled and sorted.

On the right were placed ten tiers of the Grey men, under their captain; these would seek only to hold at the edge of the fortress and not be thrown back.

At the center, Kalanin placed another six tiers, three thousand of the Grey men under Rurak and Rostov, with another six tiers of the men of the League under Dargas — these would seek to hold, but they might place some pressure on their adversaries.

Kalanin watched as the left tier mass formed: ten tiers formed by the men of Gravengate under their Steward General, with two thousand mounted men of the League under Harlond. The archers of the Mistress of Illusions marched with the men of Gravengate. Kalanin watched on grimly: here on the left, they might break them. In total numbers they were overmatched with forty-two tiers facing more than fifty pledged to Thorian and Nergal. But that would mean nothing if he could shatter the left flank of their foes.

Tiers formed, sending clouds of dust across the plain. Balardi's face was grim as he watched the sunlight pour over his ruined lands. But the death of Thorian and Nergal would bring back neither orchards nor men...the Wizard's mind struggled to come to grips with the strength of the anger that surged inside him. Men moved forward, strangely silent except for the clank of metal and the snorting of horses clearing dust from their drying nostrils.

The Eye of Merlin hovered above the dusty plain, watching as a grim, silent host shifted slowly forward in the dust, moving toward another grim mass of men. But from the corner of his farseeing eyes the eagle caught a glimpse of red sunlight; with a terrible certainty, he knew that it was his adversary, the second of the winged serpents. Desperately, the Eye of Merlin struggled upward in his climb.

Balardi glanced at the laboring wings of the eagle, and finally, his thoughts crystallized.

"Not yet!" he cried to the eagle. "Hold back for a moment!" But the eagle was beyond hearing. Balardi turned back to Kalanin and Julian. "Only the Eye of Merlin has made a final commitment to this struggle. There may still be time for the rest of you. For the sake of all these men, I will try to avert bloodshed, though every part of me cries out for revenge." Kalanin watched the Wizard warily for a brief moment, then nodded. Messengers sped among their ranks, and the tiers came to a halt, not more than a thousand paces from their foes.

A gap parted in their ranks, and three rode out: Kalanin on Balardi's left side, while Julian rode at the Wizard's right hand. It seemed a long, slow, journey, inching forward hesitantly, waiting for their opponents' response. For Kalanin, it was just another turn in a dark labyrinth, with hope now for a little, greater light; but for Julian, it seemed that they brushed the outermost strands of the *Web of Fate*, and now the Lurker in the Shadows was easing its way toward them, and the Web was beginning to quiver.

After a few, long moments, another party of three came forward from the massed tiers of Thorian and Nergal. Rafir peered out of Julian's saddle pouch: in the distance, a tall grey-haired figure with a silvery cloak approached, accompanied by another figure nearly as tall, but in dark robes, hair a deep black. These Rafir knew as Thorian and Nergal, as shown by the conjurations of Balardi. A third figure rode behind the other two and was not known to the fox. Julian leaned down to Rafir.

"It's best for you to stay visible," he whispered, "now that they've seen you." He touched Sebastian who perched on his left shoulder. "When we return, leave me for a while — stay with Kalanin and ask if there are errands you can perform." By now the two groups were closing, and they halted, leaving a gap of twelve paces. Thorian's expression was grim, lofty, and remote.

"Say what you have to say," Thorian said coldly, and his eyes were colored flint and filled with hatred. Balardi held himself in check, nodding as though to pace himself.

"I had no great wish to ride over my ruined lands to speak with you," Balardi said, and his voice was bleak, though measured. "Still, there are men full of life and strength who will live no longer if we continue. Here is my offer: Depart, and we shall not pursue. Our dead will be buried, and we will begin to restore the land you have broken. What say you to this?" Thorian was somewhat taller than Balardi, looking down on him perhaps by a hand's breath, but now he stared down from his height as though he beheld an evil being squirming in the dust.

"Even at the last," said Thorian, "the treacherous slayer seeks to avoid judgment, and it will avail you nothing. But you, Julian, and you, Kalanin, you have been deceived by this evil Wizard, and this is truly the reason I consented to parlay: remove yourselves, take your peoples and depart. The issue is between Gravengate and Stone Mountain alone."

"Merlin himself sent us to aid Balardi," said Kalanin. "We are Merlin's tools in this conflict."

"Bring Merlin forth then, to explain himself," Thorian said coldly.

"Merlin has been taken or destroyed," said Julian. "Even he did not foresee the extent of the snares laid for the League."

"You mean that even Merlin has been caught in this traitor's web," Thorian snarled, then his voice rose. "Do you think me a fool? Do you think that this false Wizard can so easily hide his deeds? By divination, by conjuration, by a call to the dead, I know that my consort was destroyed by this Wizard! I know that he has stolen away with my one child, my daughter! Here then, is my last offer: yield my child if she still lives, and the false Wizard — the rest may go."

Balardi could not restrain himself. "I know *nothing* of these people! For *nothing* have you slain men and ruined a good land! But hold...now, hold...." Balardi struggled for control. "Wait. Your quarrel is with me alone. Let us bid the others depart, and we shall settle this matter between ourselves: a contest of two magicians only, with no others suffering." At this Nergal laughed in a deep voice, and Julian was surprised by the unexpected melody of the Sorcerer's voice.

"The betrayer asks for trust, the deceiver for belief," said the Sorcerer in his rolling, musical tones. "How long shall we listen? We have seen his crimes with our own enchantments. We have not fought a bitter, bloody war, and skulked about in the brush seeking outlaws and bandits, only to be struck down by words."

"Enough of words," said Thorian, and he turned to go, with Nergal in his wake. Balardi and Kalanin also turned away, but Julian called to Thorian's back,

"Your ally is passing strange, Thorian. From him, perhaps you may discover the true reasons for this struggle!" Thorian did not reply, but Nergal leaned back and gave Julian a look with such a powerful shock of magic that the tongue of the Apprentice was stopped, and he was left speechless.

Their horses clumped slowly back to their formations, sending small clouds of dust into the afternoon sky. As they rode, Balardi shook his head back and forth, distraught, filled with shame and rage. Kalanin and Julian watched the Wizard with pity — and concern.

"It was Merlin's way to seek peace rather than conflict," Kalanin said quietly. "It was right that we tried to reason with Thorian — although Nergal's part remains a mystery."

"We spoke for *nothing!*" said Balardi. "For *nothing* except the end of all honor. In the middle of my land's destruction, I sought peace, only to be scorned by filth!"

Around Balardi the air began to crackle with energy. Julian and Kalanin fell back a few paces.

"It cannot be borne!" cried Balardi, and winds began to whip the dust of the plain into their faces. "It will not be borne!" cried Balardi, and now as Elementals and Spirits drew toward the great Wizard, a dust storm held their tier ranks in place, as men hunched down against the wind, covering their faces with mailed hands. Julian and Kalanin halted on the plain, peering into the swirling dust, searching for the Wizard. But Balardi's voice came from a height above them, speaking in clear tones that rose above the storm's noise and echoed over all four corners of the plain.

"Now, stand back! I was asked to draw the Mad Wizard away. This I will do but in no gentle spell test! There will be death and destruction!! And flames in the Heavens!!" Blasts of power rattled over the plain, shaking the ground. Cries of pain and terror rose from the storm struck tier masses of their foes.

Kalanin shielded his eyes from the dust, murmuring to Julian, "What now? This was not what we planned. Do we break off, or hold our ground?"

"Hold for a moment," said Julian. "I do not believe that Thorian can restrain himself." More blasts shook the ground so that Julian and Kalanin dismounted. Now, similar noises rose from their enemies' position, with Thorian's voice emerging, calling for destruction and revenge. Sounds from the plain began to lessen, but above them came wild sounds of battle and warfare in the skies. The storm that had swept the plain died as quickly as it had begun. Kalanin and Julian remounted, gazing upwards. Through the dust could be seen the vague images of sky chariots, one drawn by an array of glittering phoenixes, the second by gleaming griffin shapes.

"Those are the chariots formed by the Elementals of Air and the Elementals of Fire," Julian spoke, his face turned upward as though in a trance. "It was never thought that they might be used against one another."

Sheets of light began to roll over the skies above Gravengate: sudden lightning storms radiating hues of crimson, azure, and gold. All the eyes of the Mid-World began to flee or collapse shrieking to the ground. Yet as the Wizards ranged farther and higher, the air began to clear over the Plain of Gravengate. Kalanin and Julian reached the lines of the League, watching as men pulled cloaks from their faces, still coughing, and wiping dust from their eyes. Others raised their heads slowly, as though waking from a dream.

"It's all still part of the *Game*, isn't it," Kalanin murmured grimly to Julian. League tiers were beginning to reset. "Two Powers are locked together in some distant corner of the Field of the Masters, while others must play out their own moves unsupported," Julian said nothing, but he opened the chest of Merlin and drew out the last two pouches, placing them in deep pockets within his cloak. Tier captains gathered about Kalanin.

"We'll do our part as planned," said Kalanin. "And now, it's too dusty for speeches. We must only finish what we've begun." Dargas looked up into the distant sky battle and said nothing. The forces of the League began to move slowly across the Plain of Gravengate.

On their right, the Grey Captain led five thousand of the Men of the Dragon's Teeth. As he strode forward, he cast his human name aside — and chose the Mid-World. He would build his power over many ages, defining his pleasures in the long afternoon of Earth's Sorcery. But first, there was a battle to win. His men picked up their pace in response to his mental command.

In the center, Dargas rode forward, his horse kicking up dust from the ruined plain. It was good that he'd been given Rurak and Rostov, but twelve tiers were not enough. Though he would do his best, and maybe, just maybe, he would have a cut at the filthy backstabbers who had killed the Baron.

Harmadast rode behind his mass of ten tiers, a full five thousand of the garrison of Gravengate. Nergal's colors were flying from the fortress, and Harmadast could feel the anger surging through the tiers supporting him: rage was good. And it was good to have Harlond serving under him, with two thousand of the men of the League — that lad would obey orders at least. He wished that he might say the same of Géla, who led the archers. She was hotheaded so he would need to watch her closely. He stood in his saddle so that he could see that she kept her position.

Behind the three tier masses, Galad rode with two mounted tiers. Just behind him were four tiers of two thousand of the Grey Men, and these were silent as they marched through the dry, dusty air. At Galad's side, the Tarnished Sword began to stir in its sheath as it sensed the blood and metal of their foes.

Julian rode beside Kalanin, and a great feeling of sorrow swept over him, that Thorian had not listened, that men would die, that Merlin could no longer counsel him. Even the Eye of Merlin was gone, fighting in the skies, or falling crippled with the other beings of the Mid-World. Dust was beginning to rise again as the tiers clanked forward. Rafir rode at Julian's side and Sebastian was on his shoulder, but the Apprentice now placed them on a pack horse.

"Listen," he said. "After the first crush of battle, see if you can help as messengers. But your most important task is to stay alive. There's malice in so many of our enemies and rage in Thorian. Nergal would probably kill you outright and keep your stuffed bodies as trophies. Do you understand?" They nodded, watching Julian with large eyes.

Julian turned his attention from his small friends. Movement across the Plain of Gravengate seemed to be taking forever. Was it fear that made it longer? Men seemed to labor with each step — the Gift shot a bolt of alarm through him.

Julian looked toward the mass of adversaries arrayed before the great fortress, and he perceived the enchantment: it was a spell that he had never felt before, one of enormous power...slowly, it was bringing thousands of men to a halt...the strong willed captains of the League were pushing a little farther, before freezing into the dust...Kalanin and Galad were still moving forward, as though riding in their sleep. Galad halted, hunched and frozen, then Kalanin faltered, his head partly turned as though seeking Julian. At the last Julian halted, with fear causing beads of sweat drip down over his forehead.

Silence reigned over the plain. Across from Julian, the men of Thorian and Nergal also seemed to be frozen. All the charms, all the potions of Adepts, the sorcerous herbs of Sanguine, and Dragon's Breath and Goblin Rush, and Serpine, and all the amulets that turned aside Mid-World Sorcery, all these proved to be nothing. Here, at last, was a Power that would not be charmed.

Julian struggled to free his hands, while his eyes searched for the figure of Nergal.... But the Dark Sorcerer was also searching, and suddenly, over the enchanted battlefield, the eyes of Nergal found Julian, the last mortal human still conscious on the frozen Plain of Gravengate.

Julian found himself in the presence of a being of great power, cowering before it as a shrew might before a lion. And the Gift perceived Nergal's intent, how he looked upon all the humans on the plain with contempt, amusement, and deep malice. Slowly, Julian's hand reached into the third of the pouches sent by Merlin, and he felt an incredible cold fill his hand, while the enchantment over his own form was broken. To the amazement of Nergal, Julian the Apprentice rode forward a few paces and spoke in clear tones over the stillness of the plain.

"The emptiness comes for the darkness..." and Julian reached forward with his left hand — and his hand had become as dark as the night, growing so that it reached, like a great cloudy shape over the expanse of the Plain, stretching toward the Dark Sorcerer: the Gauntlet of the Void, that imprisoned its opponents in nothingness, far from all sources of magic.

Nergal leaped back in alarm...his form changed, and he had become wraithlike, with great bat wings. A Portal flashed just behind the Sorcerer, and he leaped through. The Gauntlet pursued, drawing Julian behind it, into the deep enchanted substances of the Mid-World, and far from the battles of men.

· X ·

Masses of men began to slip from their enchantments, into great confusion. Horses woke, filled with surprise and fear, and men on both sides stood bewildered. The men of the Dragon's Teeth had been less affected — they were on foot and were themselves beings fashioned by magic. They began to move forward toward their opponents, and in a few moments, men of the League followed.

Galad looked up as mists began to lift from his mind. He drew his sword. The blade gleamed with bright metals; dull metals gave off a somber glow. Beside him, Kalanin murmured in a low voice, "It begins." The left flank of the League, with fourteen tiers, closed against the lines of their enemies.

"Break the destroyers of the land!" the men of Gravengate called out, and men of Thorian and Nergal called back, "Death to the betrayers! Death to the backstabbers!" On the left came the first bitter blows as the great weight of the League began to force back the men of Thorian and Nergal. Galad's face turned to Kalanin, but no sign was given.

Now the two centers met, and Dargas hurled twelve tiers against their foes, and the right flanks struck with the Grey men of the Dragon's Teeth speaking no words but wielding grim spears against their foes. Galad looked up into the air: even with the din of battle, the Wizard's struggle rumbled through the skies like the sounds of distant thunder. Julian had vanished. On the left and in the center, the weight and fury of the League began to force back the men of Thorian and Nergal. Galad pulled to Kalanin's side.

"I won't try to advise you," he murmured, "but is it not time now?"

"You hold," said Kalanin, not looking away from the battle. "It's time for the horsemen and their spears." Then two tiers of mounted men were sent crashing into the battle on the left.

"Break them, break them!" Kalanin muttered, and a few around him could hear his teeth grind with tension. The left pushed forward, at first quickly, then more slowly. Dargas, in the center, smashed back a counterattack. The push on the left slowed, then stopped, as their foes threw more tiers into battle.

"Here is what we feared," said Kalanin. "Now we begin a long afternoon." He reached for a messenger. "Call back the mounted tiers. Tell the Steward General that he must hold his ground — giving way only if he must."

"It's the center, then," said Galad.

"Yes," said Kalanin, "but give me a few moments." Mounted tiers gathered again, and many of the riders were stained with red, and more than a few horses bled beneath their armor.

The left flank of the League was now overmatched with fourteen tiers facing more than twenty, and they began to be forced backward, but Harlond was rallying them, and there were cries of "Hold! Now, hold!" And the Steward General would not yield, as the men of Gravengate fought back, giving ground only a few steps at a time.

Then, against the center, Kalanin hurled the main strength of the League. To the twelve tiers led by Dargas, he added four tiers of the Grey Men, with Galad beside them, now on foot, wielding the Tarnished Sword. As the pressure grew, Kalanin drew two tiers of the Grey Men from their right flank, where their adversaries had not sought to give serious battle and launched them against the center.

Galad swept forward, and the first rank of men went down before the Tarnished Sword, and the second rank backed away, as the Mid-World Weapon struck at them. Men of Nergal and Thorian pulled back, but through their ranks, as though long designed, poured two sub-tiers of men with long pikes, and Galad again was hacking and hewing through a vast, impassable forest — yet, as he slashed, Galad could hear the heavy crush of armored horse striking at the center of their foes, and now all around him formed a company of Grey Men, armed with spears, forcing aside the long wooden pikes of their enemies. The lines of their foes began to shudder as if a great shattering would soon take place.

Men of the League pushed forward, their opponents fell back...and in the middle of their ranks appeared a tall figure, gleaming and golden, with his head bowed in sorrow. Dargas halted and cursed.

"It's that fornicating Angel," he muttered, as all along the lines, men were faltering. "A First Servant, and the death bane of the Baron." The Seraph raised his head and fixed his eyes on the men of the League.

"Leave now, mortals," he murmured, "and trouble me no more." In his right hand, the Seraph held a long rod. Men of the League hesitated.

"It's the Baron's killer," Dargas cried. "Now, let's cut him down!" But the men of the Dragon's Teeth held back, murmuring, "He is one of the Firsts…we are sworn to serve the Maker, not his Adversaries." Galad slashed against the pikemen, seeking to break through. Kalanin felt the hesitation and sped to their side. Dargas was filled with fury and battered his way forward to the tall, once holy figure.

"It's more foul than the monsters!" he cried, and he hurled a javelin at the Seraph, but the tall figure brushed it away with a flick of his fingers, and reaching forward, touched the old warrior with his long cane. Dargas fell like a stone. Like jackals, the men of Nergal leaped from behind the Seraph and hewed at the fallen figure. As bodyguards of Dargas pulled his body from the press, Rurak shouldered the men of Nergal aside and struck at the Seraph, but his sword would not bite. Men of Nergal hewed him with axes; Rurak fell dead to the plain. The Seraph looked to the sky, face filled with great sorrow.

"What have I done to be so compelled?" he murmured. But now Galad was upon him, with Kalanin just thirty paces behind. The Tarnished Sword flickered and glowed as it faced the First Servant.

"You are wielding an ugly weapon created by mongrel magic," said the Seraph. "Cast it away and depart from me."

"You are corrupt," said Galad softly, and he edged forward, his eyes following the movements of the Seraph's cane.

"Alas, mortal, you do not know," said the Seraph, casting his head back in agony. Doubt came into Galad's mind: he beheld in the Seraph's torment, the sorrow of the Lady of the Hill. In that half moment of confusion, the cane of the Seraph flicked out, striking Galad on the helm. As Galad toppled, Kalanin leaped forward, pulling Galad from the axes and knives of the men of Nergal.

Now, men backed away from the Seraph, and as battle swept away from the First Servant, his noble, golden face turned once again to the dust of the plain, as though lost in contemplation.

Kalanin watched as the bodies of Galad and Dargas and Rurak were carried to the rear. His hand drifted to his sword hilt.

Rage — and understanding, raced like lightning through his mind: he had been set on this course long ago, by Merlin, to become a captain, to leave sword and shield aside.

If he drew his sword now and struck at the Seraph, thousands would die — needlessly. He could no longer choose for himself.

Rage flailed again at his mind, but he understood, at last, how he had been shifted by Merlin as a piece in *The Game of the Masters*.

But now, he could free the others — and himself. He rose in his saddle, and hurled his sword, sending it arcing high, shining in the sunlight, and it fell harmlessly, far from the Ruined Angel.

All along the battlefield, men of the League were falling back, or dying needlessly. The day was lost. The Men of the Dragon's Teeth had lost their fierceness, and fought only mechanically, thrusting halfheartedly at their foes, as their own feet backed away from the contest. Dargas and Galad and Rurak were lost. The great thrusts against the left and center were blunted and broken. In the sky, the battle between the Wizards had grown more distant, while Julian and Nergal had vanished.

Messengers were sent racing to Harmadast and Harlond, bidding them to give way slowly and to withdraw a tier of archers and two tiers of horse to cover their retreat. Kalanin rode to the right flank, seeking the Grey Captain.

The Grey Captain stood behind the men of the Dragon's Teeth, staring in confusion at the gleaming Seraph. All around him, the men of the Dragon's Teeth were faltering, milling, and dying in confusion. Kalanin slipped from his horse and jerked the captain's body so that it faced away from the Seraph.

"Hear me!" cried Kalanin. "Tell your people not to contend with the Seraph, but to resist the humans. Do you understand? Fight the humans!" The Grey Captain nodded, his eyes focusing on Kalanin, and some of the confusion seemed to pass from his mind.

Bit by bit, men of the League began to fall back. The battle was lost, but the lines of the League would not be broken. Again, and again, the captains of Thorian and Nergal hurled fresh tiers against them, but the men of the Dragon's Teeth began to stiffen, and Kalanin sent two tiers of mounted men to shore up their left flank. Archers fired volley after volley at their attackers. And the Ruined Angel would not advance but stood alone on the plain, head bowed in sorrow and contemplation. Above them, the war of the Wizards grew ever more distant, with only the faintest of tremors reaching them.

A slow, hard time passed.

Little by little, trading bitter stroke for bitter stroke, the League forces fell back, retreating but not fleeing. At last, the captains of Thorian and Nergal allowed the men of the League to break free from the battle, and the tiers of the League stumbled to the western edge of the Plain of Gravengate, and into the meadows and fields beyond its rim.

Kalanin stood at the meadow's edge, staring back out onto the Plain of Gravengate. In the distance, the red and black banners of Nergal were barely visible, as they flew from the topmost tower of Gravengate. Sebastian sought Kalanin, bringing news of the wounded.

"Galad lives, with the deep chill slowly leaving his body," the little Familiar said, "but Dargas is near death. I've done what I could, but we need Julian." Kalanin was silent, staring into the distance. Baroda, the Grey Captain, and Harmadast, the Steward General of Balardi moved slowly to his side. The face of the Grey Captain held human tears, welling from his eyes.

"We've lost, but who could have contended with a First Servant!" Real, human sorrow swept over the Grey Captain, and he became irrevocably human. "That was a Seraph, and no illusion, was it not?"

"It was a First Servant," said Kalanin, "but a broken, corrupt one, serving the Adversaries of the Maker."

"The battle was ours," added the Steward General, "until the Seraph came upon us — yet it's no shame to have lost to such an immortal."

"*You* may have lost," said Kalanin, and all the stormy wrath boiled up in him, and he tore his badge of generalship from his cloak, letting it float to the ground. "Decide among yourselves who is to lead you." He tugged the heavy plate mail from himself, keeping only light chain mail.

"As for that corrupt slayer of men, I will deal with him, if I can." Kalanin strode away from them, drawing a spear from the weapons cast on the ground, and he chose a heavy charger that looked fresh enough for the return. A sound reached into his mind, as though a voice called to him from a distant chamber.

The sword — do not forget the sword, whispered the voice. Kalanin turned, staring in all directions but no one was near him. Several paces away, the captains watched on, dumbfounded. Before they could act, he leaped on the charger, and rode to Galad's side, taking the Tarnished Sword from the stricken knight. Galad lay frozen, silent, but his eyes watched intently as Kalanin sheathed the sword and rode away.

Harmadast stood, mouth opened, seeking words to stop Kalanin, yet no words came. His sergeants surrounded him, waiting for instructions; Géla pulled herself from those around her.

"We should never have left Gravengate," she said. "My people are going back." The sergeants blocked her way. She turned back to Harmadast, her eyes blazing.

"Get your rot-brained lackeys out of my way!" she cried, "or I'll cut them!" They gave way, uncertainly. Géla pushed past them snarling and muttering.

Rostov turned to Harlond, and the youth's face was streaked with sweat and tears. "Did you see what they did to Dargas?" he asked. "They chopped him while he lay senseless. They should be destroyed, every mother's son of them! I'm not staying here." Harlond reached for his mail. The Grey Captain seemed to wake from a deep trance.

"You will not go alone," he muttered, then his voice rose. "We failed before, but we will not fail again!" All about the fields and meadows, men of the Dragon's Teeth began to rise and move toward their tier ranks.

Harmadast watched on, astonished. Some of his own men were beginning to pick up weapons and move back to the rim: the fight for the League was no longer under control. Men and women began, once again, to spill over onto the vast Plain of Gravengate.

· ⚔ ·

Kalanin walked his charger to the rim of the plain, then brought him to a trot across the dusty fields. A few scouts drifted over the plain, but they were busy looting the fallen or wandering aimlessly, staring at the skies, searching for signs of their masters. None looked for a lone rider, jogging across the plain. Not far from the walls of the great fortress, the Ruined

Angel stood, as before, his head bowed to the ruined land. One ranger called out to Kalanin:

"Have you come to parlay? Halt, and tell us your purpose." Kalanin lowered his spear and rode the man down. Some distance away, the Seraph lifted his great golden head, as though waking from slumber. Men stood between Kalanin and the Seraph. He spurred his charger; they scattered, spreading cries of alarm. Trumpets sounded from the towers of the fortress. Kalanin rode, full of fury, spear point aimed at the tall figure's chest. At the last second, the Seraph brushed the spear point aside, then his wrist flashed: his cane struck the charger's tail, and the horse stumbled, collapsing. Kalanin threw himself clear, and fell, rolling over the dead plain. He rose, his sweaty face caked with the dust of Gravengate. He was bruised, but there was a fury raging in him as he struggled to his feet. Kalanin drew the Tarnished Sword and limped toward the corrupted First Servant.

The Seraph stared at Kalanin, noble face filled with sorrow.

"Mortal, you will force me to do more evil," said the Seraph softly. "Will you not let me be?"

Kalanin advanced, watching the Seraph's cane with the eyes of a hawk. "You call me 'mortal,'" he said, "yet only one of us will die on this day," and he aimed a great two handed cut at the Seraph's neck. The cane rose and parried; a whine of strain shuddered as the two enchanted weapons met. The cane flashed again, but the Tarnished Sword turned it aside. The Ruined Angel grew more intent, his face losing some of its look of remote sorrow.

"You are fierce and warlike, human," said the Seraph. "But when all is said and done, you are but a mortal, and I am a First, one of the Masters." Kalanin did not reply, but stood on the battlefield, sweat pouring from his body. A few paces away, the Seraph stood, golden and noble, filled with grace and beauty, more than two heads taller than his human opponent.

Kalanin was dirty and bruised, grey hairs sprouted from his beard, his face was lined with age and tension — but now a fire raged in his blood.

He aimed another great cut at the Seraph...the cane deflected it, swinging back at the Tarnished Sword. The weapon leaped in Kalanin's hand and slashed at the cane — the long staff of the Seraph burst into flame and exploded. The next sweep of the Tarnished Sword hewed the Seraph's chest.

A great gasp of terror and horror sprang from the ancient First Servant as it sank to its knees on the ruined Plain of Gravengate. Kalanin backed away, watching as blood, golden blood, thick as sap, gushed from its wound.

"Maker forgive me," whispered the Seraph. With a great cry of fear, fear of the unknown, the Seraph passed into the darkness, falling face first into the dust.

Now the men of the League came streaming across the Plain of Gravengate, some moving eagerly, some with faltering, uneven steps. The men of the Dragon's Teeth felt the passing of the Seraph, and they called out together with one loud shout of triumph that echoed across the Plain. Men picked up their pace. Stragglers began to follow at the far edge of the rim. Harmadast formed the last of the tiers and led them toward the fortress.

From within the fortress, the captains of Thorian and Nergal marshaled their own forces once again, wondering what madness had come over their foes. In moments, battle lines had met again, but not with tidy tier lines, rather as one horde against another mass of men.

The Tarnished Sword flashed and glowed as it slashed through metal, flesh, and wood: a grim reaping time had come for Kalanin, and none could stand before him in the hour of his rage. Men of Thorian and Nergal began to back away, some dropping weapons. Harlond and Rostov pulled three tiers of mounted men from the press of battle. Archers loosed again. The captains of Thorian and Nergal rallied their forces for a counterthrust.

Now, Harlond and Rostov led their fifteen hundred horses into the confused, milling ranks of their foes — and broke them utterly, after so many bitter months. A great mass of men, more than nine thousand, were forced from the fortress walls. Men on horseback began to slip away. Others dropped weapons and sped east toward Stone Mountain. Again, Harlond and Rostov smashed into them. Other men of Thorian began to retreat into the walls of the fortress; Nergal's people jeered at them, but unable to locate their distant master, began to follow them.

At last, better than a full third of the great tier masses following Thorian and Nergal were broken, ruined as fighting forces. Men surrendered or fled. Others took refuge behind the walls of Gravengate, waiting for news of their Sorcerer or Wizard masters. At nightfall, the men of the League were masters of the hotly contested Plain of Gravengate.

· X ·

Many leagues from Gravengate, Julian stood on a darkening field. Night was coming. A thousand paces from Julian, the Dark Sorcerer waited, completely unafraid. Nergal had been pursued, streaking through many Mid-World kingdoms; now he rested, gathering strength. Julian looked down at the Gauntlet of the Void, still settled about his left hand. Its power was spent; the fabric of energy woven by the Great Spell was broken.

He shook off the Gauntlet, then stuffed it back into his cloak. In a moment, his adversary would rise and destroy him, but still Julian hesitated. Nothing was left except the last of the Great Spells sent by Merlin. Balardi had cautioned him to use it last, if at all. Now, it was the last spell, his final chance.

Julian touched the last pouch and within it, a sleeping Power stirred. Julian the Apprentice reached inside and spoke the spell words, then he added: "Great One, let me share your form."

He stood for a moment, not knowing what to expect, while around him, a pillar of flame formed, casting light over a darkening field. In the distance, the Dark Sorcerer stood, unmoved, as firelight danced over him.

Julian stepped out of the flames, and he was as one with a Lord of Dragons, no cunning Serpent, or giant lizard, but a first child of the Demons, and a master of the wellsprings of sorcery.

"Greetings, little brother," said the Dragon. He peered closely into Julian's mind and saw the beginnings of wisdom and power. The images of the Dreamers in their great Hall amazed him. It was true, then, that man, or a few men, would become Powers.

Above him, his Dragon senses followed the distant contest of the Magicians. Might their power yet equal his own? And outside of the struggle, with clear sight, he beheld all the many beings and Powers that observed them from the Mid World. Some of his brethren surely hid there, transformed.

"Hail, Great One," Julian murmured. He beheld the great glittering Dragon mind. In its mind were the beginnings of Magic and mystery, here in the first offspring of the Demon Princes, but here was one who chose to serve the Maker.

Above Julian, the battle between Thorian and Balardi still seemed to fill the upper air. Was there a chance to aid Balardi? Beyond the battle, he saw, now clearly, the Mid-World in its full reality filled with rich magic, with many beings, both greater like the Dragon Lord, and lesser, like himself.

The Lord of Dragons turned to his task, fixing his eyes upon the Dark Sorcerer.

"I will deal with this one, and fulfill my vow," said the Dragon. "Then, I will be free to seek the Maker beyond the circles of the sun. May you have good fortune in your Service, little brother."

The Dragon, glittering with wisdom and power, moved toward his adversary. True Sight was needed...the Sorcerer was one who was masked on many levels, layered with illusion...he was...not human, a Power... and...it was...his Master. The great Dragon Lord moved forward, placing his head on the ground before his Lord.

Julian watched Nergal, who stood silent and motionless before the Dragon Shape.

"If you are able to counter this one," said Julian, "you will transform this struggle. I will be freed to aid Balardi. May you find the Maker at the heart of universe, at the center of all understanding."

As the Lord of Dragons moved forward, Julian could feel the enormous power of mind and body ready itself for conflict with the Dark Sorcerer, and its Dragon senses were able to pierce many layers of the Sorcerer's disguise and...it was.... Almost, before he yielded his Dragon's shape, he was nearly able to discern the true shape of the Dark Sorcerer.

· ⋊⋉ ·

Julian was cold. His cell was dark. He opened his eyes, and saw before him the form of Balardi, lying on the ground, streaked with soot, caked with blood: the Wizard was alive, but not conscious, and he was breathing heavily, as though in a coma. Balardi had lost. The Great Spells sent by Merlin had been broken by Nergal. In a great mind-numbing shock of despair, Julian sank back on the floor of the dungeon: death was coming, the last and final act of *The Game of the Masters*.

Chapter Fifteen
The End-Game of the Masters

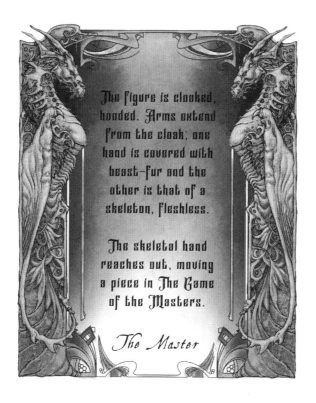

> The figure is cloaked, hooded. Arms extend from the cloak; one hand is covered with beast-fur and the other is that of a skeleton, fleshless.
>
> The skeletal hand reaches out, moving a piece in The Game of the Masters.
>
> *The Master*

KALANIN DREAMED, A VAGUE, LIGHTLESS night vision slipping over him in the aftermath of bitter fighting: a distant voice reached to him, beautiful, but evil, and it was summoning grief and death...a great cold weight, like some massive glacier, was slowly inching toward him, and already he felt the chill and shortness of breath that comes from the fear of suffocation....

But now hands were shaking him, rough, ungentle hands, breaking into his night vision. He woke slowly, then lurched up, collapsing back to the edge of his sleeping roll. Blood still seeped from his shoulder wounds, and he swayed a little as he focused his eyes on the messenger.

"Are we attacked?" he mumbled. His eyes focused and he saw Rostov standing at his side. He struggled to his feet.

"No violence," said Rostov, "but a matter you need to deal with."

"Let the Steward General or Baroda deal with it," murmured Kalanin, and he turned to topple back onto his cot. Rostov and his aide caught him and held him upright.

"That's foolish counsel, and you know it." Together Rostov and his aide pulled Kalanin away from his sleeping roll. "There's a woman who's come to our camp, claiming allegiance to our cause, offering strange advice," Rostov continued. "We could easily call her insane, and send her away, but she has the look of those with the Gift."

"Then summon the others, too," said Kalanin, rubbing his face. "Let them hear and judge as well."

"Rurak is dead," said Rostov, "while Dargas lives by a hair's breadth. Galad heals but is still not able to move. I'll bring the others."

"Just one moment," said Kalanin. "What of the Eye of Merlin, the fierce Familiar of Merlin's?"

Rostov shook his head somberly. "He may be injured, hidden in the forests, but we fear that he perished, for hundreds of winged creatures were destroyed during the Wizards' battle in the sky."

"I hope it was a clean death, a warrior's death," said Kalanin, shaking his head. He thought of the eagle, standing broken winged in the night forest, waiting for death. And there were so many others to mourn.

The captains began to push into the tent, murmuring and nodding to one another in subdued, hushed, funereal voices. Harmadast and the Grey Captain sat beside Harlond and Rostov. Using his own judgment, Rostov had summoned Géla, and now he carefully avoided the eyes of Harmadast. Rafir and Sebastian were present on Julian's behalf as no word had come from Julian or Balardi.

When they had gathered, Rostov brought in the old woman. Though Kalanin was exhausted, he understood immediately that she was a Sorceress, a being comfortable in the Mid-World. From Kalanin's side, Rafir called out, "Granny!" and raced to her like a lost kitten. The old woman knelt and rubbed the soft fur of the fox.

"I wondered if you would remember old Granny," said the woman, rising. "Rafir at least will speak for me, and so perhaps you will listen."

"I'll speak for you too, Granny," added Sebastian, and he turned to Kalanin. "She helped Julian at the first part of our journey, and she gave him those Seeking Stones that freed us."

"We'll listen, at least," said Kalanin. "What do you have to tell us?"

"Two little pieces of information," said the Sorceress, standing before them. "First, this old body has seen many good times, and it's not what it once was. Second, the courtesy of soldiers is less than in years past." Somewhat sheepishly, Harlond brought a chair forward for the old woman.

"That's better," said Granny, sitting. "Now, I'll give it to you straight: your Wizard and your Magician have lost." They all tried to speak at once, and the Sorceress held her hand up to quiet them. "Don't ask me how I know — it's our business in the Mid-World to know these things. They've lost, completely, but here's a strange thing. For some reason, the *Game* is not yet over."

"That makes little sense," said Kalanin. "They have lost, but not lost. How can this be?"

"They *have* lost," replied the Sorceress. "They are alive, but completely without power. Why there's a doubt about this struggle is a mystery to us. But I came forward to tell you this: you must withdraw from Gravengate or be destroyed. No trinkets, amulets, or prayers will protect you against the Wizard and the Sorcerer who stand before you. Withdraw into the Mid-World, and I and many other beings of the Mid-World will shield you."

Kalanin was silent for a moment, lighting his pipe, then drawing on it slowly. "You've come forward to aid us," he said. "Is there a way you and others might protect us from sorcery while we complete the destruction of their tier groups?" The Sorceress laughed, a short, bitter laugh, almost a bark.

"I couldn't hold up for thirty seconds against even one of them, much less two. If you withdraw, other forces will shield you — but you must act now." Kalanin again drew on his pipe, watching the old woman closely as the candlelight flickered about her.

"I sense your good will, and your concern," he said. "Yet I should ask: why have you come forward now? It was always said that those of the Mid-World were neutral, unwilling to be drawn into our conflicts."

Granny sighed. "How can you know what we've risked for you? We fought at the Portal to bar the Dark Emissary. The Mistress of Illusions and I lost that contest, for the summoning was too great. We sought to bar the Lord of Coils, and we succeeded, with Julian's help." The Sorceress leaned forward. "I'm risking myself right now to save you. Tonight, I'm making enemies who will likely pursue me and destroy me one dark day. Look: you've done much, so much that I'm amazed that you still live. But you must withdraw *now!*"

Géla turned to Kalanin. "Choose as you wish, but I and my archers will stay, and complete our service to Balardi." The hands of the old Sorceress searched the pockets of her cloak, fumbling a little before she found what she wanted. She stood and passed a small scroll to Géla.

"Here are your orders from the Mistress of Illusions," said the Sorceress. "Best to follow them."

"What of the wounded?" asked Kalanin. "Many cannot survive long travel."

"I'm no healer," said the Sorceress, "but we can ease their pain and hold many alive while we seek healers in the Mid-World." Kalanin looked about to the captains for advice. Only the Steward General spoke: "You choose."

Kalanin stared into the distance, trying to imagine a new struggle without Balardi and Julian. In reality, he had no choice even had he twice as many men, with a thousand charms or amulets, and a score of Mid-World Weapons, still the powers of Thorian and Nergal would easily master them.

"You bring strong counsel," he said slowly, reluctantly. "We will follow you into the Mid-World if you pledge to release us when the time comes."

"Of course, we'd let you go," said the Sorceress. "No one would want to hold a rough lot like you against your wishes." The other captains nodded.

"Then let's be gone quickly," said Kalanin, rising. "Keep the watch fires burning — they may think that we are still nearby."

"I've one final request," said Granny. "I'll have many helpers on this journey — ask your men not to look too closely at them, for few are as 'nice' as I am." She laughed again, this time with a touch of dark humor. The captains left to rouse their men, but the Sorceress held Harmadast's sleeve, keeping him in the tent.

"We'll need, all of us, to learn of events at Gravengate," she said. "I judge that this one," she nodded to Rafir, "might sneak about safely. But is there a way into the fortress?"

"There's a small passage," replied Harmadast. "We kept a guard on it at all times, afraid that it might be discovered by our foes. Still, I doubt they've learned of it yet."

"Will you help us with this?" Kalanin asked Rafir.

The fox looked up into the faces of the Sorceress and two captains. "Of course, I'll help you. Anyway, Julian will want to know that you're safe. Yes, I'll go."

· ⅄ ·

The fox pattered through patches of water that lay on the floor of the dark tunnel. Morning sunshine was creeping about the corners of the fortress, but in the depths of the tunnel, no light penetrated, only seeping moisture. From its rich, damp smells, Rafir sensed that the tunnel's sides were covered with molds and spores. So, he stayed clear of the sides, but spiderwebs could not be so easily avoided. The fox slipped lightly over the tunnel's surface, at home in the darkness; though now in front of him, the dimmest of lights seemed to glow. As the tunnel slanted upwards its wetness began to lessen. At the edge of the tunnel's mouth, Rafir, now invisible, halted and listened, letting the moisture dry from his paws: it would be foolish to be completely invisible but leave trails of wet paw prints.

Here at the mouth of the tunnel, Rafir could hear the soft sounds of men moving quietly around, with cooking smells drifting in from camp kitchens. No guards lingered at the entrance, so the fox cautiously poked his head out.

Morning had come to the occupiers of the fortress, and men were moving around, attending to their duties. Most of them moved listlessly, in a fashion that Rafir had never seen among the soldiers of the League. The fox walked among them for a while, sniffing for Julian and Balardi. Men were talking quietly, or sipping wine in silence, staring off into the distance. No trace of Julian or Balardi were discovered, but there were smells of blood — and death. One large area had been set aside for the wounded and the dying. Rafir watched for a few moments, then he began to follow a tall figure as it moved among the wounded. That tall figure was the Wizard, Thorian.

The fox found a quiet corner and watched the Wizard for what seemed a long time. Thorian's movements and care for the wounded were like those of Balardi or Julian, for now, much of the madness and rage seemed to have left the Wizard. The fox watched as the sun arced higher and the Wizard toiled on. At last, when Thorian had finished, he stood staring into the upper skies before turning back to the keep of the fortress. Rafir followed, staying cautiously behind the Wizard. The sequences of guards that Balardi had maintained were no longer in place, and Rafir slipped from passage to passage without the slightest hindrance. They climbed, then climbed higher. Thorian passed up several series of stairs, coming at last to the very topmost tower battlements, the crown of the keep. Standing upon the pinnacle, unattended, was the Dark Sorcerer, Nergal. Rafir shrank back against the fortress walls.

"Why were you not down with me aiding the wounded?" asked Thorian. "Many who served you with great loyalty were calling for you."

"I have neither the talent nor the inclination," Nergal replied in his deep, rolling tones. "We spoke of this before: you are the healer."

Thorian looked at the Dark Sorcerer intently. "I understand you better now — you are Master of Gravengate, as we agreed. Yet you sought the Spirit Lord who dwelt here, did you not?" Nergal did not respond. "You wished to add him to your collection of Powers. Perhaps it's well that the Spirit Lord escaped, and your Seraph perished. But why did you wish to destroy the young Magician, so that I needed to stop you? And why did you wish me to destroy Balardi even before we had questioned him?"

"Perhaps my people deal more harshly with their enemies," Nergal replied. "But if you would quarrel, I ask you this: why have you let our enemies escape? Great damage was done to us and to our devices, and yet now they are removed, cloaked in Mid-World shadows."

"It is too late to quarrel," said Thorian, stepping away. "Only leave off the destruction of prisoners, and your own dark Sendings. There have been enough of those. The war is over."

"It is over, and we are the victors," Nergal said solemnly. "Have you searched Gravengate thoroughly for signs of your child?"

"The search has only been started; now I will complete it," Thorian said, and he turned and walked to the stairs. Rafir followed, but as he left, he saw a look of wild glee pass over the face of Nergal, as though the Sorcerer was taking part in some outrageous farce.

The Wizard walked alone now, but Rafir followed at a distance as Thorian strode through each passage and chamber of the fortress. When the Wizard met with sealed doors, he brought his staff to the lock, tracing a shape upon the handle — then each door would swing open. Only the Great Council Chamber of Balardi was sealed, not by lock, but by enchantment. Here, after a moment's pause, a flash of anger crossed the Wizard's face, and in seconds Thorian's power burst down the door, reducing it to splintered wreckage. Rafir stood back from the eruption for a moment, then followed Thorian inside. The Wizard stood in the chamber, looking down over the long council table where Balardi had conferred and judged.

Thorian flashed his hand and stood holding a handful of ashes. Whispering spell words over the ashes, he then cast them over the long table. Divination runes were quickly traced over the pattern, and in a moment, the images of Balardi and his counselors flickered into view. The image of the defeated Wizard vibrated with power and tension.

"Monstrosities again! If they bring these creatures against us, we will match them with more monsters!" One of the counselors rose to speak, but Thorian cast his cloak over the surface of the table: both dust and images were swept away. Rafir stood frozen in the shadows, afraid to move.

Thorian then sat, and for a time watched the sunlight pour through the high windows of the Council Chamber. A great look of weariness and sorrow passed over the Wizard's face, then it softened as Thorian's mind drifted far from the fortress of his foe and from his war.

After a while, the Wizard rose and left the high-ceilinged chamber of judgment. Rafir, as before, followed a little distance behind. The Wizard went carefully through each room, now and then examining some object closely, but his shoulders were bent and weary as though his search left little hope, and no cheer could be found in the fortress, either, for all its decorations and fine things had been stripped away for the duration of the siege. Thorian's search took him always deeper and further down into the citadel, until at the very end, he reached chambers at the base of the fortress that had been hewn from its stone foundations.

Here, at the base where the stairs ended, was a long storage chamber, and its entrance was sealed by a wall of flame. Little heat seemed to come from the flames, but Rafir watched them warily. Thorian halted at its entrance; in a muffled voice he murmured a few words, tracing symbols on the flame's wall with his staff, and the fires began to die down. The fox came closer. In the dark chamber beyond lay Balardi and Julian. Each was chained to the stone floor, and each of the chain's links was inscribed with runes of sorcery so that the chains were shielded from any counter enchantment. But Balardi looked weary and defeated, beyond further Wizardry, and no hope was reflected in Julian's face either.

"You should not believe," said Thorian, "that these flames were left to bar your way. My ally is harsh in his judgments, and in his sentences. These barriers were left for your protection alone." Neither Balardi nor Julian replied. The cavern in which they were imprisoned was lit dimly by dull, glowing lights that hung on the upper walls. There were no windows. Thorian watched his prisoners grimly, but without the great rage he had shown before.

"Yet tomorrow you will be confronted with your own evil, and shown your deeds beyond denial," Thorian continued, "and if you do not then yield my own to me, *I* will be the heavy judge!" Thorian left; the flames surged back, seething, and hissing. Rafir searched for a way through or around the fires, but he was able to get only as close as a hand's breadth, then the heat drove him back. The fox turned to leave — but halted as he heard more footsteps in the passageway: Nergal had come. Rafir flattened his small body against the passage wall. The Sorcerer studied the flames for a moment, then laughed. Rafir saw that the pupils within the eyes of Nergal were unlike the grey eyes of Thorian, or Balardi, or even Julian or Granny: they were pitch black, like dark pools.

The Sorcerer extended his hands into the chamber: all trace of fire vanished.

"So, the Wizard wishes you to live for a little while longer," he said, and his voice, as before, was rich and filled with music. "But tomorrow, the Wizard himself will bring about your destruction. *I* will not contain his rage." The Sorcerer laughed again. Rafir freed himself from his fear and slipped quickly beyond the barrier, into the cavern. The Sorcerer stood at the entrance for a moment, face mocking and gloating, yet there seemed the slightest hint of hesitation. Then, the Sorcerer's hands lifted from the barrier, and the wall of fire flashed back into flame. Rafir wondered what he had accomplished — now all three of them were trapped.

Nergal departed, and there was silence again for a while, except for flames that hissed with sinister background sounds. Rafir crept closer to the Apprentice.

Julian! he whispered. Julian started, but said nothing, only reaching out casually with one hand to touch the fur of the invisible fox.

"What do you think?" asked Julian, his faint voice blending with the background flame hiss. "There are others who might penetrate this barrier. Perhaps some aid might be sent to us." The Wizard lay on his side, under the weight of many chains, and did not speak for a moment.

"No," he finally murmured. "It would seem that only our foes may pass."

"Do we need to fear being overheard by our jailers?" asked Julian. Balardi drew a deep breath.

"I am manacled," said the Wizard, "and defeated, but still, I can sense when our enemies are nearby. They are gone now, and it no longer matters." The fox flashed into view, watching the weary, scorched face of the Wizard start in surprise.

"The Mid-World Spy!" hissed Balardi. "Yet you entered when the flames were down, did you not?"

"You're right," replied Rafir, "and I can't save you — I don't have any talismans or spells, only news. First, your armies are gone. Granny helped them to get away, and she thinks they'll be safe." The Wizard pulled himself upright, sitting with his arms on his knees.

"That's good news," he said softly. "I was afraid that they would be broken — there was a Power among them that was far too great for tier groups. The bane of Baron Cadmon, the Seraph, came upon them, did he not? How did they manage that encounter?"

"We lost the first battle because of the angel," said Rafir, "but it went much better after Kalanin killed the thing." Balardi's mouth hung open in surprise.

"It was the Tarnished Sword, wasn't it?" asked Julian. "That was a fearsome weapon, linked to the *Web of Fate*. Yet I'm still surprised."

"It is the greatest tragedy that such valor was lost in defeat," said Balardi. "And we have lost, every one of us — though it's good that so many have escaped."

"But Granny said it wasn't over," said Rafir. "She said that she didn't understand why, but it wasn't over. Something else was going to happen. That's really why I came." Julian's eyes narrowed.

"Tell us everything," he said. "See if you can remember exactly what she said." Rafir began with the battle and its aftermath and continued with the counsel of the Sorceress. Then, he told of his journey to Gravengate, and how he had followed Thorian.

"Rafir's old patroness is not a great Power," added Julian, "but she is a Sorceress with a strong measure of the Gift. What do you think?" Balardi was silent for a moment.

"Clearly, the most interesting part is the conversation between Thorian and Nergal," said the Wizard. "Let me consider these matters more carefully."

Silence dragged on for moments, then longer than moments. With the darkness, and warmth from the fire barrier, and the long quiet, Rafir fell asleep. Once again, he dreamed of running over meadows and woodlands, but in his dream, something stalked him from the shadows, and it had eyes with pupils like dark pools, and it wasn't really human.

Rafir woke, nearly an hour later, as the Wizard stirred from his meditations. Balardi drew a deep breath, stretched his body, then turned to Julian, his chains clanking with his motions.

"Are you certain that the old Sorceress has a full measure of the Gift?" he asked.

"She seemed to mock her own powers," said Julian, "and yet I believe that her strength was considerable — also, it seems likely that she was a hidden ally of Merlin."

"Here, then is what I believe," Balardi continued. "At the heart of the corruption of Thorian lies this false divination that shows me committing some evil. At the heart of this false divination is the figure of the Dark Sorcerer, Nergal." The Wizard turned to Rafir. "A divination uses the power of sorcery to forecast the future or to recall events that have already passed. The nature of the enchantment within a divination is that the vision will not lie in showing events that are past. Matters may be clouded or obscured, yet clear images are truthful.

"But Nergal has found a way to corrupt even the process of divination and has grafted deceit onto truth. Why has he done this? For power, lordship of Gravengate, and for mastery over Spirit Lord and Dragon shape. And perhaps he seeks the destruction of the League on behalf of the Powers of the Mid-World..." Balardi trailed off for a moment, then he added, "this is all guesswork and conjecture — I wish now that the Ancient One had given more thought to the reasons for the corruption of Thorian, rather than to his downfall."

"It seems that the League was subjected to an attack that was utterly subtle, malicious, and overwhelming," Julian said, staring at the flame barrier. "It seems that even the Dreamers did not fully understand the nature of our struggle."

Rafir yawned. "That's all very well," the fox noted, "but what are we going to do tomorrow?" Balardi's face formed a brief smile, then grew grave again.

"They spoke of demonstrating our evil deeds," he said. "They may recreate this bent divination, thus proving my guilt — the Dark Sorcerer considers it likely that the wrath of Thorian will be rekindled, and our destruction will follow, assisted by Nergal if necessary. I suppose that our one chance, the hope of Rafir's old Mistress, is that we might separate Thorian from the Dark Sorcerer and remove Nergal from Gravengate. Then, maybe the true image of the divination would assert itself. Yet this is a feeble hope, a tiny one compared to other aspects of this great struggle."

A shadowy thought nagged at Julian's mind: there was some aspect of Nergal, some understanding he had lost when the Dragon Shape was stripped from him. Silence fell over them, and the Wizard retreated into his meditations, waiting for the dawn.

· ⋈ ·

Julian woke with a weight of metal dragging him down: his chains were heavy. His eyes opened and he turned to the entrance. Thorian and Nergal stood there, staring down at them, and behind them were many guards. Julian touched his cloak — he had covered Rafir in the night so that the fox would not be discovered by chance. The cloak was empty, and Julian pulled it around his shoulders. He struggled to his feet, the weight of chains dragging him down. Then, he reached down and pulled Balardi to his feet. At Thorian's motion, the flame wall lessened then vanished. Guards moved forward.

"Now is the time for judgment," the voice of Nergal, so rich and filled with melody, rolled through the chamber. Thorian's guards advanced, but rather than pushing or abusing their captives, they took most of the weight of the chains on their own shoulders, helping Balardi and Julian along. They began to climb from the depths of the fortress. On the breath of the guards was the sour smell of last night's wine; but there was no air of celebration in the men, rather the depression of those who have been too long from their homes.

Julian climbed stairs, then more stairs. From behind, he heard Balardi stumble a few times, gasping as he tripped. After the long climb, they reached the peak of Gravengate, the topmost tower, the crown of the keep. Julian stood at the peak, eyes blinking in the new light of day, as one of the great new mornings of Alantéa burst over them.

"Behold, Alantéa, the Land of Enchantments," he said. "Beyond our struggles, the land will survive and prosper."

"Alantéa, a plaything of the Powers, with much left to be said about its future," Nergal murmured, then louder, "Whatever Alantéa's future, your struggles are ended, Apprentice."

Balardi stood drooping under a weight of metal, breathing heavily. "Yes, for better or worse, our struggles are ended," the Wizard said slowly, struggling for breath. "We stand here at the End-Game of the Masters. This event is intended to bring a great indictment against me. Will you list your charges from the beginning? I confess that when I first heard you, I was not inclined to listen too carefully, and yet now I have been compelled to listen." A sad smile flickered across the Wizard's face. "You spoke of a consort and a child. We of the League knew nothing of these people. Will you now tell us more?"

Thorian's face was grim and taut. "She was of the Mid-World, my consort and secret ally. When our daughter was only two, my lady was struck down, struck down in the very heart of Stone Mountain!" Old tensions were flaring in the Wizard's face. "I was deceived and sought among the Powers of the Mid-World for my adversary: I was a fool. My daughter, Eléna, I hid and disguised, so that none knew of her. I raised her and treasured her; she was rich with the Gift. Like a cherished treasure, I kept her hidden, but later she was difficult to restrain, as her knowledge grew. All the while, I sought to learn more of my adversary, not thinking to look within our League.

"Then, Eléna was taken from me, and I cast aside all restraints. I called her mother from the shadows. Do you know what that means? Do you understand?" Balardi shook his head sadly.

"We have all been ensnared, and it was all done so carefully...." Thorian had not listened but stood staring at Balardi with a mixture of hatred and loathing.

"No human returns from the Long Sleep," said Thorian. "I learned then that she was not human. But she came back, and she named you as her destroyer."

"The dead immortals may still be called, yet they may remain bound to their ancient masters," said Balardi. "That is one reason why we were instructed to stay far from them, was it not?"

"*You* will not sit in judgment over me!" cried Thorian. "I have proof of your guilt. By powerful divination, I have seen you overcome and steal away with my child.... Even now, we will show you your own actions as evidence against you!"

"Hold, now, just for a moment," said Balardi in a surprisingly gentle voice. "I have come to believe that this Sorcerer is the author of our quarrel, that he has twisted this divination in order to bring about this war, and the destruction of the League. If you wish to cast this divination again, then send him away." Here Balardi stared intently into Thorian's face, as though to extend his will over the Wizard.

"The trapped criminal searches everywhere for escape," Nergal said, voice low and menacing. "No doubt he still hopes that the ancient and corrupt Spirit Lord who dwelt in Gravengate will aid him. Enough of lies!" Then Nergal, with a flash of his hand, bound Balardi and Julian with a spell of silence, so that the power of speech was stricken from their lips.

Thorian, listen to me! Julian shouted with his mind. *Turn aside, or you will meet tears of horror, tears of rage, tears of endless sorrow! Turn aside!* Thorian heard nothing, but having blocked Julian's message, Nergal's eyes glinted with malice.

The Dark Sorcerer turned to Thorian. "Come, the defeated seek to accomplish with words things that they were unable to have done with sorcery, or force of arms. Let us proceed." Rafir stood still, ensnared within Nergal's spell so that he was unable to speak or move. He could hear though, as he listened to the sounds of many soldiers moving throughout Gravengate, going carelessly about their tasks. So, their hope had been feeble, and now it was gone. Rafir struggled to escape; but he could not, and there was a curiously soft dullness woven into the spell that held him so tightly.

Balardi watched as Thorian traced the divination portal; it was as he had done, seeking Merlin. In this divination, however, the spells and devices of Nergal were interlaced, woven into the spell's design. Some of the sorcerous runes were a mystery to him. So, this was how it was done. But it no longer mattered; he had failed.

Julian was unable to speak, but in all other ways, he was free and alert. Over the tower's edge, he could follow the movements of men, tiny in the distance, as they went about their tasks, moving listlessly, and with little joy in the victories of their masters. A few soldiers glanced up to the tower from time to time, yet none watched for long. Cooking smells rose to the tower, and Julian realized that he was hungry, that it was many hours since he had last eaten, and that it was unlikely he would ever eat again.

His eyes wandered from the fortress, over the ruined plain, to the woodlands where sunlight brought splendor to the forests of Alantéa. He turned back to the divination spell: it was nearly complete. Hung, unsupported in the air, was a black frame, like that of a large window, but a window to another land.

Thorian and Nergal drew back. An image began to form in the frame, showing a picture of Thorian's fortress at Stone Mountain. The walls of the great fortress gleamed in the sunlight, unmarked by war. At the top of the tower stood a young woman of great beauty; she was painting in the sunlight, working with oils on a small canvass. Beside her stood Thorian, erect and proud, shining with power and confidence. Julian guessed that this scene had taken place more than five years ago. He watched as the scene shifted, showing Eléna on the first of several journeys — and her powers of sight and hand seemed to increase with each voyage. Even the beasts of the land were becoming aware of her, with their movements becoming attuned to Eléna's thoughts. Balardi watched, his brow furrowed in concentration.

Now, the image showed Eléna wandering farther, in different forms, taking many shapes. And the Powers of the Mid-World were beginning to take an interest in her, moving in disguise to watch her progress. Such was the strength of the divination spell, that the ancestry of the Powers was revealed: an old woman, watching Eléna, was shown as once a Spirit Lord; a careless knight revealed as a Sorceress; a gigantic carp that crested over a river, showed by its green scales the heritage of Dragon: as those of the Mid-World watched, and those at the pinnacle of Gravengate beheld the watchers, the figure of Eléna rode over the green countryside of Alantéa, without care or concern.

Then, the images grew dark...webs of sorcery began to reach out to surround Eléna's slender form. At first, she rode on, free of care, unaware of spell strands, but the hidden Powers and Watchers of the Mid-World began to draw away, sensing peril. Then, Eléna became aware of her danger, and she halted, not yet greatly troubled. She stood, staff in hand, and began to counter the forces raised against her...then a look of panic came across her face as she realized that she was greatly overmastered.

But here, the image formed by the divination spell shook and blurred.

A gasp of surprise sprang from Thorian's mouth. The image reformed, showing Eléna fleeing from the Mid-World by Portal paths toward

Gravegate. But unseen hands slammed shut each enchanted passage as webs of sorcery came ever closer.

"This is *not* as it was shown before!" cried Thorian. Eléna's horse halted as though frozen. She leaped from the horse to flee, but her feet would not lift from the ground. From the shadows came three hooded and cloaked figures — the divination spell could not penetrate their natures. Eléna fell before them senseless or destroyed; the image faded with her passing.

"What has happened?" Thorian cried to Nergal, like a man driven to madness. "What have we done? Has the ghost of the Ancient Spirit Lord twisted the spell? Or did you bend the spell even at the beginning? Do we now see the truth?"

Nergal did not respond but stared beyond Thorian to a figure perched on the tower's parapet: on that wall stood the Eye of Merlin, and the eagle spoke clearly, almost gently, in a singsong voice.

"Who summons the Ancient Creatures of the Darkness? Who bends a First Servant to his will? And who deals so easily with the Gauntlet of the Void? Who masters a mighty Dragon, and powerful Spirit Lord? And who has the subtle strength to bend a divination pattern? I name you now: you are Zikar, Prince of Demons, a first Adversary of the Maker. In naming you, I free myself." And the figure of the eagle rippled and unfolded...to become Merlin.

The image of Nergal blurred and shook, struggling to maintain itself.

"Come now," said Merlin gently, tapping the floor of the tower with his staff. "At the End-Game of the Masters, when all their pieces are checked or taken, the Masters themselves must stand forth."

The figure of Nergal vanished, and in its place, dark red, huge, and vast with power, stood a Prince of Demons, fully seven times the bulk of a man, towering over Merlin.

"After all that has passed, you still seek to contend with me?" cried the Demon. His hands flashed, and a Portal formed in the air. Beyond the Portal, a Creature of the Darkness loomed, with snakes rippling from its body.

The staff of Merlin flickered, and the Portal vanished.

The Demon touched the tower wall: it began to shake, casting slabs of masonry down on the soldiers below.

Merlin tapped the floor of the tower gently, and it steadied.

"Then let us see who the Master upon this pinnacle is!" cried the Demon, and it leaped at Merlin. The Wizard raised a fold of his cloak, and the Demon was hurled back, smashing more of the tower's stones onto the fleeing soldiers.

"So, you came prepared," said the Demon Prince, raising itself from the floor of the tower. "Will you now test yourself against me?"

Merlin shook his head. "If you remain," he said softly, "you might easily master all three of the Wizards standing before you. But what of the Gods, the Powers of the Mid-World? Are you yet ready to confront all of them together? We do not often name them, but above us *might* be Wotan, and Ahuramazda, and even Dark-Souled Set. And beyond them lies the incredible power of the Mid-World of the Truce."

The Prince of Demons glanced up into the upper skies, now gleaming with lenses, as the Powers of the Mid-World stared down through vision screens to the confrontation on the pinnacle of Gravengate. Zikar showed not even the least trace of fear.

Julian looked on in shock: the Prince of Demons was kin to his brother Voritar, but instead of the peace of Voritar, Zikar was filled with enormous power — and malice. The Demon glanced back down at the faces of the humans who radiated both horror and confusion. The Demon stood, glittering in the sunlight, a nightmare in broad daylight, and he laughed down at them.

"And so perhaps you have won this useless, little *Game*," he said, in his rolling deep voice. "But behold your pieces, all corrupt or broken, while in the greater *Game*, we have freed ourselves, and are masters of the Guardians of the World! And we have birthed the Marids! The Mid-World lies before us, rich and decaying, like a rotted garden. The Maker is gone, and we shall rule! ***We shall rule! WE SHALL RULE!!***" As the Prince of Demons spoke these last words, his great body lifted into the air, trailing ash, and flame.

A Portal appeared before him. Through that Portal, the Demon passed, and then he was gone.

· ℵ ·

The afternoon was deepening into sunset. Merlin stood by the tower walls. Balardi and Julian stood beside him, their shackles piled to one side. Thorian remained unchained, but he hung his head, face twisted in misery. Rafir stood at Julian's feet, quiet, subdued, staring out to the desolate plain.

"What of the eagle?" Julian asked, breaking the long silence. "Was he only a mask for yourself, a finely wrought illusion that none could penetrate?"

"He was as you first perceived him, the most secret and farsighted of my servants." Merlin paused, watching shadows slant over the ruined Plain of Gravengate. "No wielder of magic is pleased to reveal his innermost secrets, but for your peace of mind, I will tell you a little of what has passed.

"From the beginning of the League, I feared that the Powers might one day come against us and overwhelm all of our fortresses and cunning sorceries. Against that danger, I forged for myself a spell of Dispersal, so that at the edge of destruction all the charmed particles of my body would leap far from death, spreading to earth, to sea, and to sky. A portion of my mind, the center of my understanding, would be hidden within the eagle. Once lodged, and aware, he and I would then bring about the spell of Renewal, drawing all my particles from their hidden places.

"Yet, at our moment of need, the spell of Dispersal nearly failed me, for it was intended to counter the Mid-World Powers. Instead, I confronted the Ancient Demon Princes, and these drew knowledge from the corrupted Seraph, and other beings unknown to me. Against this force of mongrel power, the spell still functioned, and I was dispersed, but my link with the eagle's mind was for the most part shattered. Part of me, only the smallest portion, was lodged within the eagle, and what should have been my escape hatch became a prison.

"For many days, the last strands of my consciousness lay stunned within the eagle's mind. Slowly, I began to wake, at first without knowledge or link with my host. After a time, I was able to peer out from the eagle's eyes, and I watched in horror as the Dark Emissary assailed the men of the League. I was still helpless, unable to contact my host. The danger to myself remained enormous — had my enemies found my hiding place or discovered the Spell of Dispersal, both the eagle and I would have been doomed. Our greatest danger came when Julian sought me through the Portal Talisman. He found sky and sea where part of me lay hidden; yet, if the Eye had been outside of the oval of Power, then the Portal Talisman would surely have shown my hiding place inside his mind, and our link would have been discovered.

"Later, the fox found us just as I spoke for the first time into the eagle's mind: the fox saw peace settle over the eagle's countenance, where before he had seen discord and anger, and so we deflected him with a tale of wind currents.

"I began to heal then, but slowly — and I was still vulnerable. When you marched to Gravengate for a second time, I and the eagle left the struggle early, circling with our opponent high over the battlefield. The winged serpent recognized that the eagle's nature had changed; he grew wary and fearful, so I put him down, painlessly, with a Word. I turned then back to the battle, watching Thorian and Balardi enter a Great Spell test: I had never thought to see our powers so used and wasted upon one another.

"I saw the Gauntlet of the Void pursue Nergal into the Mid-World. I watched on as the corrupted Seraph broke the men of the League. I then urged Kalanin to bring the Tarnished Sword against that being. Then I sped to Julian's side, still unable to help him, but I watched as he drew on the capabilities of a Lord of Dragon. Only one power, ancient or new, might so easily master a Lord of Dragons: when Julian fell, I perceived that a Prince of Demons hid behind the visage of Nergal, and I understood another part of the *Web of Fate* that surrounded us. But at that moment, Julian was in mortal danger, and I was not yet able to aid him directly, so I sent a thought into the mind of Thorian, and he intervened to preserve Julian.

"Then, with the Seraph slain, and Nergal exposed, all of the secrets were open to me and slowly I neared power. I spoke the first portion of the Assembly spell; in a secret cavern at Sea's Edge, all of my particles began to gather: I stood upright, facing toward the distant eagle, ugly, hideous, partially formed — skeleton first, then with pulsing organs, then partial flesh, like the half alive.

"At Sea's Edge, fully formed, I readied spells that would check a Prince of Demons: I had no hope of overcoming Zikar, I could only hope to expose him to the Eyes and the Powers of the Mid-World, and force him to depart; though this Demon Prince may plan to rule Alantéa, still he is not ready to confront the many Gods of the Mid-World, otherwise he would not have trifled with the League.

"When the time came, as you reached the topmost tower of Gravengate, I spoke the last words of the Spell of Renewal, and the eagle stood at Sea's Edge, and I here at Gravengate.

"The rest you know, except for the nature of my link with the eagle. That is my own secret, one that I will not reveal, even now — each of the three Wizards held a secret, a close and unshared truth." Merlin turned to Thorian. "And what shall we do with you, and your secrets, Thorian? I find it hard to judge you kindly. Without just cause, you turned on your brother of the League. Yet you were deceived by the greatest of deceivers. You brought death and destruction to us all, yet at the last, you wavered — you were corrupted, but not utterly ruined. Have you anything to say?"

"Truly, I am punished, and my life is ruined," Thorian murmured, and he could not meet Merlin's eyes. "I seek only death and the Long Sleep — if that Demon Prince does not find a way to rouse me. But now, give me leave to aid you in your struggle with the Great Adversaries of the Maker. If we survive, I will serve Balardi and begin to repair some of the damage done." Merlin turned to Balardi.

"Can you accept this?" he asked. Balardi's face was hard.

"Some things are beyond forgiveness," he said. "But we must renew the League, and for the sake of the League and its service to the Maker, I will put aside my anger until the end of this struggle." Thorian bowed to his brother Wizards, and some of the misery left his face. The sun was deepening into the west, glowing like a fiery, red furnace.

"You have not yet spoken of *The Game of the Masters*," Julian said. "All throughout this great contest the *Game* has intervened on our side, striving to balance the great masses of power arrayed against us. Has this happened before?"

"Never in its long history," Merlin replied. "At the foundation of *The Game of the Masters* lies the Mid-World of the Truce. If the Truce is corrupted, the *Game* will lose its power; and so, *The Game of the Masters* was seeking to defend itself."

"When Gravengate was under siege," said Balardi, "the Ancient One and I could feel a great *trembling*, a sense of larger forces moving in the distance. Only now do I begin to understand that the Truce itself was being undermined. And yet the fearsome words spoken by the Demon Prince have left many unanswered questions. How did the Demons avoid the Truce? What are Marids? Who are the Guardians of the World?"

Merlin sighed. "I can only guess that these Demon Princes were sealed away before the Truce, and now they have escaped, allowing other Ancient Adversaries to arise and renew the old, bitter struggle. We stand here with our powers wasted or broken, though we were never equal to the Demon Princes. Alas for these days! Alas, for humankind to now face such a difficult test! And worse news comes, for now, there are Marids — something has stirred in the ocean depths. I judge that the Demon Princes have brought forth a new race of beings, perhaps equal in power to the race of Dragons."

"Then even the Gods, the Powers of the Mid-World may be overmatched," Balardi said somberly. "But you did not mention the Guardians of the World. What of these beings?"

"I know nothing of them," said Merlin, staring out into the darkening gloom.

Chapter Sixteen
The Aftermath

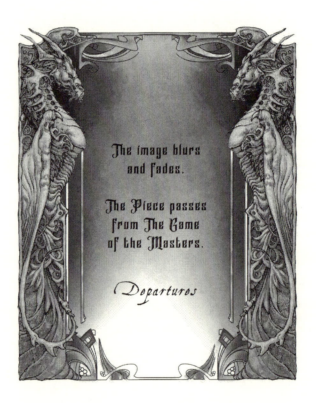

The image blurs and fades.

The Piece passes from The Game of the Masters.

Departures

T HEY ENTERED A BANK OF dry mist, a powdery smoke that glowed blue and grey from rays of distant sunlight. Kalanin rode beside the provision cart bearing Dargas, watching the face of the old soldier. Dargas hovered near death, but he lay bathed in narcotic enchantments, his wounds stopped for the moment, his mind far from the pain and torment of his body. A little distance ahead of him, Harmadast and Galad rode beside the old Sorceress as she guided them deeper into the Mid-World.

Kalanin had finally gotten the name of the old Sorcerous from her after advising her that "Granny" wasn't going to work for fighting men who were leading a procession of wounded into the Mid-World.

The old Sorceress had finally muttered, "Héna, I was called Héna, when I first began moving pieces in *The Game of the Masters,* so long, so very long ago."

She was leading a lonely procession, more like defeat than a measured withdrawal. Less than two thousand men remained, as the others had found shelter in safe portions of the Mid-World. Safe, Kalanin hoped, but with the strange spirits and Mid-World beings that guided them, it was impossible to be certain. The Grey Captain too was gone, taking the men of the Dragon's Teeth into distant regions of the Mid-World, considering the creation of his own domain. Harlond and Rostov rode a little way back, reluctant to leave Dargas and Kalanin, as though the story would end for them when they became separated from their leaders.

Overhead, the hazy blue glow was beginning to change. Kalanin watched as pieces of blue matter coalesced and began to drift downward. It was like blue snow, but dry; as crystals struck his armor, they shattered, sending a light blue powder back into the air. As they broke, the crystals made a slight ringing sound, adding an eerie overtone to the creaking wagon wheels, and the dull clopping of horse hooves.

But now the clomping sounds of hooves were growing louder. Kalanin turned: Harlond and Rostov had pulled closer, and were staring down at the face of Dargas, watching as the wagon movements jostled the old warrior, sending tremors through his enchanted sleep.

"It's taking so long," Harlond murmured. "I don't see how he can hold on for much longer."

"He may live, or he may not," Kalanin said somberly. "It's out of our control, we're at the mercy of the old Sorceress. There's nothing we can do." Ahead of them, the old Sorceress, Héna rode on through the mists, murmuring and chanting, obviously struggling in her efforts to move such a great mass of men. Rostov watched Kalanin's eyes turn away: their leader was grim and preoccupied. Rostov tugged at Harlond's sleeve, and they fell back, letting Kalanin ride on in peace.

Peace was farthest from Kalanin's mind: so many thoughts were tumbling around in turmoil, each seeking his attention. Carefully, he began to sort them. First, there were thoughts of warcraft, of arming and training men, of provisioning them, firming their morale, and moving them in tier masses from point to point. Also, concepts of siegecraft had been forming — it had seemed likely that they would need to assault Gravengate or Stone Mountain. Now, their battles were over. Carefully, he set aside all the problems of generalship.

Just ahead of them, the air was clearing a little, and the blue haze grew thinner. Flying creatures were hovering over the Sorceress; she responded in harsh tones, and the creatures fluttered away, hooting, and screeching at one another.

On another level of his mind, Kalanin found all his old thoughts of a weapons' master still active: weapons and mounts, armor types, charms against sorcery, methods of discouraging Mid-World intruders without creating lifelong enemies. But it seemed so unlikely that he would ever again resume his old tasks as an emissary of the league. Carefully, he set those thoughts aside.

Now his mind was becoming clear, and he began to focus on the great struggle of the League. The eagle, the Eye of Merlin, had understood it best, thinking of their contest in terms of *The Game of the Masters*, with men and powers and forces swaying back and forth, as the Masters countered one another. Almost, as if he floated from a great height, he could see the shifting forces sweep over the League.

In their first moves, their foes had struck at Merlin and Balardi and Baron Cadmon. Merlin and Cadmon had been swept from the Field, but Balardi had held — his secret ally, the Ancient One, a powerful Spirit Lord, had saved him. Against these strong opening moves, he, and Julian and Galad had been sent with the chest prepared by Merlin. As a countermove, it seemed so feeble in comparison, their small group riding in the mists, struggling at the ford. And yet the three of them had been catalysts for powerful forces, with every attempt to check them ending in failure: Gogra, shapeshifting Adept, tier masses, Manticore, Dark Emissary, and ruined Seraph. Even the small servants of Julian had avoided destruction in some distant time and had been put back into play as Mid-World Spies.

Why should all these thoughts trouble him so much? After all, they had done well, more than any Master had reason to expect. But he had been played, like a piece in *The Game of the Masters*, set in motion in a contest he only dimly understood, then maneuvered, and manipulated at every turn.

On the Plain of Gravengate, watching as friends and allies fell around him, he had struggled to free himself, but what had really happened? "Do not forget the sword," the voice had said. In the context of the *Game*, he had failed as Captain, so his Master had armed him with *The Mid-World Weapon*, and moved him forward again, back in his role of weapons' master and *The Charmed Knight*.

Only one thing was certain in this hazy blue portion of the sorcerous Mid-World: he would never, never, let himself be used that way again.

Let his Master, whoever he might be, however good his intentions, let him find another human to move about in his great *Game*.

Not fifty paces in front of him, the Sorceress was again arguing with some mist shrouded Mid-World being, but this time, she seemed much less certain of herself.

So, Kalanin was moving from the Field of the Masters, riding through a blue haze into the unknown. But two questions remained: who were the Masters? And how would they end their contest?

Was Thorian the Master of their opponents? Nergal seemed to manipulate the Wizard; the Dark Sorcerer seemed more likely to be Master. Or perhaps Thorian was playing a more complex role and ruled the Sorcerer. And the Master might be an unnamed Dark Power of the Mid-World.

And for his own Master? The Spirit Lord? Could it be that the Ancient One remained on Earth, concealed? Merlin? Perhaps the Wizard had survived and would emerge as Master. And again, it might be one of the Mid-World Powers — of these he knew almost nothing.

As for *The Game of the Masters*, its hold on him had faltered; indeed, its hold on each piece seemed to be slipping away. As he stared deeper into the haze of blue mists, an image seemed to coalesce, of an enormous wraith form, a colossus, reaching with a skeletal hand to move some fading piece — but then billows of blueish grey mists seemed to lift the wraith form and carry it skyward, into nothingness.

Kalanin shook his head; now his own overloaded mind was creating illusions.

A short distance in front of him, the Sorceress had now come to a complete halt. Before her, wreathed in mists, stood a huge stag, taller than war horses, blocking their path. Galad drew his sword but the Sorceress called on him to halt. The old woman stepped down from her cart and shuffled forward a few paces until she stood before the Mid-World creature; the stag dwarfed the Sorceress, with huge antlers riding on his head like an immense crown of darkened bone. Sorceress and Mid-World creature conferred in the mist, while Kalanin, Harlond, and Rostov came closer.

"This stag creature is only one of several messengers," Harmadast murmured in hushed tones. "For some reason, the Sorceress would not speak with the others." The Sorceress listened to the creature, sometimes shaking her head as if baffled. Finally, the stag finished speaking, and he turned to look at the faces of the warriors. The eyes of the stag were bright and filled with perception, and they returned for a second time to stare at Kalanin.

Then the creature was gone, leaping away in a single bound, vanishing into dry mists. The Sorceress took a deep breath, then sat heavily on the ground, forming a jumble of flesh and cloth. She mumbled to herself for a moment, then raised her voice.

"By all the Powers, I was a fool to meddle in this business!" She looked up at them. "I could believe the news about Merlin, but the rest was too much to swallow." They waited, silently, for her explanation. "You are a lot of heavyhanded, slow witted louts!" she said irritably. "Merlin was a *Power*; he was bound to emerge if he still lived...I can see that now...." She trailed off.

"So, Merlin lives," said Harmadast. "What of Balardi?"

"He lives, as does Julian," she said, nodding, "and Thorian is once again an ally of your League, while Nergal has departed — that's the good news. But the bad news is far heavier: The Ancient Adversaries have arisen to renew the struggle beyond the Truce, outside of the Mid-World. Do you understand what *that* means?"

Kalanin nodded somberly. "Yes, Demon and Dragon, there's a balance to it," he said slowly. "All the other Ancient Powers emerged in this conflict: Seraph, Spirit Lord, and Creature of the Darkness. There's a balance."

"But these have come to stay!" cried the Sorceress. "And they're making other evil ones to help them!" She took a deep breath and rose to her feet.

"All of your soldiers will want to go back. I'll have to help them," she muttered, then she turned to the litter cart where Dargas lay. "I planned to bring this one to the Mistress of Illusions, but it's not fair to him. He should be taking the Long Sleep." Slowly, Kalanin eased forward, so that he stood between the Sorceress and the provision cart.

"Is there a chance for him, if we hold him alive?" He looked down at the Sorceress and saw a flicker of menace and anger flash over her face.

"There might be, there might be," she said, "but you should have learned: it's not death and the Long Sleep that's to be feared, it's dying, dying in torment over a long time. This old soldier has suffered enough. If he could speak, he would *ask* to be released."

"Then we should ask him," said Kalanin.

The eyes of the Sorceress narrowed as she looked up at him. "Yes, you would choose that path — you think yourself so strong. Let's see how you fare in your last moments." She cleared her face and drew a deep breath. "I suppose there's no help for it. I'll try to keep the bleeding down." She approached Dargas' litter and began to chant in a muffled voice. The others dismounted and stood beside her.

As the spells of the Sorceress lifted, the face of Dargas grew troubled and grey, then filled with pain. The eyes of the old warrior darted open, shifting wildly back and forth. His body lay motionless.

"Old soldier, there's a chance," said the Sorceress quickly, but gently. "A chance to live, maybe a slim chance, maybe a lifetime's pain. Or you can take the Long Sleep — it will seem only a moment before the Maker wakes you." Dargas' lips twitched but no sound came. The Sorceress put her ear closer. "Yes, we won, we held the field." Her eyes glanced at Kalanin. "But at best the struggle was a draw. Now, listen. For peace, and the Long Sleep, close your eyes; if you wish to hang on, nod your head gently." The head of Dargas twitched — and then blood surged from his mouth and nostrils.

"No!" cried the Sorceress, and then her hands were running over his tongue and chest, and spells leaped from her lips as she tried to stem the tide of blood. The bleeding ebbed then stopped, and in a few moments, the trouble and torment left Dargas' face. The Sorceress stepped back with a sigh.

"So, after all that, I almost lost him. We'll send him on to the Mistress of Illusions, less than half a day from here. I'll take the rest of you back, but one of you will have to stay with the old warrior. You'll bear a charm to hold him alive. Who will it be?" Harlond and Rostov exchanged glances.

"I'll go," said Kalanin. "I've had enough of war and destruction for a while. I'll go with Dargas." The others stood straight in shock and surprise.

Harmadast broke the silence. "Yes, yes, if anyone deserves a leave from this struggle, it's you," he said softly. "There should be a lull, after all that we've gone through." Kalanin nodded and remounted. He sat looking down on his friends and allies.

Their faces said: *Why are you leaving us? What have we done? We will need you now, more than ever.* But no words came.

And he had the urge to speak, to say: *Don't go back, don't be fools. Again, you'll be tools for the wielders of magic — rough tools, good only for fighting then dying at the right moments. Don't go back.* But he said nothing, only giving them a half wave, and turned to lead the litter cart bearing Dargas deeper into the Mid-World.

He rode for a few moments, concentrating on the sound of blue crystals as they shattered against his armor and then he turned to look back. His old allies were only a few hundred paces away weaving along sorcerous trails. Messengers were coming and going, seeking instructions, and the captains of the League seemed to grow stronger in purpose with every step.

They were only a few hundred paces from Kalanin, weaving along sorcerous trails, but the gap now seemed more than distance, greater than sorcery.

The Game of the Masters is the second of five books.
The Grey Witch of the North is the sequel.

·𝕏·

Manufactured by Amazon.ca
Bolton, ON